THE BILLIONAIRE BOSS AND THE BARISTA

ROGUES AND RESCUERS

BOOK 5

LUCY LEROUX

The Billionaire Boss and The Barista © 2024 Lucy Leroux

TITLES BY LUCY LEROUX

The Singular Obsession Series
Making Her His
Confiscating Charlie, A Singular Obsession Novelette
Calen's Captive
Stolen Angel
The Roman's Woman
Save Me, A Singular Obsession Novella
Take Me, A Singular Obsession Prequel Novella
Trick's Trap
Peyton's Price

The Spellbound Regency Series
The Hex, A Free Spellbound Regency Short
Cursed
Black Widow
Haunted

The Rogues and Rescuers Series
Codename Romeo
The Mercenary Next Door

Knight Takes Queen
The Millionaire's Mechanic
The Billionaire Boss and the Barista
True Crime Billionaire - Coming Soon

Writing As L.B. Gilbert
The Elementals Saga
Discordia, A Free Elementals Story
Fire
Air
Water
Earth

A Shifter's Claim
Kin Selection
Eat You Up
Tooth and Nail
The When Witch and the Wolf

The Seven Families
To Hell and Back
Don't Touch

Charmed Legacy Cursed Angel Watchtowers
Forsaken

Chapter One

GARRETT

Garrett Chapman dropped the pillow onto his plush new mattress, resisting the urge to climb up and roll around on it.

"You are way too excited by a bed that doesn't stand a chance of seeing any action," Fletcher said, barely looking up from the contract he was perusing. "And I don't just mean because it's the one being installed in your office."

His partner was too wrapped up in their current deal negotiations to appreciate the joys of a thousand thread-count percale cotton sheets.

"You would be excited too if you had spent a week straight sleeping on the couch in the office."

Fletcher put the sheaf of papers down and raised a bushy black brow. "Here's a crazy idea. What if instead of spending a hundred grand on an office remodel, you go home to your luxurious penthouse and sleep in the king-sized bed there?"

He fluffed the pillow and smirked. "Easier said than done these days."

Fletcher sighed, slumping a bit so that the incipient paunch he was developing hung over his belt. "True enough, I guess," he said, somehow managing to appear around ten years older than Garrett despite being several months younger.

Next Chapter Enterprises, their investment company, was in a period of expansion. That was a line he'd said in various forms for the last two years and it was still true. Their little group, which dabbled in everything from microprocessors to real estate, had gone from him and Fletcher and thirty-eight staff to nearly double in that time. They had grown so much that they'd had to pull up stakes from their old office to their new one.

Their new office suite took the entire top floor of the new Lumen tower, a joint enterprise between his company and his friends including Rainer Torsten, Ian Quinn, and Elias Gardner.

The luxury office building had opened only six months ago. It provided many amenities including security, two state-of-the-art gyms, spacious balconies, three full-service dining rooms, and a car service. All of this was in addition to the café-slash-bakery on the ground floor and coffee carts in a communal space located on every other floor.

Add that to the modern open design, competitive pricing and location, and it was no wonder they were already ninety percent occupied with a waiting list a mile long for their small and midsized suites.

The only reason the floor underneath him was unoccupied was because Auric Security, Quinn and Gardner's private security firm, was waiting for their current lease to run out before moving their West Coast operations here.

"Just go ahead and jump on the damn bed." Fletcher sighed. "You know you want to."

Garrett snorted. "Like I'm going to do it in front of you."

His partner got to his feet. "Fine, I can take a hint."

He saluted with the contract in hand, nearly giving his eyeball a paper cut.

Refusing to acknowledge his near miss, he ducked out, leaving Garrett alone. *Finally.*

Pulling out his phone, he set his alarm to go off in half an hour. Then he pulled off his jacket and kicked off his shoes. Taking a running start, he leaped on the bed like a four-year-old. He landed, bouncing twice before his body weight sunk into the thick pillow top.

Almost moaning with pleasure, he turned over and clapped, turning off the lights, then settled in.

However, his power nap couldn't undo the last few weeks of burning the candle at both ends. With only a few minutes before he had to jump on to his London conference call, he decided to hit the coffee cart on the floor below. But the Back in 5 Minutes sign, along with the three guys ahead of him made him bite back a growl.

Wishing his assistant hadn't chosen yesterday to start their vacation, he was about to give up and head back upstairs when he caught what the guys ahead of him were saying.

"Wish she'd hurry that glorious ass up," the man with a visible bald spot said.

"You think it's good? I say she's too fat." His thinner friend paused. "Although those tits are spectacular. Even better than her lattes."

"What can I say? I'm an ass man," the first guy said. "And hers makes me want to take a big bite out of it. Speaking of her lattes, I've got some foam for her—"

"*Hey*," Garrett snapped, unable to listen to another second of their shit. "I hope you're not talking about anyone who works here."

The man in question spun around. As tall as him, the balding guy was a middle-aged example of what his best friend Rainer called *hard fat*. He reminded Garrett of an aging boxer gone to seed, but he had the air of a man who still loved to brawl.

London be damned, the arrogant and belligerent twist of the jerk's mouth was tempting him to give the man his unspoken wish.

"What's it to you?" Baldy asked, sticking out his chest like a pufferfish. Any more and Garrett would lose an eye when the buttons on his shirt popped off.

His voice dropped to the register that sent his staff running for the hills. "I think it would be wise if you kept those kinds of thoughts to yourself. We don't need *De Olla* coffee filing charges for sexual harassment—although they would be justified."

The guys rounded on him. "What is your problem, asshole? Is the fat-ass barista your girlfriend?"

He rolled his eyes and turned his back, muttering to his friend.

Garrett's body flashed hot and cold, and he hid his hands behind his back because they were turning into fists without his volition. "I would take the free advice, buddy, unless you want someone to revisit your lease…"

He looked over the guy's shoulder, reading and repeating the name of the accounting firm printed on the glass.

"Our lease?" The jerk blinked several times. "Are you fucking serious? Who the hell do you think you are?"

The other guy elbowed him, his eyes widening in recognition.

"He owns the building," loser number two hissed at his red-faced companion.

"I'm also on the board of *De Olla*," he added with the scariest smile he could summon—the one that made his subordinates run for cover on those rare occasions they screwed up. "Which means the employee you're harassing works for *me*."

"We're sorry, man," the skinny one said, backpedaling fast enough to leave tread marks on the floor.

But the first one wasn't budging, so Garrett gave him a verbal push. "I don't think you need any more coffee today."

"Nah, man, not from here." Baldy shrugged, rolling his shoulders and sniffing loudly. He jerked his head at his friend. "The coffee here sucks. Let's go to Starbucks," he said, heading to the elevator without waiting for his friend.

Garrett watched the offender go, his posture transforming the farther he went. By the time he reached the elevator, Baldy was swaggering, as if leaving had been his idea.

When he turned back, the barista was standing at the coffee cart, staring at him. But it wasn't a woman. It was a skinny white kid with a protruding Adam's apple.

The kid didn't look old enough to shave, but he had to be in college at the least. Garrett had edited the employment contract so the coffee company didn't hire underage workers at this location. Everyone had to have a high school diploma to work in his building—part of how he ensured quality service for his tenants.

Not that all of them deserved it.

"Hey, thanks for saying something to those men," the kid said, that huge Adam's apple bobbing distractingly. He was holding a package of disposable coffee cups in front of him like a shield.

"They had to change Em back to the café downstairs because of the jerks on this floor."

"They did?" Man, he shouldn't have let those two pervs go with a warning. No, this was shaping up to be a systemic problem.

De Olla wasn't obligated to let the building's management know about every little problem they were having. The way they handled issues like this was up to their discretion. But he prided himself on how his company treated female staff.

Next Chapter staff was forty-four percent women, but Garrett was determined to get it to half—and not just with the administrative staff. His analyst, legal, and accounting teams were equally well represented.

"I'll look into it, Kyle," he promised after clocking his name tag. "In the meantime, can I have a cappuccino?"

"You got it," the kid said with a wide smile. "And thanks again. Em shouldn't have to get moved because of guys like that. It's much harder working in the main café. It's so much busier."

"I'll speak to Hector as soon as I get a chance."

De Olla was a new company. Their contract with Next Chapter was one of their first supplying a major office building. Maybe Hector Ortiz, the founder and general manager, didn't know how to handle issues that brought them conflict with other businesses yet.

Garrett was going to have to step in. He wasn't about to let everyday sexual harassment turn the atmosphere around here to shit. Not in his own building.

Kyle took a little longer than Garrett would have liked on his drink, but the delay was worth it when he took the cup. The kid has somehow managed to put a Superman-style *S* on the foam of his cappuccino.

Snorting lightly, he saluted. Vowing to contact *De Olla* after his London call, he hustled back upstairs.

Unfortunately, his conference call ran long. It was well after six by the time he was done. He stopped by the café on the way out, but it was already closed, the ground floor space dark.

Vowing to speak to Hector before he started his day tomorrow, he decided to take Fletcher's advice and go home for the night.

Naturally, Garrett overslept.

By the time he got to the café, the line was out the door, lured by the aroma of roasted beans and freshly baked pastries. Cursing under his breath, he scanned the space for the manager, only to find the man hustling to fill orders along with the dark-haired barista, a woman half-hidden behind the gleaming steel of an industrial espresso machine.

Sighing, he resigned himself to calling Hector from his office upstairs—and settling for coffee from his pod machine.

Then the barista behind the machine moved into view.

Garrett blinked. *No, it can't be.*

The woman manning the espresso machine just looked like Emma, but it couldn't possibly be her.

Emmaline Mendez was a Wall Street power broker by now. In high school, she had been determined to storm those halls of power and take no prisoners. Her job would involve wearing suits and spiked heels she would use to step all over her competition. There was no way she'd be working as a bar—*shit*.

"Em," he breathed in shock. The kid had called his coworker *Em*, the one being sexually harassed.

No, this was just a coincidence. Garrett was overly tired and imagining things. A second look would prove that. But the barista had her head down, a long side braid covering what was visible of her face.

Then she turned, a sunny smile stretching plush rose lips as she set a to-go cup on the counter next to her.

"Macchiato for Evans!" she called.

The blood drained out of his head at the sound of her voice.

"*Emmy*," he whispered, the tips of his fingers going numb. He tried to walk toward her, to make sure.

He stumbled, unable to catch himself before he crashed into a tiny two-person table, jostling the coffee mug on it. He didn't hit it hard enough to knock it over, but enough of it spilled that the woman sitting at the table jumped up with a gasp.

"I'm sorry," he said, grabbing the napkins next to the cup to mop up the mess.

"Oh, that's okay, Mr. Chapman," the woman said a little breathlessly.

He blinked down at the blonde, belatedly recognizing the woman as Fletcher's new PA, the pretty young thing his partner had hired when his former assistant had decided not to continue after they moved offices.

Speaking of lawsuits waiting to happen.

"It's okay," she repeated. "Only a bit spilled."

"Here, let me get that."

Garrett froze as the Emma look-alike stepped up to the table. She held out a white towel, wiping down the table with quick, efficient strokes.

Fine dark brows, thick sooty lashes, and cheekbones that would have done a twig-sized supermodel proud—a feature totally at odds with the curves that had grown even lusher over the years.

There was no doubt about it. Emmaline Mendez was working as a barista in his building.

Garrett held his breath, the universe pausing as he waited for her to look up. Then she did.

"Did you need one too?" she asked, her caramel-colored eyes meeting his.

Garrett froze, waiting for the moment of recognition. But it never came. She just *stood* there, holding out a paper towel, that friendly but impersonal smile fading as the moment stretched. He might as well have been a stranger off the street.

"I'll take one," the blonde said when he didn't move.

Emma turned to the blonde with a graceful sweep of her hands—as if she lived to serve and be helpful!

She handed her several brown paper towels before the manager called out to her. Then she was gone, ducking behind the counter without a second glance.

"Can I get you a coffee before I go up, Mr. Chapman?" the blonde offered.

Garrett shook his head, irritated when the small motion made him dizzy.

"No, thank you, Sarah," he replied, his excellent memory providing the assistant's name. "I was going to, but I've changed my mind. Going to cut back."

Starting now.

"If you're sure," she said, looking at him with an eager innocence that didn't quite mask her interest.

But Garrett had lost his taste for dewy-eyed ingenues a long time ago.

"I'm sure," he rasped, displeased at how hoarse he sounded. "Please excuse me."

He rushed out, his heart pounding so hard and fast it was like it was trying to burst out of his chest. Staggering down the hallway, he stopped short of the elevator bank until his vision cleared.

Where the hell had his discipline gone? He should be marching back into that café and getting into Emma's face. Instead, he was hiding, trying to catch his breath like an asthmatic kid who had just seen his bully coming around the corner.

That visual image calmed him down. Garrett forced himself to walk away, but his blood was boiling, his anger and indignation growing with every step.

He didn't know what game Emma was playing. But the woman who had consistently given him hell throughout high school, skipped both freshman and sophomore year, and was voted most likely to succeed alongside him was no mere barista!

No, if Emma was working here—pretending not to recognize him for fuck's sake—it could only mean one thing.

She was up to no good.

Chapter Two

GARRETT

Fletcher spun in his chair, his face a rictus of disbelief. "Excuse me, what?"

"Emma Mendez is a corporate spy," Garrett ground out a second time.

The line between Fletcher's brows deepened, making him look like a skinny bulldog. "Where did you hear this?"

"I didn't hear it," he said, snatching the contract in front of Fletcher just so he could smack it back down on the desk. "I saw it. With my own eyes."

His friend was confused, but judging from his sudden paleness, he was starting to get the picture.

"*Here*? You saw her *here*?"

"She's downstairs in the coffee shop."

"*Oh.*" Fletcher processed this. "But you're not sure which business she's working for?"

"No. Could be anybody."

Fletcher brightened suddenly. "Well, that doesn't mean she's working for one of our tenants. Lots of people in the neighboring buildings come here since the coffee shop opened. She's probably visiting one of the investment firms across the way."

"You're not listening to me," Garrett spat. "She wasn't a customer. Emma works in the coffee shop as a barista."

Fletcher's face shifted from concern to incredulity. "Your high school nemesis is downstairs right now making espresso?"

He flung his hands in the air. "Yes!"

Fletcher's expression grew speculative. He leaned back in his chair, sinking into the backrest. "That's… interesting."

Garrett put his hands on his hips, beginning to pace. "It's damned suspicious is what it is."

"And what happened when she saw you?"

He paused, spinning to face him. "That was the most un-fucking-believable part!"

Fletcher leaned forward, his chin wrinkling the way it did when he was confused. "Why? What did she say?"

"She pretended not to recognize me."

"Huh." Fletcher stared off into space, looking at a point somewhere behind him. "That is weird."

Garrett snorted. It wasn't weird. It was fucking maddening. "Clearly, she didn't expect to run into me before she got what she wanted."

Fletcher frowned. "What does she want?"

"What all corporate spies want." He resumed pacing. "To steal company secrets."

His partner's mouth went slack. "*That's* what you think?"

"What else could it be?"

Garrett was going to wear a fucking hole in this carpet. He needed to do something more productive, like punching through a wall.

"It has to be the Danbury group," he decided. "They have been out to get us since we snaked the Montevalle Resorts deal out from under them."

Not to mention the two very lucrative deals before that.

Garrett had put it all together on the ride back from the elevator. It was too much of a coincidence that Emma Mendez, his only serious competition in high school, would be working in this very building making lattes.

But Bryce Danbury hated him enough to dig up his old high school rival and set her up to spy on him. He could feel the back of his neck begin to burn in irritation. Hell, her mere presence in this building was enough to completely knock him out of equilibrium.

Jesus, just how much did Danbury know about him?

Fletcher appeared to be on the same wavelength. He wiped his forehead, which had begun to bead with sweat. But he appeared intent on playing devil's advocate.

"So, Emma chose to base her spy operation in the coffee shop? If corporate espionage is her plan, wouldn't a janitorial position be better? She'd have after-hours access. Or better yet why didn't she apply for an analyst position where she could easily get insider information? It doesn't make any sense."

Garrett shrugged. "It doesn't have to make sense. Not to us. But I'm willing to bet it does to her. Besides, she must have known we'd never hire her as an analyst."

Fletcher sighed. "Yes, I guess that's true. The two of you were oil and water. It's a wonder you two made it to graduation without strangling each other. As I recall you two came close that one time in debate —remember when she creamed you arguing against carbon credits?"

"I recall that day differently." Garrett sniffed. "And I stand by my argument. Carbon offsets are imperfect but better than nothing."

Fletcher drummed his fingers on his desk. "Emma was the only one who could out-argue you. I swear I never saw anyone else drive you that crazy."

Garrett narrowed his eyes. "Don't get any ideas."

"What?" Fletcher's expression was suspiciously mild.

He crossed his arms. "I don't need you installing her in a job up here so you can watch her argue with me."

"Hell, I wouldn't do that," Fletcher said, his tone dead serious. "No. I'm with you. We need to get rid of her before she does whatever she is here to do. Good news is, we can do that. It's easy. You're on the *De Olla* board. That means you're her boss. Better yet, her boss' boss. Just tell Ortiz to fire her."

Send Emma packing without finding out what she was up to?

"No." He shook his head instinctively. "That's not possible."

"What? Why not?"

Good question. But the answer came to him quickly. "There was this thing with some of the guys on the floor below. I can't fire her without it looking as if I'm siding with them. I'd be inviting a lawsuit."

Fletcher scowled. "A lawsuit for what?"

"Never mind." Garrett had made up his mind. "I'm going to deal with this."

His partner picked up the contracts, holding them in front of his chest like a shield. "Why don't I like the sound of that?"

Garrett waved that off, leaving without answering. He wasn't about to explain what he had in mind.

It was better that way. At least one of them would need plausible deniability.

Chapter Three

EMMA

Emma jumped off the bus, swearing under her breath. This line was running later and later every single day. She was eleven minutes behind schedule.

That wouldn't have been a big deal last week, but it was a huge problem now. All because of one self-important jackass.

She didn't know his first name. Just the last. Chapman.

Excuse me, Mr. Chapman. Hector, her boss was adamant she addressed him properly. Not that this was an actual issue. She'd been schlepping coffee from the ground floor café to his penthouse office for over a week now and the man hadn't deigned to speak to her once.

Apparently, he had asked for her by name. Why? She had no idea. The man never spoke to her.

Kyle was sure it had to do with the troglodytes on the twenty-third floor. Mr. Chapman had heard them say something nasty about her and had reprimanded them. Her coworkers had practically canonized the man since.

"He looks after the little guy," Hassan said while washing dishes.

Kyle had promptly agreed, going on about how forceful and righteous Mr. Chapman had been. "I bet he wants to ask if you've had trouble with those assholes before."

"But HR has already spoken to me about it," she pointed out. The woman in charge had encouraged her to file a complaint if anything else happened. "There's no reason he has to drag me up there."

"Well, the man can drag me anywhere he wants." Tattooed and wiry Bethany licked her lips and danced from side to side while she washed the mugs in the triple compartment sink. "Seven days a week, twenty-four seven."

Emma suppressed a frown. "You know those two D-bags got reamed for saying something remarkably similar."

Bethany shrugged, unconcerned. "I did not objectify Mr. Chapman by pointing out he has abs you can bounce a quarter off of or an ass like a ripe apple." She had winked lasciviously. "Not yet anyway."

Needless to say, Bethany had been intensely disappointed to learn Emma alone would be delivering his coffee.

"If he asked for you, then you have to go," Hector had told her when she offered to switch with her coworker.

She'd tried to argue her way out of it, but Hector hadn't budged. He'd even pulled out a brand-new apron, so she'd 'put *De Olla*'s best foot forward.'

But none of her coworkers' high-minded and idealistic conjectures came to anything because the illustrious god of the building never even looked at her. Not once.

He also never asked her about the men who'd been leering and speculating about the size of her breasts in voices loud enough for the entire floor to hear.

It would have been one thing if she'd caught him on the phone, wheeling and dealing the way someone who owned the building was supposed to.

But Mr. Chapman hadn't been on the phone. Every single time she'd been summoned to his office to deliver his *café de olla*, the house specialty, he'd been standing behind his desk with his back to her, staring out the window at the city.

At first, she assumed he'd heard news he hadn't liked. Maybe he'd gotten a call from his luxury car dealer telling him the Ferrari he wanted wasn't available in midlife crisis red.

Or perhaps the weight of the gold toilet he'd installed in his penthouse had cracked the floor of his bathroom, sending it crashing down through the levels below.

Emma entertained herself with those excuses for a few days before the truth hit her.

The explanation for Mr. Moneybags' behavior was simple really. Garrett Chapman was plotting world domination. He was probably outlining his hostile takeover of city hall or mulling over which politician to buy next.

But when the same thing kept happening day after day, Emma knew it wasn't an accident. He was ignoring her on purpose.

Was it supposed to be a prize of some sort? Did His Highness think that getting a break from the busy café during the breakfast rush would be a treat? Was riding in the express elevator supposed to be the highlight of her day?

Kyle tried to defend him, of course. "Looking out the window could be meditation," he suggested. "I'm sure it's like really calming. He must be centering himself."

Emma didn't care if she was in the presence of a Zen master. Today was going to be the last she served that rich weirdo.

She glanced at her watch and quickened her pace. If she managed to get to the café in the next five minutes, she'd have just enough time to throw on her apron and grab the coffee her boss had been personally pouring all week.

Hector was so proud that his grandmother's recipe was so popular. Flavored with *piloncillo*, cinnamon, anise, and a hint of cloves, the *café de olla* was brewed in clay pots, giving it a distinctive flavor.

However, that flavor came at the expense of time. Brewing it the old-fashioned way took much longer than making a latte with the espresso machine. But in her opinion, the flavors didn't compare.

And it seemed Mr. Chapman agreed, she thought with a sigh.

Emma was taking a shortcut through the parking garage when she heard it. The meow. One too high-pitched and tiny to belong to a mature cat.

Forgetting all about the time and the task awaiting her, Emma crouched, checking under car after car.

She was only a few yards down from the main bank of elevators and the side door that led to the café. This was where the bigwigs had reserved parking spaces. It was a line of high-end sports cars, Mercedes, BMWs, interspersed with the occasional shiny Range Rover —the sporty kind meant to be driven in the mud but never were. Not by any of the suits in this building.

She had almost made it to the fire-engine red Ferrari next to the door when it swung open.

"Emma," Bethany called out, her mouth turning up at the sight of her least favorite coworker on her hands and knees. "Did you lose something?"

"I heard a meow. I think there's a kitten hiding somewhere here."

Bethany wrinkled her nose. "In the garage?"

"I heard it," she insisted.

"Well, there's nothing you can do about it now. You've kept the future father of my children waiting a whole—" Bethany glanced at her watch. "Seven minutes for his coffee."

"Really?" She straightened, dusting off her hands. "He didn't have someone else do it?"

"I told him it was better to send me, but he didn't go for it. Hassan took it up yesterday because it was your day off and Mr. Chapman complained."

"He did?"

Emma couldn't believe it. Was Kyle right? Was Mr. Chapman giving her space to complain about those douchebags from that accounting firm?

Or was everyone's equal rights hero the worst of the lot?

"I bet he wouldn't mind if you took it up," she murmured. Emma wanted to see if it was just her he was weird about or all women.

Bethany threw up her hands. "That's what I keep saying."

"What if I tell Hector I have a headache coming on and need to sit on my bucket?"

There were no seats in the café's small dishwashing room, just two upturned buckets they used as seats when they needed a break and the café had too many patrons for them to sit at one of the tables.

Bethany's eyes widened. "You would do that for me?"

Emma shrugged. "Of course."

Bethany threw her arms open and hugged her tight enough for Emma to feel the outlines of her nipple rings pressing into her chest.

But Emma hugged her back despite knowing the other woman's goodwill would only last until she got a real headache and needed to take an unscheduled break.

"Mr. Moneybags can't complain if I'm incapacitated," she reasoned, letting the other woman go.

"No, he can't." Bethany practically skipped to the door.

They walked into the café together feeling upbeat.

But Hector wasn't willing to let her off the hook. "We can't tell Mr. Chapman no," he said, sounding horrified.

She tried to change his mind, pointing out they were keeping the billionaire waiting every minute they argued. But Hector had seen her at her worst enough times to know that she wasn't quite at bucket-level pain yet.

"It has to be you," he said, handing her the coffee cup.

Resigned to her fate, Emma took it and trudged to the elevators.

And once again, Garrett Chapman stared out his window and didn't say a word.

❧

GARRETT LISTENED to the door close behind him. Disgusted, he banged his head on the glass.

He didn't even need to look at the security footage to know that Emma hadn't even glanced at his carefully laid trap.

Instead, she'd said, "Here's your coffee, sir!" Then she set the cup on the only clear corner of his desk, leaving without a backward glance, just like she had every day since this farce had begun.

Emma hadn't even commented on the increasing clutter. It must have been killing her not to say anything. His high school nemesis had been incapable of keeping her thoughts to herself. Her smart mouth had gotten her in and out of trouble more times than he could count.

But did she take the bait this time? That was a big fat hell no.

Pivoting, Garrett surveyed the carefully laid-out disaster before him. Almost every square inch of his office had been covered with piles of fake documents.

He'd spent an entire weekend dummying up contracts and sensitive financial documents to lay the perfect trap. Garrett knew entrapment was a bit underhanded, but what other way did he have to expose her?

At first, he'd merely covered his desk with them, even half turning one so she could read the name of the Montevalle development with ease.

When that hadn't proved tempting enough, he had started arranging papers on the side tables, an avalanche spreading out onto every available surface—even the couch.

And damn it, she hadn't so much as batted an eye. Not even to inform him that his office was becoming a firetrap.

Sighing, he started stacking his fake documents into a big pile. He'd have to have Fletcher's assistant shred them before his analysts saw them and demanded to know what the hell was going on.

Chapter Four

EMMA

The Stop Requested button on the bus must have been malfunctioning because the sign didn't go on and the driver blew past her stop by several blocks. It would have been fine except for the fact San Diego was experiencing a rare day of torrential rain.

Emma had marginal success staying dry, darting from awning to tree cover, hugging buildings to take advantage of that small space around them that was spared the rain.

She was across the street from her apartment building when a Tesla flew past to turn the corner, sending up a huge spray of dirty puddle water all over her cream-colored tights.

Swearing, she shook out the water that had run into her shoes and trudged up the steps to the third floor, bypassing the elevator to avoid the landlord, who had been on the rampage for the last week.

And with good reason she thought, her stomach dropping as she opened the door and it caught halfway.

"Oh God," she muttered squeezing inside as a stack of old magazines threatened to topple over on her.

Emma dripped on the doormat, wiping her feet and looking around in dismay. Pedro was rearranging again.

When Emma had moved to town, she had been grateful to have a cheap place she could stay in while working her minimum wage job. Her mother had been doubly grateful she'd be living with family, an older male cousin who could keep an eye on her as she got back on her feet after the accident.

But her mother hadn't seen her brother's only son in years. And she certainly hadn't visited him before Emma moved in to share his crowded two-bedroom apartment.

Pedro was a hoarder.

That wasn't an official diagnosis. Also, according to the stricter definitions Emma had read online, it wasn't entirely accurate. But Emma knew that's what this was.

The nine-hundred-square-foot apartment should have been spacious. Pedro's furniture was modern and in good shape. Except she didn't get to appreciate it because it was always covered in stuff.

Junk mail fliers joined piles of kitchen supplies still sealed in their original packages. These would be stacked next to brand-new paperbacks whose spines had never been cracked. There was a corner reserved exclusively for outdated computer equipment.

"This will all be valuable someday," Pedro had insisted, adding a pink plastic apple computer to a carefully constructed tower. He pushed aside a crowded clothing rack on wheels to make room.

Many of those items were new, the tags still attached, but nonsensical for San Diego, like the heavy parka rated for subzero weather. Add that to the sports equipment he never used and what she called the promotional pile: objects like frisbees, mouse pads, tote bags, and more, all branded with the names of local businesses—things most people gleefully took but rarely used.

Her cousin's collection material of choice were periodicals. Magazines mostly, but the *Union-Tribune* newspaper was a close second. It would have been first, but she had convinced him to give up his paper subscription in favor of the cheaper online one. At the same time, a few of his favorite magazines had folded.

Emma was convinced the death of print journalism was the only reason her cousin hadn't been buried under his possessions.

He can't help it, she reminded herself.

Something happened to Pedro's brain every time he came into possession of a new object. According to her research, had she stuffed him in an MRI machine and handed him a pen, something in his gray matter would light up like a lightbulb as the pen went from a random object to a precious personal possession.

Maybe it was chemical. Or perhaps there were lesions in his brain as one research paper indicated.

She didn't know. Emma only knew that trying to take something of Pedro's hurt him on an almost physical level. That was why she always checked before she threw anything away.

Pedro still spoke of the time his mother had come and cleaned this place out, throwing away every old newspaper and recycling his magazines. He described it the way another person would describe a death in the family.

To him, it was the same thing.

"Emma." Pedro emerged from his bedroom, flushed but neatly dressed in a blue button-down shirt and khaki pants. If you passed him on the street, you never would have guessed that his apartment would look like this.

"You're home already!" he said a touch too brightly.

She knew the signs. Pedro was annoyed. He usually moved his hoard around while she was at work.

"I'm late actually."

And wet but he hadn't seemed to notice that, so she didn't mention it.

"Are you rearranging?" she asked, stating the obvious. Her bedroom door was blocked by several large Tupperware containers stuffed full of miscellaneous, yet irreplaceable things.

He held up a finger. "I just need one more hour and it will be as good as new."

"Uh-huh."

Pedro bit his lip and winced, looking away. "I got your favorite Italian sausage pasta from the Pizzaz."

Emma put her hand over her heart, tearing up. "You did?"

He gestured to the kitchen table, hidden by the pile of paperbacks stacked on the table behind the couch.

Thanking him, she stripped off her shoes and wet socks, leaving them at the door. He came to the table a little later—after clearing the path to her room.

"How was your day?" he asked.

Emma told him about the kitten. "I've got to get him out of the garage."

"Try food," he suggested. "It'll be hungry."

"I will," she said, not giving her weird trip to the top floor another thought. "I have a plan for tomorrow."

The next day Emma clocked out early. The cat was right where he'd been the day before.

She crouched down behind the red Ferrari, cooing with all her might.

"C'mon, sweetie," she said, dangling the piece of turkey she'd peeled off her day-old discount sandwich. "I know you'd rather this be ham but beggars can't be choosers."

Apparently, beggars could be picky as hell because the kitten didn't budge. To make matters worse, the only thing she could see under the low-slung sports car were tiny cat paws. She would have had to lay flat on the dirty concrete to get a better look.

Why couldn't the little guy have chosen to hide under one of the Range Rovers?

At least the kitten was under one of the cars that didn't move during the day. This Ferrari was always parked in this spot when she arrived at six in the morning and would be here when she left at five.

She had been convinced the owner left it here all week. Parking was at a premium downtown. But ever since she'd discovered the kitten, she'd finally seen the vehicle's small shifts in position relative to the yellow lines, confirming that the owner did move it every day.

Emma winced as the sound of an engine roaring to life was followed by tires squealing at a high pitch.

The damn suits in the building were always doing that—peeling out of the garage like their butts were on fire. Seriously, they were going to hit someone someday.

And that somebody would be her unless she started going the long way around to the back of the building. Because, of course, his highness Mr. Chapman didn't want the café staff coming in the front doors of the complex. Building rules.

"Did you hear that?" she asked the kitten as another engine started, the post-five o'clock exodus well underway. "It's not safe to stay here or one of those jerks in a suit is going to squish you."

She couldn't let that happen to this sweet baby, no matter how difficult it would be trying to keep a pet at Pedro's apartment. How would she get the little one to use a litter box when the apartment was full of nooks and crannies only a cat could access?

"You know it's probably a rat you've been hearing," Bethany said over her shoulder.

Startled, Emma looked up.

Bethany rocked on her heels. "Not to mention the fact a pet is a spectacularly bad idea—you can barely take care of yourself."

Emma scowled at the unasked-for reminder.

"Shouldn't you be wiping down the tables inside?" Emma had done them all after breakfast and lunch to get the other woman to agree to close the café.

Bethany lifted a shoulder. "Fine. Get rabies," she said before wiping her hands on her apron and going back inside.

Emma sighed. The rest of the café staff either didn't believe there was a kitten or they didn't care, too wrapped up in their own problems. Rent. Bills. Boyfriends. Girlfriends.

Kyle had a beta fish, but that was it on the pet front. Even her boss Hector was pet-free because he was allergic to anything with fur.

Which means saving the kitten is up to you. Emma had scouted the entire garage and the immediate streets around it. There wasn't a mama cat. The little guy wasn't part of a litter. What was it surviving on?

Scratch that. She didn't want to know.

Sighing, Emma scooted closer, careful not to let the knees of her beige tights touch the dirty concrete floor. They were part of her uniform and she really needed six to get through the week, but so far had only been able to afford four. She washed them in the sink on Wednesday to cover the entire week.

One of the few blessings of Ernesto's condition was that his closet was always full of cleaning supplies. She'd also gotten paid today. Once she paid her share of rent and utilities, she'd take whatever she had left to the nearest discount grocery store to buy cat food and a bag of litter.

Unless Pedro already has litter in the apartment? It was entirely possible.

The kitten meowed again.

"Here, little baby." Emma pinched off a piece of the turkey and tossed it at the little paws, craning her head forward so far she got a shooting pain in her neck.

Swearing under her breath, she stood up just in time to see a wall of muscle in a suit rushing at her at full speed.

She barely had time to scream.

Chapter Five

GARRETT

He knew he had made a mistake the second Emma cried out, the overwhelming terror in the sound reaching into his gut to punch his lower intestine.

He had gotten a glimpse of her fiddling underneath Fletcher's Ferrari and his vision had clouded as red as the car. His wild imagination had her planting a tracking device under the vehicle—or in the insanity of the moment—a bomb.

It wasn't until she saw him and dropped the sandwich she was holding that he realized how monumentally he had fucked up.

But it was too late to stop. The paramilitary training he'd done with Auric Security had taken over and in a blink his momentum had carried them both to the wall behind the car, where he pinned her using the bulk of his body.

His only saving grace was that he'd had the foresight to cradle the back of her head with his palm before she hit the concrete, the sweet taste of vindication fleeing as quickly as it had come.

Now he was frozen in place, unable to see anything but Emma's fear-filled eyes, his mind having blanked in self-protection against his own idiocy.

Even Fletcher's shouts were barely making it through the wall of white noise his mind had created.

He had been walking his partner to his car, talking about the dinner they were about to have with a longtime client when they'd spotted Emma.

Fuck. Were those tears? Yes, they were.

Congratulations, asshole. He had terrorized his employee—*in a parking garage no less*—and made her cry.

The sob that escaped her mouth finally broke the ice that had encased him. Garrett let go, backing off before he threw up all over her.

It took Emma a minute to realize she'd been released. She looked from side to side, jerking abruptly before picking up the coffee cup he hadn't noticed.

A thousand words of apology rose to his lips, but they got trapped in his throat.

Then he saw something, a scar about an inch long peeking out from behind her hair, the thick mass of it pulled forward over one shoulder in a side braid.

He fixed on the pale line of white that appeared to thicken before disappearing behind the glossy dark-brown strands.

"How old is that scar?" he breathed, his hand moving to push her braid back.

It was another idiot move of course. Garrett had just assaulted a woman in a parking garage and was now trying to stroke her hair.

He deserved what happened next.

Squeaking as if all the air had rushed out of her lungs, Emma jerked the coffee cup up.

De Olla was a premium coffee place but even they used those flimsy to-go lids that never managed to stay on.

Garrett reared back as the still-hot coffee splashed all over his pristine white shirt.

"Shit."

He ran his hands down his chest in rapid strokes, pushing the hot liquid off. It wasn't scalding, but it was hot enough to shock him and incense Fletcher.

His partner stepped up around them, uncaring that Emma had flattened herself against the wall as two men crowded her, effectively trapping her.

"Emma! Did you just throw the coffee at him?" he asked, giving her an incredulous glare.

She didn't answer. Garrett would have been surprised if she could. Emma was trembling, her eyes wide and glassy as if she was in shock.

"Are you fucking kidding me?" his partner continued yelling as Garrett yanked off his navy blazer and ruined tie. "What is wrong with you?"

He turned his head to glare at his partner. "Calm down. This is my fault."

Garrett shouldn't have taken his eyes off her.

Emma pushed past him, hitting him in the shoulder like a tiny linebacker. Surprised, he leaped back at the same time, knocking Fletcher into the side panel of his prized Ferrari.

"Emmy, wait, I'm sor—" he began but she was running too fast to hear.

Emma was already at the garage entrance, cutting off a tricked-out Jeep about to exit.

The driver leaned on his horn, but it wasn't loud enough to drown out Fletcher. He shouted at the two security guards Garrett hadn't realized were there, waving at the fleeing girl.

"Don't let her get away!"

❦

THIS IS OFFICIALLY A CLUSTERFUCK.

Garrett was a sticky mess, surrounded by people talking at him—Hector, the manager of the coffee shop; Kyle, the skinny barista; the building's manager, Catherine; and Celeste Myers, his head of HR.

Emma was being held in Celeste's office under the watchful eyes of the two security guards. He could see her through the open door, cowering in a chair while the guards stood like prison wardens on either side of her.

He thrust a hand through his hair, his stomach roiling. Shit, they had dragged Emma inside like some sort of criminal.

"She is a criminal," Fletcher said, making him aware he'd spoken aloud.

"I assure you Emmaline is nothing of the kind," Hector said, his hands gesticulating as if he was pouring something, a telling nervous response. "Whatever happened here is a big misunderstanding. She has special needs—"

"I can't believe you are dragging her to HR over the spilled coffee," Kyle interrupted, his face sporting red blotches, either from anger or fear.

"She threw that coffee at him!" Fletcher was irate, his cheeks splotched with red.

He turned to Garrett with an apologetic grimace. "And I'm sorry I didn't believe you earlier. We'll get to the bottom of this mess. I promise you it ends today."

"The bottom of what?" Kyle was near tears. "I thought you were on her side. Did those perverts on twenty-three get to you? Is that what this is about?"

Fletcher scowled at the kid before dismissing him.

"Security is sweeping my car for bugs now," he told Garrett. "Once we find them, we can have her charged with corporate espionage."

"*Bugs*? You think she's some sort of corporate spy?" Hector asked in confusion. "No, that's not right."

Fletcher straightened, patting the man on the back in an awkward this-isn't-your-fault gesture.

"Rest assured we don't blame you. Whoever placed her here was very cunning," he said, his tone implying that Hector was anything but. "However, I think it's in everyone's best interests if *De Olla* steps back right now. We'll let the authorities handle this."

Kyle threw up his hands. "This is crazy. How could you even think Emma is a spy?"

Fletcher pointed an accusing finger through the door. "How could we not? We see her every day and she just waltzes past like she doesn't even recognize us."

Kyle shook his head. "Why would she…"

The kid almost tripped, stumbling in front of Garrett. "*Wait.* Did you know Emma before her accident?"

Garrett hadn't been able to tear his eyes from Emma's huddled form, but he jerked to look at Kyle now. The contents of his stomach were trying to crawl back up his throat.

He silenced Fletcher with a slash to the air when he began to speak again.

"What fucking accident?"

Chapter Six

EMMA

She took a deep breath, hating herself when a shudder racked her whole body.

Calm down, she ordered. But the adrenaline coursing through her veins was almost painful. Even her fingertips were tingling. She couldn't decide if they hurt or if they were just numb.

A tear escaped but she scrubbed it away. Emma needed to be angry now.

For a very real moment, she'd thought she was about to be kidnapped or worse.

A loud engine had started, scaring the kitten into darting under another car. Emma was following it when a wall of muscle had rushed at her full tilt.

She'd been too stunned to register the suit or recognize the man in it. She tried to scream. What had come out of her had been more like a strangled wheeze.

It would have been funny if it hadn't been so freaking terrifying.

Emma had been pinned to the wall when she realized it was Mr. Chapman restraining her.

All that heat and muscle had almost smothered her, pressing her against the wall, until he'd abruptly backed away.

Then the guards came, alerted by the balding man who always made his secretary fetch his double-shot macchiato. Baldy had been ranting something about her and the Ferrari, which appeared to be his car.

Good God, did they think she was trying to steal a Ferrari? That was both the craziest and *stupidest* thing she'd ever heard. What the hell would she do with a sports car?

Emma wasn't even allowed to have a driver's license.

And yet an accusation of grand theft auto was not outside the realm of possibility. She was a Hispanic woman, after all. What if they fired her? What would she tell her mother? Or her baby sister?

Reluctantly, she tuned back into the bald man, who was still ranting. Something about a spy.

Nauseated and clammy with sweat, she put her head between her legs. The sound of voices faded as the overwhelming noise of static filled her head.

A small touch on her arm made her jerk upright.

Mr. Chapman was kneeling in front of her, his face a mix of regret and concern.

"Emmy…" His intense dark eyes scanned her face. "You're killing me here. Do you really not recognize me?"

A middle-aged woman hovered anxiously behind him. "Under the circumstances, I would advise against physical contact."

The woman stepped forward when Mr. Chapman didn't move, putting a hand on his shoulder until he stopped touching her.

The small office was so full of people now it was getting hot. Mr. Chapman repeated his question.

"Of course I do," she rasped, frowning at him. "I took you your coffee, remember? And it's Emma, not Emmy."

Mr. Chapman's lips parted, his face going ashen. He sucked in a breath so hard it sounded like he was wheezing.

"I wasn't trying to break into the car," she added, scooting her chair back to get away from him.

There were too many bodies crowding around her. They were sucking all the oxygen out of the room.

"It's going to be okay, Emma," Hector said. He was standing at the door. "I told them what happened to you. They understand now. It's going to be okay."

Scowling, she shook her head and looked up at the woman who'd told Chapman not to touch her. "I don't know what's going on here, but I want to go home."

The woman introduced herself as Celeste Myers, the building manager. She was wearing the kind of expression one wore when trying to dance on a knife's edge. "Of course you do—"

"Right now," Emma insisted. She wanted to stand but Mr. Chapman was standing too close.

Would pushing him away with her foot make things worse? Or would they arrest her for kicking him?

"Emma, this is very important," Chapman said, ignoring everyone but her. "When was your accident?"

She blinked. "What?"

How did he know about that? And why did it look like he was going to start crying? What did he have to cry about?

"She's faking it!" the balding suit who owned the Ferrari yelled. "Seriously, who is buying this? She's messing with *all of us.*"

Mr. Chapman went from sad to mad in a blink. "*Shut up, Fletcher.*"

"But—"

Mr. Chapman jumped up and stalked over to Fletcher, grabbing his arm and hissing something under his breath.

"Are you really falling for this?" Mr. Overcompensating with a Ferrari asked in a hiss. "This is just some mind game she's playing now."

"And why would Emma pretend not to know you?" Hector asked.

Ferrari threw up his hands. "Because they hated each other in high school! Absolutely despised one another. Trust me, this is just the latest and weirdest chapter in a long war."

Emma's head was spinning. "High school?" she echoed.

"I said the client is waiting," Mr. Chapman bit out, glaring at Fletcher.

The bald man tried to stare him down, but Chapman was the alpha in the room. Sweating and swearing, Fletcher backed down, stomping out with a huff.

Emma immediately felt better, but her relief was short-lived when Chapman turned back to her, giving her his full attention.

"You don't remember anything before your accident?" he said, running his fingers through his thick dark hair and swallowing as if this was earth-shattering news. "Not even drama class?"

Emma sucked in a breath as the import of his words sank in. He was serious. He knew her.

She was over a thousand miles away from her hometown in Colorado. This was the fanciest office building in town. How the hell could someone from there be here?

"You were voted most likely to succeed," Mr. Chapman continued, his face lighting up as if this would jog her fractured memory.

Her expression must have darkened because his happy face died away.

"With me," he added in a far less enthusiastic voice. "You were voted most likely to succeed with me. We're in the yearbook together. We graduated in the same class."

"Are you sure?" Celeste asked. She sounded almost relieved. "I think Miss Mendez must look like your former classmate because I'm fairly certain you're a few years older."

Chapman didn't turn to look away from Emma when he answered.

"I am older," he confirmed. "She skipped two grades—"

Oh. Oh God. It was true. They did know each other. Or rather he knew her.

The chair hit the wall as she pushed it back. "I need to go now," she choked out.

Emma put her head down and headed for the door, ignoring the way Celeste had to physically hold Mr. Chapman back.

The man hated her so much in high school he didn't want to let her leave his sight.

Chapter Seven

GARRETT

He pulled out the last drawer of Hector's desk, stacking the manila file folders on the blotter while he ignored the argument brewing at the door.

"You tell him—" Kyle hissed.

"I'm going to," Hector insisted. But he kept silent as Garrett continued going through *De Olla's* confidential papers.

The tattooed and pierced female barista snickered. "Maybe sometime this year."

That one didn't bother to keep her voice down like the other two. Ignoring them, he flipped through the top folder.

"Oh no—not the employee satisfaction forms," the manager said in consternation. "You were rather harsh, Bethany."

Garrett suppressed a frown. Did that mean Hector let his employees rate *him*?

Doesn't matter. Keep your eye on the prize. He set that folder aside, flipping through the others until he found the one containing the health plan information.

"Her address isn't in there," Hector called from the door as Garrett pushed aside some purchasing orders.

Damn. Cinnamon was more expensive than he thought.

"I'm not looking for Emma's address," he muttered without looking up.

Garrett's private detective had sent that to him yesterday. However, after a long lecture from Celeste, he had refrained from going there last night.

But he had wanted to. At one point he'd even climbed into his car and turned it on. The only reason he hadn't driven over had been the realization it was after two a.m.

Needless to say, he hadn't gotten a lot of sleep.

He wasn't going to find what he needed on his own. Garrett pinned the trio at the door with a pointed look. "Please come in here, Hector."

The threesome in the doorway looked at each other.

"Go," whispered Kyle.

"Err. Yes, I will come into *my* office," Hector replied, walking in with an exaggerated put-upon expression. He ruined it a moment later when he sat in the chair reserved for employees.

The man was going to need assertiveness training if he wanted *De Olla* to succeed.

"Where are your health insurance agreements?"

Hector blinked. "Our what?"

Garrett sighed and held up a folder. "The agreements that spell out the medical coverage terms for full-time employees. Emma is full-time, isn't she?"

"Yes?"

Garrett scowled. "Is that a question?"

"No." The manager cleared his throat as Bethany snickered in the background. "She is a full-time employee. *My* employee."

The emphasis was not lost on him. Garrett looked over the man's shoulder. "Can you two leave us? I need to speak to Hector alone."

The junior staff melted away. When he turned back to Hector, the other man was sitting straighter, having taken the time to bolster his confidence.

"Perhaps we should switch sides here?" Hector suggested, gesturing to his desk chair. "Or not," he added quickly when Garrett gave him a flat look.

Garrett placed his hand on the pile of folders. "How long has Emma been working for you?"

Hector's brow creased as he thought about it. "A little over nine months."

"In this building?" he asked, unwilling to believe Emma Mendez had been under his nose all that time.

"No," Hector said. "She was at the waterfront kiosk for most of it. I transferred her here when we got the contract."

Garrett relaxed. It had only been a couple of months, then. But his brain couldn't help calculating the exact number of hours Emma had been in this building without his knowledge.

"And what do you know about her accident?"

Hector began to look uncomfortable—even more than he had been. "I'm not sure that's something we should be discussing without Celeste… maybe in some form of mediation?"

"That won't be necessary."

"I, um, I think it is."

"Why?"

"Well…" Hector swallowed. "You appear to have very intense feelings about Emma."

Garrett tried to play that off. "I'm not sure I would characterize it that way."

Hector raised his brows. "You broke into my office to look for her address."

"No, I used my key—the one I have as the owner of the building," he added. "And I don't need her address. What I need to know is what her health insurance covers because she sustained a major brain injury that left her with *permanent memory loss*."

He was nearly shouting by the time he finished. Aware that he'd just blown his facade of indifference, he took a deep breath and cleared his throat.

"So, it would help if you could find your medical plan information."

As for the details of her accident, Garrett didn't need to pump this man for that. His PI was already gathering that information.

Hector stared at him for a long moment before finally finding his voice. "I thought you hated her."

Garrett tossed a file folder to the side. "What?"

"Fletcher Sweeney said you and Emma hated each other."

"*Oh.*" He waved that off. "That was high school stuff. Over ages ago."

Hector's head drew back. "High school is a formative time for many of us. And if you had an issue with Emma, it's only natural that you might carry it into the present."

Guess who's been to therapy. Instead of asking Hector who had bullied him in school, he decided some honesty would serve him better.

"It was a healthy rivalry. We were competitive," he elaborated. "Sure, there was some arguing—we did debate each other. But most of it was good-natured bickering."

All right, that last part was a stretch, but he wasn't about to get into his and Emma's real history.

Judging from the look on his face, that wasn't enough for a still-skeptical Hector.

Garrett let the tight line of his shoulders drift into a slump. Damn, he was tired. What came out of his mouth next was probably the most truthful thing he'd ever said. Something he'd never told anyone, not even himself.

"I don't think I'd be here if it weren't for Emma."

He'd totally lost the man. Hector sat forward. "Excuse me, what now?"

Garrett leaned back in the manager's chair.

"I was pretty focused on sports and partying in high school." That and disappointing his absentee father. Garrett had excelled at *that*.

"I didn't get serious about school until Emma skipped those two grades. She ended up in most of my classes."

It had been a rather small school, so it had been impossible to avoid each other despite the faculty's best efforts to keep them apart after that first disastrous semester.

He smiled, remembering a not-quite fifteen-year-old Emma

pointing at him, calling him out during drama class. *"I wouldn't be his Juliet if you paid me."*

Yeah, she had been smart as hell and impossible to intimidate.

"Rather than letting her keep making me look bad, I cracked open a book."

In fact, Garrett had cracked several. And when he was done with those, he cracked some more, enough to dig himself out of the hole he'd dug coasting along freshman and sophomore year.

Because of Emma, he'd managed to get into his second choice for college. From there he'd gone on to business school and started Next Chapter with Fletcher a few months after graduating.

It wasn't an empire—yet. More like his own little fiefdom. But it was expanding. Many things were happening, all at once. Including the realization he'd had at midnight last night.

Garrett wouldn't be a success without the kick in the pants Emma Mendez had given him.

Hector was intrigued. "So you think you owe her now?"

"Something like that," he murmured, realizing he hadn't paid close enough attention when he pulled these folders out because now he didn't know where they went.

"And this payback involves getting ahold of our health insurance forms?"

Garrett chose a folder at random and stuck it in the bottom drawer. "I think, under the circumstances, I should make sure that the woman who suffered a head injury bad enough to forget high school has the best insurance possible."

"Because she forgot high school or because she forgot *you*?"

Garrett paused in the act of randomly sticking folders in drawers. He nodded, letting the man interpret that however he wanted.

Hector continued, wincing. "I'm sorry but I can't bump up Emma's health insurance coverage. It wouldn't be fair to the others. And as a new business in the process of expanding, I can't afford to give everyone premium coverage."

Garrett waved that off. "Don't worry. I'll take care of Emma."

"Oh." Hector was undeniably relieved but still didn't seem

completely on board. "Well, maybe you don't have to. You know she was a disabled hire, right? We get benefits from the state, and I know she gets some extra things too. Physical therapy and stuff like that."

It was meant to be comforting but the fact that Emma was considered disabled hit him like a punch to the gut. "I'm still going to need those papers."

"Of course." Hector stood. "But it might go faster if we switch places because the information you're looking for is on the computer. All the records are online."

Garrett flushed, straightening his jacket as he rose. "In that case, why don't you forward it to my email?"

"I'll do that."

"Thanks."

He left, racking his brain. It was one thing to make sure Emma had access to the best care. But judging from the way she'd run out of the office yesterday, it would be quite another to get her to accept it from him.

Chapter Eight

GARRETT

I should have changed before starting this, he thought as he crawled on his hands and knees, aiming the flashlight on his phone under a low-slung sedan.

"And you're sure there's a cat?"

He glanced up at Kyle, who was generously spending his break to help him look for the kitten Emma had been searching for.

Not being a cat person, Garrett could have taken or left the fate of the animal to chance. But Emma hadn't come to work the day after he'd ransacked Hector's office. Or the day after that.

When questioned, Hector reluctantly admitted that Emma had requested a switch to another location. "Under the circumstances, and on advice from Mrs. Myers, I don't think I should say which one."

Garrett lifted a brow in response, wondering if Hector thought Emma's new workplace was a great mystery.

The *De Olla* chain was expanding, but they only had three other locations in town. Their second café was still undergoing renovations. The other two were coffee kiosks. One was in Old Town and the other was on the waterfront near the USS Midway, a retired Navy aircraft carrier that had been converted to a museum.

"Well, Emma said there was one." Kyle exchanged a side-eye glance with Bethany who was openly snorting.

"Sure, there is. It's striped like a tiger and has big-ass teeth." The other barista had already clocked out, but she wasn't here to help. Her purpose was to provide snarky commentary.

"Very helpful," he muttered.

Bethany gave him a sarcastic smile. She buffed her nails on her apron. "I aim to please."

The woman had been flirtatious at first, but when he hadn't shown any interest, she had reverted to her true personality—a ballbuster with no respect for authority.

Garrett affected a casualness he didn't feel. "I don't suppose Emma told you anything about her accident?"

"A car hit her," Kyle replied. "But she doesn't like talking about it —like not at all."

"Yeah," Bethany agreed. "And if someone from her past comes around, she bolts."

His head popped up from between two cars. "She does?"

"It only happened that one time." Kyle wiped his nose with a crumpled café napkin. "Not sure it's a pattern."

"Oh, it is." Bethany leaned on a car and jumped when the alarm sounded.

Garrett took his keys out and turned it off. "You're lucky that one was mine."

And any chance of finding a cat just went to hell. But he'd keep looking if it kept them talking.

Kyle obliged a bare minute later.

"Emma's cousin Pedro comes in once in a while," he said as Bethany sauntered to the car next to his and began to lean on it instead. "She lives with him. I think that's the only reason her mom was cool with her moving out here. He is supposed to keep an eye on her. Doesn't quite work out that way though."

Bethany wrinkled her nose. "Oh, yeah. That dude is weird as hell. And he brought that other cousin that one time. That mean girl."

Garrett frowned, giving up on the sedan and crab-walking to the next car, a dark-blue Tesla. "What happened?"

She shrugged. "Emma froze up for a minute. She tried to play it off, but it was obvious she didn't feel comfortable. And I can't blame her. She didn't recognize that other cousin. So, she lied and turned down their invitation to join them for dinner. She said she had to work overtime."

Kyle nodded, his expression sad. "Once they were gone, she went and sat in the broom closet for a long time. When I asked if she was okay, she said yeah but that she doesn't like meeting people from before her accident."

"I used to think that was because of the scar," Bethany added, touching her forehead. "Until the cousin came, I didn't realize she had lost so much of her memory."

The woman sniffed. "Can you imagine how messed up that is? It must be a constant mindfuck walking around, interacting with people, and not knowing if you've met them before. Or worse—if you fucked them. You could run into an ex and not know he's a douchebag."

She narrowed her eyes suddenly, giving him a speculative once-over.

"Or maybe your high school nemesis comes round to accuse you of corporate espionage?" he deflected, making Kyle laugh.

But the kid sobered immediately. "Man, I never knew how rough she had it. The headaches are bad enough…"

Garrett mentally added headaches to his running list of Emma's symptoms.

Would it be that bad to hire a hacker to get her medical records?

He sighed, hands tied by this pesky thing called ethics. At least the accident report would be public information, wouldn't it? What was taking his PI so long to get it?

"Maybe you could be nicer to Emma now that you know how bad her accident was," Kyle suggested.

Bethany looked as if she was seriously considering the issue. "Nah, you know what? I don't think so."

"Oh, c'mon!" Kyle bleated.

"I don't think she wants to be treated any different," Bethany insisted. "Seriously, what would she do if I started being nice to her tomorrow?"

Kyle crossed his arms. "I think she'd appreciate it."

"Actually, if she's anything like before the accident, I have to side with Bethany," Garrett said, resigned. "No special treatment."

Bethany rounded on her coworker. "Ha!"

"As long as you're not actively making her life more difficult," he added, feeling the need to add that caveat. Bethany looked like the type.

She scowled at him. "I don't do that."

Kyle sniffed. "You don't make it better, either."

Garrett held up his hands when Bethany opened her mouth, ready to launch into an argument. "Which is fine. Neutral is fine."

That didn't do anything to wipe the sour expression off her face, but it didn't matter because they heard something that diverted their collective attention.

A tiny meow.

Chapter Nine

GARRETT

He nearly bit his tongue off trying to keep from shouting at the gray tabby kitten that had pissed all over his keyboard.

"What the hell?" he hissed, trying to mop it up with the spare tie he kept in his desk drawer. "The PI just sent the accident report!"

The kitten skittered to the side. It looked at the floor as if it was contemplating jumping, but it was too far.

Sighing, Garrett picked the animal up. He set it in the makeshift bed he'd made from a file folder box and some microfiber towels from the supply closet. But the little beast immediately escaped to roam the expanse of his plush cream carpet.

"Crap on that and you'll be…" He trailed off, at a loss to find a threat that didn't make him sound like a monster.

Garrett unplugged the keyboard and threw it in the trash. "Just behave kid. I'm trying to do you a solid here."

He'd already fed the animal a quarter of his lunch, some very choice tidbits from his favorite sushi place. A mobile vet was also on his way to check him out and give him whatever shots cats needed at this age.

The kitten sniffed around the couch before stopping to sit and scratch his back. "Guess I better add flea dip to the list," he muttered.

On cue, Garrett began to get itchy. Ignoring the sensation, he buzzed Fletcher's assistant to get him a new keyboard. Dismissing her as soon as he had it plugged in, he sat and opened the file.

The first blow came when he saw the date at the top. March twenty-third.

He closed his eyes for a long moment before taking out his phone to confirm what he already knew. March twenty-third had been the last Saturday of his spring break senior year of college. He'd thrown his last party in Verdant Falls that night.

The next day he'd packed his bags, going back to college, determined to kick-start his life in the fast lane, leaving the Podunk town of his birth in his rearview mirror. And not just the town but everyone in it.

He had never gone back.

Garrett shoved the keyboard aside and laid his head on his desk surface, belatedly remembering there might still be cat pee on it. Groaning, he went to find some disinfecting wipes before continuing with the report.

Fuck. It got worse. Emma wasn't *in* a car at the time of her accident. She had been walking when it struck her.

It had been a hit-and-run.

Garrett scrolled on as the vise around his chest got tighter and tighter.

The woods. Emma had been found at the bottom of the incline on one of those unnamed dirt roads that ran all through the woods. Her mom had been the one to find her a little after midnight, long after she had been expected at home.

The report didn't say what road she had been on when she was run down. Where had she been going?

Jumping up, he began to pace. This was not enough information and at the same time too much.

Some asshole had hit Emma with his fucking car and left her for dead. He knew the men of Verdant Falls were always gunning it down those fucking dirt roads in their 4x4s.

Hell, the driver didn't even have to hit her to do the damage they had done. A lot of those roads ran along steep ravines. Emma might have seen headlights and jumped out of the way, the driver passing none the wiser that he'd almost killed her.

God, he couldn't imagine what Emma's mother Mariana had gone through.

Back then Mariana Mendez had a reputation. Garrett had always thought it was unfair, the way people had talked about her love life. Small towns disapproved of anyone single with an active sex life.

Mariana had Emma young too, at sixteen or seventeen. She hadn't been done growing up herself. Most of the town had condemned her for it. The rest—the single male part—vied for her attention.

It wouldn't have been unusual for Mariana to be out all night back then. Far more likely than her very responsible college-bound daughter. How long had it taken her to realize Emma wasn't just out with friends, but *missing*?

Unwilling to wait for his PI, he called the number attached to the police report.

"No, I never had a viable suspect," Jesse Warner said when he finally got him on the line and explained his interest in the case.

Warner, a former deputy and now the town sheriff, had been a good six or seven years ahead of him in school. They hadn't been friends but had been aware of each other in that way reasonably popular guys in small towns were.

"Did anyone get bodywork on their car in the aftermath?" he asked.

Jesse harrumphed. "If they did, it wasn't in Verdant Falls or any of the neighboring towns. We checked and made sure the local mechanics knew to call me if anyone brought in a car with damage consistent with a hit-and-run."

"Shit," he muttered. "I guess I was imagining that she saw the car and jumped out of the way."

"Afraid not," Jesse said with a sigh. "There was crushing damage to her left side."

Garrett closed his eyes, struggling to hear what Jesse said after that.

"Could you repeat that?" he asked after a minute.

"I said it could have still been a drunk. You know how people are always tearing it up on those dirt roads. And the Mendez women are tiny. The fucker might not have even noticed he hit Emma and just drove on."

Garrett wanted to protest, but he could see that exact scenario happening. Verdant Falls wasn't financially depressed, but every Colorado town had that segment of hard-drinking roughnecks.

Warner must have shifted around, the sound of fabric rubbing against the phone's receiver. "You said you ran into Emma recently and that's how you found out?"

"Yes," he said. "She ended up working in my building."

"And she didn't remember you?"

Garrett tapped the blotter on his desk with his pen. "No, she did not."

"That's a shame." Jesse sighed. "I was hoping Emma would recover her memories someday. Accident or not, what happened to her never sat well with me. I guess Mariana was right. She'll never get those memories back."

Garrett leaned back in his chair. "She's that sure?"

"She must be. She's the one who has had the most contact with the doctors, right?"

He grunted, making a mental note to check the credentials of all the doctors who treated Emma back then.

"I still wonder if Mariana made the right move," Jesse continued after a beat. "She moved one town over about a year after the accident. I know Stella was young and needed a lot of care, but Mariana did have friends here who could have helped no matter what she thought…"

"Stella who?" Garrett asked with a frown.

"Emma's little sister." Jesse hummed. "I guess you don't know about her. She's like four or five years old now. Mariana found out she was expecting around the time of the accident."

Garrett rubbed his forehead. "No. I hadn't heard about her. Do you keep in touch with Mariana?"

He wasn't aware he'd touched a nerve until Jesse hesitated, his tone changing. "I still check in with her from time to time. We used to spend time together back in the day, but I wasn't quite done playing the field yet so she moved on."

Mariana had 'spent time' with several of the town's eligible men. And a few of the married ones too. It was one of the reasons Emma hadn't dated in high school. She'd been so determined not to make her mother's mistakes.

"One thing I'm not sure you know…" Jesse hesitated. "Rumor had it she moved on with Teddy Bronson."

"Oh." Well, *fuck*…

Teddy was his aunt Phil's ex-husband. He'd been ten years younger than her. They had divorced after eight years of marriage around the time Garrett left Verdant Falls.

Jesse's grunt was clear over the line. "Yeah. I don't want to gossip because I really like Mariana, but you should know there was a lot of talk about Teddy being Stella's dad. Some even suggested the inheritance Mariana got—the one she used to buy her house—was a payoff from him."

Naturally, his aunt Phil hadn't told him any of this.

"I can pretty much dispel that last one for you right now. Geoffrey got alimony after the divorce, but nothing near enough to buy a house for himself, let alone anyone else."

"Really now?" Jesse was skeptical but Garrett didn't fight to convince him. It was enough that he knew the truth.

His aunt had used *his* lawyers to handle Teddy's settlement after the divorce.

Whatever had gone down between Teddy and Emma's mother, Garrett didn't think it had been the reason his aunt had filed for divorce. At least not the only one. Teddy was a womanizer who'd had several affairs.

"Tell Emma the case is still open, if she's interested, that is," Jesse said. "But there's no need to dredge it up if she's moved on and doesn't want to dwell on the past. Last I heard she was hell-bent on doing that."

"Yeah," Garrett mumbled. "Understandable."

He hung up a few minutes later, giving the cat a meaningful look.

"Jesse brings up a good point."

It was the same one Bethany, the surly barista, had made. Emma didn't want to interact with anyone from before her accident.

Rising, he bent to pick up the kitten, putting it in the box before it could pee on him.

"You're going to have to do me a solid and help me get my foot in the door," he told it. "Remember to be extra cute when you meet your new mom because daddy has some karmic debt to clear."

Chapter Ten

EMMA

She wrapped her jacket a little tighter around herself, but it didn't do much good. The zipper was broken, and she hadn't been able to find a tailor who was willing to fix it.

It hadn't seemed like a very big deal earlier this week when the weather had been in the eighties, but the temperature had dropped precipitously the last couple of nights.

Everyone and everything is disposable these days, she grumbled to herself.

It didn't help that the wind on the waterfront was always colder than the rest of town. It always managed to blow straight through the narrow window of the coffee kiosk like a knife, chilling her to the bone.

Which was worse? This cold or getting sexually harassed on the regular by a bunch of overstuffed suits? It didn't matter. She could never go back to the café. Not with that man there.

Which meant she needed to get a new coat. Pedro was sure to have one in those crowded clothing racks. The only trick would be getting him to loan it to her.

Yeah, you're going to be cold until summer.

The icy chill dissipated in a rush of heat when she stepped out of the *De Olla* kiosk to lock up for the night. Garrett Chapman was standing a few yards away.

Emma's lips parted with a gasp.

"Hey," he said, lifting his hand in an awkward wave.

She froze, despite his nonthreatening posture. Keeping her eyes on the threat, she reached behind her for the handle of the kiosk door, seconds away from diving back inside.

Chapman winced. "Please don't run," he said.

He took a step backward, giving her a bit more space. "I'm not here to bother you. I just wanted to apologize for scaring you."

The man looked out of place in his fancy suit and stylish wool coat. Everyone else on the waterfront was in casual clothing. Even the ones who were wearing coats didn't have anything as nice as what he had on.

"Okay, fine," she muttered, a little bit of her panic fading as she realized they weren't alone.

De Olla closed at five. At this hour there were still a lot of people out here by the water's edge. It wasn't like this was a dark parking garage…

That timely reminder straightened her spine. She was *allowed* to be mad about that. This jerk was lucky she didn't kick him in the nards. *Very* lucky.

"Apology accepted," she added in a clipped voice. "You can go now."

Mr. Chapman rocked back on his heels, his dark-brown eyes closing for a long uncomfortable moment.

"I know I deserve that," he began. "I was way out of line, making you bring me coffee and then that, um, that other thing."

Emma tilted her head to one side. "What thing would that be?"

It was hard to tell in the fading light, but she would bet money that he was blushing. "The, um, the thing. By Fletcher's Ferrari."

"Oh…" she began, fluttering her lashes. "You mean when you tackled me in a dark parking garage? Is that the thing you are referring to?"

Emma was aware she was taking no prisoners, but she was on a roll and couldn't seem to stop herself. "Because that qualifies as a serious incident, not a thing, according to your own HR person."

"Yeah." He coughed. "And it was a big deal."

Emma hadn't expected that quick capitulation.

"Yeah, it was," she muttered. "Mrs. Myers also assured me you wouldn't approach me directly. Any sit-down or apology is supposed to happen in her office, with her in attendance."

His eyes narrowed on her face. "You wouldn't agree to see me or accept my apology."

She threw up her hands. "Because I don't want it!"

Chapman clapped a hand on his forehead. "Look, I can only imagine how weird it is to be confronted by a total stranger who claims to know you."

"But you do know me," she mumbled.

That was no longer in doubt. When Emma had packed up her things and moved in with Pedro, her mother had insisted she bring along her high school yearbook. Emma hadn't wanted to, but she also hadn't wanted to argue with her perpetually exhausted mother.

The yearbook confirmed she and Garrett had both graduated from Verdant Falls High the same year. According to the inscriptions of friends she no longer remembered, he'd been class salutatorian to her valedictorian.

He'd come in second to her. *Bet he loved that.*

Which was in line with that other bombshell his business partner had shared. "Oh, also, you hate me with the intensity of a thousand suns."

"We didn't always get along in high school," he corrected, holding up a finger. "But I never hated you."

She wrapped her arms around her chest. "Your best friend said you did, Mr. Chapman."

His shoulders lifted but he jerked suddenly, looking down at his coat with a frown before returning his attention to her.

Emma's brows rose a fraction. *And I thought I was weird.*

"First of all, please call me Garrett. And yes, Fletcher is an old friend and my business partner, but he doesn't know every detail of my life. He wasn't even in most of our classes. It was my fault he got invested in the whole corporate spy theory."

"Because that was rational."

Although she had to admit, Emma Mendez, corporate spy, sounded a whole lot cooler than Emma Mendez, disabled amnesiac.

"Again, I apologize for—" Garrett began before cutting himself off to give the bulge in his coat a glare.

Emma huffed, taking another protective step back. The man was being too weird.

He cleared his rapidly reddening throat. "As for high school, we weren't mortal enemies. It was more along the lines of a healthy rivalry."

So, was Fletcher lying in the HR lady's office, or was Garrett lying now?

Emma sighed, suddenly exhausted. "Then we *didn't* hate each other?"

His mouth opened but he caught himself and appeared to flinch. "Well, you did threaten to hit me with a history book once or twice."

She raised her brows. Did the man have some sort of nervous tic?

"History? Not math?"

"History was our thickest textbook." He gave her a charming shrug. "But I assure you, I deserved it."

Emma kicked the sidewalk with the toe of her scuffed boot. "That's, um, believable."

She expected a scowl or dirty look, but Garrett Chapman surprised her. He started laughing. It transformed his features from forbidding and intimidating to open. Almost warm.

And stupidly handsome. Very stupid.

Chapman leaned forward, his face sober and serious now. "Our rivalry turned my life around. I want to pay a little of that forward."

Emma's brow puckered. Hector had mentioned something to that effect, but she hadn't expected Mr. Moneybags to follow through.

Except he was here in the flesh, being awkward and promising what exactly? Also, what the hell was he hiding under his coat?

"Let me get this straight," she said, deciding it was her turn to hold a finger in the air. "Back in high school, I threatened your manhood in science class or whatever. So you started studying so you could prove your masculine superiority. And now you think you owe me because—shocker—you, a well-to-do white male, made even more money?"

His lips flattened but he nodded. "In a nutshell."

Emma wanted to write him off as a psycho, but the reality was much more depressing.

This was pity. Mr. Moneybags felt sorry for her.

Emmaline Mendez had been valedictorian of her high school class. She had excelled at sports and math, was co-captain of the debate team, and made the Dean's list the first three years of college. She had applied to business school and secured a competitive summer internship at a major Wall Street firm.

It wasn't just her memories that were gone. That bright and shining future belonged to a stranger.

Emma had spent years doing intensive physical therapy just to get to a point where she could function. She couldn't even get a driver's license because of her frequent headaches. They were chronic and debilitating and the reason she was legally classified as disabled.

Now this handsome wealthy man had dropped out of the sky with his perfectly fitted suit and sculpted cheekbones. But this wasn't a romance movie. Garrett wasn't here to sweep her off her feet. He was here to give her a handout to assuage his guilt over living his best life while she had forgotten everything about hers.

This is why she avoided everyone from before the accident. She hadn't even visited her mom or sister since moving out here from Colorado.

Emma had enough.

With that, she took two steps forward and made the sign of the cross up and down over Mr. Moneybags' tall frame.

His head drew back. "What was that for?"

It was her turn to shrug. "You appear to need absolution. I just gave it to you. Can we call it a day now?"

He snorted, managing not to sound like a pig. That or he came from an alternate dimension where pigs were suave debonair bachelors who regularly graced the cover of *GQ*.

"Well, I'm glad to see some things haven't changed. Someone is still snarky as hell."

He may as well have hit her. Because *everything* had changed. Emma recoiled, whirling around, her instinct to leave as fast as possible.

She didn't get far.

Mr. Moneybags stopped her with one hand, wrapping his big paw around her upper arm. "*Emmy, wait.* I didn't mean anything by that. I'm not trying to mess with you. I really do just want to help."

God save me from good Samaritans.

She pulled out of his grasp. "I'm not a charity case! If you're looking for one, I suggest the Feeding San Diego food bank or a local women's shelter. Also, I'm cold and would like to—"

She stopped, nearly biting her tongue when he whipped off his coat and settled it over her shoulders.

They both froze in place. He was standing close, his hands on her shoulders.

She stared up at him, her mind going blank and very quiet—as if those dark eyes had hypnotic powers.

Emma didn't know how long they stayed like that. Coughing, he stepped back. "Keep it," he said hoarsely.

She looked down at the coat draped over her like a blanket. She didn't know fashion, but she would bet the high-end wool coat dragging on the sidewalk cost more than her monthly paycheck.

He cleared his throat. "Although now that I've given you that, I should also give you this."

Cradled in the man's big hands was a tiny gray kitten. Garrett had been holding it under his coat this whole time.

The little animal protested being held out in the cold night air with a tiny angry yowl.

Emma's lips parted. "You found him!"

Garrett stroked the furry head. "I did. He was under a little red Corvette, which I think means he loves Prince," he added with a grin.

It was gone a moment later. "Prince was a singer by the way. A pretty good one."

"How *dare you*?" Emma swept out a hand. The kitten swiped at it.

"Oh, shit. I'm sorry—" he began, regret stamped on each of his stupidly perfect features.

"Prince was not merely *good*," she interrupted. "He was a damn legend and an American treasure second only to Dolly Parton."

Garrett's expression was almost comically relieved. "Oh, thank God. You know who Prince is."

"Yeah," she huffed. "Music streaming services exist."

It was at this point the kitten decided it was done being ignored. He flexed his little claws, making Garrett wince as the surprisingly sharp nails punctured the skin of his hand.

He swore under his breath, trying to dislodge the claws, but the kitten just dug them in harder.

Emma plucked the kitten out of his hands. It must have smelled him on the coat because it burrowed in against her chest and began to audibly purr.

"Oh, so it's like that," he said, glaring at the kitten.

The fur tickled her chin as the kitten nosed around her chest, purring like a freight train.

"Aww. You're a perfect little sweetie, aren't you?" she cooed, rubbing his soft fur.

"What a little traitor," Garrett grumbled. "I gave you grade A sushi, you little jerk. And all I got was peed on."

Emma laughed. "You fed him sushi?"

"What can I say, he's a discerning little jerk. I take it you're keeping him?"

She cuddled the animal closer. "If I don't, are you?"

Garrett put his hands in his pockets. "Not going to lie, giving him up is a sacrifice. Who will claw me to shreds once he's gone?"

Probably any woman he took to bed. All he had to do was ask, she thought, snuggling the fuzzy tabby under the comfort of the wool coat.

Mr. Moneybags had to be freezing, but he wouldn't deign to shiver in front of her.

"I'll take him," she said, cheered by the thought. "Will you be able to cope without him?"

Garrett put his hand over his heart. "You know what they say. If you love something, set it free."

"You don't love cats."

"I really don't." He laughed. "Which is why you are doing me a solid taking him off my hands."

They kept their attention on the cat for an awkward amount of time. "I have to go catch the bus."

Emma had missed her regular one, but if she walked two blocks farther, she could catch the seventy-eight.

Except Mr. Moneybags had other plans. He pointed somewhere to the right. "My car's just over there. Let me drive you home."

"No, thank you."

"Emma." He sighed before changing tactics. "What happens when the bus driver says you can't bring Prince on board?"

"Prince?" she echoed.

"Prince Rogers Nelson," he elaborated with a completely straight face. "Our cat."

"*My* cat," she corrected. "And I've seen way weirder things on the bus."

"Funny how that doesn't make me feel even a little bit better."

No, for some reason he looked like she'd just force-fed him a lemon. "C'mon, Emmy, let me drive you and the little beast home."

Emma bit her lip, mulling it over. The bus driver wouldn't kick her off for having a kitten, would they?

"I guess a ride this one time wouldn't hurt," she mumbled. "This baby needs to get out of the cold."

"A great point," Garrett said as a particularly cold blast of air swept over them.

"Speaking of which, is your hate for cats keeping you warm? Is that why you don't need your coat?"

"That's it exactly," he said, taking her elbow to steer her in the right direction. "Also, I have some stuff in the car for him, a cardboard box with holes, and some drops the vet gave me for fleas. I had someone examine him. He's healthy. Just underweight."

He proceeded to give her the vet's summary on Prince, talking nonstop until she forgot that as little as five minutes ago, she'd been against getting inside his fancy Ferrari.

Except the Ferrari was a Range Rover, and before Emma knew it, she was being buckled in like a child into its toasty interior.

"I don't need help to buckle up," she protested indignantly after he reached around to secure the fastening.

But he was already pulling away, leaving a hint of expensive cologne in his wake. "I'm giving back this coat the second you stop."

"Just hold on to that cat," he ordered. "Don't let him claw up my interior."

She wanted to reply with a snappy comeback but the brief surge of energy she'd gotten when he appeared tonight was dwindling.

Emma sank into the warm seat, feeling unaccountably tired. The purring kitten in her arms did nothing to keep her alert.

"This is a nice car," she observed, wondering where all the potholes downtown had gone. "It must have a great suspension."

"It does," Garrett confirmed before turning the conversation to health insurance of all things.

He talked about it the entire ride. Emma was too tired to ask if that was one of his businesses. It was rude not to listen, but the cozy interior and smoothness of the ride were more effective than a glass of warm milk.

She managed to stay awake, refusing his aid when he tried to help her out of the car and again when he offered to carry her up because he was a psycho.

It was only after she was standing alone in front of Pedro's building with a box full of cat that she realized she hadn't told Garrett Chapman where she lived.

And she was still wearing his coat.

Chapter Eleven

GARRETT

He dropped the extra-large bag of cat litter a second time, regretting taking the stairs up to Emma's apartment instead of waiting for the elevator.

The small Asian woman who'd been checking her mailbox in the lobby caught up with him. "Do you need help with that?" she asked.

Grateful for the assistance, he lifted the smaller bag containing the cat food and toys he hadn't dropped. "Could you take this one?"

He tossed her a self-deprecating smile. "I'm afraid I overdid it at the pet store."

"I can see that," she said, taking the lighter bag from him. She moved the feather-tipped toy so it wouldn't tickle her face. "I take it you just got a cat."

"My friend did," he said, glad that Emma appeared to have friendly neighbors.

There was a private elevator to the penthouse level of his building, which meant the only neighbors he ever saw were his friend Rainer and George, his girlfriend.

Garrett didn't mind that, of course. After making the Forbes list, he had learned to treasure his privacy. But for a normal person like Emma, friendly neighbors could only be a good thing.

This was San Diego, where people smiled and meant it, unlike New York, where he'd briefly lived after business school. There, your neighbors would only concern themselves with your well-being when the stench of your decomposing body became unbearable.

Of course, that wouldn't happen to Emma, he reminded himself when an unwarranted surge of panic made him miss a step.

Emma lived with her cousin, a gainfully employed computer programmer four years older than her. According to his PI, the man didn't appear to have much of a social life, but at least that meant he was home on those nights when Emma wasn't feeling well.

Like last night. She'd been so feisty sparring with him outside the coffee kiosk. It had felt so familiar and right, despite his repeated attempts to cram his boot in his mouth.

But then her energy level had drained so quickly in the car. It had been like watching a balloon deflate before his eyes.

That sudden wave of exhaustion had given him an advantage, letting him bundle her into his vehicle so he could talk to her about his plan to provide her with premium health insurance. Not that she'd paid much attention.

Maybe that was for the best. He could try and convince her that she'd agreed to it during the car ride.

"This is very kind of you," he told his companion when they finally reached Emma's apartment. "If I'd known it was on the fifth floor, I would have waited for the elevator. And I definitely wouldn't have gotten so many cat toys."

Nine was excessive. Especially for such a small cat. Yeah, he should cancel the extra-large cat tree. Judging from how close these doors were to each other, the apartments were on the small side.

"Think nothing of it," the woman muttered.

He wasn't paying close attention to the stranger but something in her tone made him swing his gaze to her.

The woman's features hardened. He didn't understand why until the door of the apartment swung open, revealing a full-blown hoarder's den.

Emma had called in sick to work and put herself to bed after recognizing the signs of a swiftly approaching migraine. But she hadn't quite succeeded in sleeping it off when the shouting woke her.

Sucking in a deep breath, she forced herself to her feet, holding on to the bed frame for support. Long experience had taught her she had to wait for the ceiling to stop spinning and the nausea to subside. Then she made her way to the living room.

"What's going on?" she asked, her voice hoarse from sleep.

Pedro spun around, his eyes rimmed in red. The reason became clear when she registered who was standing behind him.

"Having a cat is a violation of your lease!" Hannah Cho crowed, the vindication on her face out of proportion with her petite features.

Garrett Chapman was standing next to her, unable to hide his stunned dismay as he took in the stacks of broken outdated computer equipment, magazines, and stacked boxes of new household appliances.

"But this building allows pets." Emma turned toward Hannah, her head beginning to pound. "I know I've seen Mrs. Moore on the first floor carrying a Maltese in her purse. And the big, bearded man on the floor above us had that huge German shepherd. We can hear it barking sometimes. The building must allow pets."

Hannah pointed at Pedro, her head wagging side to side. "Not for him it doesn't. The updated lease you signed last March explicitly forbade you from having any sort of animal."

"It did?" Pedro frowned. "But you can't have separate rules for one person and another set for everyone else."

Hannah put her hands on her hips. "We can for problem tenants like you."

The sick feeling in Emma's stomach grew with Hannah's jubilation. The landlord's daughter was almost dancing, she was so excited.

Unlike most of the buildings owned by faceless corporations, Pedro's apartment building was owned by a single family.

Her cousin made some comments about the Chos not being fans

when she moved in, but Emma hadn't realized they were actively gunning to get him out.

"Look at this place," Hannah yelled. She waved at the crowded stacks with a frenetic air. "This is not *normal*. Letting you introduce animals into this mess would be criminal."

Emma's head was killing her at this point. "But it's not his cat," she said, her voice far weaker than intended.

"Emmy, what's wrong?" Garrett was suddenly in front of her. She recognized him by his size—she could barely make out details now, her headache was so bad.

"Migraine," she whispered, bile rising in her throat as she struggled not to throw up. No other words were possible. She couldn't even speak to chastise him for getting her name wrong again.

"Christ, this is bad," he muttered before his voice grew distant.

She knew he was speaking to Pedro and Hannah, but her world was pain. Staying upright required every ounce of energy.

Emma stifled a cry as she went horizontal. For a second, she thought she'd lost the ability to stand. It took her too long to realize she was being carried.

Garrett set her down on her bed, turning off the light and crouching next to her head. "Close your eyes and rest. I'm going to get someone over here right away."

"*What*?" Who was he going to call?

"Just rest."

The words were kind, but the tone was an order.

"But Hannah is going to kick us out..." Emma had to do something.

She jerked when a heavy hand touched her forehead. "Shh. That's my fault for pointing out the cat. I clean up my messes. So rest. I'm going to take care of everything."

The door closed behind him.

On some level, Emma must have believed him because she let go, closing her eyes until sleep finally claimed her.

Chapter Twelve

EMMA

Dr. Saha, a neurologist who'd driven down from Cedars-Sinai in Los Angeles, was there when she woke up.

Emma was in that weird hungover and depleted state she always experienced after a bad migraine. Docile and weak, she submitted to a physical exam before she realized what she was doing.

"I don't think you're covered by my insurance," she said as the doctor took her vitals.

The Indian woman gave her a bright smile, putting her stethoscope aside. "Don't worry, this consultation has already been paid for."

She straightened. "Sorry—is Mr. Chapman your boss or your boyfriend?"

Alarmed, she shook her head, but that made it swim. "Neither."

"I see…" the doctor said in a tone that implied otherwise.

She gently held Emma's head still, checking the reaction of her pupils with a penlight. "Did this headache begin after the incident he mentioned where he jostled your head?"

"Is that why he called you?" Emma asked, relaxing. "Because of the parking garage?"

The doctor's brows rose a touch, but her focus remained on her examination.

"He was concerned it was related. But your cousin mentioned a long history of migraines after your accident. I had a quick peek at your medical records, so I saw that for myself, but their overall duration is not as well-documented. On average, how long would you say they last?"

She tried to clear the fog by yawning. "A day or two but I try and sleep when they're really bad so it's hard to say."

The second part of the doctor's words registered. "Wait, how did you get my medical records?"

"I believe your cousin gave them to Mr. Chapman and he forwarded them to me."

"*Oh,*" she said, nonplussed.

Her mother had insisted Pedro have the power to make medical decisions for her, in case Emma needed to be hospitalized again. That meant her records were at his disposal. But she hadn't expected him to share that information with anyone, let alone some strange man.

Although she shouldn't have been surprised.

Pedro didn't have an assertive personality. An alpha male like Garrett Chapman would steamroll right over him.

What in the world was she going to do about him?

Emma had expected the kitten delivery last night to be the last time she ever saw him. She had gone out of her way to let him know he was off the hook. But he didn't seem to be getting the message.

Weren't billionaires supposed to be assholes? Wasn't that a universal truth? Could it be he was taking this secret of my success-debt-thing seriously? Or was this all fueled by his pity?

Of course, it's pity.

There was a reason Emma had a no-contact policy with everyone who knew her before the accident. Not that many of her old friends had been beating down her door since she'd woken in the hospital.

Her mother was still angry over the way so many of them had dropped her after the accident. But in retrospect, Emma was nothing but grateful. That handful of painfully awkward visits with old friends had taught her an important lesson.

For some people, there was no going home again, even when you still lived there.

The doctor began putting her equipment away. "I understand you've had a recent CT scan, but I would like you to come in for an MRI this afternoon."

Emma blinked. "Today?"

The doctor nodded. "Mr. Chapman has already arranged it, but if you can't make the scheduled appointment, we can find a slot for tomorrow."

Just how much money did Garrett Chapman have? Because in her experience, no doctor was this accommodating. Come to think of it, they also never made house calls.

"Do you need to move the appointment?"

Emma shook her head. "No. I wasn't scheduled to work today."

"Perfect."

Emma thought they were done, but Dr. Saha continued asking dozens of questions, noting down the answers on her tablet.

Finally, the visit wrapped up. Despite her lingering headache, Emma walked the doctor to the door, eager to speak with Pedro.

Her cousin wasn't there. The kitten was gone too.

Emma gingerly lowered herself onto the couch, trying not to worry. Garrett had promised to fix the Hannah situation and he would do it. If he tried to wash his hands of it, she would force him to keep his word.

Feeling better, she tried to be productive. Emma hated when her headaches kept her in bed, preventing her from accomplishing all but the simplest tasks. Setting her sights lower, she did some light cleaning in the kitchen, waiting impatiently until Pedro finally returned.

She was all over him the moment he walked in the door.

"Thank God you're back."

Pedro took off his windbreaker and gave her a weak smile. "Is the doctor gone?"

"Yes." She bit her lip. "I'm so sorry about Garrett coming here and telling Hannah about the cat. I had no idea he even knew where I lived. Someone at *De Olla* must have told him."

Pedro sat on the couch. "Yeah, he explained what happened,

confusing you for some sort of corporate Mata Hari. But he is determined to make up for it."

To anyone else, that wouldn't sound ominous. "It was nice of him to arrange for the doctor," she acknowledged.

Dr. Saha was a specialist with a long list of credentials she was pretty sure her regular HMO doctor had never even heard of. Getting her down here for a house call was on par with the odds of winning the lottery.

"He has a gorgeous penthouse. It's bigger than any house I've ever been in."

Emma's lips parted. She sat next to him. "You went to his place?"

"Yeah." Pedro lifted a shoulder. "That's where I was. I went to get the cat settled. He said it was half his anyway."

Unbelievable. "We're not sharing Meowmus Maximus."

Her cousin's brows rose. "I thought his name was Prince."

"I changed it because he is *my* cat whom I do not share with anyone."

"Except he lives in a penthouse with someone else now..." Pedro sighed, looking down. "Look, about what Hannah said..."

"Again, I'm sorry about that. I knew she wasn't a fan, but I had no idea the Chos were looking for an excuse to get rid of you. Hannah seemed so happy when I moved in."

Pedro looked down at his hands. "I guess the cat was a bridge too far."

Emma felt terrible. She reached out to touch his arm. "I can talk to her. I'll tell her the cat's gone. It will be all right."

He shook his head. "I think it's too late for that."

"No, it's not. I know Hannah was upset, but the Chos can't kick you out because of the kitten. Not when they allow other tenants to have pets. Especially since Meowmus won't be living here anymore," she added, unable to keep the sadness from her voice.

"They are the landlords. They make the rules."

She held up her hands. "Renters have a lot of rights in California. If Hannah and her parents try and make an issue of this, we can get help from one of those tenant rights groups."

It wasn't as if the apartment posed a hazard to the other residents. There was no food waste. No chance of vermin beyond silverfish.

Not yet anyway.

"*Em.*" Pedro rubbed a hand over his face. "I don't think this is working out."

The little ball of anxiety that had been sitting in her stomach since Hannah's explosion grew exponentially. "What isn't?"

Her cousin looked down at his lap. "You living here. I don't think it's a good idea anymore."

His words were so unexpected she didn't process them for a long moment. When she finally did, it was like the ceiling had fallen on her. "You're kicking me *out*?"

He held up his hands. "It's not like that."

Her head was spinning. "Then I can stay?"

Pedro swallowed, but he straightened his shoulders with uncharacteristic firmness. "No."

"Please don't freak out—you're not going to be homeless. Garrett is finding a place for you."

"Oh God," she groaned. That was the last thing she wanted. How could Garrett do this?

Then she remembered the look on his face when he'd seen the piles of things in the room.

"*Wait.* Did he offer to take me off your hands first? Is that why you're doing this?"

"I know this is a shock," he said, ignoring her questions. "But I'm trying to do the right thing here."

He broke off, his voice cracking. Pedro's shoulders rounded back up as if he was drawing in on himself. "It was different... seeing this place from someone else's eyes."

Emma's panic quieted, sympathy welling at the palpable despair in his voice.

She didn't need to ask if he was referring to Garrett, not Hannah. Not that the younger woman's low opinion wouldn't have decimated him under normal circumstances.

But everyone else faded into the background when Garrett

Chapman was in the room. His presence would have thrown the hoard into sharp relief.

Emma had only known Garrett a few days in this post-accident incarnation of herself. But this awareness of him felt older, as if she had been pre-tuned to pick up his frequency.

What an idiotic thought. Emma rubbed her forehead. The stress was making her stupid. She had Garrett's number because he was a white alpha male who thought his money and power entitled him to run other people's lives. The US government was full of them.

No. Her shy, troubled cousin wouldn't be able to stand his ground against him.

His next words confirmed that conclusion. "Garrett spoke to Hannah and convinced her not to evict me but there were conditions. One of them is that you and the cat are going to be relocating to a new apartment."

Emma could barely believe her ears. Garrett had negotiated her out of her home.

"So it's not enough for the kitten to go," she said. "I have to leave too."

Pedro was near tears as well.

"I'm not well, Em." He gestured to the mess around them with a broken half wave. "And if I can't take care of myself, how can I take care of you?"

"I take care of you too!" she protested. "We take care of each other."

Or at least they tried. But even she had to admit they did a piss-poor job of it sometimes.

She swallowed, wiping under her eyes. "What if you get worse after I'm gone?"

"I might. I can only try. I'm going to start therapy."

Emma sucked in a surprised breath. She had broached the subject countless times, but Pedro had always dismissed the suggestion or changed the subject.

Well, of course he wouldn't listen to her. She was more messed up than he was. Yet the moment Superman walked in the door…

But he was finally getting help. Was she even allowed to be mad?

"Garrett and I had a long talk about it," he continued, and she decided yes. Yes, she was.

"He has found someone who deals with people like me. A specialist, like he found Dr. Saha."

"That's good," she said, trying to stay positive despite her fears for herself.

Where would she live? Would it be near a bus line? Or in a safe neighborhood? San Diego wasn't the most dangerous place, but every city had bad spots.

And what would she tell her mother? If Mariana found out she was no longer living with Pedro, she'd be on the phone every night.

Her mother wouldn't pressure her to come home, but she would want detailed rundowns of her day. Mariana would have helpful suggestions and thousands of unfounded worries.

Emma would be a basket case in a matter of weeks.

She bowed her head. What if she couldn't hack life in the city without Pedro? Maybe she *should* go home?

Her cousin's phone buzzed. He lifted it and bit his lip. "Garrett is on his way."

Standing up too fast, Emma leaned on the couch to steady herself. "Why is he coming here?"

Pedro stood too, scanning the room as if he wanted his precious piles to disappear. "He's going to take you to the doctor to get an MRI. Then he's going to take you to look at a few places after."

He gave her a bright smile. "I'm sure they are going to be amazing apartments."

Apartments, plural? Was she going to be living alone? Emma didn't know what to think about that.

There was nothing she wanted more than to regain her independence. But what if a debilitating migraine took her down? True, there hadn't been much Pedro could do when that happened, but his presence had been a comfort.

"Pedro, we don't even know Garrett." He'd met the man today for

Pete's sake. A few scant hours with him and he was ready to hand her off to the man.

"But he knows you."

The flinch was involuntary.

"*Hey*." Pedro's arms came around her. "I know it's difficult for you to be around people who knew you before. But the situation with Garrett is different."

"Because he hates me," she scoffed.

"No, he doesn't." Pedro sounded surer of that than any of the other things he'd said. "He obviously admires you. He told me all about debating you in class and how smart you are."

"The old me was smart." Emma couldn't hide the dejection in her voice. She looked away so she wouldn't see Pedro's hangdog face.

How had this happened? A few days had passed and suddenly everything in her life had turned upside down.

Emma rubbed her damp hands on her leggings. "I don't want this. He just feels sorry for me."

"It's not pity. I don't know what it is but it's not that."

Pedro leaned forward, covering her hand with his. "I know you're skeptical, but Garrett Chapman is important and powerful. He's the type of man who makes things happen. If he wants to help you, then you should let him."

She started to shake her head when he interrupted her. "Em, I know this is going to sound really shitty, but I have to be cruel to you to be kind to myself."

Emma leaned away from him. "What?"

He closed his eyes. "Some people are coming to pack up your things while you're at the doctor."

Holy shit. Emma gripped the couch to keep the room from spinning. But this time her headache was not to blame. "This isn't a conversation, is it?" she asked. "I don't have a say in moving out. The decision has already been made."

Irritation flashed across her cousin's face. "It's not like I'm throwing you out in the street. Your new place is going to be way nicer than this one."

He broke off when his phone buzzed again, not meeting her eyes. "He's here."

Chapter Thirteen

EMMA

Pedro was right about one thing. Garrett Chapman made things happen. Weird things. Like the MRI. His presence at her side transformed an otherwise routine and taxing medical visit into a surreal experience.

Emma had spent the better part of the last five years in and out of different doctors' offices and hospitals. She'd had good experiences with professional and sympathetic doctors and nurses. But she'd also had plenty of bad ones with people who treated her as less than human.

To them, Emma wasn't a person. She was a condition.

Long-term amnesia like hers was rare enough that she was inevitably paraded in front of every medical resident and student in the building. Then she'd be poked and prodded. Tests would be ordered that she was convinced had nothing to do with her condition. Meanwhile, her real issues would be glossed over or outright ignored.

Funny how a hovering millionaire overseeing her appointment made all those issues disappear.

Garrett picked her up and whisked her to the Jacobs Medical Center in La Jolla, where Dr. Saha had medical privileges. Before Emma knew it, she was in a hospital gown, lying on a conveyor belt, being rolled into a big white tube like a bunch of groceries. That was followed by a blood draw, X-rays, and a long consultation about her current medications.

She left with a sack of new ones. Emma was still examining their labels, doing her best to ignore the hypermasculine presence next to her.

That proved to be a poorly thought-out plan when he pulled his shiny Range Rover into the subterranean parking lot of a new high-rise.

Emma shoved the pills back into the white pharmacy bag and craned her neck to examine the sterile half-filled lot.

"Where are we?" she asked. "And if you say, *This is where I murder you,* I will punch you in the testicles."

Garrett covered his face, making a sound that was half-snort, half-wheeze. He took a moment to compose himself before turning to her. The impact of his clean-shaven good looks and sharp suit was a visceral push to her senses.

"Home."

Frowning, she followed him as he got out of the car and led her to an elevator. She didn't protest until he put his hand on a high-tech black panel. A light went on at the bottom along with an electronic message.

Welcome home, Mr. Chapman.

He pressed the top button, and the car began to rise.

"*Wait.* This is your place? I thought we were going to look at apartments for me."

"I thought about it but after that consultation, I think setting you up in your own place might be a bad idea. So, you'll stay with me instead."

Her scowl was instant. "Excuse me, *what*?"

Garrett turned to face her, gesturing to her sack of prescriptions like it was a bag of spiders.

"Em, I was hoping that the consultation would help you cut back on the amount of medication you have to take. But Dr. Saha made it clear you're not in a place where that's possible. And a lot of these are heavy-duty. I can't in good conscience let you live alone."

She stared at him in disbelief, refusing to budge when the elevator stopped and the doors opened. "Then why did you run me out of my apartment? Or did you forget I had a place to live until you showed up?"

He didn't even have the grace to look ashamed of himself. "You and I both know Pedro has enough to deal with on his own. I'm going to find him a great therapist who will help him. But he needs the space, both physical and mental, to tackle his problem."

"That makes no sense," Emma snapped. "Me leaving just gives Pedro another bedroom to fill with things!"

Garrett's sigh was long and drawn out. "I didn't mean space that way. Pedro has been in denial about his condition for a long time. He's only now starting to face it. Acknowledging it is a huge step. So is seeking treatment. He's fragile. And rooming with someone who is fragile in another way..."

"All right. I get it," she bit out, tears stinging her eyes. "I'm a burden."

"You're *not*," he said. "You just need a roommate with more emotional bandwidth than Pedro has now. Which is why you are going to let me—the person who owes you—set you up in a new situation."

His measured, even tone grated on her. Also, why did he have to be both rational *and* handsome, damn it?

Someone with his hairline and chiseled features should have a low IQ or at least smell bad. But no, he had to run a billion-dollar company and smell like citrus and cedar.

"I hope you're right," she muttered. "But also, don't make it sound like that."

"Like what?"

"As if I'm the old-timey mistress you're setting up with an apartment." She swept her hand out. "I lost my *home* because of you. That's the only reason I am agreeing to let you find me a new place. But it's not supposed to be *with* you!"

He took her hand and tugged her out of the elevator into a plush carpeted hallway with one wall that was entirely made of glass. Two doors stood at either end.

Garrett ushered her toward the door. "At least see the place first."

She parted her lips to protest but he was pressing his thumb to a discreet black panel on the door. This fingerprint lock was smaller here and it didn't spit out a welcome message. It just flashed green.

"My closest friends are authorized to enter but they won't unless it's an emergency. It will be no trouble to add you to the database. But you can also have a key fob that will open the smart lock," he explained, pushing open the door to reveal a space worthy of a magazine cover.

"This is one of two penthouses on the top floor." He entered and gestured for her to follow him inside. "It has six bedrooms, so there's plenty of room. I turned one into an office but that's still four big bedrooms up for grabs."

The sunken living room was outfitted with two overstuffed couches and a fireplace. The shiny mahogany bar effectively acted as a separator at the top of the two steps behind which was a swinging door that appeared to lead to a kitchen.

Moving behind the bar, he lifted a cut crystal glass. "Want a drink?"

He took out a sphere of ice from an under-counter freezer she couldn't see and poured himself a few inches of something amber gold. He paused, giving her bag of drugs a considering glance.

"On second thought, mixing alcohol with your meds is a bad idea. How about a Shirley Temple?"

Her brows crept up. He was either going to be the best roommate she'd ever had or the worst.

"You're the one who asked the doctor to have my old prescriptions re-evaluated," she said, examining the glamorous space. The glass he was holding must cost more than her entire wardrobe.

Dear Lord, what if she broke something? She would be in debt to him for *years*.

"Could you drink on the old ones?" he asked, leaning forward and resting an arm on the bar.

"No." She bit her lip, giving their surroundings a skeptical once-over. "I'm not sure about this."

His sigh was long and drawn out. "Man, I wish you could drink," he muttered.

"I heard that."

Garrett grinned, his entire face warming with both welcome and reassurance. "You were meant to."

Emma narrowed her eyes at him. "You are not as cute as you think you are."

His grin only deepened. "Yes, I am."

She hated that it was true. But she'd sooner chew her own arm off than admit it.

He continued after a beat. "Along with the spare bedrooms and my office, this place has a gym, a state-of-the-art kitchen, and a formal dining room in addition to this living room area. You can have two bedrooms if you want. Or change to a new one every week. Rotate the whole month if you want."

Wow, he was giving her the hard sell. "Next you'll tell me you're never here, that I'll hardly ever see you."

Garrett rocked back on his heels. "Oh. No. I'm not going to do that."

Did this man conform to *any* expectations? Emma flattened her hand on the satiny wood surface of the bar. "You're not?"

Garrett took a swig of his drink, the tightening around his eyes testifying to its strength. "Nope."

Unsurprisingly, he got more relaxed with every sip. "I'm going to be here a lot. I would never bring you somewhere to live that didn't have supervision."

That was meant to be comforting. His words shouldn't make her underarms sweat. "But it doesn't have to be you."

A strong emotion flashed across his face before he could hide it. It almost looked like… hurt.

Emma immediately felt guilty. Yes, he'd inadvertently ruined her life, but he was trying to fix it. "I mean, don't you have to work?"

Garrett set the glass down. "Many of our current projects are moving out of the planning stage. I'll still have quite a bit of work, but far fewer meetings. Which means I can telecommute for the next couple of weeks. If anything urgent comes up, the office is only a short drive away."

"Oh." A new thought occurred to her. "You said a few weeks. Does that mean this housing situation is temporary?"

Was a few weeks enough time to find something she could afford?

Even with the assistance she got from the state, that would be a challenge. Her hours at *De Olla* were supposed to be full-time, but with her frequent absences, she worked part-time most weeks—something Hector considered when drafting the schedule.

"*No.*" Garrett took a deep breath, frustration creeping into his tone. "Like I said, you living alone just isn't possible right now—your mother was right about that."

The look of horror on her face made him laugh. "Before you ask, no. I didn't speak to her. We grew up in the same town, but I never met her. Not officially. Your cousin spoke of her quite a bit though. He said she was a little high-strung, and the only reason she slept at night was because you lived with a family member."

"Which you aren't," she said, pointing out the obvious.

Garrett acknowledged that with a gruff nod. "We've been over this. In a perfect world, you could have stayed with Pedro, but sweetheart… you know he's a mess. He needs to focus on his health before he can be responsible for yours."

The endearment was unexpected, but she was too irritated with his choice of words to let her surprise show. "You make me sound like a child. I can take care of myself."

His eyes were serious and soft. "I know you want to. But you're not there yet."

Ouch. Guess who wasn't pulling their punches?

"Also, I hate to be the asshole who points out you weren't helping Pedro either."

"You don't know that," she shot back, stung.

"Emmy." He sighed. "Introducing an animal into a hoarder's home was a terrible idea."

"I know that now. But—"

He held up a hand. "I know you claimed Prince as your own, but it was just a matter of time before Pedro began to think of him as his pet as well. Trust me when I say that would have been the worst-case scenario. Because one cat would have inevitably turned into two and then three. And then a dozen."

She shook her head. "I wouldn't let that happen."

"Could you stop him?" Abandoning his drink, Garrett came around the bar, stopping just a few feet from her.

His posture wasn't hostile. Garrett had even slipped his hands into his pockets to downplay his intimidation factor.

It didn't work, of course. His sheer size made her want to keep a piece of furniture between them. But she was too stubborn to let him see that.

"Tell the truth. Have you been able to stop Pedro from accumulating more stuff since you moved in with him? Or even slowed it down?"

His words hurt like hell, mainly because she'd asked herself those same questions before.

"I'm not trying to hurt you by saying these things." Garrett's big hand engulfed hers. "That's the last thing I want. But the fact is that you *weren't* going to be able to stop him. He needs professional help."

Emma pulled away from his touch. "How do you know so much about hoarding?"

"Honestly, I don't. I've just started to investigate it, but what I've found is depressing as hell. Pedro is a hoarder, Em. It's a serious and badly understood disease. And he's going to need more help than you can give him."

The tear that fell took her by surprise. Damn, had she gotten so used to pain that the fact that she was about to cry didn't even register anymore?

Garrett crept closer, opening his arms.

"I don't need a hug." She sniffed, swiping under her eyes with the cuffs of her sweatshirt.

Garrett stepped back, giving her more space, but damned if he didn't look disappointed. "Just as well. Celeste would have my balls in a sling."

The mention of the HR woman brought the absurdity of the situation home. What the hell was she doing here? If he was trying to avoid a lawsuit, this was a weird-ass way to go about it.

Emma gnawed on her lower lip. "Why does my high school nemesis want to help me? Do you have a secret white knight fetish?"

His smile was like one of those glowing orbs that sometimes appeared in her vision. Fascinating and distracting, but it didn't bode well for her well-being.

"I know you don't want help, especially from someone who knew you when. But I'm here now and I've got a debt to repay. In fact, given my recent track record, those debts are multiplying."

The parking garage incident replayed itself on fast-forward in her mind. "Yeah, I guess you are racking them up."

Garrett snorted. "So let me pay them off, please. For the sake of my karma." He gestured to the opulent space around them. "It's not like it'll be a sacrifice for me."

"All right, Mr. Moneybags," she groused, grateful for the chance to resent him again. "Want to take five to go dive into your vault of gold coins a la Scrooge Mc Duck?"

He cocked his head to the side. "How do you even know about Scrooge McDuck?"

"Memes," she explained.

Researching them had been her mother's suggestion, a quick way of discovering what was in the zeitgeist. Emma had spent the first few years after her accident doing a comprehensive if haphazard study of the world.

His head rocked back in understanding. "I see. So can I show you the bedrooms now?"

Did she have a choice?

It's no different from finding a room online, she told herself. It was probably safer.

Yes, Garrett had barged into her life in the most suspect and intimidating way possible. But he'd done it publicly. Their names were on HR reports together that had all sorts of red flags all over them.

"What are you thinking about?" he asked suspiciously.

"That if anything happens to me, the police will look at you first."

He snickered. "That's true. Also, bonus—tabloid TV would have a field day."

That was a very good point. Handsome billionaire embroiled in a scandal with an amnesiac would be a juicy story.

"I suppose it's not in your best interests to murder me and chop me into little pieces."

His eyes crinkled at the corners. "Believe me, if I had murderous intent for anyone, I'd save it for someone who deserved it. Like a politician."

Emma nodded sagely as if that was a given.

"All right. I will consider staying if you can answer one question. And I want the truth. No lies. No excuses."

She put her hands on his forearms, lifting on her tiptoes to look directly into his eyes. She fell several inches short, but he responded appropriately—freezing in place as if dreading what she might say next.

"Where's my damn cat?"

Chapter Fourteen

GARRETT

Startled and relieved, he laughed. "He's next door," he said. "My neighbor and best friend is watching him."

He held out a hand. "C'mon. I know Rainer is here today. We can pick up Prince now."

Emma gave his outstretched hand the side-eye. "His name is Meowmus Maximus now."

Putting his hand down before it got embarrassing, he cocked his head at her. "So, he's not royalty? Instead, we're setting him up to be a dictator?"

She shrugged. "He *is* a cat."

Damn, she made him want to smile. He wasn't used to that sort of thing anymore.

"I'm not sure it's a good idea to acknowledge his dominance over us."

"That's dogs. Cats automatically assume we're their servants."

Garrett pressed his lips together, acknowledging the truth of that. "Makes me wish you had found a puppy in the garage."

With that, he led the way next door, telling her a little bit about Rainer and George.

Garrett used to live across town but when his old college roommate had told him the penthouse next to him was opening up, he'd jumped at the opportunity to move in next door.

He'd had a few misgivings about it. Being divorced, he'd been worried about crowding Rainer, who had just gotten engaged to his girlfriend-slash-mechanic Georgia. The last thing he wanted was to be a third wheel. Or worse—a gross serial-dating divorcé who changed women every few weeks.

These were just a few of the reasons he'd throttled down on his social life.

It might have been his imagination, but his best friend's girl had warmed considerably as a result. Not that George had ever been icy. She wasn't capable of that. But there had been some awkwardness in the beginning. Which was understandable, given how they'd met.

Note to self, don't ever tell Emmy you accidentally saw Georgia naked.

He also recognized the irony—despite that rocky start, Garrett was counting on the woman now.

If ever a woman was earmarked as a future best friend, it was Georgia Hines. Cute as a button and super friendly, she even had a cool job that required greasy coveralls. Yes, she might live in the penthouse next door, but George didn't have a pretentious bone in her body.

Garrett wasn't above using whatever tools he had at his disposal to make Emma want to stay put in his apartment.

His speculation that Emma and Georgia would hit it off proved spot-on. They got along so well it quickly became obvious that he and Rainer were superfluous, especially once Georgia emerged from the bedroom with the newly christened Meowmus.

He and his friend retreated upstairs to the office, where they could look down on the women in the living room through the glass wall as they fussed with the kitten.

Rainer glanced down at his fiancée of almost a year and heaved a heavy sigh. "Now I have to get a cat. Thanks for that."

His lips twitched. "Sorry, it had to be done."

Like Georgia, the kitten was part of his plan. Fortunately, the little beast was cooperating. The fur ball appeared to recognize Emma and was hamming it up for her, welcoming her as if she had just come back from a war.

He was so engrossed watching her that he didn't notice Rainer's scrutiny until the man nudged him.

"Are you ready to tell me what the hell is going on here? Why did you invite this woman to live with you?"

He raised his brows. "You don't believe it's out of the goodness of my heart?"

Rainer snorted. "Look, I know you have a good heart, despite what people say. But the Garrett I know is a commitment-phobic divorcé who would sooner chew his leg off than invite a woman to live with him, even in the short term."

What people? Garrett scowled. He wandered over to the drink fridge Rainer kept in his office, grabbing a soda. "In case you didn't notice, I haven't exactly been tearing it up lately."

Rainer frowned as if just now realizing that his closest friend had no social life to speak of. "I guess that's true. You've been busy expanding your business."

Rainer only had part of the answer. It wasn't just Next Chapter that had led Garrett to kill his dating life off. It had been Rainer and George and their true and vibrant love for one another.

He'd been happy for them, of course, but he'd also been envious.

"So, obviously, you didn't tell me everything yesterday," Rainer prodded.

Garrett passed a hand through his hair. "Things happened so fast, there wasn't time."

He broke off, his mouth open as he wondered where the hell to start. His relationship with Emma was a clusterfuck over a decade old. He finally shrugged. "It's complicated."

The understatement of the year.

"Yeah," Rainer mused. "That's kind of obvious from the way you look at her."

It was as if a bright spotlight had just been pointed at him. "How do I look at her?" he asked.

Rainer was nothing if not brutally honest. "Like you want to leap on top of her. So, unless you want her to run away screaming, I'd work on that."

Fuck, that wasn't good. He cleared his throat. "Noted."

Rainer took the soda from his hand, switching it with a beer. "How long have you known her?"

Pivoting, he narrowed his eyes. "Did Fletcher call you?"

"No." Rainer laughed. "But color me intrigued. How do you and Fletcher know her? And why is she living with you?"

Unable to help himself, he went back to the window to watch the women play with the cat.

Don't kid yourself. Garrett had eyes for only one woman below.

She was so guarded now, but still so… Emma.

"We went to high school together," he finally said. "During spring break of her senior year of college, she was the victim of a hit-and-run while walking to a party. She was hurt."

Rainer joined him at the window. "Bad?"

"Real bad. She lost her memory."

Rainer frowned. "Of the accident?"

"Of everything. Her entire life before the accident is gone."

Rainer shoved his hands in his pockets, his face tightening. "Fuck. I had no idea. She seems so normal."

"It was a couple of years ago now. I found her working at the coffee shop at the Lumen last week."

Garrett explained his idiotic theory of Emma being a corporate spy and what happened after, the landlord fuckup that had put her here, in his power.

He didn't phrase it like that, of course. But his best friend could read between the lines.

Instead of peppering him with questions, Rainer simply waited, a quiet nonthreatening presence who wasn't shy about telling you when you were going off the rails.

"I hate to say it but I'm with Fletcher. Moving her into your place is a recipe for disaster. Find her someplace else to live."

He shook his head. "No. I can't do that."

Rainer rolled his shoulders and shot him a look. "Why the hell not?"

Garrett was glad the kitten was so damn distracting. If Emma glanced up and saw his expression right now, she'd pack her bags.

"Because there's more," he confessed, intent on getting everything off his chest. "The night of the accident, the party Emma was going to…"

"Yeah?"

He swallowed back bile. "It was at my house."

Chapter Fifteen

EMMA

"I can't believe you restore cars," she told George as Meowmus climbed all over her lap. His little nails were puncturing her yoga pants, but she didn't care. He was too cute.

"That's so cool. I've never met a female mechanic. Not that I remember anyway," she added wryly.

Emma had known Georgia for an hour, give or take ten minutes. But the small black woman's warmth and sweetness had touched her. She'd felt enveloped by it, and before she knew it, she was telling Georgia her life story—the bit she remembered.

Needless to say, it hadn't taken long.

"We're not as rare a breed as you might think." George offered Meowmus a ball with a bell inside. "But I admit I'm biased. I've been tinkering with cars since I was a kid."

"That's amazing, finding your calling so young." Emma sighed. "I wish I knew what I was going to do with my life."

Holding down a regular job had felt like an insurmountable goal after her accident. Emma had fought tooth and nail to become a barista.

It was the first step in the long road to reclaiming her life. Unfortunately, she didn't know what the second one was.

Georgia leaned over, putting her hand on her arm. "You need to give yourself time. You're still healing. But once you do, you'll find something you love as much as I love fixing up old junkers." Georgia's eyes lit up. "Hey, do you want to learn how to do an oil change?"

Emma beamed at her. "Yes!"

"You're on! Next time I need to do one, I'll come get you."

Giggling, Georgia launched into an anecdote about her latest customer at the car restoration place, a former rom-com actor who'd found unexpected success as an action star in his sixties.

They got so lost in conversation Emma didn't notice how much time had passed until the men came back downstairs.

Rainer invited them to join them for dinner. Emma was pleasantly surprised when Garrett checked with her before accepting. And though she was a little tired, she wanted to spend more time with George.

By the time they were done with the five-course meal, she was ready to crash.

"Just roll me to your guest room," she yawned, cuddling Meowmus to her chest as Garrett ushered her back into his penthouse.

"Will do," he said, taking the sleeping cat from her arms when she stumbled on his absurdly shiny marble floor.

Taking her hand, he took her deeper into the inner sanctum, past several very nice bedrooms, to a truly spectacular master suite done up in greens and pale beige.

The bedroom he took her to was across the hall from it.

Garrett set the kitten in the little bed someone had thoughtfully placed next to a brand-new litter box. "I'm through here," he said, jerking his thumb behind at a pair of double doors leading to the master bedroom—as if it wasn't obvious that the palace suite was his.

"I can sleep with the door open if you think you might need something."

Emma's brain was half-asleep but that woke her up. "No thanks, weirdo," she said, kicking off her shoes.

"Funny," he said a touch defensively. "Here I thought I was being considerate."

"Nope." She gave him a pointed look. "Just weird. Also, I'll be sleeping with my door closed. Please don't come inside here in the middle of the night to smell my hair."

Garrett snorted, choking on nothing. "I'll try to resist," he deadpanned.

He glanced at the kitten, who snuffled when he laughed. "What if Meowmus pees on the floor?"

She looked down at the marble floor. "I'll clean it. Speaking of the floor, why is it warm?"

"There are heating coils under the stones." He pointed at the boxes in the corner. "Your stuff is still packed up. Want me to grab you a T-shirt to sleep in?"

Emma pursed her lips, looking down at what she was wearing. Her outfit wouldn't be the most comfortable to sleep in and she was perilously close to passing out. "Okay. Thank you."

Leaving the double doors open, he disappeared into his bedroom.

Curious despite herself, she angled her neck, trying to see more of the room beyond the doorway. But it must have been humongous because despite the wideness of the opening, all she saw was part of the bed, a fancy leather chair, and a bit of the dresser.

Garrett came back with a long T-shirt emblazoned with the words, Ironman Mallorca.

Oh, for Pete's sake. "If you tell me you have this because you finished a triathlon, I will stab you with a pencil."

Pursing his lips, Garrett backed away with exaggerated slowness. "You know you're a little violent when you're tired."

"Good. Remember that." She pointed at the door. "But if you want sweetness and light, you better leave so I can get some sleep."

"Sweetness and light?" He raised a dark brow. "It's a regular bed. It's not infused with the waters of Lourdes or anything like that."

"Ooh, solid burn," Emma trilled, giving credit where credit was due.

Then she shut the door in his face.

Chapter Sixteen

GARRETT

He ducked, narrowly missing Rainer's right cross. He returned it with a quick jab, but Rainer danced away, crossing the mat that divided this corner of his home gym from the weightlifting gear.

He smacked his boxing gloves together. "And then she ordered me not to sneak into her room to smell her hair in the night. As if I would ever do that!"

Rainer snorted. "I hate to break it to you, but you already did exactly that."

"*What?*" He dropped his hands, letting Rainer land a solid right cross.

"Afraid it's true," his friend insisted, gesturing in the direction of the entrance. "Just after dinner, you opened the door on the way out and held it for her. She turned to say bye to George. You leaned in and took a deep whiff."

"Did not," he muttered, not at all happy with the fact he'd regressed to a six-year-old.

He expected Rainer to continue mocking him, but the other man shook his head and sighed.

"Look, it's obvious your mind is set on helping Emma out, but do you honestly think having her live with you is a good idea?"

"In case you forgot, she got kicked out of her place."

"Because of you," Rainer added helpfully.

"Exactly. I owe her."

Rainer blocked his uppercut. "And you could easily repay her by arranging for a new apartment. Hell, there are still some empty ones in this building."

Gesturing to the clock, he began to strip off the gloves. "Do me a favor and don't mention that to her."

"Garrett."

"I can't do it, man," he said, tossing down one of the gloves. "She gets such bad migraines, she needs supervision."

"Maybe, but does it have to be you? Find her a roommate. Or better yet, she could find one herself. Because the woman I met yesterday seemed to have definite opinions on things."

"I thought you liked her."

"I do. And George loves her," Rainer assured him. "I'm just worried by how badly you *wanted* me to like her."

Garrett drew himself up to his full height. "A completely normal amount."

Rainer scratched his head. "Your divorce was final ages ago, but then came the partying, and after that, you insisted on the two of us getting paramilitary training with Auric—"

"That came in handy for you," he interrupted, pointing the glove he'd removed at him.

"And so it did, but it was still a weird move for you."

Rainer began to tug off his gloves so he could grab a couple of towels. He tossed one at him. "But the last few months it felt like you were coming down, starting to get back to normal."

"I turned into a workaholic with no social life," he groused.

Rainer shrugged. "You like your work and were making a killing doing it. Still are. But you also seem more centered. But now this thing with Emma is… I don't know."

"Yes, you do," he said, making a *get on with it* gesture. "Spit it out."

Rainer winced. "I'm not saying it's going to blow up in your face…

but when it does, it's going to be catastrophic. Like H-bomb huge. You know that, right?"

"Yeah, I know." He wiped his face with the towel, wondering if he should strangle himself with it. "I should offer her one of the places downstairs, shouldn't I?"

"I'm not going to tell you what to do. But also, yes. Do that."

Tossing the towel in the laundry chute, he grabbed his water bottle. "Fine. I will. And despite what a pain in the ass you are, I'm glad you're concerned about her."

His friend had what his grandmother used to call good moral fiber.

"With everything Emma has been through, I'm glad she has decent people in her corner. You know, just in case."

"In case of what?"

His heart picked up, aware of how much he was revealing. "In case something happens to me."

Rainer grimaced. "Garrett, man…"

"Yeah, I know." He bit his lip, blinking against the sting burning his retinas. "But you didn't see her before. Emma was a ballbuster who took no prisoners. She was going to burn down Wall Street. Now she can be sparring with me one minute, and then she'll just crash and it's…"

He shook his head.

Rainer leaned against the rail of his VersaClimber. "It's hard for you to see her in pain."

That was the understatement of the year. "Yeah."

"Look, I'm not saying Emma doesn't need a hand. But it's not like the ballbusting is in the past. She was giving you shit like a pro last night, wasn't she?"

"Yeah, she was." And he had loved every second of it. "But I still worry."

Rainer threw in the towel. Literally. He closed the laundry chute door after tossing the sweaty one inside.

"I know what that means. You're obviously dead set on keeping Emma next door, for her sake. But I gotta tell you, man, she's not the one I'm concerned about."

"Yeah," he muttered. "I know. And I get it. This could get ugly."

With that rousing pep talk still ringing in his ears, he headed back to his room to shower. Only to run straight into Emma coming out of hers.

She was wearing a towel and nothing else.

Dear God, I take it back. Not ugly. The opposite of ugly.

Chapter Seventeen

EMMA

She was used to feeling hungover after a migraine, but the dry mouth she felt upon waking, accompanied by the weird sensitivity of her brain as if it had shrunk, was new.

The likely suspect was the two glasses of wine she'd had with dinner last night.

She couldn't drink because of her many meds, but if she was going to transition to a new medication, Emma needed to wean herself off the old one first. It gave her an unexpected window to enjoy herself a little. Which was why she had the answer to a question she'd never needed to ask.

Emma was a lightweight.

Maybe she'd had a higher tolerance before her accident. Since she'd been in her last year of college, that was a good bet.

Climbing out of her comfortable bed, she blinked and took a good look, the daylight revealing details she hadn't noticed last night.

I can't believe I'm staying here.

This guest room looked like a fancy hotel suite with its huge sleigh bed, posh furniture, and little conversation nook. Her middle-of-the-night visit to the bathroom had shown her a dimly lit space where everything was subdivided. There was a sink across from a big tub and a separate shower stall with more nozzles than the human body had parts.

Even the toilet had its own little room.

This morning she discovered her nightstand had a built-in mini fridge full of snacks and drinks.

Unreal. Emma took a bottle of water and drank, but the unsettled feeling in her stomach didn't dissipate. If anything, it got worse.

This just proves what you suspected. She was not normal.

Any other woman who got a chance to spend a few weeks in a place like this would feel like she'd won the lottery. But it just made Emma anxious, her equilibrium shot.

That feeling intensified when she left her room in search of her clothes.

Clutching the towel, she backed up to avoid mowing down an almost-naked Garrett.

The man was wearing a very short pair of shorts and a pair of sneakers. Nothing else.

His sweat-sheened pecs were hypnotic. But why were his hands all bandaged? Had he hurt himself?

Concerned, she shifted to grip her towel with a single hand and pointed. "Did you burn yourself?"

Seemingly startled, he lifted his hands. "No."

The combination of his answering smile with that muscled chest was lethal. "They're wrapped because I was sparring with Rainer."

Her brows drew together. "Sparring?"

"Boxing. We box." He began to peel the bandages off, completely unselfconscious of the fact he was half-naked in front of her.

So are you, her damaged brain reminded her. "Oh, um. That's stupid."

His head jerked back. "What?"

She pointed at her head. "Risk of traumatic brain injury."

The expression on his face was almost comical. She doubted this suave playboy had ever looked more uncomfortable.

Garrett coughed. "Well, we don't hit each other *that* hard. Not enough to do any serious damage."

"Must be nice." Emma tilted her head at him, stretching out the awkward moment for all it was worth.

He narrowed his eyes at her, suspicion making their hazel depths as bright as polished topaz. "Stop enjoying my discomfort."

She couldn't help but smile. "I will as soon as you tell me where my clothes are."

His brows drew down. "In your room," he said in the tone kind people reserved for talking to the mentally impaired.

Emma put her hand on her forehead. "There must be a box missing because I can't find my work things."

His face curdled as if he'd smelled something bad. "You're going to work?"

"Yeah," she said pointedly. "Why? Do you have an opinion on that?"

"Nope," he backpedaled for all he was worth. "Of course, you're going to work. So am I."

Emma immediately knew that Garrett Chapman had taken the day off from whatever it was he did in that penthouse office.

Her brows drew together. "What did you expect us to do here all day?"

Garrett puffed up indignantly. It did very interesting things to his chest. Not to mention the six-pack over the waistband of those tiny shorts. "I *said* I was going into the office."

"Uh-huh."

Rolling his eyes, he stalked off, presumably to shower. Emma's giggle followed him, but her amusement didn't last long.

As much fun as it was to torture the man, she couldn't let herself get too comfortable around him. Or this palace.

By the time Emma managed to find the box with her work clothes, Garrett had showered, dressed, and cooked breakfast. She followed the enticing smell to the kitchen. It was, as the scent promised, a full-service kitchen that would have been at home in any small or midsized restaurant.

Garrett seemed at home in it too, which was a bit of a surprise. He set a plate stacked with half a dozen coaster-sized pancakes. "Eat," he growled.

"*Buen provecho* to you too."

His handsome face darkened further. "I ate already," he said. "But thanks."

"Are you fluent in Spanish?" she asked, lifting the fork that had accompanied the plate and taking a bite.

Damn him, the pancakes were perfect. Fluffy on the inside and golden brown on the outside, they had perfect crispy edges. Combined with a fat curl of gold butter on top, they might have been the best she'd ever had.

"It's Southern California," he said by way of explanation. "I'm driving myself to the office, which leaves my driver free."

He took a card out of his pocket and set it in front of her. "That's her number. She can drop you off at work and pick you up. You should call and give her at least twenty minutes' notice. Maybe a little longer if traffic is heavy."

Emma hurried to swallow. "You're kidding, right? I can walk to work in ten minutes."

"Then aren't you lucky?" he said, tilting his head in an echo of her earlier move. "You don't have to."

What an obnoxious ass.

Emma pointed her fork at him. "Can I say something?"

He passed her a napkin. "Is there any way to stop you?"

Emma shifted her grip on the utensil menacingly. "If you're going all Christian Grey on me, I will stab you with this fork."

He wiped his hands on a handy kitchen towel and tossed it down with a little too much vigor. "You wish."

With that snappy comeback, he left.

Guilt nibbled at her the moment he was out of sight. Or at least it did until she remembered the cat.

Meowmus had been asleep in his basket when she went hunting for her clothes, but he was gone when she returned with them to the room to change.

It took twenty minutes, but she finally found him behind a baby gate Garrett must have had installed in the guest bathroom next to hers. A note taped to it informed her that someone from the building's concierge service would be by to walk him around lunchtime.

"Good Lord." She laughed, picking the kitten up and cuddling him. "Does he think cats get walked?"

The kitten purred in response.

Comforted by the little creature's warmth, she kept stroking him as they walked around. "Maybe I should have told Mr. Moneybags that I don't have to go in until ten thirty. Do you think we should explore?"

The kitten continued to purr. "Agreed, we definitely should."

Garrett had neglected to give her a tour, and though the basic layout was like Georgia and Rainer's apartment, the bits she'd seen were furnished and decorated with a completely different aesthetic than their place.

Next door was modern comfort with fun, edgy pieces. This place was a straight-up bachelor's paradise with an almost embarrassing amount of leather. Not to mention the glass and dark polished wood.

It was like living in a cigar bar. Or at least what she'd always imagined one looked like.

And so began their explorations. In addition to that suspiciously well-stocked bar and gourmet kitchen was a plasma TV so large it could have replaced a classroom projector in a very wealthy school district.

She also found the gym, which had a dozen intimidating exercise machines, a motorized lap pool, and a hot tub. This was in addition to the spare bedrooms and the office-slash-library where she found a stash of magazines in a drawer.

Garrett graced the cover of each one. Most were business or real estate related but there was one with Most Eligible Bachelor emblazoned on it. He looked disgustingly hot in that one, sitting in a chair with his tie undone, she admitted with a frown.

His pose was that of a man about to call it a night and go to bed. The beautiful woman who would accompany him was not shown, but in Emma's mind, she was strongly implied.

She took that one out of the drawer, snapping a pic of the cover in case the magazine mysteriously disappeared after she hung it on the refrigerator like a child's art piece.

That task done, she wandered a little more, ending her self-guided tour in front of the master suite.

"For shame, Meowmus," Emma chided as they contemplated the closed double doors. "We can't go rifling through our host's underwear drawer. That would be highly inappropriate. And we're not going to go through his medicine cabinet either."

Besides, his wouldn't be anywhere near as interesting as mine.

She stroked the cat, her mood nose-diving as a rain of multicolored pills fell in her mind. "Great. Now I'm depressed."

Shaking it off, she put Meowmus down on the floor. "Come on. Let's go rearrange something and not tell him."

Chapter Eighteen

GARRETT

He spent the entire drive to the office planning Emma's move to one of the downstairs apartments. As soon as he got upstairs, he'd call the building concierge to arrange it.

"Christian Grey," he muttered, stomping his way through the parking garage. "I'll give her Christian Grey."

An image of Emma tied to his bed flickered through his mind and he swallowed, pausing with his finger over the elevator button.

Yeah, don't go there.

Except his uncooperative brain insisted on painting that picture in graphic detail, adding the memory of Emma in the towel just to torture him.

That toasted almond skin wasn't a tan. No, it was too even, her upper arms the same shade as the tops of her breasts and lower thighs. He made a mental note to buy bigger towels. For the sake of his sanity.

Damn. He wasn't going to call the concierge, was he?

Fletcher didn't take the news of his current living situation well. "You moved her into your apartment? Are you *crazy*?"

"It's a good deed, Fletch," he said, dropping into his leather chair with a grunt. "Ever heard of one?"

"This is exactly what Celeste warned you about." His partner buried his face in his hands. "This is wrong on so many levels, I can't even count them. She is your *employee*."

He straightened the pens on his blotter, not meeting Fletcher's eyes. "She works for *De Olla*."

"Which means she works for you because you accepted a seat on their board!"

"It's an advisory position," he stressed. "It's not as if I'm her actual supervisor."

Fletcher's sarcastic laugh had never grated on his nerves more. "No. You're just her boss' boss."

"Only on paper. In practice, I'm a world away from being her employer."

"We're not talking about hypotheticals here," his partner scoffed. "On paper is all we care about. Unless you plan on talking her into quitting."

Fletcher drummed his fingers on his knee. "Yeah, that's a much better plan. Get one of your buddies to give her a job at one of *their* businesses. Doesn't matter if it's on the other side of the country. In fact, that's preferable."

The idea made his body alternate hot and cold. "You want me to send Emma away? Are you serious?"

Fletcher passed a hand over his face. "I cannot stress this enough. *Yes*. I am dead serious."

Hell, he isn't going to let this go.

Garrett shook his head. "I don't get why you have such a problem with me helping Emma out," he said, taken aback by his partner's vehemence. "This is someone we went to school with. She has *brain damage* for fuck's sake."

His argument momentarily derailed Fletcher who lapsed into an uncomfortable silence.

"You used to eat lunch with her sometimes, don't you remember?" Garrett reminded him.

Fletcher scowled, a line forming between his brows. "No. I don't think I ever did. At least not on purpose."

Really? Because Garrett could have sworn he'd seen them eating at the same table several times.

Maybe he doesn't remember because, unlike you, he wasn't hyper-focused on Emma Mendez's every move back then.

"God, you made her sound like she was a pariah," he muttered. "She wasn't."

"That's not what I meant, and you know it." Fletcher closed his eyes, abject frustration on his face. "Emma was nice enough. But her rivalry with you didn't win her any popularity contests. Don't forget, you were the big man on campus. People followed where you led."

He stopped, scratching his chin. "I'm not saying *I* did that. I didn't have the same issues with her that you did, but I also can't say I really knew her. And despite how often you two bickered, neither did you. She didn't move in our circles."

"What a nice way of saying she was poor," he said, displeased with that cold summation of their high school life.

"Hey, I was poor too!" Fletcher snapped.

"Compared to your family, everyone was," he added more gently. "But her lack of money had nothing to do with it. She may have been in our classes, and we may have sat together a few times. But that doesn't mean much for a school that size. We didn't engage. Which isn't surprising given she was years younger and kind of immature."

Immature was the last word he would have used to describe Emma, but he didn't have a leg to stand on here. If people thought Emma was immature, it was because she had always been arguing and sniping with him, for fuck's sake.

He'd sniped right back, their back and forth integral to his existence back then.

He would have said as much but Garrett didn't need to get into that argument with Fletcher right now. Not that his partner needed help. He was just getting warmed up.

"I'm not saying don't help her at all. But you need to do it from a distance. Every moment you interact with her is exposing you and this entire company to an incredibly destructive lawsuit."

"She's not going to sue. She wouldn't do that."

Fletcher went beet red. "For fuck's sake, Garrett! You don't know her anymore. *She doesn't know herself.*"

Damn. That one almost got him. Thankfully, Garrett was a fucking stubborn bastard.

Fletcher wasn't wrong, but he also wasn't right. Not morally. There were things he didn't know, things Garrett couldn't tell him…

"My ability to judge someone's character is the reason we do so well as a company. When a potential investment walks through that door, it's me you count on to decide whether the principals are on the up and up. Have I steered us wrong yet?"

"No," Fletcher admitted with a grunt. "But there's always a first time."

"I'm not wrong. Emma hasn't changed that much. Trust me on this."

Emma herself might disagree, but in this limited set of circumstances, his judgment was more reliable than hers.

Hell, the phrase 'I know you better than you know yourself' might apply here. Or was that his wishful thinking?

Well, for better or worse, he was resolved to find out.

Fletcher's groan was loud enough for people outside his office to hear. In retrospect, it was a good thing Garrett's assistant had decided to extend their vacation.

"I cannot stress this enough: you are making a huge fucking mistake. The Emma Mendez of today is not the same one we went to high school with, which is something she has gone to great lengths to make clear. You have no idea what she's capable of."

He slapped his hand on his blotter. "All right, that's enough. I know what I'm doing."

Fletcher got to his feet. "I wish that were true. The least I can do is not help you fuck up your life. From now on, you're on your own. I'm not going to help you."

Garrett scowled, leaning back in his chair. "What the fuck does that mean?"

"It means anything that involves Emma Mendez, count me out. If she's working downstairs, my secretary can fetch my coffee. If she's at your apartment, don't expect me to go over there. If you take her out, don't invite me, and don't bring her anywhere I am. That includes dinner with Magdalena tomorrow."

His expression darkened at Garrett's blank expression. "You *forgot?*"

"No, I didn't," he lied. He was a busy man who was dealing with a major personal situation. He could hardly be expected to remember every little detail.

Fletcher made a grumbling sound. "You already canceled once. Do it again and Mags is going to take it personally."

Fletcher and Magdalena had been dating a couple of months, enough for him and Rainer to have dined with the couple over half a dozen times. He'd only canceled last week because a work meeting got pushed back.

"I didn't forget and I'm not trying to get out of dinner, but I have…" He trailed off in expectation of the coming explosion.

Fletcher slapped a hand over his eyes. "Go ahead and say it."

"Emma just moved in," he said. "She has chronic health issues. I'm not comfortable leaving her alone."

His partner swore under his breath. "Unbelievable."

"She gets terrible migraines."

There was a long moment of silence as Fletcher stared at him in silent judgment.

Garrett took a deep breath, aware the next truth wouldn't help his case either. "Also, I have a kitten now. I don't think you're supposed to leave those alone for long periods either."

The laughter took him by surprise. Ignoring Fletcher, he began to pull out the contract he was supposed to review.

When Fletcher was done chortling to himself, he made his way to the door, yanking his jacket into place with a bit too much drama.

"I can't believe you're making me say this, but I guess I have to. For all intents and purposes, Emma Mendez is a stranger now. Not only do you not owe her anything you haven't already given—namely an apology for the garage—but she doesn't want your help. Not at all. She doesn't want anything to do with you. She never did."

Those words were still ringing in his ears when Fletcher slammed the door behind him, leaving Garrett alone to stew in his thoughts.

Chapter Nineteen

EMMA

"You are seriously the luckiest bitch alive."

Emma winced as Bethany handed a mom with her two elementary school-age daughters a latte through the waterfront kiosk's service window.

"Could you maybe not swear in front of the customers?" she murmured after the woman shot Bethany a dirty look. "Or at least do it more quietly? Hector will get pissed if you get *De Olla* another bad Yelp review."

Bethany popped the gum she was chewing as the woman and her kids moved on. "You're such a Pollyanna."

Emma frowned. Her internet dives had covered a lot of ground but there were still huge gaps. "Who is that?"

Her guess was a singer. It had that ring. Rihanna, Pollyanna…

Her coworker deflated her hopes with her usual diplomacy. "I forgot you have brain damage and no Disney channel subscription."

"You've got me on the Disney stuff. I only have Pedro's Netflix password." Emma wiped the espresso machine's steam wand with a hot towel. "But my brain is mostly recovered, thank you very much."

"Not enough if you don't remember tall, dark, and delicious," Bethany pointed out, lowering herself on the upturned bucket they kept for when they needed to sit out of sight of the customers. "Forgetting a snack like that *would* require serious brain damage."

Emma swallowed. This conversation was starting to give her a headache. "Can we stop talking about my brain? And Mr. Chapman?"

Bethany cocked a hip. "Let's compromise. I'll stop with the brain stuff, but we keep on dissecting this *Mister* Chapman thing."

She cocked a hip, giving her a conspiratorial eyebrow waggle. "Does he make you call him that? Because if he does, it's only a matter of time before you end up tied up in that guy's sex dungeon."

Emma threw up her hands. "That's what I said!"

"To who?" Bethany was frowning. Then her eyes lit up. "Not to him!"

"Of course to him. I told him if he turned all Christian Grey on me, I'd stab him with a fork."

They both laughed but Emma stopped first, subsiding with a sigh. "But it was a joke. I know he's not interested in me that way."

"Yeah, right." Bethany smacked her lips. "The man tackles you one day and then boom! He's moving you into his penthouse the next."

"Only because nearly got my cousin evicted and then had Pedro kick me out," Emma said darkly before frowning. "Or was it the land-lady? I'm not sure how it went down."

"Which just proves how badly he wants you in his clutches." Bethany waved a finger to encompass her body. "He's obviously into the T&A."

Emma scowled and looked down at her size Ds. Bethany might have a point. Garrett *had* checked her out in the towel. That didn't mean much, of course.

Garrett was a red-blooded man under eighty. Most men looked. The few who did anything about it usually restricted themselves to gross comments. A handful tried to cop a feel. Or they rubbed up against her on the bus—one of the many reasons she preferred to walk home.

But a man as wealthy and good-looking as Garrett Chapman wasn't going to go for someone like Emma. Not that she wanted him to be interested. She could never be with someone who knew her before the accident.

"It's not like that," she repeated in a flat voice. "He…"

"Wants some of that booty?"

Emma held up a hand. "Let me finish. He feels guilty for accusing me of corporate espionage and going ballistic in the garage. He's just trying to avoid a lawsuit."

"If that were all it was, he could have gotten you a studio somewhere. He could certainly afford it. Hector says ours isn't the only building he owns. Chapman has property all over the world. The dude is loaded."

"And with that money comes a god complex," she scoffed. "Garrett thinks he knows what's best for everyone. Pedro and I weren't perfect, but we were getting by. And then Garrett came in and blew that up. And you want to know why? It's because he thinks I need supervision. More than Pedro can give because he's a hoarder."

Bethany stopped restocking. She turned around, making a face. "He *is*?"

She rolled her shoulders uncomfortably. "Yes. Kind of."

"Wow." Bethany leaned against the side of the espresso machine. "I didn't know that. Was it like gross? Like maggoty and stuff?"

"Not really. It was just very cluttered. He's not as bad as the cases on those TV shows. Not yet."

And really, who the hell was Garrett to decide what was best for her? Or for her cousin?

"It's because he used to know me, how I was before."

Emma stared down at her hands. Her palms had faint scars from the accident. She didn't even know what had made them. Morose, she focused on the glimpse of the water out the service window.

Wouldn't it be nice to sail off on one of the boats on the horizon? It beat being second-guessed, what little independence she had snatched away.

Her shoulders slumped. "Garrett compares the old Emma to the current one. He sees how broken and less I am, and he feels sorry for me."

The words fell like bricks, almost thudding in the little space.

Bethany winced. After a minute, she raised her shoulders. "Are you sure you were that great before?"

Emma almost choked on her sudden laughter. Bethany might have been a monster, but Emma liked her brutal honesty.

"It's pity. There's some guilt too, but it's mostly pity," she said, but without the incipient tears. "Lucky me, I get to be his new charity project. Once I've improved to his satisfaction, he'll move on to the next one."

For once, her snarky coworker appeared at a loss for words.

"Not that I plan on waiting for him to decide," Emma added. "I'll be out of his place as soon as I find a roommate situation that's not too far or too gross. Something affordable."

Bethany held up her hands. "Don't look at me. I already have two roommates."

Also, it would have been a disaster. Bethany was best in small doses.

"Maybe Kyle," Emma thought out loud. "He's been saying he wants to move out of his mom's house. Maybe we can find a cheap place together."

"Dude, you think you've got guy problems now? Move in with Kyle and see what happens."

Emma pursed her lips. Bethany had a point. Kyle was sweet but he had a puppy dog crush on her. That could get awkward very quickly.

"There's always Craigslist. I'll find something."

Bethany rolled her eyes. "Better than a penthouse?"

She shrugged. "More permanent at least. Garrett's white knight complex won't last. I've got a week or two, a month tops, before he gets tired of me cramping his style."

The other woman looked disappointed. "It does seem a little too Cinderella to be real."

Finally, a reference she knew. "Hey, I've seen that one!"

Emma had watched both Disney versions of the movie last year with her little sister. Then their mother made them watch *Ever After*, which was her favorite film version of the fairy tale.

Bethany smirked and shook her head.

"I'm not wrong about Garrett, either. You should see his place. It screams Playboy bachelor so loud you can hear it."

"Playboy, huh? I take it back. You are so going to end up in a sex dungeon." Bethany smirked and rocked back on her heels. "Make sure he knows how to tie you up properly. If they haven't practiced, they end up cutting off your circulation."

Emma groaned. "I don't want to know how you know this."

The blonde preened, popping her gum again. "You really don't."

Chapter Twenty

GARRETT

He choked down a second antihistamine, seriously hoping it wasn't possible to overdose on the things.

"This is all your fault," he growled at the cat twining between his legs. "Get off me before I turn you into earmuffs."

The kitten gleefully ignored him. It continued to rub up against his pant legs, really grinding his fur all into the lightweight silk blend.

By the time he dragged his ass home tonight, Garrett had been exhausted.

Then this little fucker had greeted him at the door, smushing his little face against him. The animal proceeded to complain in high-pitched kitten speak about the audacity of being forced to live in a three-thousand-square-foot penthouse instead of a busy parking garage.

Because getting catered to hand and foot, or paw to paw, was such a hardship.

"I know what you're doing. Your instinct is to mark your territory. But it's not going to work," he said, picking up the beast when he began to simultaneously claw and headbutt his ankles.

"I will feed you, vaccinate you, and provide flea medication. But there will be no cuddles and no kisses to your wee furry face. I'm not falling for your wiles, so save that shit for Emma."

The kitten meowed as if in protest.

"That's right. I don't even like cats. You're too furry and you shed over everything and I'm not on board with that whole licking yourself clean thing. It's unhygienic. But I'm willing to put up with you as long as you keep up your end."

The cat tilted its head almost as if it was listening to him.

"That's right," he added with a significant look. "I'm not doing this out of the goodness of my heart. You're a working cat. Your job is to make Emma love you so she doesn't want to move out."

It wasn't manipulation, exactly. At heart, Garrett was a businessman. He knew how to craft a good deal.

Out there was a world of crowded, overpriced apartments, too many roommates, and long commutes. Here, Emma got her choice of bedrooms, a kitten, and if all went well, a cool mechanic best friend next door.

Not that he'd asked George for any special treatment of his guest. But his best friend's girl was a naturally sweet woman who already seemed to like Emma a lot.

After pumping both Kyle and Pedro, it became obvious that Emma didn't have many friends. Those two might be it for her. Unless you counted Bethany, which he didn't. No one should.

For years, Emma had been focused on her recovery, but expanding her social circle could only help her. She needed a stronger safety net. Which was why it was odd that Emma had moved so far from home, away from her mother and younger sister.

Yes, it must have been uncomfortable being around people you didn't remember. But to distance yourself from your family? And why had her mother let her leave?

Garrett's own mother was long dead, and he didn't have the best relationship with his father. But despite the occasional tension her mother's reputation caused Emma, he knew that on a personal level, they had gotten along. At least they appeared to be close when he'd seen them around town.

Regardless of why Emma had come here, she had done it, inadvertently landing in his sphere of influence.

Some people would call it chance. But Garrett was growing increasingly convinced that the hand of fate was involved. How else could he explain Emma ending up working for a company he owned?

If anything, he was *obligated* to keep an eye on her. He had to because of... reasons. Things she didn't need to know about and wouldn't be receptive to hearing yet.

He was just trying to do right by her. She might not like it now, but she'd come to understand that. Eventually.

Garrett rubbed his eyes before remembering he'd handled the little beast and hadn't washed his hands. "*Shit!*"

Hurrying to the sink behind the bar, he quickly washed his hands before repeatedly splashing his face, eyes open, until his eyeballs began to burn.

"If you want me to move out, just ask. There's no need to drown yourself."

Grabbing a bar towel, he wiped his face before turning to face Emma, who was just pulling off a black windbreaker as the heavy door swung shut behind her.

"This is your cat's fault," he informed her.

"Oh, so now it's *my* cat?"

"It's like a kid," he said, shrugging philosophically. "When it's good, it's our cat. But when it's bad, it's all yours."

Emma snorted in response.

Tossing the towel aside, he examined her windblown hair and checked his watch. It was almost half past six, a gap reasonably explained by the busy downtown traffic. But it was also enough time for her to walk here, even if she closed the kiosk a few minutes late.

His eyes narrowed on her face. "Did you call the car service to drive you home?"

Emma hesitated, jacket in hand. It was all the answer he needed.

Sighing, he went to take the windbreaker from her, hanging it in the coat closet next to the door.

"It takes less time to walk," she protested.

"Debatable given the foot traffic at dinnertime."

"Are you going to give me a hard time about this?" she asked, her voice pitched a touch higher.

Warning lights began to flash in his brain, but he couldn't stop himself from being honest.

"I know a lot of people are still out at this hour, but downtown's not a great place right now. You'd be much safer waiting for the car service."

"Sure, dad."

Garrett shuddered. "Don't call me that."

The light brown skin of her cheeks deepened in color. "I meant dad in the normal mocking way, not in the daddy sense. Don't make it weird."

He shook his head in despair. This woman was going to drive him insane. "Dinner is in half an hour."

Emma's head drew back. "Uh, do we do that together?"

Garrett thought about it. "Probably not every night. I often work through dinner, eating in my office when work is especially busy. But as I explained before, things are winding down there. Mohammed, the chef, is pretty good, though. You ate his food yesterday."

"Rainer's chef works for you, too?"

"He works for the building. He used to service the penthouses exclusively, but Rainer and I didn't keep him busy enough. I eat at the office or out at business dinners often. Which is why Rainer and I decided to let the other tenants book meals from him too. It works out if they do it a couple weeks in advance."

Her brow puckered. "Do you own this building too?"

"Me, Rainer, and two other old friends," he explained.

Garrett regretted telling her immediately. Everything Emma was thinking was written on her face.

"That's, um, nice," she said, her expression a touch nauseated. "Is one of the other guys Fletcher?"

"No, these are friends I met in college. I lived with both Rainer and Elias in a condo at one point. We met his cousin Ian a little later. They're my closest friends."

"Oh. That must be nice," she said, picking at some invisible lint on her sleeve. "Being in business with your friends."

"It is," he said, trying his best to forget he'd likely separated her from one of her few friends by busting up her living situation. Unless you counted her coworkers, but who in their right mind would count Bethany?

Glossing over the momentary discomfort, he soldiered on.

Garrett jerked his thumb in the direction of his kitchen. "I let Mohammed prepare the meals for the rest of the building here. He leaves me something to heat up when I ask. But he's been at Rainer's more since he and George got together, preparing family meals. Did she tell you her dad lives in the building too?"

Emma nodded. "She did. It's nice she and her dad can live so close."

Was that wistfulness he heard? Why the hell had her mother let her leave home?

Emma blinked, refocusing on him. "George said she and Rainer are getting married in a couple of months. She invited me over tomorrow night to help her fix up some wedding favors. Since we're telling each other our plans and all."

"Keeping me informed isn't obligatory," he said, trying his best to sound breezy and unconcerned. "Neither is dinner. But you may as well join me if you're free. I don't think Mohammad likes cooking for one."

Emma considered that. "I guess that makes sense. So would you like me to text you if I have plans outside the building?"

He knew 'no' was the right answer. This would work so much better if he kept things casual, letting Emma come and go as she pleased.

But Garrett couldn't do it. All his concerns about her health aside, there were too many things that could happen to a beautiful young woman on her own.

Hell, bad shit *already* had happened. Bad enough to erase him.

"Did you check in with Pedro?" he asked, ignoring the strangled quality of his voice.

Emma lifted a shoulder, her cheeks duskier than normal. "There wasn't a need. He was always home."

That blush was killing him. It helped when Garrett reminded himself Emma was recovering from a major head injury.

"Let's be practical," he said, ignoring the fact his chest was trying to collapse on him. "We're roommates now. I think touching base is reasonable."

That way he didn't have to worry she was lying in a ditch. *Again.*

"You really do sound parental."

He sent a little prayer of thanks that she didn't call him dad again. Daddy, however, was still on the table.

Emma lifted a shoulder. "Okay, I'll do the same. Or I'll try to."

He shrugged with a nonchalance he didn't feel. "Sometimes I lose track of time at the office. But you can text me so you don't have to wonder if I got kidnapped like Rainer almost did."

Her mouth dropped open. "Rainer almost got *what*?"

Garrett jerked a thumb in the direction of the kitchen. "I'll tell you during dinner. Ready in fifteen?"

She grabbed his arms. "Good God, man! Tell me now."

Laughing, he reluctantly peeled her hands off him. "Fifteen minutes. I need to shower your cat's fur off."

Emma raised her hands, miming choking him.

It was the most enthusiastic she'd been for his company.

Yeah, he might have tricked her into wanting it, but he'd take anything at this point.

"See you in fifteen."

Chapter Twenty-One

EMMA

Garrett's suite doors closed behind him. Emma decided she should clean up too.

Quickly stripping off her clothes, she jumped in the shower, setting a personal record. She toweled off with one of the new plush cotton towels.

Emma didn't know why Garrett had replaced the old ones, but these were twice as big and even thicker, so she wasn't complaining.

She contemplated her closet while wrapped in the sheet-sized towel.

By rights, her bedroom should be a disaster. When Garrett had her stuff moved here, Emma had intended on leaving most of it in the boxes. It would have made moving out in a few weeks easier. But someone had come in while she was at work and unpacked all her belongings, putting them away in the walk-in closet.

It was strange, seeing her cheap and utilitarian clothes in this palatial closet with its multitude of shoe shelves and clothing rods. Her things occupied less than a quarter of the space.

Shaking off that nagging sensation of being somewhere she shouldn't be, Emma grabbed a clean bra, leggings, and an oversized T-shirt. This place might be fancy as hell, but she wasn't going to pretend to be someone she wasn't.

Also, she only had one passably formal dress. She had to save it for Georgia and Rainer's wedding, which she had been invited to.

Emma had been bracing herself for some side-eye judgment from Garrett over her outfit. Then he walked out of his room in gray sweatpants and a plain white T-shirt. The cotton stuck to his damp skin, showing every ridge underneath.

His feet were bare.

Feet were not supposed to be beautiful. Especially male feet.

"I think we're both underdressed for your dining room," she said when she finally found her tongue.

He stuck his hands in his pockets, accidentally pushing the waistband on his sweatpants lower down his hips.

Flushing, Emma averted her eyes from the packed muscle outlined with hard-won definition.

"I was thinking of something less formal," he said, seemingly unaffected by her glamorous outfit. "I had a long, weird day at work and want to veg out in front of the TV with something easy to watch—a comedy or mindless action movie. I don't care which."

Emma tucked her damp hair behind her ear. "That sounds good to me."

His sudden smile was startling. It was like seeing the sun after working in a windowless room all day.

Luckily, he didn't linger long enough to notice her reaction. He disappeared into the kitchen, returning with two steaming plates of something that looked like a pasta burrito covered in a pink cream sauce. He set them on the coffee table.

"Mohammed left these crepe cannelloni in the warmer before he left to prep something next door, so I might need a hand getting the rest of the stuff."

"Sure."

Following him, she fetched the utensils while he grabbed a bottle of unfiltered apple juice from the fridge and a bottle of beer.

She sat next to him on the couch, taking her plate as he settled in, fetching the remote and handing it to her after activating a video-playing app she didn't recognize.

"Go ahead and search for whatever you like. If I don't already own it, we can buy it. Just press the button."

Her brain hiccupped at the casual mention of buying a movie and then realized in this scenario, *he* was the normal one. At her age, an adult woman should be able to download and pay for a movie without thinking twice.

Thanks to her accident, she was no better than a teenager perpetually saving up for a night out.

"Emmy?"

Blinking, she found Garrett staring at her.

Movies. Right.

"Hold on." Putting her plate on the table, she stood and ran to her room, snatching up her media journal. She returned, flipping through the pages until she found the section on must-see movies.

"What is that?" he asked, not bothering to hide his curiosity.

She held up the notebook. "It's one of my journals."

"Like a diary?"

Emma fingered the pages, taking comfort in their slightly rough texture. "Not exactly. I mean, I write some things down, an event or something I want to remember."

"So, it's a diary?"

Without looking up, she picked up a throw pillow and threw it at him, counting on his reflexes to knock it away before it hit his plate and made a mess.

He snickered but started eating, making enthusiastic noises about the meal.

"For the last couple of years, I've been doing a study, trying to figure out what the hell people are talking about. Cultural references and pop culture callbacks. Stuff like that."

He put his fork down, studying her intently. "It must be difficult, starting from zero."

She shrugged, glossing over those first few painful and confusing years after the accident. "I have a lot of lists of books and movies that I should read or see. It helps me make sense of the world."

"That's good," he said, scooting a little closer so he could see the list.

She held up the page filled with names, a score rating, and the occasional line that explained why people still talked about the movie or referenced it in a particular way.

He reached out, running his fingers along her crowded printed lines, a touch as gentle as his tone.

She waited to see if he would say something else, something that would cross the line from sympathy to pity. But he didn't. He just smiled and asked, "So what's next on the list?"

The tension that she'd been holding dissipated. She did that a lot, she realized. Braced herself.

You need to chill out.

He was waiting for an answer so she ran her finger down the page. "I'm currently wading through the Bill Murray *oeuvre*. I just saw *Caddyshack* and had *Reds* on while I cleaned once. Up next is either *Ghostbusters* or *Groundhog Day*."

Garrett's eyes lit up like it was Christmas morning. "Both. Let's watch both."

A corner of her mouth lifted. "I don't think we'll make it through both."

"Oh, come on. It's Friday!"

She didn't have the heart to tell him that she had another shift at the kiosk the next day. Weekends meant nothing to people in the service industry.

Deciding harmony was more important, she shrugged. "*Ghostbusters* it is," she said, finding it high up in the options.

Emma curled up at the other end of the long couch with her plate and picked up her fork.

The pasta burrito was, in a word, sublime.

Filled with chicken instead of beef, the dish was perfectly prepared. Not that Emma had a whole lot of experience with fine dining, but this had to be one of the best things she'd ever eaten. It was so good that when Dana Barrett got possessed, Garrett went back for a huge second helping instead of watching her pant all sexy and animallike.

When the marshmallow monster attacked, he timed it just right, bringing out dessert and handing it to her.

Emma burst into laughter, picking up the marshmallow and tooth-pick creation stuck to the top of a berry and cream dish served in a little pot.

"How did you do this so fast?" she asked, comparing her marsh-mallow man to his big brother rampaging on the screen.

"Very sloppily," he said. "Else it would have a little hat. Out of what, I'm not sure."

Emma bit her lip, giving him a coy glance before biting the head of the man-made monster.

"Be careful of the toothpicks," he warned, looking away quickly when she sucked one of the miniature marshmallows off the stick.

"Okay," she said, frowning when he wouldn't look at her. Wondering why he seemed uncomfortable, she finished her dessert.

When the credits began to roll, she expected him to retreat to his room, but he surprised her by insisting on starting the second movie, which was equally entertaining.

But Emma had worked on her feet all day. She was also full of deli-cious food and sitting on an absurdly comfortable couch. Soon she could no longer fight the fatigue and her eyelids closed without volition.

She felt the plate being removed from her hand.

"I'm up," she mumbled.

The voice came from far away. "Debatable."

There was rustling fabric, and then she was levitating.

"Don carry."

"I'm not carrying you," he whispered.

"Def carrying." She yawned, her lids too heavy to open and confirm. The rocking motion and warmth of strong arms weren't helping.

"You're dreaming."

"Weird dream."

"Nice dream," dream Garrett argued as her body landed gently on the mattress of the guest room.

"Nice," she acknowledged, deciding that opening her eyes would be counterproductive at this point. "But weird. For worst enemies."

"*Alleged* worst enemies." The door clicked closed.

Emma slept like a rock.

Chapter Twenty-Two

EMMA

She sat cross-legged next to Georgia, packing tiny custom-made die-cast cars into special acrylic cases engraved with the date of their wedding.

Georgia's adoptive father, Ephraim, leaned over and tapped the case when she was done.

"That's a 1949 Talbot Lago," he said, smacking his tongue against his yellow but minty fresh teeth. "The car used to belong to my father. Georgia was restoring it as a gift to me when she met Rainer. She took a picture of it so his security folk would let her into his office so she could warn him someone wanted to kidnap him. We call it the family car now."

"Oh my God!" Emma gasped. "That story is true? I thought Garrett was pulling my leg."

He'd given her a brief account of the kidnapping plot while grabbing the silverware last night, but he'd been so matter of fact, she'd thought he was kidding.

George recounted the tale, starting with overhearing the kidnappers lay out their plan while cleaning the bathroom at the car dealership she used to work at. It ended when she moved in with Rainer.

"That is the most incredible story I've ever heard."

"It was quite the adventure," Ephraim said, patting George on the shoulder. "And even though I had my doubts, Rainer ended up being a very nice young man."

Ephraim kept talking, packing a few more boxes before excusing himself for a meeting at his office across the street.

Emma leaned toward the bride-to-be. "Okay, now tell me all the good stuff you left out!"

Laughing, Georgia obliged, giving her the PG-13 version that involved hiding out in a snowbound cabin where the inevitable happened.

"I never imagined this when we first met," she said, gesturing to the wedding fripperies around them.

"Rainer was so handsome, with all these glowing magazine articles describing his charity work. He seemed so high above me, so unattainable. It didn't occur to me that he was a flesh and blood man who wanted love and affection like everyone else. I'm so glad I found him."

Emma put a hand over her heart. "I bet he says the same thing about you."

She had spent very little time in Rainer's company, but it was enough to see his complete and utter devotion to the woman who would be his wife. "He's obviously a smart man. Explains why he's so eager to put a ring on it."

Georgia's smile lit up the room. It made Emma want to lean in and bask in the warmth of it.

"Not to change the subject," George said with a little flash of her very white teeth. "But how are things going next door? I know you were a little weirded out that first night."

Where did she begin?

"Well, it's a bit weird, but not as bad as I thought it would be."

George bit her lip. "And you're still determined to find a new place?"

Emma pulled the corner of her mouth up. "I know that tone. You think I should stay."

Her new friend swept out a hand. "It's not like he doesn't have the room, and talking about how Rainer and I met brought back how dangerous the world can be. But you know that already," she said with a wince, gesturing to the place on her head where Emma's scar was.

George straightened sharply. "I'm sorry. Should I not bring up your accident?"

"No, it's fine." Emma packed another box and realized she meant it. "I admit I used to avoid talking about it. I didn't like how people looked at me afterward. But now everyone I know is aware of it. All my coworkers had to be told because of my chronic headaches. Some of them are nicer than others about it, but I almost enjoy the ones who are mean about it."

"Why?" George asked, laughing a little.

"Because they don't give me special treatment or act weird." Emma reached for another tiny car. "I don't remember the accident or anything before it. Plus, people don't like hearing about what came after—the hospital stuff, physical therapy, *therapy* therapy."

Georgia reached out to take her hand. "Well, I do want to hear about it. And anything else you want to talk about."

"Thanks." She pursed her lips. "You're the second person to say that to me. Garrett wants to know every little detail about my recovery, too. Almost intrusively so."

Emma wasn't sure if she found his interest comforting or disconcerting.

"Honestly, I'm a little surprised." Georgia tilted her head. "Garrett is Rainer's closest friend, but I have to confess I didn't think that highly of him when I first met him."

Was it terrible that she was dying of curiosity? "Why not?"

"He was on the tail end of his post-divorce partying binge. But I guess he's calmed down a lot since then. It's good to see him concerned about someone else this way."

George wiped her hands on her pant legs. "And this may sound weird to you, but it appears to be cheering him up. Which surprises me less. Deep down, I knew he and Rainer were friends for a reason."

Whoa. Way to bury the lead.

"Garrett was married?" she asked, refusing to acknowledge the rock that had just materialized in her stomach.

Georgia hesitated. "He didn't mention it?"

She raised her brows. "No, he did not."

Emma didn't know why this was so shocking. Garrett was handsome and rich. Lots of women would want to be with him. "There's no trace of a wife in that apartment."

Shouldn't there be signs of a former relationship somewhere in that huge apartment? Pictures of them tandem skydiving that he couldn't bear to put away? His and her coffee mugs tucked in the back of the kitchen cabinet?

Unless he kept the proof of his former relationship in his bedroom, close to him…

There might be a wedding picture on his nightstand. He could spend an hour staring at it every night before bed. Who the hell knew?

"I don't think it was an amicable split," George said, unaware of the bomb she'd just dropped. "I don't know too much about it other than she was an heiress. A socialite with ties to European royalty."

Royalty? Emma had never felt so pudgy or so scarred in her life.

Her self-doubt lasted until she remembered Garrett was not a romantic prospect. He was merely an unexpected roommate, one who insisted on meddling in her life because of an overinflated sense of responsibility.

Less than a week living at his place and you're already having to remind yourself of that. This had *slippery slope* written all over it.

Emma picked at her sleeve. "He must have been sorry to lose her."

Georgia burst out laughing. "I don't think a man that parties that hard is sad. That was a celebration. But again, it seems to have run its course," she added. "He's been so busy at Next Chapter. I doubt you're going to have put up with that kind of shit."

"He did mention being very busy with work." Emma couldn't help but worry now. "Maybe he'll start partying again once his busy season is over."

"Maybe," Georgia acknowledged. "But I'm hoping not. For Rainer's sake and his own. I didn't get the impression he was happy when I first met him."

She paused, looking at Emma from under her lashes. "Not like this morning anyway."

"This morning?" she echoed.

"We ran into him in the lobby. He was grinning even before he spotted Rainer. And he's not exactly what I'd call a morning person." She winked at Emma. "I gathered he was still in a good mood from last night."

Emma tossed a bit of ribbon in Georgia's direction. "Nothing happened. Not like you're implying."

George's smile was smug now. "But something did happen?"

"A scintillating night of dinner in front of the TV? You're right, it was the thrill of a lifetime for both of us," she said, deciding to leave out the part where he carried her to bed.

It hadn't been a big deal. She *was* heavy but Garrett had muscles she'd never heard of.

Seriously, someone should study him. They could make more accurate anatomical drawings with that man as a model.

"He's not interested in me that way," she added.

Georgia held up her hands in surrender. "I didn't say he was. But even if things are strictly platonic, Garrett may be enjoying having someone to come home to. Even if it's just to veg out in front of the TV. We all need human interaction—and no. Work doesn't count."

Well, crap. "Except for my cousin, and now you, the only people I'm even remotely friendly with are people from work."

"I didn't mean you can't have friends from work," Georgia clarified. "My best friend Judy was a friend from my old job until I stole her to work for my new business. But I was thinking about Garrett's business. I've met the top execs at Next Chapter and they're not what I would call *outside of work* friend material."

"What about Fletcher? I thought he was Garrett's oldest friend."

"Well, he has known him longer than Rainer," she said with the enthusiasm of someone discussing a dead trout.

Emma's lip twitched. "You don't like him?"

"Fletcher's fine," George said with a little moue of her lips. "Don't pay attention to me. I just get a vibe from him."

"What kind of vibe?"

Georgia shook her head. "I can't even explain it. It's…"

"A bad vibe."

"A… discordant one. I think he feels out of place sometimes among Rainer and the other guys."

Emma reached for more ribbon. "Which other guys are these?"

"Ian and Elias. They are other high-powered bigwigs around the same age. The four are tight and do a lot of stuff together. Their business takes them out of town a lot but I'm sure you'll meet them soon."

Emma was going to nod but stopped herself. Best not to acknowledge she might be living here a while or the universe would make it happen.

"Fletcher's a fifth wheel and knows it?"

George wrinkled her nose. "Yeah, I think so. Ian and Elias own the private security company that trained Rainer and Garrett."

The what now? "They have military training?"

"Yeah, with a security force team. Auric is all ex-military, but they work private sector now. Rainer and Garrett still go out and run their grueling obstacle course for fun."

Emma's face twisted as if she had tasted something sour. Georgia laughed. "Exactly! My idea of exercise is a light jog. Maybe a leisurely swim."

"I walk to and from work," Emma said. "That's it."

"A woman after my own heart." Georgia started packing up little cars into a bigger cardboard box. "Speaking of, do you like coffee or just sell it for a living?"

Emma leaned forward. "Coffee may be the sole reason I came out of the coma."

Georgia's eyes widened.

"My hand to God," Emma continued, putting her fingers over her heart. "The nurses and my mom were always drinking it. The smell of it…"

She fell over onto her side dramatically, continuing the conversation from her prone position on the floor.

"On my first day in town, I passed by a notice on a *De Olla* kiosk that said they were hiring. I took it as a sign from above."

"Hmm." Georgia bit her lip. "Can I ask you something terribly personal?"

Well, Emma had asked some pretty personal questions today, too. It was only fair. She raised her hand. "Shoot."

"Why did you move here? Away from your hometown and family?"

"Ah." Emma let out a gust of air. "That."

"It's okay if you don't want to tell me."

She waved the other woman's concern away. "No, it's fine. I moved because my mother wanted me to."

Georgia dropped a hot wheel on the floor. "Shit. Sorry."

Emma laughed. "No, I didn't mean it like that. I'm on good terms with her. I called her and my baby sister right before I came over today."

"Then why did she want you to leave?" she asked, picking up the fallen car.

Emma wondered if this was going to make her sound like a basket case. "She was worried. Because my accident wasn't really an accident. It was a hit-and-run."

"Shit. That's right." Georgia winced. "They never had a clue who did it?"

Emma shook her head. "Some drunk is the best guess. But my mom always worried that the driver sobered up and realized what they'd done afterward. It made her paranoid. She thought we were being watched."

Not that this was anything new. The good people of Verdant Falls had always watched her mother, the better to criticize her. Presumably Emma too, by extension. But she had no memory of it. Her chief recollections of home were of the people who'd come to see her at the hospital. How awkward each interaction had been...

Her visitors had expected the stories they shared to jog her memory. They couldn't seem to understand that her brain was permanently damaged. She wasn't ever getting those memories back.

"It was a mutual decision in the end. Home was a place of unspoken expectations, ones I had no idea how to interpret, let alone fulfill. It got so bad I could barely talk to people at all. That's why I came here. My cousin had a spare room. He charged me half of what he would have charged anyone else. Of course, he turned out to be a hoarder, so it wasn't that great a price after all."

Georgia pursed her lips. "Are things okay with him now? You seemed kind of mad at him before."

"I was," she admitted with a sigh. "I mean I am. I thought he could have fought for me a little more. But he has to fight for himself first. Garrett was right about that. He found him a good therapist. I've texted him but he doesn't feel up to speaking yet. Which, honestly, is sort of a relief."

Georgia nodded, her eyes a little distant. "A refractory period can be helpful. Especially if it's family."

Emma sensed there was more to unpack there, but then she looked at the time. "Oh God. I need to get ready or I'm going to be late for work."

George scanned the room for the clock. "Eek! Sorry to keep you so long but thank you for helping!"

Her hostess saw her to the door, pausing at the threshold of their shared hallway. "Hey, has Garrett mentioned bringing someone to the wedding?"

Emma froze. "Like a date? No."

George shrugged. "I'll get Rainer to ask him. It's a little awkward asking if we can take back his plus-one, but a few Auric people want to come that we didn't originally count on. They were supposed to be out of town on a long-term assignment, but it wrapped early."

"There's also me." Emma winced.

George touched her arm. "You are officially team wedding. That makes you a lock."

"Aww, thanks." She risked a quick hug and was gratified when Georgia warmly squeezed her back. "I can come back later if you need more help."

"That would be great," she said with genuine enthusiasm. "I know I should let the wedding planner do more of this stuff, but I want it to feel like *my* wedding, ya know?"

"I get it. You want it to have a personal touch."

"Yes! Rainer agrees. But it's gotten busy at work, so I haven't had as much time to spend on our little projects as I wanted."

Emma smiled. "Well, consider me drafted. I love the little cars and your dad is so sweet."

"Yay!" Georgia hugged her again. "Now scoot or you'll be late for work."

Shit, she was right.

"Ahh," she called behind, hustling down the hall. "Gotta run!"

Chapter Twenty-Three

GARRETT

Emma was talking a mile a minute when he opened the door.

He took off his coat, expecting to see her with Georgia, but the living room was empty. They must be in her room.

The pair had become inseparable over the last month. Emma spent a lot of time next door helping with wedding stuff or just hanging out. That part of his plan was working out just fine.

The cat was doing its job too. Emma adored the ornery little fuzzball. So long as that was the case, Garrett would tolerate him.

But the animal was getting older and sleeping a lot less. Garrett frequently found the little beast in his suite. Meowmus stalked him, his cat's sixth sense alerting him every time Garrett forgot to close his double doors.

Either that or the demon seed had figured out how to open the doors on his own.

Intellectually, he knew that was impossible for a cat that size. But Meowmus Maximus was a diabolical fiend. Garrett frequently found fur on his pillowcase, right in the indentation his head made. Not a lot, but it didn't take much to set off his allergies.

If he didn't change the pillowcase and sheets before bed, he woke up with swollen eyes. He kept popping antihistamines and started taking allergy drops. But they could only do so much when the damn cat was taking over his bed.

Many showers and having the housekeeping service change his sheets every day, just in case, were helping. But he was still going to have to double his efforts to keep the cat out of his room.

"Em, is George staying for dinner?"

Emma popped out of her room, pointing to the phone. "No, my *preciosa*, it's not Pedro. I have a new roommate now. His name is Garrett, remember?

She paused, grinning. "Yes, I agree it's a very weird name."

Garrett chuckled.

It was a good thing Ian had been out of town for so long. He'd laugh his ass off if he could see Garrett right now, so stupidly pleased to be in a platonic relationship.

Elias would get it. He understood about debts that needed to be paid.

Emma had thawed considerably in the weeks since moving in. Despite her initial misgivings, she had settled in just fine, as he knew she would. The woman was incapable of holding a grudge. She was too warm and good-natured for that.

It helped that Garrett went out of his way to be a considerate roommate. He gave Emma her space when she needed it, providing meals and conversation as she grew more comfortable around him. But when Emma was feeling unwell, he was there, ready to administer meds and consult with specialists whenever he felt it was required.

Emma did give him shit sometimes. But that was a part of their dynamic, as familiar to him as she was. And no, he didn't feel the need to enlighten her on that fact.

"No, he's not another cousin." Emma beamed at the phone screen, her face as animated and happier than he'd ever seen it. "He's just a friend. He grew up in Verdant Falls where Mama and I used to live."

She paused. "Oh, really? Well, I guess it does have nice pancakes."

Emma continued to talk to her sister for another ten minutes, mouthing 'yes' when he pantomimed eating dinner.

By the time she was done with her call, he had the meal served in front of the TV.

They had moved on from Bill Murray to Keanu Reeves. Emma hadn't been the biggest fan of Bill and Ted, but she loved Keanu in anything action because she was the most perfect woman in the world.

Except *Johnny Mnemonic* wasn't Keanu's strongest work. Emma was flagging by the midpoint, and he wasn't doing much better.

"In retrospect, taking the extra strength Benadryl for the cat dander might have been a mistake." He yawned.

There was no response. Emma was already asleep.

It was time to carry her to her room. He was just going to close his eyes for a minute…

THERE WAS a hand on her breast. It was very warm and very big.

This was around the time Emma realized she wasn't in her bed. She had fallen asleep on the couch again.

But Garrett hadn't done that thing they didn't acknowledge. He hadn't put her to bed. Instead, he'd lain down with her, curling around her body so that her back was to his front.

And now his arm was wrapped around her, his big hand underneath her T-shirt, cupping *underneath* her bra.

Dear God, her nipple was diamond-hard. It was throbbing and for once that word didn't mean pain.

Her inhale must have been too deep because Garrett began to stir.

"*Baby*?" he muttered sleepily, squeezing her breast.

Emma pushed out of his arms so fast she fell off the couch, landing on the hardwood floor with a thump.

"*Shit*." That had hurt. Emma picked herself up with a groan.

"Emmy." Garrett's voice was slurred. He was still half-asleep. Blinking, he pushed himself up on one elbow.

He swore under his breath when he realized where they were. Then his eyes slowly focused on her. "Did we fall asleep on the couch?"

Did Garrett not realize he'd been feeling her up in his sleep moments ago?

"I guess so," she mumbled, flushed, her skin itchy. "God, look at the time. I have to get ready for work or I'll be late."

He frowned and started to ask a question, but she was already rushing out of the room.

Hurrying, Emma showered and dressed, ducking out of the apartment as soon as she heard the doors to Garrett's room close. Then she left for the shift that wouldn't begin for another two hours.

Emma's mind was racing the whole ride down the elevator to the lobby.

Baby. He'd called her baby.

Obviously, he'd been thinking about someone else. Who was it? His ex-wife? Or was it someone new she didn't know about?

Hold up. That was crazy. Garrett wasn't seeing anyone. He would have told her. Relished doing so in fact.

Unless he's sneaking around.

That didn't seem like Garrett. But he was the type to be protective of a new partner. Maybe he didn't want to bring it up to her before he knew it was serious. Men did that sort of thing all the time, right?

He was divorced. It was only natural he'd be gun-shy and careful with a new partner. Unless it was his former wife he was thinking about after all?

Her stomach tightened. Emma didn't know which idea she disliked more. They all sucked.

She didn't ask herself why.

"Excuse me, are you Emmaline Mendez?"

Emma stopped halfway across the black marble tiled lobby.

A white-haired man in his late fifties or early sixties walked over. He was wearing a tie and gray suit, but it wasn't nice and fitted like Garrett's. No, this one screamed cop or insurance salesman.

It turned out she was half-right.

The stranger flashed a badge at her. She had time to register the state seal and Investigator over some other smaller letters before he closed it.

"Ms. Mendez, I'm Richard Folsom. I investigate insurance fraud for the state of California."

"O-okay." She moved her tote bag in front of her like a shield. "Why are you here?"

"I came because your file was recently updated, triggering some warning flags." He pursed his thick lips. "Can you confirm that you're receiving MediCal for your health insurance needs?"

Emma's adrenaline started to pump, tightening her chest. "Uh, yes. I am."

His bushy white brows raised as he gave their surroundings a cursory and contemptuous once-over. "And you live here?"

"Yes, but it's temporary."

He ignored that, his nostrils flaring as if he'd smelled something foul. "Ms. Mendez, are you aware that *you* are supposed to report any change in your living situation to the state right away?" he asked, stressing the *you*.

Emma frowned. "I…"

There had been something about that in the application her mother had helped her fill out when she moved here. But she couldn't remember the details.

"I'm not sure," she whispered.

"The address we have on file for you is on 23rd Street, is it not?"

She nodded. "That's my cousin's place. I had to move out because they didn't allow pets with his pre-existing condition. But I don't *live* here in this building. I'm just crashing with a friend… from high school."

It was the first time Emma had claimed a pre-accident relationship. But the investigator had no way of knowing the significance of the moment. Instead, he scowled, as if she was hesitating because she was lying.

"But it *is* temporary," she continued. "I'm just a guest."

"You're crashing on this man's couch?" His bushy eyebrow raised superciliously.

How was it that her mouth was *this* dry? "No, I'm in his spare room."

Richard Folsom sighed, looking at her with a mix of disappointment and contempt.

"Ms. Mendez, insurance fraud is a very serious crime. It costs the state of California millions every year. The benefits you collect in addition to your medical coverage come to a sizable sum. If you don't make restitution, the state has no choice but to prosecute for fraud."

"*What?*" Emma sucked in a shaky breath. "Prosecute? But I'm not committing fraud. I was in an accident. I need my health coverage and the benefits. I can only work part-time. I have the medical evaluations to prove it."

The investigator looked down his nose at her. "The legitimacy of your medical issues is not in question. It's your ability to pay for your own coverage that is the problem. That will be the case as long as you live here in this luxury building."

Emma couldn't believe this was happening. "But I'm not on the lease. I don't even pay rent."

Folsom retrieved something from his pocket, a rolled-up magazine. He opened it to a page marked with a sticky note.

"Is this the penthouse that you live in?"

Emma's head jerked, her mouth dropping open at the glossy spread.

It wasn't exactly Garrett's apartment. Not as it was now. It had the same layout, but the space pictured in the glossy pages had different furniture and decorations. Either Garrett had done a dramatic redecoration or the magazine spread was from before his time.

A neighbor stepped out of the elevator. The elegant octogenarian slowed, rubbernecking the train wreck in progress. But one hard look from Folsom and she hurried along.

"Well, Ms. Mendez?"

Emma was sweating now. "I told you, it's not mine. I'm just a guest."

Folsom flipped the magazine shut. "Like I said, so long as you live here, the veracity of your claim will be in question. My report will reflect that. Your insurance coverage and benefits will be suspended starting Monday."

Chapter Twenty-Four

EMMA

She could barely process the words over the ringing in her ears.

"Monday?" she echoed.

"Yes, for the duration of the investigation. You are welcome to appeal, of course." Folsom gave her a derisive once-over and sniffed. "Good luck with that."

"Wait, you can't do that!" Emma staggered, trying to follow, but the man had already turned his back. Nearly wheezing in panic, she tried to follow him, her heart pounding so fast it was making her vision tunnel and her head pound. "I *need* my insurance."

The investigator wasn't listening. By the time she made it out the lobby doors, he had melted into the dense pedestrian traffic on the sidewalk.

Where had he gone?

Emma picked a direction, running to the right. She changed directions, sprinting until she had a stitch in her side. But Folsom had disappeared.

Still struggling to breathe, Emma stepped out of the busy flow of foot traffic. It was that or get trampled.

What was she going to do? Feeling numb and on the edge of tears, she wandered until she ended up at the coffee kiosk over an hour early for her shift.

Kyle was there with Bethany. He took one look at her face and guided her to sit on the upturned bucket they used as a chair, coaxing her until she was able to explain what had happened.

"Damn, that sucks," Bethany said, preparing a pumpkin spice soy latte for their sole customer.

"I just don't understand how they can suspend all my benefits," Emma mumbled. "They have no proof I'm hiding income. Shouldn't they have proof?"

"It might be standard procedure," Kyle said. "My cousin used to get food stamps. When she moved to another county for a new job, she told them she didn't need the help anymore, but another payment went through anyway."

His chin dipped down, wrinkling. "She thought it was procedure, a sort of buffer payment. But it turned out to be a clerical error. They were late stopping her payments. And even though it wasn't her mistake, they made her pay all the money back."

Emma could feel the blood draining from her face. She wasn't on food stamps. Her aid helped subsidize her rent, but the bulk went toward her medical expenses. And those were insanely high without insurance.

"How do they even know I moved?"

Emma hadn't been at Garrett's that long. Her mail still went to Pedro's, but Garrett must have had someone pick it up because it showed up at his place with the old address printed on it.

Emma would have had her mail forwarded by the post office, but she hadn't believed she'd be staying at Garrett's that long, so she'd put it off.

Bethany popped the gum she seemed to be addicted to. "Someone must have reported you."

Emma's head snapped up.

Kyle nodded. "It was the only way they could have found out so soon."

He was right. Emma didn't care how many gung ho investigators the state employed. Bureaucracy at the state level would have taken a lot longer to investigate a claim. Unless someone lit a fire under them.

"Who would hate me that much?"

As one, both she and Kyle turned to look at Bethany.

"Hey, I wouldn't do that!" the other woman snapped.

She shook a sponge at Kyle's skepticism. "I *wouldn't*. First off, I didn't know that moving somewhere nicer was a crime—which just figures, doesn't it? It's all about the one percent keeping their boot on the neck of the ninety-nine. And with Emma having to drop shifts, I *know* for a fact she makes less than I do."

Bethany twisted to face her. "Unless the rich dude has decided to pay you for your services? Have you started hitting that yet?"

Emma's shift hadn't started yet, but she was already exhausted. And a little grossed out.

She was honest enough to admit that her relationship with Garrett had more than its share of sexual tension. But it wasn't sordid. "I'm not sleeping with him."

Bethany was visibly disappointed. "Why not? It's been over a month!"

Kyle made a choking noise in his throat, but it wasn't laughter.

"I know you're not going to like hearing this, but I think you should tell Garrett right away," he said. "There's got to be something he can do."

Emma rubbed her temple, trying to stave off a possible headache. "He'll just offer to pay for everything. I don't want to owe him any more than I already do."

Bethany pulled off her apron. "Of course you should let him pay. He'll bend over backward to do it, you know after he bends you over," she added, thrusting her hips suggestively.

"*Bethany.*" That was all she managed before the other barista threw her apron on the floor, her face reddening around her piercings.

"I can't believe how fucking stupid you're being! You have a gorgeous billionaire at your beck and booty call, but you don't even entertain the idea of letting him help you. Because poor brain-damaged Emma keeps trying to prove she doesn't have brain damage. But you do! So take the fucking help! And once you do, give the desperate fucker the reward he's obviously waiting for—a good long fuck. Maybe if he pounds you hard enough, he'll shake some sense out of whatever functioning brain cells you have left!"

She stalked out the door, slamming it behind her.

Kyle winced. After a long minute of silence, he shrugged. "Her shift was over anyway," he said in a quiet voice.

Emma closed her eyes. Then she took a deep breath and stood, picking up Bethany's apron and hanging it on the hook next to the door.

"I will tell Garrett about the investigator."

She didn't have a choice. Folsom would contact him next, wouldn't he? But she doubted Garrett could get her health insurance reinstated right away. This was state bureaucracy. No, he'd just throw money at the problem.

Did billionaires pay for their health expenses out of pocket?

No, Garrett likely had the Ferrari of health insurance. Paying out of pocket would be like burning money for no reason.

Except he *would* do that for her.

The idea made her stomach twist up in a huge knot. Garrett was already doing so much for her by letting her live with him.

"I'm sure he'll find a solution," Kyle said, his hero worship front and center. "I know Hector told him he couldn't bump you to a better plan through work, but circumstances have changed now."

Huh? She blinked up at Kyle's pale shiny face. "When did they speak about my health plan?"

"It was right after the garage thing. The day after he found out about your accident."

"I gathered, but why would Hector talk to him about that?"

Didn't discussing her paperwork together constitute some sort of privacy violation?

That didn't make sense. Her boss had never met a rule or guideline he didn't love. It was practically his religion.

"I know he owns the building, but Hector shouldn't be discussing my insurance with him."

Kyle scratched the back of his head, the paleness disappearing under a tide of red. "Uh, well, it makes sense in light of…"

"In light of what?"

"Well, Garrett doesn't just own the building and the finance company on the top floor. He also owns controlling interest in *De Olla*."

Emma's stupid brain processed the information with the speed of a sloth.

She was quiet for so long, Kyle became concerned. Crouching, he waved his hand in her face. "Are you okay?"

"No. I'm not." Emma buried her hands in her hair. "I live with my *boss*."

And this morning, she'd woken up with his hand squeezing her breast.

Chapter Twenty-Five

GARRETT

His pacing was threatening to wear a groove in the hardwood floor. This morning had been a disaster.

Sure, it had started good. Fantastic, in fact. That hazy minute where he'd been in between sleep and waking had been surreal, a stolen moment from another timeline. The life he hadn't gotten a chance to live.

But that voluptuous warmth, the rich softness of Emma's skin had gone to his head. Both of them.

Hard as a rock and half-asleep, he'd taken things he had no right to claim. Emma had bolted, making an excuse and running out the door two hours early for her shift at the coffee kiosk.

What she should have done is crack him one over the head.

And there he went again, thinking about his dick. At least he hadn't said it aloud.

Could you stick a foot in your brain? He should just punch himself in the groin and save Emma the trouble.

His downward spiral was interrupted by the kitten. Garrett had been vaguely aware the beast had been following in his wake, claws scraping the floor's finish. The little shit thought it was a game.

He'd spent the entire day on edge, drafting and erasing texts to

Emma. In the end, he'd decided to wait to speak to her until she got home.

That should have been a half hour ago. Garrett knew that because Hector had sent him her schedule yesterday. Garrett didn't even have to ask for it anymore.

Fifteen minutes later, he lost the battle with his patience. He ordered his driver to take him to the waterfront.

He jumped out when he spotted Emma sitting on a bench, facing the water.

Wordlessly, he sat down next to her. All his worst fears about that morning were confirmed when she didn't turn around. Emma refused to look at him.

Garrett sucked in a deep breath, his carefully prepared speech gone, completely forgotten at the sight of her.

"Emma, I know I fucked up this morning. But you don't have to be afraid to come home. What happened was an accident. I took some Benadryl last night and it knocked me on my ass. It won't ever happen again. Even if the antihistamines render me unconscious, I'll make sure to go to my room. And if I don't make it and end up sleeping on the floor halfway, just leave me there."

The joke fell flat. Emma kept her eyes on the water. He glanced in the same direction and was startled to see the end of a sunset so spectacular it belonged in a movie.

But it paled in comparison to Emma. The golden glow transformed her caramel skin into a fiery bronze. She was a golden goddess, but one warm and alive.

It physically hurt not to touch her. And it made his heart hurt that he couldn't tell her that. But enough boundaries had been crossed today.

Emma twisted to face him. The confusion and hurt in her eyes damn near killed him. "Is it true that you own *De Olla*?"

Okay, a line *had* been crossed. Just not the one he thought. And Emma was just realizing it now.

"Was this news?" he asked, unable to hide his surprise.

Her mouth dropped open. "It's true?"

He raised a shoulder. "I thought you knew. The first *De Olla* café is in my building."

Her lips parted. "I thought the owner paid rent!"

He shook his head. "*De Olla* doesn't pay rent because it's a partnership. And yes, I have controlling interest. Or Next Chapter does."

Emma's brow puckered. "You and your partner own it?"

"Our company does," he stressed. "But I did accept a seat on the board at their invitation."

"Why?"

"Hector's boss Hilda, who is also his wife, wanted to partner with someone experienced at expanding businesses." Garrett turned so he was facing her. "Don't get me wrong, Hector is a decent manager, but he's a perfectionist. His chief interest is in making sure the recipes he's using are authentic when mass-produced. Which is a good thing because they make money, but he can't handle the logistics of more than one café."

She processed this slowly. "But you can."

He nodded matter-of-factly. "I push boundaries and excel at seeing the big picture. They decided sacrificing controlling interest was worth having someone like me on board, directing from the top."

"I did know about Hector's wife," Emma said slowly as if the memory had come from a long way away. "I knew she was the company president. But I didn't know about you. No one mentions it."

"I wasn't keeping my position a secret," he promised. "I'm on the board of many businesses. I don't do any of the day-to-day. And I won't have to, so long as they stick to the expansion plan I drafted."

He waited for a response, but Emma didn't have one. "Are you upset about this?" he asked.

She closed her eyes. "If you have controlling interest, that makes you my boss."

His brain filled in what she didn't say aloud—that this morning her boss had been pressing his cock to her lush ass and fondling her bare breast.

"*Hector* is your boss. I don't intend on interfering." Not any more than he already had.

Emma looked down at her lap, her hands tightly gripped together. She turned to him, blinking fast.

Fuck, this was bad. He was a monster. Garrett was going to have to sell *De Olla*.

"I don't want to ask you for help." Her breath was shaky. "But I might need it."

Oh. *Oh… Wait.* "Did something else happen?"

She nodded, a tear sliding down her cheek.

What the fuck? Had someone messed with her?

Garrett slid closer to her, sliding an arm around her shoulders. "Hey, you can ask me for anything. You know that, right?"

He expected to be rebuffed. But Emma shocked the hell out of him when she gripped the lapel of his suit jacket, burrowing her face in his chest.

Emma was crying but he hadn't caused it. She was turning to him for comfort. Garrett's shoulders straightened, puffing up involuntarily even as he pulled her into his side, comforting her.

He didn't know if he should be pulling out his wallet or getting ready to kick someone's ass. Whatever she needed, he'd do.

She sniffed. "There was this man."

Garrett went from zero to sixty in nothing flat, heat coursing through his veins. "Who is he? *Did he touch you?*"

Emma raised her face. A tear track stained her cheek.

"No, it wasn't like that," she said. But she hesitated, worrying her lower lip with her teeth.

Garrett ordered himself to calm down, but he couldn't seem to. "Baby, you need to tell me what the hell happened 'cause I'm this close to tearing this bench apart," he said, holding his fingers a hairsbreadth apart.

She was so fucking upset she didn't register the endearment.

"It's concrete," she whispered.

"What?" he breathed.

"The bench. It's concrete."

"Then prepare for a Hulk-level smash," he replied from behind gritted teeth.

That surprised her into a laugh. The sound relaxed his tense muscles a notch, but he stayed alert, battle-ready.

"This man was waiting in the lobby of the building," she began, launching into an unexpected tale of a state investigator and accusations of insurance fraud.

Garrett processed it all in silence, tapping his fingers on his thigh. "This Folsom said he worked for the state?"

She lifted her hands. "He showed me a badge. Someone must have reported me. At least that's what Kyle thinks."

He scowled. "And you have to prove you don't have money because you live with me?"

"I guess." Emma sighed miserably. "How does a person even do that?"

"Bank statements, income tax records?" he guessed. "The state must have forensic accountants that would authenticate them."

Garrett didn't know much about the inner workings of California bureaucracy, not outside the areas where it intersected with his various business enterprises.

Never in his wildest dreams would he have thought he'd be wishing for expertise in health insurance of all things.

'Health care for all' is starting to sound better and better.

"They're jumping the gun cutting off your insurance before their investigation is done," he said with a scowl. "Your medical record alone should be sufficient to let you keep it."

She looked at him with her heart in her eyes. "Do you think I could get the coverage I need through *De Olla*, even though I don't work enough hours?"

Well, shit. "I'm sorry. I don't think so. You see, I already spoke to Hector and we realized that's not a viable route."

He reached for her hand when her eyes welled with tears. "But I don't want you to worry. Because there's no fucking way I'll let you go without the care you need."

The tremor that passed through her was enough to get him mad all over again.

"I don't want you to just pay for everything," she said, wiping under her eyes. "I should have insurance. I need it."

"I know, baby, I know." He pulled her close again, squeezing her tight. "I'm going to make sure you get it. Hell, we'll get married if we have to."

Her breath puffed against his chest as she laughed. A small fist hit him in the back. "That's not funny."

"It wasn't meant to be," he said. "But don't worry. I'll find a solution—like switching jobs. Something great that will come with a fantastic health plan."

She pulled away abruptly. "I have to stop working for *De Olla*?"

Garrett showed her his teeth. "I don't see a better path but give me a chance to ask–" he broke off and pressed his lips together when he realized he already knew an insurance expert.

Emma's hand fisted in his shirt. "What is it?" she asked.

"Nothing."

She poked him. "*Garrett.*"

He let out a frustrated noise. "This isn't a problem. It's just that Fletcher is the guy who handles the nitty-gritty paperwork side, including the health plans."

She studied him for a moment. "And he doesn't like me."

"He doesn't *not* like you," Garrett assured her. "What he has a problem with is me."

Emma blinked those impossibly long lashes at him. "I don't understand."

He tried to think of a better answer but was forced to settle for the truth.

"Fletcher has been trying to warn me away from you since the parking garage. He was convinced you're going to sue us into oblivion."

Garrett's eyes lit up. "Which you are welcome to do. Just be sure to ask for a big-ass settlement. A couple of million dollars would cover your medical expenses, with or without insurance."

Emma shook her head in despair. "Why are you like this?"

Laughing, he tugged at her hands, coaxing her up from the bench. Overwhelmed, she let him bundle her up and take her back home.

Drained, she even let him put her to bed.

Garrett promised to have the issue resolved by lunch the next day. But thanks to his partner, it didn't work out that way.

"What don't you understand?" Fletcher threw up his hands. "Living with you is putting her coverage in jeopardy. The solution is simple. Find her a new place. Something that would normally be within her means."

"She works minimum wage part-time in Southern California," he ground out. "Her means equal a shack by the side of the road."

"Then set her up in a nice two-bedroom with her cousin, preferably across town. You can subsidize their rent in a way the insurance investigator can't object to—you know, the setup she had before you ruined it for her."

A less stubborn son of a bitch would have crumpled under that direct hit. "Then there's nothing I can do as her employer? Not even if I gave her a new job?"

"What job? Cat sitter?"

Garrett leaned back in his chair. Hell, that wasn't a half-bad idea. If he could pay Emma to keep the little shit off his bed, then he could—

Fletcher was incredulous. "Are you fucking kidding me? You're thinking about it!"

Garrett irritated him further by shrugging. "It's outside the box, but it's not the worst idea I've heard. I hate that animal."

"Unbelievable," Fletcher muttered. "Why do you insist on making everything so damn hard? Any new insurance plan you find her will likely deny her because of pre-existing conditions. She has to keep her *current* coverage. Just find her a more modest place, so it doesn't look like she has a sugar daddy too cheap to pay for her aspirin."

Fletcher stalked out, leaving Garrett to come to the same conclusion. And he did… in a way.

Emma did not need a sugar daddy. She needed a husband.

Chapter Twenty-Six

EMMA

Emma kept replaying Garrett's words of reassurance. He was going to find a solution, hopefully one that didn't involve charity or breaking any laws.

"He will fix it," Georgia had insisted over coffee earlier, a to-die-for Yemen blend Rainer had ordered from a roaster in Berkeley. "The thing is you have to let him."

Emma sipped the coffee. "Don't worry. I'm not about to shoot myself in the foot. This time, I will take the help."

It was only fair. Garrett had gotten her into this mess. He could get her out of it.

She didn't care what kind of job Garrett got her. Emma was prepared to scrub the toilets of this apartment if it meant keeping her insurance.

However, when Garrett got home, his expression told her things hadn't gone well with his partner. "I guess Fletcher didn't have good news."

Garrett shook his head. "He excels at being the voice of doom and gloom. But there's no cause for concern. I said I was going to take care of everything, and I will."

Emma thrust a hand through her hair. "I can't let you pay for everything."

"Oh, I'm not. I have a new plan." He covered her hands with his, guiding them down because she'd started making fists, pulling her hair.

He tipped her chin up so she couldn't avoid his eyes. "I think we should get married."

Emma groaned aloud. Seriously, there was a time and a place. "I told you that wasn't funny."

He squeezed her hands, the earnest light in his downright terrifying.

Emma straightened, her heart beginning to hammer in her chest.

"Emma, I'm not joking. Marriage is the fastest and most reliable solution. You have pre-existing conditions, which makes things complicated. But there is no way the insurance company that covers Next Chapter would deny my spouse coverage. Not when it could jeopardize our entire corporate account."

He rubbed her arms, chafing warmth back into them. "The contracts we have with them are worth mid-six figures and growing. Not to mention the business I could throw their way in the future. Hell, they'd bend over backward to add my wife to the plan."

His wife? A frisson passed down her body, making her skin tingle. Mrs. Garrett Chapman. What would that even look like?

It would look like a Wall Street wolf went slumming.

With that apt assessment, she snorted and shook her head. "Please stop talking nonsense. We can't get married."

"People do it every day."

"Because they're in love."

His cheek twitched.

"True," he said, looking at his feet as if to make sure they were still there. "But they also do it for a lot of other reasons. Money and green cards to name a few."

"Are you comparing this to a green card marriage?"

He perked up suddenly, and she realized she'd phrased it as if she was considering his crazy plan. "I'm pointing out that there's a long and varied list of reasons people marry other than love. Practical reasons."

Garrett led her to the couch. But he didn't sit next to her. Instead, he sat on the coffee table in front of her.

"I know you have a million arguments against it but trust me when I say I've given this a lot of thought, and the benefits outweigh the costs."

Emma had to be careful. A wheeler and dealer like Garrett needed just a crack, the tiniest of openings to work his magic.

"For me," she pointed out. "Not for you."

What would he get out of this? She was afraid to ask.

Garrett rubbed the back of his neck. "I'm the one who jeopardized your current health plan. So let me fix it. And not just temporarily. By marrying me, we can guarantee your coverage for life. It can be part of your prenuptial agreement."

Emma sat up. "A prenup?"

"Yeah. One with special considerations for both of us. That's legal speak for the things we get out of it."

Christian Grey's contract sprang into her mind. With effort, she pushed that visual away. "Mine is health insurance. What would yours be?"

"Protection."

"Huh?"

He gestured to the space around them. "We would spell everything out in writing. In the event of a divorce, you wouldn't have a claim on my fortune, businesses, or properties. You only get insurance, and perhaps a small stipend to offset any expenses a divorce would cost you. That kind of thing."

Garrett leaned forward, patting her knee. "I know you are leery of accepting money but it's important you don't come out *owing* money because of this."

His logic seemed reasonable. Or was she just grasping at a shiny piece of straw?

"Oh."

"Can I get another syllable?"

She kicked him in the shin, not hard. "Hey, this is a lot to take in."

"I know," he admitted. "But I don't see any downsides."

Emma blinked with exaggerated slowness. "You're kidding, right? What about your social life?"

"What about it?"

Seriously? Emma was tempted to kick him harder.

"You're a young single man. How will it look to the many models vying for your time if you suddenly get married to some nobody?"

He gave her the strangest look.

"I'm marrying to help out a friend," he began in a halting voice. "Any woman I dated would understand. Besides, I haven't been divorced long. It'll be years before I think of tying the knot for real."

His words were like a punch to the stomach. *It's a paper marriage*, she reminded herself. Garrett wasn't proposing anything real.

"Then the third time will be the charm?" she asked, attempting a snicker and failing miserably.

He lifted a hand. "Why not? I'm wealthy enough for a string of wives. It's expected. In the meantime, you'll help me keep the gold diggers away."

Garrett gave her a hapless grin.

He was joking, but she really wanted to kick him now. Emma was still contemplating it when he put his hand on her arm.

"I realize this is a big decision. Why don't you call your mom and baby sister and ask them what they think?"

"My sister is four and thinks boys are gross."

He chuckled. "I see. I didn't realize how much younger she was."

"Yeah, well, my mom's still pretty young herself." Emma had been a teen pregnancy.

He rocked back on his heels. "You know that's a bonus I hadn't considered. You paid Pedro rent, right?"

"Yeah. A little," she muttered, already suspicious. Emma was starting to recognize Garrett's crafty look.

He tilted his head to one side. "It must be expensive for your mom, having such a young kid at home. I guess she's never been able to help with your expenses or vice versa."

"No. Neither of us earns much."

He nodded sagely. "Well, if you take me up on my offer, you'd have no expenses. Any money you made working would be freed up. You could send a bit of it home."

Emma sucked in a breath, her thoughts roiling. What could she do with her wages if she didn't have to pay rent?

Damn the man. He had her and he knew it.

"You might also think about enrolling in college classes again," he continued. "I'm not sure if a degree in business is still interesting to you, but you had all your core classes done. I'm sure it wouldn't be too difficult for you to finish up your bachelor's. No need to stick to business either. With your core classes done, you could pursue a degree in any field. There are any number of high-paying jobs available."

But the one thing they all required was a degree. Or a technical certificate of some kind.

Emma pictured going to a job that earned more than minimum wage. It almost hurt.

Then she thought of the room at her mother's house, the one full of boxes containing awards, trophies, and old report cards. The memorabilia of a past life.

The likelihood of getting back to a place where she could reclaim a solid future had been so distant yesterday. It was hard enough for Emma to maintain her status quo and to keep the sliver of independence she'd managed to carve out the last few years.

By accepting Garrett's offer, she would be giving up some of that independence. She would have to rely on him. But if Emma agreed to marry him, she'd have time, some space to breathe and rebuild.

She could find a new calling.

It was what Georgia had done when Rainer came into her life. George had accepted Rainer's help and built a successful business with it. She and Garrett might not be a real couple, but he was a friend now. Sort of. This wasn't that different.

Well, it was completely different, but the benefits outweighed the costs. If she married Garrett, there would be a legal contract—the prenup. Once they both signed it, he couldn't change his mind and withdraw the support for her medical expenses without consequences.

Emma studied him for a long moment, but Garrett didn't appear to be fazed by her scrutiny. Nope, he was cool and collected, the picture of a steadfast and confident man.

He had to practice these expressions in the mirror. How else did they get so perfect?

"Are you sure you want to do this?" she asked, a distant ringing beginning in her ears. That detached feeling was back as if she were watching herself from the outside.

"As sure as death and taxes," he said with a charming grin.

Emma narrowed her eyes at him. He'd brought her back to the here and now with a few choice words.

"I'm going to kick you now."

He pressed his lips together before nodding. "Yeah, well deserved."

Inviting his friends to his wedding would only scare Emma. But Garrett couldn't stop himself from asking Elias, Rainer, and of course Georgia.

He would have asked Ian as well. Unfortunately, Elias' cousin and Auric Security co-founder was out of the country on a mission, providing security to a Danish royal on a global goodwill tour.

Garrett greeted the trio at the door, gesturing to the tray of drinks and hors d'oeuvres. "Emma is going over the prenup with the lawyer in my office. We'll get started as soon as the justice of the peace gets here."

Rainer did a double take halfway to the drinks. "Prenup? Justice of the peace? I thought this was just dinner."

"A quick civil ceremony, then dinner," he corrected, patting his best friend on the shoulder. "Sorry for not telling you sooner. We decided to move on this last night. I think it's important to do this as quickly as possible before Emma's current health insurance lapses."

Rainer recovered from his shock first. "*This* is your solution to her insurance issue problem? You're getting *married*?"

"Yeah, for the insurance," he said, checking Georgia's reaction out of the corner of his eye. "It'll be just the three of you acting as witnesses. I'm not trying to steal your wedding thunder or anything here."

Rainer twisted, catching Georgia's eye. She was just as confused, her lips a round *O*.

Elias, who'd ignored the specialty fig cocktails he'd had Mohammed fix up for the occasion, proceeded to spill the precious liquid all over his mahogany bar. "Come again? Who's getting married?"

"Me." Garrett threw his arm up, then quickly put it back down so George wouldn't catch on to how enthusiastic he was.

"I reconnected with an old friend recently—well, sort of a friend," he explained to Elias when Georgia crossed her arms and stared him down. "Emma needs health insurance. She has several pre-existing conditions. Matters got a little complicated but it's going to be fine because we're getting married."

Elias blinked. "Emma who?"

Georgia held up a hand, interrupting what promised to be a grand inquisition. "This isn't a joke? You're serious?"

"Like a nun," he said, picking up one of the figgy cocktails and taking a sip.

He would have normally opted for the single malt himself, but Emma used to be quite fond of figs. He was hoping she still liked them.

"Are nuns serious?" Elias asked, bemused. "According to the last trivial pursuit game I played, there was one who flew and was quite silly."

Georgia's sharp hazel eyes drilled a hole through him. "This is what Emma wants?"

"She's on board," he said evasively. "It solves a lot of problems."

He took another sip of his drink. Mmm, he could grow quite fond of these.

"She might be feeling a touch overwhelmed with the lawyer," he added a bit more truthfully.

Emma's eyes had almost crossed when he first gave her the

contract. He'd decided to call his lawyer to come explain it to her before the size and breadth of it scared her off.

"Maybe you can join her and share some insights on the process?" he suggested to George. "Tell her how it went for you."

"George didn't sign a prenup," Rainer informed them.

"She didn't?" Elias asked, wide eyes rounding on George. "You didn't?"

"Hey, don't look at me like that." She held up her hands. "I offered to sign one."

Elias was immediately contrite. "I didn't mean it like that."

"Of course you didn't," she said skeptically, rolling her eyes at Rainer who didn't smile, although his lips quirked. "I think I will join Emma and the lawyer despite my lack of expertise."

She turned on her heel, but Rainer intercepted her, giving her a quick kiss before whispering something that softened the expression on her face.

Elias waited until she had disappeared before turning on Rainer. "You're marrying her without a prenup?"

"I trust George with my life," Rainer said with the confidence of a man who'd struck gold in the relationship department. "By the way, you're not my emergency contact anymore. She is."

Elias threw up his hands in surrender. "Well, of course she is. I'm just surprised about the prenup given…"

He trailed off, deciding discretion was the better part of valor.

"Because my mother was a gold digger?" Rainer asked, his face carefully blank.

"Hey—" Elias broke off, waving them on. "Fuck it. I said nothing and know even less about relationships than Ian so have at it."

"True." Rainer smirked. "As for me, being a product of that kind of marriage makes me even more sure of George. She'd never try anything shady."

"I don't doubt it…" Elias conceded, surprising them both. "But I don't think I'd ever be able to trust anyone quite that much, let alone a woman who'd have *me*."

Elias took another swig of his Scotch. "At least this one is crossing the *T*'s on his fake marriage by getting a prenup signed."

"The hell it's fake," Rainer laughed.

"What?" Garrett affected innocence. "I told you, Emma needs health insurance."

His friend gave him a knowing look. "I know that's true, but tell me—and be honest—what does she get if the marriage sticks?"

Garrett swept out an arm to encompass the penthouse. "I've listed all my assets in the prenup and spelled everything out. All she gets is her health insurance and a small stipend. Plus, a small cash settlement if the marriage dissolves."

"*If*?" Elias was nearing meltdown—well, as close as the former SEAL got to one. "Not when?"

"Yeah," Rainer drawled. "Again, what happens if it doesn't dissolve?"

"No dissolution means the prenup's clauses never go into effect." Garrett laughed. "Or do I have to explain basic contract law to you?"

Rainer picked up a swizzle stick from the bar and threw it at him. "Let me rephrase—do you have an end date for the marriage codified in the prenup?"

Garrett took another sip, declining to answer.

Elias waited a beat, then whistled. "Now I have to know who the fuck Emma is."

Rainer held up a hand. "In a sec. I have one more question."

Garrett put his hands in his pockets, rocking back on his heels. "Shoot."

"Are there any provisions for children of this blessed union in the contract?"

He waited a beat, but Rainer continued to stare at him in challenge until he caved.

"Well, obviously, any children of the union would become my heirs."

Rainer guffawed, while Elias shook his head, mouthing, *Wow*.

Garrett dismissed their obvious concern. "It's a moot point. This is a strictly platonic arrangement. But you know lawyers—they insist on covering every possible contingency. The bit about kids is all hypothetical."

"Uh-huh. What are the names of these hypothetical children?"

Garrett scoffed, reddening. "I didn't *name* them."

Rainer gave him a smug smile. "Yes, that was very believable."

"Shut up," he muttered.

"I need another drink, and the two of you need professional help." Elias staggered to the right, reaching for the bottle of whiskey. He picked it up, pointing his index finger at him and Rainer, managing to wag it without spilling this time. "Being so eager to get leg shackled is not normal. Neither is *wanting* children. They're loud, they smell, and you can't just leave them at home to hop on a plane to Europe or Japan whenever you want."

"You mean South America or Africa." That was where Auric business generally took him, not the vacation hotspots he'd named.

"Whatever," Elias replied, exasperated. "My point is you're going to do what you're going to do, so go with God and be grateful Ian is the one who drew the short straw on this royalty-sitting gig. Because if he was here instead of me, he would hog-tie you until he could get Doherty up here."

Garrett frowned. "Doherty?"

Elias waved his glass at him. "He's the deprogrammer we subcontract when we extract someone from a cult."

Rainer snickered.

Garrett shook his head, letting amusement color his tone. "I can't wait for a woman to take you out at the knees. That's going to be incredibly satisfying."

"Never going to happen," Elias said with a snort. "But you go right ahead and put that yoke on with my blessing. Just remember this: when those rug rats start arriving, you're naming one after me. Because I am never having one of my own."

Chapter Twenty-Eight

EMMA

"Should I reread that clause to you?" the lawyer asked Emma, concern lining his face.

She gaped at him. "How much did you say?"

"Five mil—" the man began when the door opened.

Emma twisted to see Georgia entering the office. From the look on her face, Garrett had already filled her in on what was going on.

"George!" she squeaked, reaching out to invite her friend to join them at the small conference table. "He's trying to give me five *million.*"

Georgia tripped but caught herself before she face-planted. "Dollars?"

"Yes!"

Her friend turned to the lawyer with a sugary smile. "Hi, sorry. Can you give us a minute?"

Emma's head slumped to the table. The sound of retreating foot-steps signaled the lawyer's departure.

She turned her head without lifting it from the shining dark wood.

"*Five million dollars,*" Emma breathed, slurring because her face was still pressed to the table. "He's trying to give me five million dollars."

George raised her brows. "I thought he was making you sign a prenup."

"He is!" Emma pushed the thick contract toward her, pointing to the part the lawyer had highlighted with a sticky note in the shape of an arrow.

"Wow." George lifted the contract to get a closer look as if she couldn't believe what she was reading. "In the event the marriage dissolves, you get five million dollars in the form of a one-time alimony payment."

"Just like that!" Emma exclaimed. "Five million! It's automatic too."

The lawyer had explained it was hers by default the day after the divorce was final. There were no conditions, which he seemed to find remarkable.

Georgia blinked with exaggerated slowness. "Here I thought Garrett was doing the cutthroat CEO thing, making sure you got nothing."

She slumped. "So did I when he mentioned the prenup."

Emma was still reeling. It would be one thing if the five million was earmarked to buy health insurance, but it wasn't. The insurance was guaranteed for life and separate from the alimony payment.

"There's something wrong with him."

Chuckling, Georgia murmured her agreement while flipping pages. "Are these always so long?"

How was Emma supposed to know? "I guess you didn't get one of these?"

"Nope." George pulled open a page that folded out, accordion fashion. "What is this? It looks like some kind of inventory."

"Those are his assets."

It was a complete listing of properties, bank accounts, stocks, bonds, and who knows what else.

"That part was actually comforting because it spelled out explicitly that he keeps all that stuff."

Which was fine. That was normal. She didn't want Garrett's assets.

This was a deal for health insurance and a little breathing room from bills and other expenses.

Georgia's head drew back, her eyes widening as the list unfolded a comical number of times. It stretched to the floor and beyond, spilling around her chair like a frothy wave. "Uh, this is kind of…"

"Psycho?" Emma finished, still incredulous. She lowered her voice to a whisper, wondering if the wall had ears. "Is this how all rich people do things?"

"I have no idea. Rainer was the first rich guy I met and he's a marshmallow—so gooey inside."

Emma brightened at the touch of humor. "I don't think he's like that with anyone else."

Sure, Rainer was perfectly polite to her. But she had noticed a reserve to him, a little standoffishness that told her he usually held the world at arm's length. That innate distance went out the window only when Georgia was around.

Suddenly she was depressed. What would it be to be *that* for a man?

Emma might never get the chance to find out. With her medical issues, her prospects for love had never been good. Now she was going to be in a fake marriage with a man too handsome for his own good.

That might sound good if this was a movie. But Emma lived in the real world.

There would be other women.

The contract hadn't come right out and said anything about infidelity for either party, but of course, he'd start dating eventually. That was going to be weird and uncomfortable.

Georgia grabbed her hand, the touch pulling her out of her spiral. "Are you going to sign this?"

"I should, right?" she asked, taking the contract back from her. "If I'm going to marry him?"

Georgia studied her expression. "And that's settled? You're going through with the ceremony?"

Emma pushed her hair back from her eyes. "It seemed like a good idea last night. Especially since Garrett was the one responsible for getting me in trouble with the state in the first place. But I never expected him to add millions of dollars to the mix. Living here rent-free is one thing. Taking his money is something else."

"Well, technically you only get the five million if you divorce," Georgia pointed out. "So, the solution is simple. You need to stay married."

"Ha ha," she said in a flat voice. "I didn't realize you were so funny."

Georgia snickered, continuing to flip through the contract. But she didn't appear to understand the legalese any better than Emma did.

"How did Garrett get you in trouble with the state? I missed that part."

Emma explained about Folsom, the insurance investigator, and Garrett's subsequent conversation with his partner. "I'm not sure why it was so complicated getting me work-based insurance, but nothing will be as good as the insurance Garrett can get me as his wife."

"That's crazy. Who do you think reported you?"

"I have no idea."

At this point, finding out who was responsible was moot. The report had been made and now it was either marry Garrett or risk going without insurance.

Georgia handed her a pen. "Honestly, the fact you have so many reservations means you deserve that divorce settlement. You should think of it as winning the lottery."

Emma bit her lip and leaned forward to stroke the petals of the potted orchid decorating the table. "It seems too good to be true. Promise me if Garrett ends up chopping me up into little pieces and using me for fertilizer for these, you'll avenge me."

Georgia put her hand over her heart. "I promise if my man's bestie ends up being an axe murderer, I will run him over with whatever car I'm restoring at the time."

Smiling weakly, Emma flipped back to the beginning of the contract, signing and initialing wherever the little sticky flags indicated.

When she was done, she and Georgia went to change.

Emma had planned on wearing her blue dress. It was the nicest one she owned. But that was no longer true.

Lying on her bed was a gorgeous white lace A-line dress. Transfixed, Emma touched the lace, wondering how something so intricate could be so soft. Then she found the note.

THOUGHT YOU MIGHT NEED THIS 😊

–G

"He made a call and had it delivered," she reminded herself, stroking the edge of the sweetheart neckline.

Finding a stunning dress in her size was very easy for him. Garrett had people for all sorts of tasks, including personal shoppers. But she couldn't help being touched and surprised.

It fit perfectly. Of course.

Emma was still staring at herself when Georgia returned in a green silk wrap dress.

"Damn, girl. You look amazing." The shorter woman took her hand and led her into a twirl, making the skirt flare out.

"How do these shoppers know my size?" Emma asked, bemused. "No one came to measure me."

And with her waist-to-hip ratio, not to mention her cup size, finding a dress that fit like this off the rack was like finding the Hope Diamond in the gutter.

"Rainer has surprised me more than once with a perfect outfit, so I asked him. Someone riffles through your closet and checks your measurements against your current wardrobe. That or they send multiple sizes."

"*Oh*. Weird."

Georgia wrinkled her nose. "I know. You'll get used to it."

She helped fix her hair into a cute half-updo, applying makeup with more skill than Emma possessed.

When she was done, Emma barely recognized herself. "I have never looked this nice," she said, smoothing the skirt of the dress. "Well, that I know of."

Had she ever stood before a mirror all dolled up, anticipating a date with a hot guy? Wouldn't it be sad if the answer was no?

"Plus, it's not a date," she muttered under her breath. She was getting fake married for the sole purpose of securing health insurance.

Emma had a feeling she would need to remind herself of that fact quite a bit in the coming months. Being around Garrett meant blurring lines. Only, she couldn't tell which one of them was doing it.

"Are you ready?" Georgia asked.

Emma took one last look at herself in the mirror. "Hell no."

But she followed her friend out the door and got married anyway.

Chapter Twenty-Nine

GARRETT

He took the breakfast plates out of the warmer, bracing himself for the sight of Emma in her *De Olla* gear.

They had been married a week, and she was still working at the coffee kiosk.

Things weren't going to change overnight, he reminded himself. Baby steps. He closed his eyes, cursing because now he was imagining Emma pregnant with his baby.

"Fuck," he muttered, setting the plate on the counter with more force than was necessary. This was turning into a major problem.

Garrett prided himself on always having his shit together. Even during his post-divorce party days, he'd never gotten sloppy drunk. As for drugs, he avoided them like the plague these days, having learned the hard way never to relinquish control of the reins.

But that was before Emma. His life began to careen out of control the moment he first saw her in the café. His head had been a mess from then on. But after watching Emma walk toward him in that white dress, he'd been done. Stick a fork in him done.

Garrett had instructed his clothing buyer to find something tasteful that worked for a wedding but wasn't a formal bridal gown.

They'd sent him a picture of a knee-length lacy number straight out of the fifties. He'd approved the retro look because it was sufficiently casual.

Trust Emma to transform a simple dress into a religious experience.

It wasn't her fault. Her curves turned even the simplest of silhouettes into showstoppers.

But having such a flamboyantly sexy woman living with and now married to him was like a trial by fire. At the very least he should have to pay a fine when he stared too long. And he'd stared way too fucking long when Emma stepped out of her room in the dress.

Fortunately for him, his bride had been too nervous about getting married to notice. Hell, she'd been terrified, and he knew it. So had everyone else.

Elias had been so taken with Emma that he'd taken him aside to ask if he thought getting married right then was a good idea.

"Maybe if you give her a couple of days she won't look so freaked out," his friend had muttered as the justice of the peace freshened up before the ceremony.

The words had sounded kind and protective, up until the point Elias had straightened his sports coat and run a hand through his hair. "That way she has a chance to look around and weigh her options."

Garrett had mock-punched Elias a little too hard in response. He knew Elias had been joking, but he hadn't wasted any more time. He'd hustled Emma in front of the justice of the peace a few minutes later.

Emma had been shell-shocked during the brief ceremony, which was why Garrett had kept their vows to a simple *I do*. Fortunately, Emma had recovered somewhat by dinner when they were eating Mohammed's exquisite duck tajine, the one with the figs and apricots she loved.

The flowing wine hadn't hurt either, although he'd made sure she hadn't taken any serious medication beforehand.

"I liked your friend Elias," Emma told him at the end of the night, once everyone had gone home. "Are the rest like him and Rainer?"

"Yeah." Except for Fletcher, of course.

That was probably why he'd waited until after the ceremony to text his business partner, informing him of his nuptials after the fact.

He'd gotten a string of head-exploding emojis.

Then fifteen minutes later he'd received another one.

> Fine. Problem solved. Congratulations.

"Hey."

Garrett raised his head. As anticipated, Emma was dressed for work.

He suppressed a sigh. At least she was wearing the new parka he'd gotten her. Fall in San Diego wasn't exactly demanding, but the wind on the waterfront could be biting.

"Good morning," he said. He pushed a plate forward. "Mohammed made you a cheese frittata."

Lighting up, Emma hopped onto the barstool at the end of the kitchen island. She closed her eyes at the first bite and swayed, making happy little noises.

"Dear Lord. How does he do this to eggs?"

Her sounds of pleasure were both a blessing and a curse.

"I asked him once. He said the egg was the ultimate challenge for a chef. Lots of people eat eggs in all sorts of ways. But to take an egg and make it an experience—that's true talent."

She hummed, her mouth too full to speak. "You should give him a raise."

"He makes a very healthy salary. I assure you."

Her ponytail was coming undone. A lock of it was flipping forward until it was almost to her mouth. Should he tuck it behind her ear so she wouldn't get egg in it? Or would that be weird?

Yeah, it would be weird. Which is why he was kicking himself for doing it anyway.

Emma's breath hitched, but Garrett just charged ahead, carrying on as if he wasn't a giant freak. "You're on till four today, right?"

She nodded, taking one of the glasses of fresh-squeezed OJ to wash down her eggs.

"Good, good. By the way, your credit and debit cards are here," he said, taking them out of his pocket and sliding them across the kitchen counter to her.

Emma blinked. "My what?"

"Your Amex Black and the Chase Sapphire. They're already set to autopay from your stipend," he said, nodding at the credit cards. "For expenses."

Her lips pursed in confusion. "You do remember the stipend you get?" he reminded her.

"Stipend?"

"Five thousand, paid out every week." He frowned at her deer-in-the-headlights expression. "It was in the prenuptial contract."

"*It was?*" Emma gasped. "I get five thousand every *week*?"

He wiped his mouth before putting his glass and plate in the dishwasher. Emma looked like he'd just asked her for a kidney.

"You don't have to spend the stipend if you don't want to," he pointed out. "You can invest it. Or send some home."

She toyed with her fork. "I thought when you said I could send my wages home, that would be it. That was more than generous."

Not really. He knew how much she made an hour.

"You can send that too," he said, trying to sound indifferent. "But the stipend gives you options. We talked about you going back to school. Or you can pick something else. It's up to you."

He stopped before telling her the world was her oyster.

"Are you done freaking out?" he asked after a minute. "Because we can get Meowmus one of those tiny service animal vests. He can be your emotional support animal."

Emma's face transformed, anxiety shifting to mild irritation. She balled up a napkin and threw it at him. "Smart aleck."

He grinned. "Do you want me to swing by and pick you up after work? There's a good steakhouse a block down from the kiosk I've been wanting to try."

"Oh…" Emma blinked. "Okay."

"Great. I've been craving beef Wellington all week."

Still affecting disinterest, he checked the time on his phone. "I better run to the office. I'll meet you at the kiosk around closing. See you then."

Quitting while he was ahead, he said goodbye, running into Rainer on his way out. They discussed a few last-minute pre-wedding plans.

Tomorrow night was the stag party.

"Make sure Ian doesn't get his way about the strippers," Rainer told him as they boarded the elevator. "Else, George will have my balls."

Once upon a time, having a stripper at a stag party would have made the night complete. But that stage of his life had come and gone before Emma came back into his life. Nevertheless, his nose wrinkled, wondering how she would react if Ian got his way.

She probably wouldn't care. Which, if he was being honest, would be disappointing.

"I'll make sure," he promised.

It didn't matter that they weren't a couple. Not partying with strippers was Garrett being considerate to his roommate, a woman legally bound to him for insurance reasons.

The fact he was taking Emma to a highly acclaimed restaurant whose reviews never failed to mention the dim and romantic lighting… Well, that was something he wouldn't be mentioning to any of his friends.

Chapter Thirty

EMMA

Bethany nudged her so hard, Emma nearly fell off the bucket.

"*Hey,*" she protested. But it was weak, her heart not in it.

"What's eating you?" the other barista asked.

Emma pressed her lips together, wishing Kyle hadn't traded with the other woman because of a last-minute dental appointment.

Damn, I'm going to regret this. "I'm having dinner with Garrett tonight."

Bethany put her hands on her hips. "If you are about to complain about that hot piece of ass—"

She held up a hand to forestall a diatribe. "It's not that. We… got married."

Bethany's mouth dropped open. Nothing came out.

"I should write this down in my calendar." Emma smiled despite herself. She took out her phone and pretended to make a note. "Bethany is speechless."

"Holy shit!" the other woman burst out.

"Don't get excited," Emma warned. "It's a platonic arrangement. I was going to lose my health insurance, remember? That's how he fixed it."

"*By marrying you?*" Bethany screeched, the piercing sound scaring away a customer who'd just walked up to the window.

Emma rubbed her ear. "*Yes.* But like I said, it's strictly platonic. He made me sign a prenup and everything."

"Oh." Bethany's excitement dimmed. "Well, you still get something. Free room and board at least. Have you fucked him yet?"

"No. And it's not going to happen," she added dejectedly.

"Huh." Bethany turned to face her. "You almost sound sorry about that."

"No… but I guess I sort of thought we were getting closer. Then he mentioned dinner and I almost asked him if it was a date."

"Is it?"

She shook her head. "He was out in the hall with his friend and neighbor Rainer, talking about his wedding right after we spoke. They were discussing hiring strippers for the bachelor party. Garrett said something about making the call, so I guess he's taking care of it personally."

Emma doubted he had a specialty buyer for strippers. Unless his fancy concierge service found hot women for him.

"That doesn't mean your dinner isn't a date," Bethany pointed out with surprising kindness.

Emma grunted. "I wouldn't want to date someone who turned right around and made plans to hire a stripper. Besides, he's probably taking someone else to the wedding."

She lifted a shoulder, shaking off her unwarranted melancholia. "I have no cause for complaint. Married or not, Garrett is doing what he told Hector. I gave him a reason to study and get good grades back in high school and now he's paying it forward."

"Hmm." Bethany smacked her lips. "That's way more boring. Well, prenup or not, you're still the luckiest bitch I know."

Emma nodded because it was true.

She had been doing her damnedest before Garrett but trying to work part-time with her condition meant not having the time or energy for anything else. Certainly not college classes.

Emma was barely working at all now.

Hector hadn't come right out and said he was cutting her hours, but she had been scheduled to work a mere two days this week. That was something that would have made her spiral and freak even with the free room and board. But now she was getting five thousand dollars a week she didn't earn.

She wasn't going to touch it, of course. But the money was sitting in her bank account right now. Emma had checked her balance on her phone before starting her shift. Even if she never spent it, she could do what Garrett suggested and invest it. Then she could spend the dividends it made guilt-free.

It didn't matter how she got this chance. Emma owed it to her family to make the most of it.

As for Garrett, he may be her husband, but it was a marriage of convenience. A paper marriage. It meant nothing to him. His convo about strippers made that clear.

The thought of going to the wedding this weekend and watching him dance with his date made her stomach hurt. But she would do it with a smile, because after all he was doing for her, Garrett deserved to live his life however he wanted, with whomever he wanted.

GARRETT EXAMINED the bow he'd just made in his tie and swore. He walked to the door of his bedroom and called out for Emma.

She emerged from her room in a new dress that skimmed her curves so perfectly he nearly swallowed his tongue.

Her dress was a deep emerald green made from some silky synthetic material that alternately gathered or flowed over all the right places. Her hair was loose, falling down her back in shiny waves. She was holding a brush in her hand.

"I don't suppose you know how to tie a bow tie?" he asked when he recovered.

Panic flared in her eyes for a second before she laughed. "Not unless it's a clip-on."

Yeah, he was an idiot. Even pre-accident Emma wouldn't have had bow-tying experience. She didn't have a dad or a granddad. And if he found out that one of her mom's boyfriends had asked her to fix their tie, Garrett would go after them with a baseball bat.

"There is a clip-on option," he confessed, "but I wasn't quite prepared to admit defeat just yet."

Her brow puckered adorably. "I thought you went to black tie events all the time."

"I do, but I make it a point not to wear a bow tie. I think they're outdated as hell. But it's different for a wedding. I don't want to ruin Georgia's pictures."

He began to back away. "No worries, I'll wear the clip-on."

"Thank God." Emma wiped her brow in faux relief. "But since you're here, I wanted to ask if it's okay if Kyle rides with us?"

He paused in the doorway. "Kyle?"

"Yeah." Emma ran her palms down her skirt. "Georgia said I could have a plus-one because I wouldn't know anyone at the wedding besides you."

Her voice grew hesitant when he didn't speak. "Is that okay?"

"Oh." He cleared his throat. "Uh, yeah."

It made perfect sense. Garrett was in the wedding party and would no doubt be occupied for a big chunk of the festivities, posing for pictures and giving the toast.

"Good, good." Emma swung her brush around, accidentally smacking it into the doorframe of her room. "But if you need to leave early because you're in the wedding party, don't worry about it. You and your date can take the car."

His what? Had she said *date*? No. He must have misheard.

Emma misinterpreted his confusion because she held up her phone. "Don't worry. We won't take the bus. I signed up for that luxury Uber like you asked."

He nodded absently, wondering if he should ask her to repeat herself.

"Is everything all right?" she asked when he stayed quiet too long.

"Yeah. Don't worry about the car service. I do have to be at the church early, but the car can come back for you and Kyle with plenty of time."

"Okay," she said and hesitated, waving her phone. "We can still get a ride after if you and your date want to go out afterward."

Christ. She *had* said date.

Garrett needed to nip this in the bud. "No need. I don't have a date."

"Shit," Emma muttered under her breath, her cheeks turning rosy. "Were we supposed to go together?"

"No," he lied. "I figured we'd carpool but given my best man duties, it makes more sense to have you hang back with Kyle. I don't think George is going to require that many photos, but she hired some big-name photographer so never say never."

Emma put her phone away, her relief obvious. "Okay, great. We'll have your car come back for us if it's not too much trouble."

He pasted a smile on his face. "No trouble at all. And it's a good idea to take another friend along since I'll be busy. I should have thought of it myself."

At least she had invited Kyle. He'd rather pluck out several nose hairs than willingly spend time with Bethany. And God forbid Emma try and bring a real date.

Wait, why hadn't she asked Pedro?

"Are you upset—" He trailed off, deciding it wasn't in his best interests to point out the rift he'd caused.

"Upset about what?" Emma asked in a lower voice.

He thought quickly. "That Georgia didn't ask you to be a bridesmaid."

Her features relaxed, making him wonder what she thought he was going to say.

"Oh, no. I completely understand. She'd already chosen her bridal party before we met. And Judy has been doing an awesome job as maid of honor. I'm just happy to be invited."

"Yeah, Judy is great."

And now that Georgia's top salesperson and business partner was dating someone, she'd finally stopped hitting on him. Which was utterly fantastic as far as he was concerned.

Not that there was anything wrong with Judy. But staring at Emma in that dress now, he realized why he'd never responded to the petite Filipina's flirtation.

Garrett had a type. It had been stamped into his psyche during his most formative years.

Through some quirk of fate, the woman who'd inspired it was standing in front of him now. Wearing a dress he wanted to rip off her with his teeth.

Swallowing heavily, he made a production of checking his watch. "I guess I should get going. I'll see you at the end of the ceremony. You and Kyle can ride with me to the reception."

"Sounds good." Emma beamed at him. "I'm so excited! This is going to be so much fun."

Garrett forced a smile that quickly became genuine at her enthusiasm. They had only been married for a few weeks.

"It's early days yet," he said aloud. "There's plenty of time."

She looked confused for a second. "Days? More like a couple of hours. And that becomes less true every minute. Now scoot. You can't keep George waiting."

She waved the brush in the direction of the door. Saluting, he went down to meet the car.

Chapter Thirty-One

GARRETT

What the hell is that kid doing?

Garrett forced himself to keep his seat as he watched Kyle flail, taking a wild swing that was probably supposed to be dancing.

The wedding reception was in full swing. The oceanfront grand ballroom of the Caislean San Diego was a three-hundred-person venue, but Rainer had wanted a more intimate celebration so he'd invited less than a third of that number.

The elegant room spanned the entire length of the floor, boasting views of both the ocean and the city. The Pacific-facing side had the traditional dining tables and dance floor, while the other end was set up as a chic conversational lounge serving cocktails and coffee against the jeweled backdrop woven from the city's lights.

He was parked on a couch in the lounge area, watching Emma try to corral Kyle on the dance floor.

She was having a hard time with it. The kid was all elbows on a good day. Add alcohol to the mix—and someone unwisely had—and it was shaping up to be a disaster out there.

He has to stop trying to do the Renegade. Or whatever the TikTok that was supposed to be.

Good Lord, the boy needed help. Dance lessons, followed by

weight training until he put on at least twenty pounds of muscle. It was like watching a scarecrow dance.

A hand clapped Garrett on the shoulder. "Did your wife bring a date to this wedding?"

He turned to shoot Ian a dirty look. His friend had recently returned from the complex protection detail he'd been coordinating for some obscure royal house.

Garrett had introduced Ian to his blushing bride at the church, just before the ceremony, which thanks to Georgia and Judy's extensive planning had been short and sweet.

Georgia had been flawless in a long white dress designed by one of Judy's friends. Rainer had been so proud and so damn full of joy Garrett couldn't help contrasting it to his farce of a first marriage.

And maybe my second.

"Kyle is her work bestie."

Ian laughed and twitched up his dress pants before sitting down next to him. "Bestie? Are we in high school?"

Garrett shrugged. "Emma wasn't the one to christen him that. I think that was Stella."

Ian took a healthy swallow of his glass. "And who is Stella? Don't tell me—the future Mrs. Chapman the third? Or is this like a sister-wives thing where they run concurrently?"

Gross. "You know you're old and slow when you're relegated to supervising Auric missions instead of participating in them. That's when a man gets sloppy."

Ian snickered, hitting his rock-hard abs hard enough for him to hear the slapping sound. "Sure, it is."

Signaling a waiter, he asked for a second Cognac, his drink of choice. When it arrived, he handed it to Garrett. "Looks like you need this more than me."

Sighing, he took the glass. "I'm fine. This just didn't go the way I thought it would."

Ian looked at him over the rim of his glass. "Because of your sister-wives situation?"

Garrett grimaced. "Stella is Emma's four-year-old sister."

"Oh, ick. Sorry." Ian shook his free hand out as if getting rid of some unseen muck. "Forget I said anything about your bizarre situation."

"Good." He took a large swig of the Cognac, focusing on the welcome burn it made going down.

"So does the kid live with you too?"

He smiled. "I knew you wouldn't be able to keep your opinions to yourself."

"'Cause it's weird."

Ian glanced across the dance floor at Emma and the wildly gyrating Kyle. "And out of character. I know you give to charity but you're not exactly what I would call a humanitarian. Not the kind that gets into it, face-to-face. So why the hell did you do it? Pre-existing conditions or not—you're a fucking billionaire. You could have just bought her a fucking health insurance plan. You didn't need to marry her."

Garrett leaned back in his chair, unable to look away from his wife.

She used to be a better dancer. Downright hypnotic in fact. Now she was winging it, but she still looked good on the dance floor because she had been blessed with natural rhythm. A little more practice, maybe some lessons, and she'd be back to form.

Yeah, he snorted to himself. She and Kyle could take lessons together. "You know it's more than that," he muttered.

"Well, obviously." Ian tilted his head, following his gaze. "One look at the little woman explains a lot. Most of it in fact. But not all. I have questions."

Well, he could answer one of them.

"Her sister Stella lives with her mother back in Colorado. The rest will have to wait for another time," he said when he saw Rainer signal him from across the room. "It's time for the bouquet and garter toss."

Ian somehow managed to gag while keeping a straight face. "Promise me you won't do these things at your wedding."

He turned to frown at his former business school roommate. "Did you forget I just got married?"

Ian rose, straightening his tie as he went. "Yeah, I meant the next time."

Garrett elbowed his former roommate in the gut before shoving him forward. "Just for that, I'm going to tell Rainer to aim that garter at you."

Ian turned a look of genuine horror on his face before straightening the sleeves of his tux. "Don't forget. I know Krav Maga."

It was Garrett's turn to smirk. "Thanks to you, I do too."

Chapter Thirty-Two

EMMA

Emma kept a smile plastered on her face as she tried and failed to drag Kyle from the dance floor. Thinking she was trying to take his hand, he pulled her close before spinning her out in a wild circle that sent her on a collision course with another couple.

"I'm so sorry," she cried, rubbing her stomach where the man's elbow had driven into her. She gave Kyle a hard yank. He stopped gyrating, belatedly noticing her doubled over.

"Oh, Em, what happened?" he asked, the picture of concern.

The man whose elbow had left a permanent impression in her gut blinked, his bushy eyebrows creeping sky-high.

Unable to suppress a wince, she pushed Kyle toward the exit.

"We need to find you some coffee," she said once they were clear of the ballroom. "It'll be a drip, but I'm sure the quality is excellent here."

Kyle stumbled and grabbed her arms.

"Em, I have to tell you a secret," he shouted before whipping his head all around as if to check and see who was watching.

He dropped his voice to a whisper. "I *hate* coffee."

Emma was shocked enough to stop walking. "*What?*"

She knew this was just the alcohol talking. It had to be. "We work at a coffee shop!"

And the coffee was good! Some of the best she'd ever tasted.

"I know, I know. But it tastes like dirt to me." Kyle waved too wide, managing to make himself off-balance. He ended up on his ass, looking up at her and blinking like an owl.

Judy, Georgia's maid of honor, materialized on her left, hip checking her. "I think someone needs coffee," she said.

Kyle groaned, turning noticeably paler. "*No.* God, no."

Emma turned to Judy, her features contorted in disbelief. "He hates coffee."

Judy laughed at the expression on her face. "You look like he just kicked your puppy or something."

"Because it's *coffee.* The nectar of the gods. The smell alone is…" Emma trailed off, deciding it was too dramatic to say the scent had roused her from a coma. Even if she believed it.

"Stop!" Kyle held up a hand pleadingly. His face had taken on a waxy look, and he was sweating. "Please stop."

Judy gave her a sympathetic glance. "Thank you for getting him off the dance floor. Do you think you can keep him off it while I go get him a Coke?"

"Yes. And thank you," she told her, feeling chastised as the maid of honor slipped away. And rightly so.

Emma shook her head at the prone teenager. "How the hell did you get so drunk?"

The wedding had two open bars at opposite ends of the room. But it had never occurred to her that the bartenders would serve him. Kyle was almost twenty but looked sixteen.

She had been wrong. Judging from his current state—and his breath—those soft drinks he'd been drinking all night had contained mostly alcohol.

Resigned to babysitting a sloppy mess, she managed to haul Kyle up, ushering him to a plush chair in a small lounge adjoining the ballroom.

Judy came and handed her a glass of soda, immediately getting called away to put out another fire.

"Drink this," Emma told Kyle, pressing the glass into his hand.

He sipped it gingerly. "Needs rum," he muttered, slurring a little now.

"*No.* It doesn't." Emma covered her face with her hand.

A tingling at the back of her neck made her spin around.

Garrett was coming down the hallway, a distinctly annoyed look on his face. He wiped it clean when he saw her watching.

He stopped next to her, staring down at her plus-one. "He needs to throw up."

Emma frowned. "But I've been trying to keep him from vomiting."

"That's the wrong move. Trust me, as a former teenage boy, I know whereof I speak. He needs to get it all up. Then he should have some of this."

Before she could stop him, he thrust the cup of coffee she hadn't noticed in his hand in Kyle's face.

"Oh no."

Emma jumped back as Kyle smelled the coffee. He jerked forward, proceeding to spew all over Garrett's very shiny shoes.

Garrett closed his eyes, muttering something under his breath. He looked down at his ruined bespoke Oxfords and spattered dress pants with an icy calm.

"Well." Emma wanted to fall through the floor, but she touched him on the arm. "I think he got it all up."

Chapter Thirty-Three

EMMA

Disasters were different when they happened to rich people. For the normal unwashed masses getting puked on at a wedding usually meant a very smelly and stomach-churning ride home.

But for people like Garrett, it meant getting escorted to a nearby suite while the concierge ran out to his place to pick up one of his other suits and a pair of shoes.

As for the hallway carpet, the hotel's cleaning crew took care of the mess with a speed that must have set some kind of record. Another member of the wedding party volunteered to hose Kyle down, providing him with a pair of sweats and a T-shirt branded with the hotel's name.

By the time they got into the limousine, both men were squeaky clean.

Garrett didn't say a word the entire ride to Kyle's mother's house. It would have been a painful, awkward silence were it not for the fact that Kyle was still drunk. He sang several off-key and garbled renditions of Taylor Swift songs the entire way.

When they got to the house, Garrett told her to stay put while he escorted Kyle up the walk of the modest one-story home.

They were almost there when Kyle grabbed Garrett's shoulders and appeared to be speaking very earnestly.

That didn't last long.

Kyle bent over and threw up again, making enough of a racket to rouse his mother.

Emma sank deeper into the upholstery when a middle-aged woman appeared at the threshold. She began to shout at Garrett, gesturing at her inebriated son, raging visibly.

"*Oh nooo!*" Emma squeaked, covering her face.

But she peeked out from between her fingers, unable to stop watching the train wreck in progress.

At least Garrett wasn't losing his temper in return. She wouldn't blame him at this point. But he kept his cool despite being harangued by a woman wearing adult onesie pajamas.

Kyle staggered up the steps to interrupt his mother's tirade. Whatever he said calmed his mother down. Garrett said a few words that seemed to mollify her further. Then they went inside.

"I'm sorry," she burst out when he climbed into the car.

His face could have been carved from stone. "For what?" he asked in a silky voice.

Emma bit her lip. "She shouldn't have spoken to you like that. It was my fault. She should be mad at me. You both should. I'm the one who let Kyle get drunk."

"You think I'm upset because you let Kyle drink?" he asked, face still infuriatingly impassive. "Well, I'm not. You weren't the one behind the bar serving Kyle booze all night so let's forget it."

"I can't."

Garrett getting yelled at for something that wasn't his fault may have been the worst thing that happened tonight. "I should have gotten out of the car and explained the situation to Kyle's mom. She already hates me anyway."

This got his attention. Garrett turned away from the window. "Why? What's her problem with you?"

"I'm not sure." Emma had never been able to explain it. "She picks Kyle up sometimes and…"

"She took an instant dislike to you?"

Emma didn't pout but it was pretty damn close. "Yeah. I'm not sure why."

Because Bethany had been there too, being her extra-charming self. Yet it had been Emma Mrs. Channing had given the side-eye to.

"It's not your fault," Garrett assured her. "You're…"

She waited but he didn't seem inclined to continue. "I'm what?"

Garrett yanked up his pant leg and crossed it in that weird male power-pose way. "You're too sexy," he said matter-of-factly.

"*What?*" Emma's voice rose so high it squeaked.

Coughing to clear it, she tried again. "That's crazy."

Garrett laughed, raising a sardonic brow. "How many times has a woman taken an instant dislike to you?"

Emma opened her mouth to argue. She closed it slowly after counting in her head.

"It's not your fault," Garrett said, his tone kind. "Some women are like that. They see your face and figure and it triggers something. If they're younger, it's jealousy. If they're older, like Kyle's mom, it's judgment. As if you could help what your body looks like."

Emma scowled, glancing down at her breasts. She felt an urge to cover herself, but she hadn't brought a wrap.

Across from her, Garrett sat up, putting his foot down and leaning forward. "I didn't mean to make you self-conscious. But you seemed genuinely confused."

Yeah, she was confused. He was telling her fellow women were threatened by her because she was too *sexy*. A code word for slutty.

Except Garrett had never tried anything. Not while he was conscious anyway. He must not find her sexy. Or he found her too slutty. She didn't want to know which.

"Well, thanks for explaining things so clearly."

His mouth opened. She sensed a lecture coming but he closed it. They rode in silence the rest of the way.

Inside the penthouse, Garrett ripped off his coat and tossed it on the back of the couch as he passed it on the way to his bedroom.

"Good night," he said.

Emma bit her lip, hurt by the clipped tone.

Damn it. She chased after him, grabbing his arm. She stepped back when he turned to face her. "I'm sorry for ruining the wedding for you."

Garrett's jaw flexed. "You didn't ruin it. The wedding was beautiful. Everyone laughed at my speech. It was great."

"The end wasn't." She raised her hands placatingly. "And that *was* my fault. I should have kept Kyle in check."

He sighed. "That wasn't your fault. He's a grown man. You aren't responsible for him."

Grown man was a stretch. "If you're not mad about Kyle, why are you so upset?"

"I'm not upset!" he shouted.

Emma froze, tears stinging the back of her eyes. "Of course, you're not. Silly me."

Garrett groaned, a whole world of frustration in the sound. "All right. I guess I am a little…"

"Upset."

He thrust a hand through his hair. "Disappointed."

Oh, that's way worse. Emma would have preferred anger. "I said I was sorry about Kyle."

"No, it's not about the kid."

She stared at him, waiting.

He lifted a shoulder. "Look, it was my best friend's wedding. I was celebrating with the men I call family. We had amazing food and even better booze. Everyone who mattered to me was there and I…"

Emma held her breath, waiting for the next body blow.

He tilted his head to the side, giving her a thorough once-over. "I just wanted to dance with my wife."

Chapter Thirty-Four

GARRETT

He didn't wait around to see Emma's reaction to his too-honest reply. He went to his bedroom before she could say anything else, closing the door behind him.

And just what the hell were you thinking telling the truth? It was the last thing he should have done.

Yeah, Garrett wasn't a patient man. But he'd known going into this that Emma required very special handling—and a hell of a lot more patience than he'd just displayed.

He had forgotten himself after a frustrating and slightly disgusting night.

Garrett was playing a long game. But Emma had caught him in a moment of weakness, keeping at him with her trademark stubbornness until he snapped.

And now he may have ruined everything, letting on just how much she affected him.

Emma was understandably skittish. And not just about him. About everything. And he didn't blame her. Imagine having to rebuild your whole life. He couldn't think of a single person who would trade places with her, not even him.

Except he would have. If he could somehow save her the pain and anguish of not knowing who she was, then yeah. He would rather it had been him hit by that car.

Still riled up, he stripped off the rest of his clothes. He'd managed to stay clean the second time Kyle threw up, but that didn't matter. Just thinking about it made another shower necessary.

He took care of that in short order and was roughly toweling off when there was a tentative knock at the door.

Closing his eyes, he counted to ten. But the knock came again.

He should have known Emma wasn't going to let that dance comment go.

"Just a sec," he called out, pulling out a pair of sweatpants.

"Can you meet me in the living room?" she replied loud enough to be heard through his thick door.

Shit. This night was never going to end, was it?

"Sure," he yelled back, grateful the entire penthouse was sound-proof. He'd hate to think of Rainer and George hearing whatever was happening on this side of the floor.

Garrett slipped on the sweatpants, not bothering with a shirt. He'd just get it wet. Grabbing a fresh hand towel, he went out to the living room, trying to rub his hair dry so he wouldn't have to bust out a blow dryer.

He didn't notice the candlelight right away.

Emma was standing in the middle of the living room. Her hair was also wet, and she wasn't wearing her little black dress anymore. She was wearing a nightgown, standing before him in bare feet.

As nightgowns went, it was a simple affair. A sleeveless shallow V-neck that came to her knees. But even simple cuts like this transformed on Emma's body.

Yeah, every woman in the world should hate her.

Garrett ignored his itchy palms, clearing his throat. "What's going on?" he asked, gesturing to the romantic lighting.

"I wanted to make tonight up to you."

He raised his hand, about to tell her she didn't have to do anything, but she'd already turned away. She ran to the back of the couch, picking up her phone and fiddling with it.

A distinctive jazzy saxophone began to play through his Bluetooth speakers.

He burst out laughing.

Emma stopped the song, frowning. "What? What is it?"

"You chose Kenny G for our first dance." And he *loved* it.

Hurt flashed across her expression.

Garrett rushed to her side. "Hey, I didn't mean it in a bad way. I love that you chose Kenny G."

She rolled her shoulders to dislodge his hands. "I'm sorry, I don't know music. Not the slow stuff."

"It's an inspired choice," he assured her, taking her phone and setting it aside on the nearest table. "You went for one of the classics."

Emma shrugged. "People are more lenient when you don't know music as long as you know some of the big names."

Well, Kenny G was that in certain circles. It also explained her love of Dolly Parton, the Stones, and Cream, whose music he'd heard coming from her room on and off since she'd moved in.

He really should send her back to her room. But Garrett lacked the willpower to turn her away. Instead, he held open his arms in a classic waltz pose. "Shall we dance?"

Emma hesitated for an endless moment. But she took that first step and then another.

Finally, she was in his arms, soft curves pressing against his chest and abs.

Garrett closed his eyes, letting himself feel every luscious inch before canting his hips so his rapidly thickening cock wouldn't touch her.

He wasn't going to make it weird. But no force on God's green earth would make him let Emma go right now.

"I shouldn't have changed," she whispered, her breath fanning his collarbone as she looked up at him.

God, he'd forgotten how much shorter she was than him.

"You're allowed to shower," he managed, swaying them from side to side.

"But was the dress part of the…"

Part of the fantasy? Yes, it had been. Until he'd seen her in her nightgown. Now he had a new fantasy.

Emma's skin felt very hot against him. "Because I'm realizing now, I probably shouldn't have taken off my bra."

Garrett groaned. She was killing him. He was close to passing out because all the blood in his body was rushing south so hard and fast.

The saxophone crescendo broke, making him smile despite the discomfort in his pants.

And then Emma melted against him, cuddling his cock against her soft belly.

"*Emmy*," he groaned.

"Garrett?" she asked, her voice tremulous as he spun her in a slow circle.

"Yeah?" His voice was hoarse, a telltale sign but one he didn't worry about. The stiffness of his cock was a dead giveaway and Emma was pressing against it willingly.

She shuddered, her breath faster as she tilted her chin up, a glazed look in her eyes. "Why?" she breathed.

Unwilling to break the spell, he ran his hands down her back, letting them come to rest on the curve of her ass. "Why what?"

"Why did you really marry me?"

Chapter Thirty-Five

EMMA

Emma held her breath as she waited for Garrett's answer. When he didn't speak, she risked looking up.

It was a mistake. Garrett's gaze snared hers, holding her entire being immobile. "Because I wanted to."

Her lips parted, her instinct to argue with him. But he reached down, running his big hands down the curve of her butt and thighs. He took hold of her just behind the crease of her knee.

His gentle but uncompromising grip opened her legs. He dragged her up his body, not stopping until they were wrapped around his waist.

Emma gasped at the heat and hardness touching her so intimately.

He walked forward with her in his arms, carrying her effortlessly down into the sunken living room.

Her ass landed on the back of the couch. Garrett propped her up there, his hands cupping her cheeks and kneading with firm strokes.

She parted her lips in silent invitation.

His hand took hold of her long hair, wrapping it around his fist. Then Garrett's taste exploded in her mouth.

Emma made a noise both feminine and desperate. Her vision blurred so she closed her eyes, focusing on the feel of his heat and the roughness of his roaming hands.

Garrett tore his mouth off hers, pressing a line of kisses to the side of her neck and up her cheek to her ear. "It's okay, baby. I've got you."

He pressed her into the couch, grinding his hard length between her legs. It was like he ignited a fire. The heat of it radiated from her pussy out to the rest of her body.

Emma's mouth gaped as she clutched at his shoulders with shaking hands. "*O-oh.*"

That dark gravelly voice came again, wrapping like rough velvet all around her.

"Feels good?" he asked, rubbing more of himself against her until he was abrading her sensitive nipples with his pecs through the silky material of her nightgown.

"Yes," she moaned as he rolled his hips, hitting a sensitive spot just right.

Whimpering, her fingers went slack. She would have fallen backward but his strong arms wouldn't let her. Instead, they guided her over the back of the couch in one smooth, controlled move.

Desire made her nipples harden and the walls of her sheath clench. And he knew. Garrett was aware of his effect on her, his every touch calculated to make her melt.

"Don't worry, Emmy," he murmured, lowering over her in a wave of heat and muscle.

"I know what you need," he said, holding her hands down by the wrist and rubbing his cock against her panties, which were so wet at this point they may as well not have been there.

Soon that didn't matter. Garrett backed off moving down her body, taking her cotton briefs with him.

She expected her nightgown to follow, that he would pull it up and off her. Instead, he pushed it down, baring her breasts while trapping her arms at her sides.

"Fuck, you're perfect."

His fingers caressed her right mound, tweaking her nipple until it throbbed.

Garrett's eyes glowed like coals in the candlelight, reflecting the dim light in such a way that it appeared as if they were lit from within.

But it wasn't just hunger in his eyes. There was something else. Something almost reverent.

One of his fingers grazed the dip of her cleavage.

"Absolutely perfect," he breathed before that big hand fully settled on her breast, squeezing gently.

The sensation of his rough hand on her bare breast was too much to process. She trembled, heart aching when her shiver seemed to pass through him as well. And then his hands were gone, replaced by his mouth.

Emma moaned, her legs drawing up convulsively. They tightened around his waist, a move she thought he didn't even register until he pinned her down with his weight.

She loved it. The heat, his rough silky skin, and the pressure of all that muscle bearing down on her. It filled an ache she hadn't known she'd been feeling.

Garrett was licking and sucking her breast, whispering words of praise about the softness of her skin and how perfectly her curves filled his hands.

But it was the press of his cock against her wet folds that was causing those urgent little sounds to escape.

He was still half-dressed. Emma pushed at the waistband on his pants, only to have him remove her hands.

"I won't last, baby," he said, pinning them to the couch. "Let me do this first, or I won't get the chance later."

Emma raised her head to protest. She didn't want to wait. She needed him now. Every cell in her body was demanding it. But he kept holding her hands, working his way down until his face was buried between her legs.

Emma's brain immediately skidded, going off the rails.

"Oh, oh, that's not right," she said with a gasp, her hips jerking as Garrett sucked and nibbled at the petals of her sex.

He stopped, muffled laughter floating up from between her legs.

"Is this better?" he asked, his fingers caressing and opening her more fully. His tongue lapped up her slit, teeth grazing at her clit.

Pleasure punched through her with the force of a bomb. Hips

pumping involuntarily, she writhed under his ministrations, the onslaught long, wet, and wild.

Emma was out of control and would have fallen off the couch had Garrett's arms not pinned her to the cushions. Her muscles tightened all at once and then released with wave after wave of pulsing pleasure.

The throbbing beats of her orgasm were dying when Garrett crawled up her body. Taking himself in hand, he rubbed the head of his cock through her slick folds.

"Do you really want this?" he asked, his breath hot against her ear.

Emma wrapped her legs around his hips. Her fingers dug into his back, pressing him closer. "Please, Garrett."

His hands tightened on her. "Good, that's good, Emmy. Keep saying my name."

Thick heat forged inside her, pushing past the ring of muscle at her entrance. Emma braced herself against the blunt pressure, every nerve in her body sparking, eager to be claimed. But her body wasn't cooperating.

Garrett swore, the tip of his cock buried a few inches. "Fuck, you're so tight, baby. Am I hurting you?"

Was this pressure pain or pleasure? Emma didn't know. Her body was confused but the ache was still there. "Yes, make it go away."

That was probably confusing him, but the way she wrapped her legs around him, forcing him deeper wasn't.

It broke what little restraint he had left. Murmuring something incoherent, he pressed his face into her neck before surging up, driving his hips until they were flush against her pussy.

Her body arched up as if she'd been shocked with a strong electric current. Panting, she clutched at his back, trying to get used to the foreign invasion in her body. This was nothing like she'd imagined.

Emma's sexual experiences since the accident had involved a dark room and her phone playing a specially curated list of videos. She hadn't had the energy or the opportunity to pursue much else. She didn't even own a real vibrator. Just one of those tiny lipstick-sized buzzers.

And this… Garrett was huge inside her. She had no frame of reference for him, no way to prepare.

Emma thought she was at her limit of sensation. Then he started moving. Slow at first, Garrett continued to whisper praise in her ear, increasing the tempo until he was rocking into her steadily.

She caught his rhythm, letting instinct guide her.

"That's it, baby," he whispered, his voice thick and hoarse. "That's it. You're right here with me, aren't you?"

Emma clutched at his shoulders. "*Yes.*"

"Yes, what?" He pinched her nipple. Not hard, but enough to sting.

"Yes, Garrett."

"That's right, Emmy. Keep saying my name." He punctuated his words with a firm thrust. "You're never going to forget it again, are you?"

With that, he thrust again. And again, twisting his hips.

Holy shit, that was… wow.

"I won't. God, *Garrett,*" she gasped, her breasts beginning to shake as he rode her faster and faster.

"Do you feel that?" he panted. "Do you feel how hard I am? It's because of you. Because of the way my wife's sweet pussy wraps around me, squeezing tight, trying to keep me inside her."

Holy shit, he played the W-card. Emma moaned, licking at the only part of him she could reach, his neck.

"*Fuck.* You want to taste me, baby? You're going to get your chance. But first, you're going to come while screaming my name."

Emma's mouth gaped, her lips open against his skin. She wanted to lick him again, but she was already at the edge of another orgasm. The only thing she could do was hold on as he surged, pounding her hips into the cushions.

Emma's hands flung back over her head like she was on a roller coaster. Her body was moving without volition, arcing up whenever he retreated. His body was like a magnet. She had to touch him, skin pressed to skin, or she was going to die.

"Garrett, *I can't, I can't,*" she panted nonsensically, unsure of what she was saying. Her orgasm was right there, but she couldn't reach it.

"Don't worry, baby. I've got you."

Catching her flailing hands, Garrett held them down as he let his weight press her down into the cushions. Impaled by his thick length, she shuddered as he ground against her. "Take… what you need."

So Emma did. Obeying, she clenched around him as she came and came and came.

"That's it, Emmy," he panted, his hips hitting a spot that made her black out. "Milk me dry. Come all over that cock like a hot little wife should."

He slammed her down onto the cushions one more time, exploding with one last convulsive thrust. Warmth flooded her as his seed spurted inside her.

Garrett collapsed on top of her, shaking and out of breath. Emma wrapped her arms and legs around him again, ignoring the sudden ache in her chest.

But her heart was beating so hard it filled her ears. Emma twisted her face, pressing a kiss to the side of Garrett's neck.

Calm down, she told herself, willing her heart to slow.

It was just the exertion and residual arousal. She wasn't terrified. Not at all.

Chapter Thirty-Six

EMMA

She woke up pinned to the mattress. Drowsy, she wondered what the hell had fallen on her when Garrett's voice rumbled in her ear.

"I'm not a coatrack."

Startled, she froze. His arm tightened around her.

"You said 'When did I get a coatrack'?" He shifted in the bed but still didn't let her go. "I can only assume you thought one fell on you."

Emma wiggled, turning on the mattress very slowly.

Her sharply indrawn breath at the sight of a naked Garrett stretched out next to her was involuntary.

His muscle definition was unreal. And did that tan go *everywhere*?

"Hi," she said.

He gave her a sleepy grin. "Hi. And before you freak out, yes, we had sex."

"I know. I was there." Emma smacked him on the arm. "Did you think I forgot? Because of my head?"

"No, baby, it's not that." Strong arms squeezed her. "I just wanted to be clear. I wanted you. You wanted me. We wanted each other. And we had sex."

He closed his eyes. *"Finally."*

Emma laughed, some unnamed tension in her melting away. "So, this was inevitable?"

She expected a glib, jokey answer but Garrett turned, staring into her eyes with intimidating resoluteness.

"Yes," he said quietly. "Yes, it was. We were always going to end up here."

The expression on his face was starting to unnerve her.

"In your bed?" she asked tremulously.

"In a relationship."

"In a—" Emma sat up.

He followed suit, the sheet pooling at his waist. The move inadvertently revealed her breasts. Squealing, she snatched the sheet up.

Garrett reached out, tugging the cloth down a touch. He traced the line of her décolletage with an unfocused look that made her temperature creep up by several degrees.

"We are in a relationship, one that just took the next step into intimacy. And you never have to hide your body from me. I love it. Every inch of it."

Possessive hands ran down her body, moving the sheet to cup her butt without any barriers.

Emma could feel her tension melting away. Her body was responding, the way it always did around him.

"You know you're doing this whole playboy bachelor thing wrong," she informed him. "You're supposed to be breezy, cracking jokes so I won't take what happened last night seriously."

Except he kept calling you his wife. Garrett had also called himself her husband more than once, claiming it like it was some sort of royal title.

He never behaved the way she expected.

"No. That's not what we're going to do," he said, watching her intently to gauge her reaction. "I don't want to backtrack. Because I'm happy about last night. And I hope you are too."

Emma flushed, both confused and pleased. "I… I think I am."

The smile that spread across his face was enough to knock the air from her lungs. Damn it, he was so beautiful.

"Good. That's good."

She cast about for what to say or do next but couldn't think of anything. "So… what do we do now?"

Garrett's face lit up, the heat in his eyes going from zero to a hundred degrees in the blink of a eye. He was reaching for her when his stomach growled. Very, *very* loudly.

The hunger transformed into humor. He laughed. "Okay, we're going to revisit that after breakfast."

With a wry twist of his lips, he sat up, hopping out of bed completely heedless of his nudity.

"*Oh*! Shit," she muttered.

Garrett froze, noting her discomfort.

"Hey, sorry." He grabbed a pillow, covering his privates. "I shouldn't have assumed parading around naked was okay. I can put some clothes on."

"No, that's not it." Grimacing, she pointed at his cock. "Look."

Garrett glanced down and did a double take.

"Shit," he said, dropping the pillow to examine the rust-colored smears on his cock.

And then his confusion turned to concern. "Fuck. Em, I'm so sorry."

Emma held up a hand. "No, I'm okay."

"Are you sure?"

She waved his concern away. "Yeah, I'm fine."

Garrett kicked the pillow aside, coming to the bedside to crouch next to her. "Let me see, baby." He pulled the sheet away from her waist.

Okay, what should she freak out about? The fact she was exposing her entire naked body to a billionaire in broad daylight, or that there was dried blood smeared on her thighs?

"Should I call a doctor?"

Emma clapped a hand over her mouth. "No!" she squealed. "This is nothing. I'm fine."

Garrett's brow creased, unwilling to let it go. "Are you sure? I couldn't live with myself if I hurt you last night."

He straightened. "Unless you're on your period?"

She hated to crush the hopeful note in his voice. But there was another, far more embarrassing explanation.

Standing, she pulled the sheets in front of her, stain and all.

"Well, I guess that answers that question," she muttered, blushing from head to toe before returning to the stains. "A little bleach and they'll be good as new."

"Em, I don't give a shit about the sheets." Garrett's hands flexed. "What can I do? Should I run a bath?"

Flushing from head to toe, she clutched the sheet to her. "I was a virgin."

Garrett's face transformed, sobering. "No, baby. You weren't."

She was about to contradict him, but the inexplicable sadness in his expression stopped her.

"Oh."

Emma stared at him, a little black hole opening in her stomach and sucking in everything she had believed about herself into it.

Again, someone knew more about her than she did. Although she wasn't sure how. Had he seen her with Edward?

"I guess my mom was right."

"About what?" Garrett asked, looking lost.

She closed her eyes, wishing she was dressed for this.

"She hated my college boyfriend. He didn't come to see me after my accident. He said we'd broken up months before and he didn't feel right coming because we had never been very close anyway. But we must have been serious at some point."

In light of today's revelation, Edward's actions were cold as hell, but she guessed she couldn't blame him for not coming. Not that she would have wanted to see him. She'd had bigger things to worry about back then. Like learning to walk again.

Garrett scrubbed his face with his hands. "No, sweetie. It wasn't him. It wasn't Edward."

Emma straightened. "You know my ex-boyfriend's name."

He tilted his head a fraction to the left. "I hated his guts. But I never met him."

"Then how do you know—"

"I *know*." Garrett put his hands on her shoulders, urging her to sit on the bed. Oh shit, this was bad. This was his *I have messed up shit* to tell you face.

"You didn't lose your virginity to Edward."

Emma blinked, sucking in a bracing breath. "I see. Then who was it?"

Had it been the boy her mother had referred to as the mouth breather in the yearbook? Or was it sensitive ponytail guy from her English class, the one who brought her flowers at the hospital and had bolted when the nurse came to change her colostomy bag?

Garrett's lips parted but he didn't answer.

She frowned as a new thought occurred to her. "Do you not know because there was more than one guy?"

Maybe she had more in common with her mother than she'd been led to believe.

That's okay. She would own her sex life as proudly as any other modern woman. The only difference was that she didn't remember it.

Whatever the case, she could deal with it. "You can tell me."

"No, Emmy. You don't understand…" He trailed off, closing his eyes as if he was in pain.

Emma registered the guilt on his face with a sinking feeling in the pit of her stomach. But she tried to play it off.

"No," she said, laughing. "We didn't sleep together. We were enemies."

Garrett held up his hands. They flexed as if they wanted to grab her. But he was careful to keep some buffer distance between them.

"We *were* enemies. And then we weren't."

Garrett put his hand on her knee. "Emmy, you lost your virginity to *me*."

Chapter Thirty-Seven

GARRETT

Emma's face bleached of color as his words sank in.

She shook her head. "I wouldn't have with you. The way you reacted in the garage—you *hated* me."

This was such a fucking tangled knot; he didn't know where to begin untying it. "Never. I *never* hated you."

She gave herself a little shake, rubbing her hand over her eyes. "But you said—"

"I didn't."

That had been Fletcher shouting the party line. Because Garrett hadn't told him the truth. He hadn't told anyone.

He knew why now, of course. Hindsight was twenty-twenty. Even if he'd been sure of his feelings, he hadn't been sure of hers.

That insecurity of being a child unloved by his only parent hadn't warped him, thanks to the support he got from his aunt Phil, but it had left its mark in other ways. Ways he hadn't even been aware of when he and Emma had first gotten involved.

Not even Rainer knew the complete story.

"Just let me explain. I can tell you everything. About *us*. About the accident."

Shock slackened Emma's already pale features. "The *accident*?"

Fuck, this was killing him. "Yes."

Garrett felt like he was choking, the lump in his throat was that big. "I think I know what happened that night."

Emma shuddered, looking at him like he was a stranger. Or worse. A monster.

"Was it you?" she whispered, her face ashen. "Did you hit me with your car?"

"What? No!"

How could she think that? Garrett stood up, wishing he was dressed for this horrendous moment.

"I'm fucking this all up, I know that!" he bit out, pacing. "I've been practicing in my head and it's still coming out all messed up. But you have to know I would *never* hurt you."

He rushed to crouch in front of her. "I'd sooner cut my own arm off. You need to believe that."

Emma's wide eyes searched his face. She pushed his hands away. "I—*I don't know.* You've been lying. Oh my God, you made me marry you! But it wasn't about the insurance, was it? You felt guilty because of the accident."

"*Emmy.*" He stumbled back. She may as well have stabbed him in the heart. That would have hurt less.

"No, Em. I wasn't there! I wish to God I had been, but I wasn't."

She sucked in a shaky breath, wrapping her hands around her waist. His words seemed to penetrate.

"Okay," she breathed. "But if it wasn't the accident, then why did you marry me? What are you making up for?"

His brain stuttered. "I… It's because I love you. I always have."

Emma's head drew back. The longer she stared, the less confused she looked.

"No, that can't be right." Her fingers shook as she snatched up his discarded shirt, pulling it on with jerky movements. "You're still lying!"

She ran out of the room.

"No, Emma, wait!"

He didn't know how she'd moved so fast. Emma was at the front closet, shoving her feet into sneakers and grabbing the first coat that came to hand, his trench coat.

She swung the door open, revealing a startled Rainer and Georgia.

"Hey, guys!" Georgia called out, but the words died as she saw the state Emma was in.

Emma pushed past the newlyweds, getting into the elevator the couple must have just exited. The doors closed before he could stop her.

"*Fuck.*" He started to run but Rainer almost clotheslined him.

"Garrett, man, you can't go out like that."

"No, I have to stop her," he choked out.

"You're *naked.*"

Rainer forcibly turned him back, herding him back into his apartment as Georgia averted her gaze. "You go out like that, and you'll be arrested."

Garrett looked down, surprised to see his cock out.

"Fuck." He slapped a hand over his face. "I forgot."

Georgia put one hand up to cover her eyes and used the other one to point at him. "You go back to your room and get dressed. I will find Emma."

"You have to bring her back here," he called, ducking behind Rainer for a little cover. "I need to talk to her. She may not want to hear what I have to say but she has to this time."

Georgia turned to the elevator. "I will, if that's what Emma wants."

"You don't understand what happened," he yelled after her. "And neither does she."

She threw up a hand, not bothering to turn around.

"Oh, I think *everyone* has a pretty good idea what happened," she called behind her as she stomped into the waiting elevator.

Chapter Thirty-Eight

EMMA

Tightening the coat more securely around herself, Emma avoided eye contact with the other pedestrians on the crowded downtown sidewalk.

She knew what she looked like—a cross between a crazy homeless woman and one on a particularly rough walk of shame. The mirrorlike reflection of the office suite around the corner had shown her as much.

But Emma didn't bother to smooth her hair. She just kept walking blind, no direction or destination in mind as a torrent of thoughts filled her brain, each one more disjointed than the last.

Emma ended up going in circles, having walked around the block only to end up in front of Garrett's building again.

Someone grabbed her arm. "*Emma.*"

She blinked as Georgia's wiry strong arms pulled her into a hug. "Oh, Em, I'm sorry."

"I'm okay," she mumbled, not sure if she meant it.

Georgia shook her head, her face hard. "If he hurt you, I swear to God I'll take a socket wrench to his privates—I don't care if he is Rainer's best friend."

"He didn't hurt me." Not the way George thought he had.

"Last night was wonderful," she added in a mumble.

And it had been. Her one and only sexual experience was worthy of a romance novel. Except it wasn't the only one, it seemed. This morning had taken a sharp turn into the horror suspense genre.

George's head drew back. "Oh! I thought—well, never mind."

"It's what he said this morning that turned everything to shit," Emma began as Georgia's phone began to ring.

"Hold that thought." Wincing, the other woman picked it up.

"Not a good time," she hissed into the receiver.

Emma could hear Rainer's voice coming out from the other end.

"Yes, I found her," she told him. "*No*. Keep him there."

She said a few more words before hanging up, taking Emma firmly by the hand. "Come on."

Two minutes later they were in the underground parking structure, heading to a fenced-off area hidden behind a privacy screen attached to the metal links.

"What is this place?" she asked as Georgia opened the padlock securing the area.

"My first workspace."

She pushed the door open, revealing a couch and several racks of tools. "Rainer set it up for me while the warehouse that stored his car collection was renovated into a proper space for my car restoration business."

She led Emma to the couch and sat. "I'd offer you a drink, but we moved the mini fridge over to the showroom."

"It's okay. I'm fine."

A small hand covered hers. "Sweetie, you're really not."

Emma's eyes filled with tears. Her face crumpled. "Yeah, I know."

George's concern and sympathy just made the tears come faster. But Emma couldn't stop herself. She buried her face in her hands and cried stormily for a few minutes.

Then the worst seemed to pass, and she was able to breathe. Dashing her tears away using one of the coat cuffs, she hiccupped.

George pressed a crumpled towel into her hand. It had a little grease on it, but beggars couldn't be choosers.

"Do you want to take it back?" she asked carefully. "About last night? If what you did with Garrett wasn't consensual, I will support you in whatever way you wish. Just because he married you doesn't mean he automatically gets sex. You know that, right?"

Emma hadn't known Georgia long, but she was already her best, most amazing friend. "I think I seduced him actually."

He'd been so sad that he hadn't gotten the chance to dance with her at the wedding. Maybe she hadn't consciously planned it, but at no point during the evening had she felt like stopping.

Garrett was right. A sexual relationship had been inevitable.

Emma shook her head, looking down at her hand. "This is because of my stupid broken brain. You see, I thought I was a virgin. According to everything I'd been able to piece together of my life before my accident, I was. This morning, I thought I had physical confirmation... a little blood on the sheets."

"Oh." Georgia's expression lightened in understanding. "*Ooooh.*"

"Yeah." Emma sighed. "It wasn't a lot, but I thought it confirmed what I knew. Till Garrett informed me otherwise."

Georgia drew a line in the air. "And he knew this because the two of you..." She trailed off, scribbling in the air as if connecting the dots.

"He said *he* was my first," Emma whispered, a faint ringing beginning in her ears. "I lost my virginity to him. Before the accident."

Georgia didn't make a sound. When Emma turned to check her reaction, the young mechanic was staring, open-mouthed.

"I thought you were enemies."

She threw up her hands. "That's what I said! But it seems we weren't at each other's throats the whole time."

Georgia bit her lip, processing the new information faster than she had. "Was there a truce and it didn't last?"

That was a good question. "I have no idea. I don't know the circumstances."

Georgia sat on the couch arm, facing her with her hands propped on her thighs. "He didn't explain? Were you a couple?"

Emma was starting to feel bad for another reason. "I didn't let him tell me. Once he started talking about the night of my accident, I freaked out."

Or rather freaked out further, because she had already been right on the edge of losing it.

How pathetic did she look right now? "I couldn't process anything after that."

"Whoa, *wait*, hold the phone." George hopped down onto the couch cushions. "I thought he didn't know what happened!"

She shrugged helplessly. "I don't know what he knows. Like I said, I didn't let him explain."

Emma chewed on her lip, trying to break through that wall to her past. One memory—a flash that could explain what Garrett was. What he had done…

Georgia grabbed her hands and squeezed them, anxiety in every line of her face. "Did he run you down?"

Emma fell back on the couch cushions. The ceiling was turning above her ever so slightly. "I don't…"

I wasn't there. I wish to God I had been, but I wasn't.

The knot in her chest eased, letting her breathe. "No."

George squinted at her. "Are you sure?"

She pushed herself upright, but her body was weak. This time with relief. "What he said is that he *wished* he was there."

George made a face. "Weird, but also not the same thing."

"No," she admitted, the shakiness still with her. "But he looked so guilty when he said it. I don't know why he feels that way if he didn't cause the accident."

George considered that before laying a gentle hand on her arm. "Shit, Emma, I can't believe I'm saying this, but this is too big. You need to talk to him. Get the whole story."

Emma closed her eyes. "I know. It's just hard, you know."

"Why? I mean, why beyond the obvious?"

Slumping, Emma tried to find the right words. "The past isn't just gone for me. It's obliterated."

Flopping back on the cushions, she twisted to face her. "My mom has this little room in her new house. It's full of my old books, school papers, and all the prizes I earned in school. Before I left, she made me go through it all—the report cards, prizes, and letters of recommendation. I even read the copies I made of my college application essays."

George's eyes were soft and sympathetic. "And it was like someone else wrote them."

She nodded. "There were so many accolades. Boxes and boxes of them, representing an insane number of man-hours. Verdant Falls was a small pond but I was a big-ass whale in it. But none of *her* work was familiar."

"*Her* is you," George insisted. "You were a badass. And you're still one."

If only that were true.

"Not anymore," she said, tired of putting a brave face on things. "I used to want to work on Wall Street. That ambition defined my life. I was in every club and extracurricular activity that would beef up my college applications so I could get into a top-tier school. I busted my ass for scholarships so I could afford it."

"And now you're a barista," George finished.

"Oh. I'm the last person to knock a job in the service industry. I know exactly how hard it is and how terrible people can be to you when you wear a name tag every day."

She smiled weakly. "It's more about not recognizing that girl from before, the driven one that thought math was her love language and treated everything like a competition. She may as well be an alien. But everyone who knew me before expects *her*."

She caught Georgia's look of consternation and cut her off when the other woman opened her mouth to protest.

"Oh, they always pretended they didn't. The counselors and the psychiatrists in the hospital had coached them on what to say. They parroted the same phrases, pretending to want nothing from me. But I knew better."

The couch and garage ceased to exist, her memory supplying the image of a series of sterile white hospital rooms.

"Every single person who came to see me in the hospital would look at me with this unspoken expectation. In the back of their mind, each one of them thought that *they* would be the one to unlock my memories, to be the person I remembered. In their unspoken fantasies, they would kick open the floodgates and bring it all back for me. And when that didn't happen, they inevitably left disappointed. Most stopped coming back after one or two visits."

Georgia sobbed unexpectedly.

"I'm sorry," she cried, waving her hands at her teary eyes as if she could fan the moisture away. "But that is so messed up."

Hell, she shouldn't have been so honest. "I didn't mean to make you cry."

Emma was weeping by this point, too. This was a pity party she shouldn't have invited anyone else to.

"I guess Rainer didn't know Garrett and I had something before the accident," Emma decided. "Or he would have told you."

Georgia blinked as if waking up. "If he does know, I'm going to strangle him."

"That would be a bad way to kick off your marriage." Emma laughed before frowning. "Wait, why aren't you on your honeymoon?"

George brightened. "I had an unexpected commission. A spectacular 1960 Shelby Cobra came in."

She laughed suddenly. "Rainer is salivating over it and plans on making the owner an offer. He didn't want me to feel rushed with such a fine specimen, so we decided to give ourselves a couple of extra days at home before leaving. We're supposed to fly out on Friday. But we won't go if you need me here."

Emma felt awful. "No, you have to go on your honeymoon."

The thought that her drama was derailing her new friend's plans shook her. "I'm making too much of this."

"No, you are not! You're making exactly the right amount of fuss. However you choose to handle it, that's the right amount."

Georgia wiped the shining streaks off her cheeks. "Are you going to leave him?"

Why did the mere mention of leaving Garrett suck all the air out of the room?

"I don't know," she said, feeling short of breath. "I guess it depends on what he has to say."

Hell, they were married. Even if she wanted to, she couldn't just pack her bags and leave. They would have to divorce.

Not that Garrett would agree to that. He would fight her every step of the way. She knew that with a certainty she didn't feel for anything else.

"Unless he gives up when I don't get my memory back," she muttered, her stomach swirling unpleasantly.

Could she live with him and watch him lose whatever hopes he was harboring? Because he would.

Emma disappointed everyone eventually.

"He's spoken to your doctors. He's known from the start that it's not likely you'll ever recover your memories." Georgia squeezed her hand. "And I can't believe I'm defending him right now, but he's trying to build something with you. Something new."

Emma pulled the coat tighter around herself with her free hand, unaccountably tired. "He still should have told me about us."

"Oh, I agree." Georgia shook her head in disgust. "I can't believe he didn't. You know—before last night."

"But?" She knew there was one.

Georgia gestured up in the general direction of the penthouse.

"I see how he looks at you when you're not watching. I was there the night he married you. Garrett had the suave playboy bit down to perfection. I never thought I would see him willingly put on that leg shackle. But that night he was… eager. And like stupid-level happy."

She clicked her tongue. "I didn't know what joy looked like on Garrett until you came back into his life. And granted, I haven't known you that long, but the last few weeks you seemed happy too."

Emma groaned. "Are you suggesting I forgive him?"

"No." Georgia was adamant. "I think you should go back and kick his ass for keeping secrets. But maybe after that, you should let him explain. Because there is a lot you don't know."

She scooted closer and wrapped a thin, strong arm around her. "I get why you didn't want to get entangled with someone from your past. Your reasons for that are one hundred percent valid. But not knowing is hurting you more."

George was right, of course.

Emma laid her head on the shorter woman's shoulder. "Can we just sit here for a little? Five minutes. No more."

She couldn't in good conscience take a second longer. Georgia had gotten married yesterday. She needed to be with her husband instead of consoling an amnesiac mess.

"Are you sure?" George asked. "We can go to brunch instead. That's what we were doing—coming to invite you over."

Okay, Georgia might actually be a saint.

"That is so sweet, but you got married *yesterday*." And *not* under false pretenses.

"Go on your honeymoon," she ordered. "I'll be fine."

Georgia narrowed her eyes, studying her. "All right. You seem better so I'll take you back up. But if you need anything, I'll be right next door."

She got up and wiped her hands on her shorts. "Just make sure if you kill Garrett, do it before Friday. The body won't fit in the Shelby's trunk, but I've got a rare T-Top Caddie in the shop with a big ass that will do the job nicely."

Emma laughed, wiping the traces of tears off her cheeks. "You've got a deal."

Chapter Thirty-Nine

GARRETT

Rainer's phone buzzed. "They're coming back up."

Garrett, dressed in last night's shirt and pants, jumped up from the couch, only to be pushed back down by a firm hand.

"Garrett, I say this with love," Rainer began. "But you have to get a fucking grip. Emma may be coming up to pack her clothes for all we know."

His displeasure must have shown on his face because Rainer scowled at him. "Hey, none of that shit. You need to be calm and collected and most of all *honest*."

"I will be."

Rainer held up a finger. "Not your version of honest."

He deserved that but Garrett couldn't help getting defensive. "What the hell does that mean?"

"It means that your instinct is going to be to withhold shit that will upset Emma. I don't think you should do that."

Rainer ran his hand through his hair. "I'm not saying dump everything on her all at once. But make sure she knows you're willing to tell her whatever she wants to know when she wants to know it."

The sound of the door opening interrupted his lecture. Garrett sprang up again but stopped himself from running to Emma when Rainer surreptitiously shook his head.

She walked into the penthouse behind George almost tentatively, her hands in the pockets of his trench coat. Her hair was mussed, and she still looked pale and shell-shocked, but she was there.

Thank Christ. The relief took him down at the knees, so it was a good fucking thing the couch was close at hand.

She came back. And Garrett was ready to do just about anything to keep her here.

Too bad it was a head injury and not a bum kidney. Because he had two kidneys and she could have either one.

There was a long silence.

Rainer cleared his throat. "I guess we should be going," he said, signaling his new bride.

Garrett tore his eyes away from Emma long enough to turn to George.

"Thank you," he said, the words heartfelt.

George stepped forward, her pixie face all up in his.

"Emma wants to talk to you but if she changes her mind at any point, she knows she's welcome at our place—even after we go on our honeymoon."

She twisted to look at her husband. "I gave her a key."

Rainer flicked his eyes to Garrett, but he nodded at his wife.

"I understand," he murmured.

"Good,'" George said, her pixie face incongruously hard. "I'm trusting you here. Don't fuck this up."

She stopped to hug Emma on the way out, whispering something about a Cadillac. Then he and his wife were alone.

"Emmy," he began.

She held up a hand, her eyes narrowed on his face. "Why do you do that? You know that's not my name."

He opened his mouth and then quickly closed it. "Uh, I don't think we should start there."

Emma crossed her arms and glared at him. For some reason it instantly made him feel better.

She took a step back and he compensated, edging closer. "Thank you for coming back."

"Like I could leave… you have my cat."

"That's a very good point." Garrett tried a smile. "In the future, please consider Meowmus Maximus and the lifestyle he's grown accustomed to."

She didn't smile back. "Are you stalling?"

Instantly sobering, he shook his head. "No, I swear. I want to explain. I was just trying to lighten things up."

Her brows rose. "Should they be light?"

"Some parts are. But others are… upsetting." He swallowed hard, blinking. "Really fucking upsetting."

Her lips parted, reacting to his show of emotion.

She licked her lips. "How did we end up sleeping together if we were enemies?"

He held up a finger. "Rivals," he corrected.

Emma fisted her hands. "*Garrett*!"

"I'm trying to explain here," he said. "But there's so much. I don't even know where to start."

Emma moved, edging around him. She sat on the ottoman facing the couch.

Shoving his hands in his pockets to keep from reaching out, he sat down across from her.

She looked him up and down. "Let's start with the elephant in the room. You realize we just consummated our fake marriage, right?"

His face went slack as images of the previous night flooded his brain.

Emma kicked him with a sneakered foot. "Stop that, Mr. Most Eligible Bachelor. You're supposed to be freaking out right now."

His lips twitched and she shook her head, annoyed. "You're lucky I signed a prenup. Else, I could take your mega-millions and waltz out that door and no court would stop me."

He sobered, letting her see what he was feeling—what he had *always* felt for her—on his face.

"You can have it all. Just don't leave."

Judging from the apprehension in her eyes, that was the wrong thing to say. When she spoke, her voice was hoarse. "Start at the beginning."

God, that felt like a thousand fucking years ago. "The beginning *was* in high school."

"Okay." Emma took a deep breath. "Start in high school."

He closed his eyes, letting himself go back in time to that first day.

"You had just skipped two entire grades. The school admin transferred you into half of my classes. That wouldn't have been a big deal, but one of them was drama and we were covering Shakespeare's major works that semester."

From her expression, it was clear she didn't understand. "Why was that a problem?"

"Because Mr. Joyner, our drama teacher, didn't let us choose our scene partners. He drew names out of a hat." He sighed. "And I chose yours."

The corners of her mouth tightened. "I know I'm not supposed to take offense, but offense."

He huffed. "Yeah, that was pretty much your reaction when I asked Joyner to let me swap partners."

Garrett leaned forward when she continued to scowl. "Emma, we were doing *Romeo and Juliet*. We got the kissing scene."

"Again," she said in a clipped voice. "*Offense*."

"You were *fourteen*, Emmy," he said gently, trying to explain. "But you sure as hell didn't look it."

"Oh," she muttered, looking down at her lap. Or rather her chest. She had been almost that developed at fourteen.

He also remembered a similar look on her face in Joyner's office that day.

"The age difference between fourteen and seventeen was too damn big. And there were enough people who were gross and inappropriate about you." He gritted his teeth. "That and I knew if I started kissing you in any context, I would never stop."

She raised a brow. "Because you didn't want to be one of the gross people."

If only she knew the hell she'd gone through. He'd wanted to put his fist through every mouth breather who'd eye-banged her.

He gestured to his chest before dropping his hand. "You have a figure like your mother's. Very… hourglass. And she had a reputation. When you were in middle and high school, she ran through a lot of men. Not boyfriends. Hookups."

She sighed, looking at the ceiling. "So that reputation spilled over on me."

Garrett grimaced. "Did she tell you any of this?"

Emma shook her head. "No. But I'm not surprised. She still… dates."

He nodded, steering the conversation back to safer ground. "You overheard me asking Joyner for a new partner and became angry. Justifiably. Things deteriorated fast. And I didn't help matters improve. I intentionally made them worse by being standoffish."

"You were an asshole."

He sighed. "Avoiding someone because you're deeply in lust and can't do anything about it looks remarkably like assholeness."

She almost smiled. "I'll bet it does."

He raised a brow. "In my defense, you took that ball and ran with it. From zero to mortal enemies in a matter of days."

"I can't imagine that," she said, laughing suddenly. But her humor subsided quickly.

"You're not that different," he said, reading her thoughts. "The core of you has not changed."

She didn't look convinced, but she appeared willing to let things slide in favor of enlightenment.

"But we did," she said. "We became much closer."

"Yes." He let out a long exhale. "Our need to keep competing and sniping at each other finished when I graduated and went off to Stanford."

She tilted her head. "I thought we graduated high school the same year."

"We did," he clarified. "You went from freshman to junior and ended up in over half my classes because it was a small school. There weren't many classes to begin with. But you blew through the available curriculum too quickly. You technically graduated with me. But your mom thought you were too young to go away for college. That was why you took courses online in the library for another couple of years before leaving Verdant Falls—I'm not sure what your status was."

He knew that because he still kept tabs on her back then, although he'd been thousands of miles away.

"That's right. I took a gap year," she said softly. "The school assumed I was going to travel but I was working and saving up for living expenses and preparing. I wanted to go to business school."

He nodded. "As did I. I was on my way. And then you graduated and went off to New Haven for college. Your aim, and mine, was to graduate and go to Wharton or Harvard for business school. But that was years away yet for both of us.

"We had to get through college first. You somehow managed to come home for most of the holidays and school breaks. I think you drove down with a friend who lived in another part of the state and took the bus for the last leg."

He leaned back on the couch, reminiscing for a moment. "I remember the first time you came to one of my parties."

Surprise flared in her eyes. "I did? Without being invited?"

"Not by choice." He grinned. "Your friend Katie dragged you."

Her brows rose.

He shrugged. "There wasn't enough to do in that town, so we made our own fun. I was having a spring break blowout at my family's cabin on the Verdant River. A few of us had family cabins out that way, and we took turns throwing parties. It was a regular circuit, but my place was the biggest, so we typically ended up there. Most everyone under the age of twenty-five made an appearance sooner or later.

"You didn't come inside at first. You were avoiding the crowd in general and me in particular. But Katie told me she'd brought you, kind of running it by me—as if I would mind—so I went looking."

His voice softened as his mind replayed the memory in his head. It had been the first warm week of the year and she'd been wearing a yellow and white checkered sundress with a halter top neck.

He'd wanted to strip it off her and lick every inch of her body. But he'd played it cool that night.

"You were at the edge of the hill, looking down at the river. I walked up to you and we spoke for a few minutes. We called a truce."

Emma frowned. "Just like that?"

"We were no longer classmates." And she was eighteen going on nineteen and he no longer felt like he had to gouge out his eyes for looking at her the way he did.

"I asked you to bury the hatchet. You were reluctant at first, but the mosquitos were eating you alive, so you came into the den and we had our first real conversation over a glass of wine and a tube of Benadryl cream."

Her lips parted. "And I slept with you."

"No." He shook his head. "Not for *years*. We became friends first."

"Friends?" she echoed in disbelief. "*Years*?"

"It's not as hard to believe as it sounds," he told her, willing her to sit closer to him. "We had more in common than not. We were both driven, gearing up for careers in business. We also liked the same movies and food. I had traveled to places you wanted to go to."

He paused before biting the bullet. "You grew up without a dad and had a difficult relationship with your mom. I grew up without a mom and my father barely spoke to me."

This last visibly shook her. "Oh," she said with tight cheeks. "Sorry. I get along with my mom now."

"You did most of the time back then too," he was happy to share. "But not always."

She was so confused. "What did we fight about?"

"The men."

His cheek twitched at her expression of consternation. "For the record, I don't think her reputation was deserved. Had she lived in a big city, her love life wouldn't have been the subject of so much gossip."

"But we lived in a small town." Her mouth was hard.

"That's right."

Fuck, he didn't want to be the one to tell her this. But Emma was finally listening to details of her past. She wasn't shutting him down. And this was part of the things she needed to know.

"There were rumors of her being involved with married men. Including this scuzzbucket named Theodore Bronson… my aunt's then husband."

Emma blinked, her face reddening. She recognized the name. "*Shit*."

Yeah, he felt the same way. "We didn't know about that liaison at the time. We didn't talk about our parents that night at all."

Those confidences had come much later. "That night we discussed your first year at school and the classes we were taking. And when you came back for the next party, during summer break, we spoke again, and I finally asked for your number. We started texting."

Her full lips pursed. "If we got so close, why does everyone still assume we're enemies today?"

Chapter Forty

GARRETT

"I'm not sure everyone does," he said finally. "We were seen speaking at my parties often enough. But Fletcher is probably not alone in thinking we still hate each other. Most people didn't pay close attention."

Garrett shrugged. "We partied hard, and everyone was there to hook up or get wasted."

He had brushed off the few who had teased or made comments, dismissing the old rivalry as ancient history but obviously not strongly enough.

"I guess I was too focused on spending time with you to care or notice that people still thought of us that way."

She tilted her head. "When did things change?"

He smiled, but it was tight. "When you got a boyfriend, at the start of your senior year of college."

Emma's lips parted.

"I know how that sounds." Garrett wasn't proud of himself, but he'd do it again.

Her lip twitched. "Like you were jealous."

"Oh, I was," he freely admitted. "But I guess I did a decent job of hiding it, because when the two of you started having problems—rather quickly I want to add—you confided in me."

The corners of her lips twitched. "Did you tell me to break up with him?"

He nodded, his heart picking up at the confession he was about to make. "Not straight out and not right away. But I had plans for us, and he was in the way."

Her eyes widened apprehensively. "What did you do?"

"Nothing overt," he promised her. "I didn't sabotage your relationship. But the guy was… difficult. He made your life harder instead of easier. It wasn't hard to identify and exploit the cracks in your relationship."

Her head tilted up as she examined the ceiling for a minute. "His name was Edward. I don't know much about him, aside from what my mom told me."

Garrett knew everything there was to know about Edward McNair thanks to the extensive background check his PI had done. But he stuck to what she had told him all those years ago.

"He was from an old Southern Baptist family. Eddie wanted to be a lawyer. You met him in your Econ class. You said he had good manners and always looked you in the eye when he spoke to you, instead of your chest."

"Huh." She considered that a moment. "That must be why he got so offended when my mom implied he'd hit it and quit it."

"She did?"

Emma nodded. "In those exact words. She called him when I was in the hospital, expecting him to rush to my side. But he didn't. She's badmouthed him ever since."

Even if they hadn't been intimate, Edward had completely shut her out after the accident. Even if she hadn't been his anymore, Garrett thought that was pretty fucked up.

So much for so-called Southern manners.

"I was in my first year at HBS and was helping you with your application, including steering you toward an internship I knew the admissions committee would love."

Emma sucked in a breath, flushing. "I got into Harvard Business School. My mom showed me the letter."

"Yeah." He'd nearly burst with pride and relief. They were going to be at the same school again. Only this time she would be in her early twenties, and a peer.

"Most of it would be paid by scholarships and financial aid. But you were worried about the cost of living. Only a third of students get on-campus housing and you were stressing out about having to rent a room in such an expensive city. That's when I mentioned my spare room."

Emma leaned forward. "You wanted us to move in together?"

"I did," he said, not bothering to hide the possessiveness he felt. "Like I said, I had big plans for us."

She froze and her skin flushed, this time with true heat. The air pulsed with unspoken need.

Garrett had to fight the urge to reach for her. They needed to get through this. He wouldn't be worthy of her touch until she knew everything. And forgave him.

"And then it happened," he ground out.

"What?" she asked wide-eyed when he paused.

"You broke up with Edward," he said. "You told me all about it. We were talking on the phone a lot because texting wasn't enough for us anymore. The tenor of our conversations had changed. The calls were more personal. Intimate. We didn't acknowledge it openly, but the two of us understood that the next time we saw each other, things would be different."

She was watching him now like she wanted him to demonstrate, to feel his hands on her. But he couldn't derail this conversation. She needed to know everything or she wouldn't trust him.

"Our winter breaks overlapped, two entire weeks that I was determined to spend with you. When you got home, there was an engraved invitation waiting for you."

She did a double take. "A what?"

"A party invitation," he said, rubbing the back of his neck. "I had it specially made, making sure to note that it was for a very exclusive event. But you still seemed surprised when I opened the door and there was no one else there."

"So, it was a private party?"

He grinned. "No one knew I was coming home. I snuck in at two in the morning in a sedan rental. I didn't want the grapevine to activate or else I would have had a crowd of people show up, expecting one of the usual blow-out parties."

And he would have strangled every one of those unfortunate souls.

Garrett leaned forward until there was a scant few inches between them. "The invitation said it was a formal dinner. You showed up wearing this incredible red velvet dress. I couldn't wait to take it off you, but I wanted to do things right. I led you to the living room… I had the fireplace going."

Emma's eyes had taken on a slumberous look. She was picturing the scene of her seduction. It wasn't his imagination because her voice was breathier when she asked, "Is that why you wanted to have sex on the couch last night?"

The urge to reach out and take her all over again was almost unbearable now.

"No," he said, his voice so hoarse he was surprised the words were intelligible. "I had dragged a mattress from the nearest bedroom and laid blankets over it. We had a picnic in front of the fire."

Unable to resist, he reached out to rest his hand on her upper thigh. "We ate appetizers and had bread, cheese, and wine. And then you kissed me. Our first kiss."

He could see the increased rise and fall of her chest under his trench coat.

Garrett slid off the couch, settling on his knees in front of her. Slowly, methodically, he undid the belt of the coat, pushing it open. But he didn't touch the button on his shirt. Not yet.

"That's when I told you why I call you Em*my* and not Em*ma*, even though it made you mad in high school."

He looked into her eyes, snaring them with his own. "It was because you were *my* Em. *Mine*. Even back when our age difference meant I had to keep you at arm's length, I was laying a claim. I just never told you. I had to wait."

Garrett shifted, leaning over her. Emma leaned back, her body following the line of his. But he kept a crucial inch of space between them.

How did her lips get so moist-looking?

"Is that true?" she asked, her pupils visibly dilated. "I was your Em from the start?"

"Yes. I've always wanted you. *Always*."

He waited a beat, holding his breath. Waiting for permission. And she gave it to him, reaching up and wrapping her arms around his neck.

His resolve broke, and he gave in to the urge to put his hands on her.

Garrett pulled her off the ottoman, landing on the couch behind him with her in his lap.

Her hands shook as she undid the fastenings of the shirt and pants he'd put on to wait for her return. He yanked open the lapels of the coat and cupped her breasts with a groan. But it turned into a hiss when her small hands reached out and pulled out his cock, stroking and squeezing him.

"No, baby, you're too sore."

"Not sore," she breathed, her open mouth on his. She rubbed against him, incinerating what little resolve he had.

He swore under his breath as one sinuous undulation nearly made him explode.

"Tell me the rest," she said in his ear, pressing her breasts against his bare chest. "Tell me about our first time."

Chapter Forty-One

GARRETT

Fuck, he could barely think. The only reason he could recite those details now was because that time with her was burned into his brain.

"I took your dress off and kissed your breasts and belly," he whispered, starting to breathe faster. "Then I laid you down and licked you between your legs until you begged me to stop."

Emma whimpered, wet heat sliding along his hard length, the sensitive head positioned at her tight entrance. "Because I wanted your cock instead."

"*Yes*." He clutched her to him. "You chose me as your first. I was so fucking honored and excited. Your naked tits and tight pussy nearly made me come—the only reason I didn't was because I beat off in the shower before you got there so I wouldn't lose my shit before I satisfied you."

Emma giggled, burying her face in his neck. "Oh my God."

"It's true," he said, tightening his hold. "I'd been dying for you for so long. I didn't want to embarrass myself. And believe me, the sight of you naked, offering yourself to me—that would have destroyed a stronger man. Not everyone has my incredible foresight."

Her lips moved against his neck. "But you had prepared."

He swallowed, running his hands over the curve of her hips. "And thank God I did or I wouldn't have lasted. Instead, I was able to hold off until you were shivering in my arms. Then I covered you with my body and penetrated you real slow."

"Like this?" she breathed.

Garrett shuddered as she raised her hips and then slid down on his cock, her slick wet heat sliding over him like hot velvet.

"Yeah," he moaned, a vise around his chest. *Fuck that.* It was inside his chest, gripping his heart. "Just like that, baby."

He took her hips in his hands, urging her up and down until she was riding him, her pussy clamping him with every downstroke.

Time slipped by slowly, each second endless and perfect.

"You're so fucking good at fucking your man," he praised in one breath, making sure she wasn't hurting the next.

She may not have been a virgin, but it had been years for her and even though she denied it, she was probably sore. Because there had been no one else. *He* was the only man she had ever been with.

Garrett had always been possessive of Emma. Their short relationship had been so intense, so precious to him he hadn't told anyone about it. It had been fucking selfish, but they'd only had their school breaks together and he couldn't bear to share her with anyone else.

But Emma was his wife now. His obsession with her was now legal and binding. Their vows hadn't included the love and honor part. He hadn't wanted to push it, so he'd asked the justice of the peace to leave it out. But he would ask Emma to do the ceremony again sometime, so he could hear those words from her lips. And he'd be able to say them back.

Thankfully, judging from the way her fingers were digging into his shoulders, that day felt much closer now.

Emma groaned into his neck, her breath hitching as her tight pussy slammed down on him, grinding away. He gripped her ass, taking a delicious handful.

"Hold on to me, baby," he warned, white sparks lighting the corners of his eyes.

He slammed his hips up, fucking her hard from beneath. Garrett lost his sense of time. The only thing he could hear were Emma's cries. They punctuated his thrusts as they rocked together.

"Yeah, that's it," he breathed. "Grind up on your man. Get him all wet with your cream."

Emma sobbed, pulsing and throbbing all around him. Unable to hold it, he stopped fighting, letting his orgasm rip through him. His cock spasmed, flooding her and soaking his lap. But his Emmy wasn't done yet. His hand worked between them, drawing out her climax for as long as he could.

"*Garrett.*" Emma put her hands on either side of his face as they undulated together, two bodies in perfect sync.

He'd only ever experienced that with her.

Emma pushed against his hand, his thumb working her sweet plump clit even as she clenched everything. Her hands fisted in his hair as she shuddered in his arms.

Or was that him? Hell, it was difficult to tell, but judging from the way his heart was hammering, he was the culprit.

Her body released on a sob, and she threw her head back, trusting that he would hold her through the storm.

It rolled over them both until they were both panting to catch their breath, still locked in each other's arms.

Garrett pressed his face against the side of her neck. "That explanation went a lot better than I thought it would," he mumbled.

Emma raised her head. She was still breathing fast, but now that their mutual hunger had been fed, she was sobering quickly. He could see the doubt creeping back into her eyes.

"We're not done talking yet," he said.

Emma started to rise, intending to climb off him, but he shook his head, holding her fast.

"Like this," he insisted, his voice barely intelligible. "With me inside you."

That way she wouldn't forget that she belonged to him when he told her the rest.

Emma settled back down and nodded, the slight sheen of her sweat making her glow.

He hugged her to him, relishing in the weight of her. "Your skin is unreal. It's so soft. I've never felt anything this fine."

Emma knew he was stalling. She poked him in the ribs. "The rest."

"All right." He pressed a kiss to her cheek, the soft down next to her ear. "You spent the whole night with me. Woke up after dawn in my arms."

She pulled back to look into his eyes. "I didn't go home?"

"Your mom was working two jobs back then," he explained. "As long as you were home between her shifts around lunchtime, she was none the wiser."

He tilted her chin to make sure she met his eyes and could read the sincerity there.

"I never intended for our relationship to be a secret from her. But things between us were extremely new and already intimate. It seemed reasonable that you didn't want to tell her where you were sleeping that night."

"Did I at least text her?"

"Yes, of course," he said. "You told her you were sleeping over with a friend."

"Oh." Emma didn't know how to process that. "Seems a little thin. She wasn't suspicious?"

"You never mentioned her asking any questions about it."

He shrugged apologetically. "You have to understand she was busy, overworked. Plus, you thought she was seeing a new guy. Mariana was preoccupied with her own love life at the time."

She took a deep breath and nodded. "We continued seeing each other?"

He closed his eyes, stroking her back. "It was an amazing night. The best night of my life, which turned into the best few weeks of my life."

She tilted back to look at his face. "We spent the whole break together?"

"Every minute we could."

He traced the plush line of her lower lip. "I would drive you home so you could see your mom when she wasn't at work, but then she'd leave, and I'd drive over as soon as you texted me to pick you up. I even snuck in one night when she was asleep and slept with you there. But you felt so guilty about it in the morning that we agreed from then on, you'd come with me to the cabin."

"And where was your father during all of this?"

His shoulders straightened, the tension in him impossible to hide. "Where he usually was. Away on business."

Grant Chapman had eschewed all parental responsibility after the death of his wife. He left Garrett in the care of a nanny and less frequently under the supervision of his mother's sister, his aunt Phil.

"You and I were joined at the hip all of winter break," he said, smiling at the memories of plans and waffle breakfasts—the only meal he could make himself at the time. "But we hashed out a lot of stuff. Made plans. You agreed to move in with me when you started business school."

Emma squeezed his shoulder. "What went wrong?"

"Me."

The panic and self-recrimination rose, his constant companions. Garrett clutched her to him, his grip a little too hard.

Emma pushed away, but she was still wrapped around him, his cock embedded in her.

He held her hips, not wanting to let her go. "Go ahead and ask."

"Was there someone else?" she whispered.

He knew she meant another girl. But that wasn't it. "Your ex, Edward."

She tensed in his arms. *"Edward?"*

He didn't blame her for her incredulity. "Please keep in mind that I was a card-carrying moron back then."

"I don't understand. What did Edward do?"

"You headed back to school. I missed you so fucking much. I called you every day. We made do. But the month before spring break, you were different. Distant. I had a hard time getting you on the phone and your text responses were short. When I asked you what was wrong, you said midterms were stressing you out."

"But?"

He told her the truth he so desperately wished he could undo. "But one night I called you. It was late. Edward was in your dorm room."

He suddenly clutched her to him, half-worried she'd run away when she realized what a raving idiot he'd been.

"It was late—almost midnight—and he was in your room. You explained that the two of you had been paired on a project for your advanced Econ class and that it hadn't been your choice."

He shook his head, wanting to go back in time to kick his own ass. "But I was so fucking jealous I couldn't see straight. I jumped down your throat when you tried to explain. I was convinced Edward was the reason you hadn't been answering my calls."

Emma pushed back against his hands as if unconsciously trying to get away from him. "Oh. That's um…"

"Shitty. I was being a major league asshole," he apologized. "We spoke a handful of times after that, and each time we fought about that piece of shit."

Garrett hung his head. "I was being unreasonable. I knew that at the time. But being long distance was so fucking hard and I was insecure about us. I was convinced Edward was trying to get you back, so I issued an ultimatum."

Bewilderment clouded her expression. "What did you say?"

"I told you that once your project was turned in, you had to stop speaking to him," he admitted with a wince. "I tried to dictate who you could be friends with. Bullshit you very justifiably called me out on."

He rubbed her back, grateful she was still here, listening to him. "That's when you told me something else was wrong, but you had to talk to me about it in person."

"What was it?"

"I don't know." He shrugged helplessly. "Spring break arrived and you didn't come home. When I asked your friends, they didn't know where you were. Days passed and I heard nothing from you. And I was too proud to keep calling you over and over. In my head, you were the one in the wrong. A few days later, I decided continuing to call would be like begging."

Emma pushed away and this time he let her go, even though the loss of her physically hurt. He didn't even care that his cock was out, soaked, and still half-hard from being so close to her.

He zipped himself up as she scooted a few feet away, sitting on the other side of the couch.

Too far.

"As far as I was concerned, you had ghosted me," he said, determined to finish to the bitter end. "Like a jackass, I threw a party that last Saturday. I told myself it was a celebration of my new freedom because I was now a single man."

She curled her arms around herself. "Did you hook up with another girl at the party?"

"*No.*" His eyes widened. "No, I was still waiting for you. In my head, you showed up in another sundress, armed with a fabulous excuse for your silence, ready to promise never to speak to your ex again."

Her lips barely cleared her arms, muffling her speech. "I guess that didn't happen."

"No. What happened was worse."

He turned, raising a knee so he could sit sideways, facing her. He reached out and took hold of her upper arms, rubbing the delicate skin with his thumbs.

"Emma… that night of the accident was the night of the party. You were found by your mom halfway between my place and yours, on a small access road that would have taken you straight to my family's cabin."

Emma took a deep shaky breath, her eyes brightening with the telltale shine of tears. "I was coming to see you?"

He studied her stricken expression, his chest so tight it felt like he was going to explode.

"You must have been. But I had no idea because you never made it there."

He cleared his throat, the self-recrimination nearly choking him. "I couldn't see past my hurt to consider any other reason for your absence. I assumed the worst."

Her voice wavered. "You thought Edward and I had gotten back together."

He nodded. "I tried to drink my sorrows away that night but couldn't even work up a buzz. I packed my bags and left early the next morning. I haven't set foot in Verdant Falls since."

She took several shallow breaths. But her voice still quavered when she spoke. "You swear you didn't know about the accident?"

Garrett edged closer, pressing her against his side. "If I'd known, I would have been there."

Taking care of her would have become his life's mission that much sooner. "But you didn't return my calls."

She closed her eyes, giving herself a little shake. "Wait, you called me *after* you left town?"

"A few dozen times," he admitted. "Maybe more."

He swallowed over the lump in his throat. "I had no idea your phone had been shattered that night."

Emma leaned forward, grabbing his hand. "It was?"

He nodded, still ashamed that he hadn't done anything else.

"I have a picture of it," he shared. "The screen was smashed. The investigators couldn't get it to work again. That was all detailed in the accident report."

Her head jerked back. "You have that?"

"I got it from the sheriff in Verdant Falls." Garrett passed a rough hand through his hair. "So, you see, I've known what happened to us for a few weeks."

"To me, you mean." She shivered again, twisting the knife he could feel in his gut. "You knew what happened to *me*."

Garrett scooted closer. "Emma, I may not have been there, but that doesn't change the facts. My asshole behavior led to your accident."

Chapter Forty-Two

EMMA

The need to comfort Garrett was almost visceral. She could feel his pain and his panic. He was worried she was going to walk away from him.

His eyes and nose were red, and he kept making fists as if he were checking the impulse to reach for her.

She wanted to crawl back into his lap, but he'd just shattered her world and remade it at the same time.

"It wasn't your fault."

She had to believe that, to believe everything he'd said. The alternative was too unbearable to consider. Her heart couldn't take it.

"Emma, if I hadn't been such a colossal asshole, you wouldn't have been in those woods at all!" Garrett pointed out, not done with his self-flagellation.

"I would have picked you up and we would have been at the cabin talking things through—*alone*. I wouldn't have thrown a party at all. But I was so up my own ass that I didn't do what I should have done, which was fly to your school to help you with whatever you were going through before bringing you home."

The question must have been all over her face because he shook his head.

"What that was, I still don't know. I've come up with a million possible explanations. Maybe you'd had an issue with one of your classes or dorm mates that got out of hand. Or maybe you lost one of your grants for business school and you didn't want to tell me because money was a touchy issue between us."

She snorted lightly. "I'll bet it was."

Emma had been fortunate to have a roof over her head while his family had multiple homes in their *hometown*.

How many did he have now? Five? A dozen? They simply weren't on the same level and never would be.

But that was her issue, wasn't it? Neither of them could help the circumstances of their birth. And judging from Garrett's *what's mine is yours* attitude, he had never looked down on her because of it.

"I don't think money alone would have upset me the way you described."

Because now that she was in a relationship with him again, she just couldn't imagine freezing him out for any reason.

"You still think Edward was a factor, don't you?"

He stared at her for a long moment. "I had been in love with you for years, Em. It made sense that he would have some difficulties letting you go too."

This time she didn't stop herself. She climbed into his lap, intending to hug him, but the dam burst without warning, and then she was sobbing, crying against his chest.

He cradled her to him, rocking her in his warmth. "I know, baby. Me too. Me too. But we have a chance to put everything right. *Stay*. Let me make it up to you. Let me give you the life you deserve."

Emma stared at him, wondering if she should be mad. Because she knew now this had been his plan all along.

Yeah, he'd said all the right things about paying it forward and balancing the scales because she'd motivated him to succeed back in high school. But in the back of his mind, this idea had always been there. *His wife*. With all the benefits that entailed.

Part of her still didn't believe it. "You married me," she whispered. "You went *that* far."

Garrett looked at her as if she was everything that had ever mattered to him. The terrifying part was that it might have been true.

"I was always going to ask, Emma."

"You were going to propose?" But it wasn't a question. Not anymore.

He cupped her face, nodding.

"It was a vague plan, but a real one. I was going to ask you when I graduated from business school, or a year later when you did, depending on how things worked out. I was going to get my mother's ring from my aunt."

He lifted a hand when she gave him a horrified look. "It *is* mine. My mom had willed it to me for my future bride. But she died when I was so young. My aunt keeps it in her safe back home. I've been meaning to ask her for it, but I haven't had time. I will get it though. It's important to me that you have it."

That she didn't doubt, but Emma could feel her heart sinking. Didn't her mother have an affair with his aunt's husband?

"I don't suppose you have many aunts?" she asked weakly.

He shook his head, a wry light in his eyes. "Just the one, on my mom's side. Her name is Philomena. I call her Aunt Phil. My father had a brother too. His name was Frank, but he was much older and passed already. I also have two cousins: Frank's kids, and their grandchildren. But the brothers weren't close, so I saw them maybe twice a decade growing up. Phil didn't have any children."

Emma tried to calculate the odds. The woman holding her future engagement ring was the one whose husband had cheated with her mother, Mariana.

And of course, his aunt Phil didn't have any children of her own. She just had Garrett.

His hand closed over hers. "The ring is mine, Emma. What our parents' generation did is their business. We're not a part of it."

Emma wanted to shake some sense into him. "How can you say that? From what I've been able to piece together, your aunt Phil is the only relative you are close to. Do you speak to her? Visit?"

His shoulders straightened and she knew she wasn't going to like his answer. "Phil isn't going to hold what happened between your mom and her husband against you because I won't let her. You are my wife now. She will respect that."

Was he really this naive? The woman probably despised her mother. He was likely his aunt's pride and joy.

Any woman would have been proud to call the man her nephew. There was no way she'd accept Emma as Garrett's wife.

From her conversations with George and Rainer, she knew Garrett had been born to a successful and self-involved businessman. After his mother had died, the man had focused on his work, leaving Garrett in the care of housekeepers and less frequently his aunt.

Garrett had never told them he resented his father's frequent absences. Not in words. But his actions since then spoke volumes. Because Garrett didn't simply become a better businessman than his father. He became a mogul, completely eclipsing his parents' accomplishments.

Today Garrett operated on another level, one where financial magazines wrote about his deals.

According to Rainer, people vied to do business with Next Chapter, bringing opportunities other companies like his didn't get. He was a shining star. And because he wasn't his father, he would have stayed in touch with his aunt, caring for her in whatever way she would let him.

They were probably extremely close.

No, there was no way this Aunt Phil would welcome her with open arms. The best she could expect was grudging and teeth-gritted politeness. Emma didn't want to imagine what the worst-case scenario would be.

"Problem for another day," she muttered, feeling a little dizzy. She made a move to climb off his lap, but he didn't release her.

"One that I will deal with," he said. "*Me*. This isn't your problem. All you should be focusing on is your family, continued recovery, and whatever job you decide is worth your time."

Her family and recovery she could deal with. But that yawning gap in the road up ahead that was her future career was just too much on top of these revelations.

The future in general was frightening to contemplate.

Which brought up another issue. "What happens if you change your mind?"

He raised his eyebrows. "How can you possibly think that is going to happen?"

"You never know someone until you live with them. We never got that chance. What if you decide you can't stand the way I chew a few months down the line?"

His face cleared, warming. "Emma, we *have* been living together for months. I already know how you chew."

"What if you snore and I can't sleep? I could snap and go after you with a baseball bat."

Garrett chuckled silently. "That is very specific. Also, I don't snore. You didn't use to, either. If that's changed, I will buy some earplugs. Problem solved."

His grip on her tightened and suddenly she was being carried.

"You do, however, bring up a very good point. The most significant change is going to be our sleeping arrangements. Why don't we go see how much you like my bed? I think you'll find it very comfortable."

Emma couldn't stifle a giggle. "You say that like we'll actually be sleeping in it."

Garrett grinned down at her. "See, your memory may be faulty, but it hardly matters. You already know me better than you think."

Chapter Forty-Three

EMMA

Georgia was glowing about as much as you would expect a woman fresh off her honeymoon with a handsome virile husband who adored her.

Emma smiled at her friend and slipped on a pair of shades that were completely unnecessary in this corner of the café.

Today they were drinking at the competition, a national chain with a location right across from their building. Although technically, she wasn't a regular employee of the *De Olla* anymore.

She'd allowed Garrett to talk her into considering finishing her college degree, but she hadn't let Hector take her off the books completely. She was still taking the odd shift, filling in when someone else called in sick.

Garrett hated it but didn't argue. They'd been married less than two months, and he already knew when to choose his battles. That and he understood her in a way no one else seemed to.

Emma had a hard time quitting anything.

It was the personality trait that had gotten her out of her hospital bed years ago, but it had some downsides too. At least for her husband.

"Why the shades?" George asked after taking what appeared to be a long and satisfying sip of her vanilla latte.

"With these, I won't be blinded by that honeymoon afterglow."

George snorted and pointed her spoon at her. "You realize that's the pot calling the kettle black, right?"

Red heat crept up her neck, but she grinned and set the lunch menu she'd been holding to one side with a flourish.

"I do," she said primly. But Emma couldn't keep a straight face and burst into giggles.

Being on the same wavelength, George joined her. The waiter took one look at them, rolled his eyes, and decided to give them more time.

George subsided first, taking a sip of water before straightening her shoulders. "I know you said everything was good and I could go on my honeymoon with a clear conscience, so I did."

She waved a hand to encompass Emma. "You're obviously enjoying married life. But tell me the truth, are things okay? Are you completely satisfied with Garrett's explanation of everything? Your past relationship? The accident?"

Emma took a deep breath and nodded. "I am. Well, as much as someone who doesn't remember any of those things can be."

She gave George a condensed version of everything Garrett had told her, including all the details of her accident that he knew.

"That fucking sucks," George said when she got to the part about her phone being smashed beyond repair in the accident. "If he'd been able to get through…"

She trailed off with a wince. "Sorry. I shouldn't be speculating. It's in the past. The important thing is your future. I know Garrett must be thrilled to have a second chance. He came to see Rainer this morning. I've never seen him so smugly happy."

Emma swallowed some of her cold brew, smiling despite the fact her throat was a bit tight. She too had played the what-if game the last few weeks. But the fact Garrett's friends had noticed a difference in him was good.

She was collecting all these little moments, small proofs of his affection and care, hoarding them like gold coins.

Emma wrote down her bright and shiny new memories in a digital diary. It was backed up to the cloud and she printed it out twice a week.

Just in case.

"I'm glad to hear that. I feel that same way too," she acknowledged. "Although I can't help waiting for the other shoe to drop. I guess I'm suspicious of happiness."

"I get that," George said, a flicker of an uncharacteristic world-weariness in her expression. "It's hard to let down your guard. To trust. But it's worth it."

"Yeah," she agreed. But saying and doing were two different things.

Trusting Garrett was easy. Almost effortless. But what about her? Could she trust herself?

What the hell had happened to her to push him away before the accident? What had she done?

"Hey, did you ever see Pedro again?"

"He came over for dinner while you were on your honeymoon." She widened her eyes. "You'll never guess who he brought with him."

George took a bite of her chocolate croissant and wiggled her hand mid-height to indicate it was meh. "Who?"

"Hannah Cho."

"What?" Her friend's voice was so high it broke. Clearing her throat, George hurriedly took a sip. "Really? The landlord's daughter?"

Emma flung a hand in the air. "I guess his therapy is going well because they're dating now."

George tsked. "Unbelievable."

"I know!" Life was weird. But it also explained the strange tension between those two.

Emma was still a little annoyed with Pedro over how quickly he'd jettisoned her as a roommate, but she couldn't deny it hadn't worked out for both of them.

"So why did you choose this place?" George asked, gesturing to the space around them. "The coffee is decent enough, but it doesn't compare to *De Olla*."

"No, it doesn't," she acknowledged. "But this chain is spreading everywhere."

George raised her brows. "Studying the competition?"

She shrugged. "More like trying to find my place in it."

"Then you've decided to try and take on big coffee? Is it on behalf of *De Olla* or will you start your own chain?"

Emma blinked at the mention of a chain. "Nothing so grandiose. There is plenty about running a café that I have no interest in. But a few things I do like. Like when we get a fresh pastry shipment. Or you get good butter to go with the artisanal bread."

"Mmm. Butter." George got a dreamy look on her face. She picked up the menu. "Think they have the good stuff here?"

"Nope. Theirs tastes like wax."

"Well, never mind then." She put down her menu. "But I'm all for better butter. You can start a creamery."

"Not sure that is the right thing either," Emma said. "Although it's closer, I think. I have to do more research."

"Does that mean we'll be hitting more coffee shops?"

Emma loved that George automatically volunteered. "If you're willing, then yes."

She had a list of places to go, some successful and some that weren't but deserved to be.

George picked up her coffee mug and saluted with it. "In that case, I'm happy to be of service."

She waved at the waiter so they could order. "I knew I could count on you. Let's get started."

Chapter Forty-Four

GARRETT

He wiped the scowl off his face in the elevator. He was still frustrated over missing Emma's doctor's appointment, but today's meetings had been too important to cancel. They'd also been too sensitive for Fletcher or any of his subordinates to handle without him.

The coming week wasn't looking any better either. He resented every minute he didn't get to spend with her. He'd missed too many of them as it was.

"Emmy," he called out, noting the now familiar sight of coffee shop pastries lined up on the bar.

Garrett allowed himself a brief smile. He'd eaten more pastries these past few weeks than his entire life.

He had compensated by adding some time to his normal workout, but in truth, his new favorite form of exercise was sex with his smoking hot wife, whenever and however she wanted.

The thought made him hard, and he was already stripping, hoping she wasn't hungry after her coffee shop research. But all amorous thoughts died when he found her in bed, awake but pale and in obvious pain.

"*Hey*." Kneeling to the side, he grew calmer when she focused on him and smiled, even if it was weak as hell.

"Hey," she rasped. "Don't worry. I slept off the worst of it."

"Another headache?"

Her headaches weren't frequent but when they struck, Emma went down hard. "Did you speak to Dr. Saha about them?"

"Mmm, yeah," she said, rising sluggishly. "But it wasn't Saha. She wasn't available to fly down. It was another doctor she recommended. Some French guy."

Garrett scowled. He'd paid a considerable sum for Dr. Saha's services. However, it wasn't a contract in the traditional sense. Another doctor could take charge of her care when Saha wasn't available, but he didn't like it. "I'll call the hospital."

"I don't need another exam."

He meant that he'd be doing a background check on the new doctor, to verify the worthiness of his credentials, but didn't say so. Emma didn't need to know how thoroughly he investigated everyone who treated her.

"Did he at least give you a refill of your pain meds?"

"I took one of my old ones," she said, touching his arm when he made a face. "They work better."

Garrett sighed. "It's because they're too strong."

It was a traditional analgesic with a significant percentage of an opiate to make it effective.

Emma's skull had been fractured in the accident, so Garrett understood the need for such a strong painkiller in the beginning, but the newer formulations would be better for her in the long term.

But that wasn't good enough. Not when she kept going back to the old pills for real relief.

"What can I do?" he asked, settling down more comfortably on the floor.

"No, here." She patted his normal spot next to her. "Come lie with me for a minute."

He didn't need to be asked twice. He finished undressing, leaving his boxers on before climbing onto the bed next to her, grateful he'd sprung for the deluxe mattress. It barely moved when he climbed next to her. But he was still careful not to jostle her.

To his surprise, she turned toward him, cuddling up against him. His muscles relaxed, some of his tension dissipating. If she could move, her pain wasn't as bad as he thought.

Garrett wrapped an arm around her, pressing his lips to her hair. "I know you don't like the new pills, but perhaps we can try again. Find a better formulation. Perhaps DNA testing might help. That's the new frontier for drugs—finding the ones that work for you on a genetic level and tailoring the dosage to you."

She hummed, tilting her head up a touch to face him. "Can I ask you something?"

"Sure." Emma could ask him anything. "Do you need a kidney? If you think it will help, I've got a spare."

She poked him. "See, it's things like that. You do so much for me, but I'm not sure why you're so hell-bent on changing my meds. I'm not saying that isn't a good idea. It is. But you seem so invested in it."

"Ah." He let his head fall back, tightening up again despite himself. "Caught that, did you?"

Her fingers shifted to rest over his heart. "You're not as subtle as you think you are."

Yeah, she had him there. He hadn't done a good enough job hiding the anxiety and discomfort he felt whenever she took certain pills.

"Did I ever tell you about my ex?"

Emma didn't react, just a small betraying twitch of her stomach muscles that he wouldn't have noticed if he hadn't been holding her.

He didn't call attention to it. He just stroked her until she lay quiescent in his arms.

"No. You never speak of her."

There was a hint of something in her voice. Curiosity, of course, but also caution.

He couldn't reassure her fast enough. "It's not because she's special. I married Ekaterina Hermes in the European equivalent of a drunken Vegas weekend."

Her eyes widened. "For real?"

"Not my proudest moment," he admitted. "I wasn't in love."

"Then how did it happen?"

"Too much booze, a big boat, and a jaded captain who had seen it all. He was happy to take the tip-slash-bribe Ekaterina slipped him to marry us despite the copious amount of alcohol we'd imbibed."

A line came and went between her brows. "It was her idea?"

"I think it was one of her clique actually, although I can't be one hundred percent sure. But Ekaterina adopted it as her own with the enthusiasm only the truly wasted can have."

He could laugh about it now, but it had taken a whole week to come to terms with what he'd done. That was around how long it had taken for him to sober up and figure out that joke ceremony he only half remembered on deck hadn't been a drunken hallucination.

"Surprisingly, Ekaterina stuck to her guns afterward. She started introducing me as her husband to everyone and I… I just sort of went with it."

Emma's brows drew together. "*Why?*"

He hated discussing his marriage, for so many reasons, but Emma deserved an honest answer. "I guess I wasn't bothered by it."

"That's it? You decided to stay married *because you didn't mind?*"

He wrinkled his nose. "I wasn't in a real good place back then. Sardonic amusement seemed a fitting response. Of course, her father found it less than amusing when he found out."

She raised her brows. "He disapproved?"

"On the contrary. He wanted the marriage to stand."

Emma blinked. "What?"

He couldn't blame her for being startled. "Ekaterina's father Andreas was a Greek shipping magnate. He was tired of his spoiled daughter's antics. She shopped, drank, and partied with no thought of the future."

"He was disappointed in her?"

It was so much more complicated than that. "He didn't expect anything from her. He was too busy running his empire to parent, leaving everything child-related to his wife. But Ekaterina's mother was an older version of her. Pretty, shallow, with no aspirations but to do as they pleased."

"Why did her father want you to stay married?"

"I wasn't the Greek millionaire he'd hoped she'd land. My father was small potatoes compared to him, but he had made a name for himself in certain circles. I had gone to business school and done well there. Andreas came to see me as clay to mold. After thinking it over, I decided I was willing to get shaped."

"That's surprising." She poked his pec with her index finger. "Don't take this the wrong way, but you're not exactly what I would call malleable."

He chuckled. "I'm not, but I was ambitious enough to recognize that Andreas was a damn fine businessman, and I could do worse than learn at his feet."

"And what about your wife?"

He jerked reflexively. "You are my one true wife. Ekaterina was a drunken mistake and then an obligation."

Damn, he hadn't even thought about his ex in over a year and now he had to sum up his entire relationship with her.

"Ekaterina didn't love me and I didn't love her. But she was fun, bubbly, and she didn't ask difficult questions. I wasn't intentionally seeking that out, but it ended up working for me."

Emma's lips parted. "How long was it after my accident?"

"Almost eleven months," he said. "Most of which I spent drinking my way across Europe, under the guise of studying different business enterprises so I could broaden my horizons."

"No looking back, right?" she asked evenly.

"No," he whispered. And there was nothing he regretted more.

"Did you enjoy being married?"

"For a little while. A very little while."

She leaned toward him. "What went wrong?"

Chapter Forty-Five

GARRETT

He thought about the end of his first marriage, trying to pinpoint the reason it was over. It was an embarrassment of riches. Just not the good kind.

"So many things," he said. But he stuck to the highlights.

"In addition to the drinking, Ekaterina was fond of drugs. Lots of Ecstasy and other party drugs. I dabbled, but I wasn't that into it."

"Waking up married after too much drink might have soured you," she said philosophically.

"You have no idea," he agreed. "Sobriety had more appeal after that. I cut everything out but alcohol."

"That explains a lot."

"I'm sorry," he said and meant it. "I don't mean for this prejudice to affect you. I hate seeing you in pain and I know that you need the medication."

Emma nestled in his arms, getting more comfortable. "I don't like that it bothers you so much."

"It's my issue, Em, not yours. Please continue to do what is best for you. I want you to take your pills whenever you need them. But I also want to make sure that they are the best option available."

"I get it. You're worried I'll become an addict because you've seen someone go down that path before."

It had been far too late for that. "Ekaterina was already an addict before I met her. But she hid it under a lot of glitz. And what she didn't —well, her wealth absolved a multitude of sins."

"Wow." Emma blinked up at him. "That sounds… messy."

"It's not a pleasant tale," he said, leaning in to smell her lemony shampoo. Talking about this usually made him feel soiled, used, but being with Emma felt cleansing. That was the miracle of her.

With Emma, there were no unspoken expectations. Even with her health issues, she didn't make unreasonable demands. In fact, her independence meant he had to chase her, to ensure she leaned on him when she needed help.

But even that wasn't a drain. Their relationship renewed him.

If he hadn't already married her, he would propose right then and there.

"A few months in, I realized I was not a husband. I was Ekaterina's caretaker, her fixer, and her cleanup crew."

Another woman's sympathy would have grated. But coming from Emma, it was a healing balm. "That must have been disappointing."

"At the time it felt more like…" He stared into the distance. "A suitable punishment."

Emma sat up. "How so?" she asked.

He was never going to live this down. "Well, it may have reinforced some stupid ideas I had at the time on the trustworthiness of women and letting your guard down around them. These are things I do not currently believe. At all."

"*Ah.* I'm sorry." She reached out to stroke his cheek, automatically absolving his past idiot self. He leaned against her like the damn cat staring and judging him from the foot of the bed.

Garrett needed to figure out a way to keep that animal out of their bedroom.

"Don't be sorry. I learned a lot from Andreas. And even though Ekaterina frustrated the hell out of me, I don't hate her or bear her any ill will. But even after rehab and counseling, she showed no signs of maturing. I didn't want to be responsible for her my whole life. Especially after what happened in Mykonos."

Her eyes widened. "That sounds ominous."

"Only a little," he said, downplaying what had been a monumentally triggering episode for him.

"You see, I was working on a project with her father. I didn't officially work for him, but he was pleased with how I'd handled some smaller things and wanted to see if I could play in the big leagues. It was the most complicated negotiation I'd ever taken charge of at that point. There were multiple parties with conflicting interests and huge profit potential."

"So, basically, Garrett's wet dream?"

He laughed so hard she winced because he'd jostled her head too much.

He stopped immediately, stroking her hair. "Oh, I'm sorry, baby!" he said, pitching his voice low to avoid adding to her pain.

She breathed in and out slowly before collapsing on him a little more heavily. "It's okay now. Let's just avoid moving that part of me."

"Deal," he said from behind clenched lips, staying very still.

"I meant big movements," she snickered, poking him. "Just don't laugh that hard or push me off the bed and we'll be fine."

"Okay." It took him a minute, but he finally relaxed, continuing when she pressed him for the story.

"I worked on that pitch for weeks," he said, recalling his earnest enthusiasm. "I honed and refined that plan until I had every angle covered—even some that would never come to pass. Then the night before I was supposed to fly to Athens for the meeting, Ekaterina slipped some Ecstasy into my drink at dinner."

"Oh my God!"

Garrett gripped Emma's arms, holding her still so her shock wouldn't hurt her.

"I can't believe she did that."

Neither could he at the time, but it made perfect sense to him now.

"I had tried Ecstasy once or twice before then, but I didn't understand what was happening to me at the time."

"God, I can only imagine," she said. "One minute you're fine, digesting your souvlaki, and then the next, the room is melting."

"I think that's more a symptom of dropping acid, but close enough. All I knew was that I felt very wrong. I became convinced I had botulism or had been poisoned. I called emergency services and ended up in the hospital, getting my stomach pumped."

Emma's hand gripped his arm, alarm and anger in her expression. "Did you call the police too?"

"No, but it's okay," he soothed. "Because I called the ambulance, I was never in any real danger. It wasn't that large a dose. I just didn't have enough experience with E to tell the difference."

If Emma had been capable of moving, she would have gotten out of bed and marched out to the airport to hunt his ex down. That was how angry she was. "She should *never* have done that to you."

"I agree. It was a violation."

He still felt that way, although the anger and bitterness he felt over it was gone.

"Why the hell did she do it?"

Again, he boiled it down to what he considered the essential take-aways. "She didn't like that I was accepting her father's help or the praise he occasionally bestowed on me afterward. Which was a little two-faced. She happily spent his money and played the dutiful daughter whenever he was around. She just didn't want me to be on good terms with him."

"And she probably wanted her boy toy back," Emma observed. "I bet she didn't want you to have any other ambition but pleasing her."

"Yes and no. I think she wanted it both ways—a doting husband at her beck and call. But also a successful one she could point to with pride. A man in the same mold as her father."

Emma scowled. "Then she shouldn't have sabotaged you."

He no longer agreed. "In retrospect, I'm glad she did. I filed for divorce in the aftermath. And because of what happened, Andreas didn't argue, for which I was grateful. He could have made things difficult but chose not to."

"Really?" she asked, incredulous. "He would have tried to talk you out of it?"

Garrett had thought about that quite a bit. If his daughter hadn't put him in the hospital, Andreas *would* have fought him on the divorce, squeezing him until he caved.

The man had wielded a lot of power when Garrett had none by comparison. And Andreas was used to getting his way.

"Of course he would have," she said, answering her own question. "He was losing his free caretaker."

"Exactly," he agreed. "But it also helped that I didn't ask for money. I was happy enough to escape with what I'd brought into the marriage—and the things I'd learned from him."

Andreas couldn't take those away, although he might have tried had he not felt his daughter had shamed him with her actions.

Emma understood perfectly, as usual. "He knew he didn't have the right. Not after what she did. But how did she take the divorce?"

"She threw a screaming fit. Broke a few priceless antiques."

He'd been caught off guard at the violence of her reaction. Unlike many of the other tantrums he'd witnessed, that last one hadn't been performative. Ekaterina had been genuinely upset.

"I still don't know why she wanted to stay married to me. It wasn't as if she respected me."

Emma ran a hand down his bare chest, tracing the lines and ridges of his six-pack. "Gee, I wonder. What could it have been?"

He laughed while trying not to move, a surprisingly difficult task. "She didn't regret me for long. Believe it or not, there's a long line of handsome wannabe playboys eager to be at the beck and call of a rich heiress."

"I doubt Andreas liked them as much. Do you ever hear from him?"

"We exchange Christmas cards, but that's about it. He's getting on in years, but he remains a powerful figure overseas. He's not the type to dwell on past failures. If he learned anything from the experience, it was that Ekaterina needed help. I told him I wouldn't sue for alimony if he sent her to rehab. It was a ploy, of course, and he saw right through it. But he acknowledged it was time to do something."

"She went?"

"Twice actually, to avoid being cut off. She remarried after the second time, to a fellow patient. Needless to say, it didn't last. But I have no doubt she'll marry again."

"How do you feel about that?"

"Mostly relieved. Also a bit guilty for feeling that way," he admitted. "She was a mess. But I wasn't qualified to help her. Not really. With addiction, you need to decide to help yourself."

"No one could expect more from you than what you did," she said, tightening her hold on him. "Tying yourself to that kind of selfish narcissist would have eaten you up inside. It's good that you broke it off when you did. You would have been surrounded by vice and excess. Little by little, you would have ended up compromising more and more until you were at the bottom of the slippery slope, wondering how the hell you got there."

"I'm afraid I didn't learn my lesson on that score right away," he confessed. "There was a hard partying phase after my divorce too, I'm afraid. But it passed on its own—no matter what Rainer says."

"Okay, I'll bite. What does Rainer say?"

"He thinks I was inspired to clean up my act by his grand romance with George. That it made me realize there was more to life than partying and making money. In truth, it was a phase I'd outgrown before they met. He was just too busy to notice."

She shifted, her soft skin stroking his. Damn, he hoped her headache was gone because she was getting him too hot. He was supposed to be comforting her, damn it.

"I am glad you were done with that phase before I met you," she said. "Especially all the women who were no doubt all over you during that period. I wouldn't have liked the competition."

Wow, she still had no idea.

Garrett pressed his lips to her hair, settling her more comfortably against him.

"Emma, baby," he said, "you have *never* had any competition."

Chapter Forty-Six

EMMA

Emma adjusted the *De Olla* apron and hefted the coffee carrier higher so she could rebalance the weight of everything she was carrying.

Her overnight bag wasn't heavy, but it was awkward with the carrier and the puffed sleeves of her wool coat.

She'd almost put on a trench coat. Thanks to Garrett's penchant for buying her things, she now had three to choose from. But a trench would have been a dead giveaway.

Instead, she'd put on her apron and coat and grabbed a few empty recycled coffee cups that one of her bean suppliers had sent, stuffing them into the carrier to make it look legit.

Juggling everything, she pushed the button for the top floor, hoping the office was deserted. It should have been, but Next Chapter's employees were too dedicated. Especially the boss.

Garrett had called her less than an hour ago to cancel their dinner plans. "I have at least two more hours of work ahead of me," he said, sounding so despondent she'd started packing a bag as soon as he'd hung up.

Her body flashed hot and cold the entire elevator ride. This seemed like a great idea back at the house.

She wasn't an impulsive person. Her condition tended to crush spontaneity. But now that her marriage was real, she felt freer to be a little crazy and act her age.

Who her life partner was certainly helped. Garrett Chapman was a hell of a safety net. Of course, having an impulse and acting on it were two very different things.

Please let his staff be gone. Fulfilling her husband's fantasy was one thing. Doing it knowing she had been recognized by his employees on the way in—or worse, that Fletcher guy—made her cringe.

She got half-lucky. The outer offices of Next Chapter Investments weren't deserted yet, and people did glance up from their computers. But they didn't look beyond the apron peeking out from under her coat or the branded baseball cap she'd used to cover her hair.

She looked like a café employee, making one last delivery on her way out the door.

Emma ran those last few steps into Garrett's office, plastering herself against the door to close it shut. Her breath was ragged and she was hot enough to be perilously close to sweating.

Not sexy. Not sexy at all.

Garrett looked up from his desk and laughed at the sight of her plastered against the door like a fly someone had swatted.

He too was rumpled, wearing only his white button-down shirt, rolled up at the sleeves, the collar open and a little wrinkled.

Damn, he should adopt the scruffy look every day. Garrett was stupid hot with his usual polished perfection worn away. The five o'clock shadow alone was worth the price of admission.

"What are you doing here?" he asked, rising to meet her. "Did you come all this way to bring me a coffee?"

All this way was approximately fifteen minutes *with* traffic.

Emma let the strap of her bag slip off her shoulder so she could take one of the coffee cups and turn it upside down. "Sorry, love. I don't come bearing that particular gift. I brought another."

She looked over her shoulder to make sure no one was watching them through the glass. The coast was clear, but she still flushed so hot it was surprising she didn't spontaneously combust.

"Babe, are you all right?" Garrett started walking toward her but stopped when she held up her hand.

Emma bit her lip and opened her coat wider, showing him his surprise.

The "shirt" she was wearing under her apron was a cleverly folded silk scarf. Emma whipped it away, revealing the next to nothing she was wearing underneath.

Garrett froze, the only movement the rise of his chest as he sucked in air so hard he wheezed.

The tight, breathless feeling she'd been feeling dissipated as she kicked off her shoes and began to walk toward him.

Emma had no plan beyond this point. But her confidence grew when she looked into Garrett's glazed-over eyes. Biting her lip, she pushed on his shoulders until he collapsed back onto his chair.

Shifting the papers he had been working on, she cleared a space before hopping onto it. He was already lunging for her. But her new confidence sparked a newfound playfulness.

Giggling, she pushed Garrett back with her bare foot. He took hold, cradling it in his hands before kissing up the side of her leg.

"I thought we would stay here tonight," she whispered when he got to her knee. "In your office bedroom."

His eyes lit up. "Really?"

"If you'd like."

Catching her up in his arms, he urged her to wrap her legs around his waist. "Oh, I like. I like it a lot."

The world blended in a joyful whirl as he spun her around, turning them several times until her head was spinning.

He wouldn't have done that as little as a month ago. But Garrett paid close attention to her. He'd learned to recognize the signs of a headache coming on and when she was fine. When it was safe to play.

And play he did. He was almost bouncing her in his arms as they entered the bedroom she wouldn't have known was there if he hadn't told her about it.

The hidden bedroom echoed the masculine lines of his office, only more. Here the walls were dark wood, as if someone dismantled his desk and made panels out of it.

"Why is it so dark in here?" she asked as he set her down at the edge of the bed.

His brow puckered. The lights were on after all. But then his confusion cleared. "I only ever intended on staying here when I had to work late or had overextended and needed to crash during the day."

He gestured to the space around them. "The designer optimized this room for sleeping. Kind of like a man cave—since I don't have one at the penthouse."

Emma snickered. "That entire apartment is a man cave."

He bent over her, pushing down the sides of the raincoat, leaving her in the dark green apron and nothing else.

His eyes were like banked coals, but she could see the fire growing in them. "Change anything you want. It's your home too," he whispered.

He'd said something like this before, back when she was still sleeping in another room. But this time was different. His tone made it a vow.

This was essentially an open invitation into every aspect of Garrett Chapman's life.

"I want it all." Her hands moved up his shirtfront, making it clear she didn't mean his home.

With slow and deliberate movements, Garrett pulled the apron over her head, revealing her bare breasts and the skimpy black lace panties she'd left on just so he could remove them.

She liked it when he undressed her.

He made a rough sound in his throat before shifting, the back of his hands grazing her already stiff nipples. The teasing lasted only a moment before his palms cupped her. He squeezed lightly while rotating his hands, creating a delicious friction that made her gasp.

Garrett knelt in front of her, the expression on his face an odd blend of hunger and solemnity. "Everything that is in my power to give you, is already yours."

Emma's hands tightened on his shirtfront, pulling the clean white cloth out of his waistband. "I just want you."

He started to undress, pulling the buttons of his shirt apart.

Emma pressed closer, parting her legs so he stood between them. "Let me."

But she didn't stand to help him with his shirt. Emma remained sitting, going for his belt buckle instead.

Eyes flaring, Garrett stopped moving as she undid the belt and zipper of his pants. She traced his length through his boxers. "You're already so hard."

"Emma, you showed up in a raincoat, apron, and nothing else." He laughed. "I've been rock-hard since you walked in the door."

She fiddled with the waistband of his shorts. "Good, that's very good," she said, smiling wickedly. "Let's see how long that lasts."

"What—"

He stopped talking when she pulled down his shorts, taking his length in her hands.

GARRETT LIKED to be in charge during their sexual encounters, his naturally dominant personality setting the pace. She didn't mind that. On the contrary, she liked that he was the aggressor. But it was satisfying to turn the tables on him this time. Especially when it put a prize like this in her hands.

Emma examined his cock with great curiosity, testing its heft and thickness.

Garrett stood very still as she stroked him experimentally before pressing her lips to the head. It was silky and very hot.

"Hell," he rasped when she flicked her tongue out and took a long slow lick. Emma peeked up to gauge his expression and nearly melted when she saw the raw intensity there. He looked like a man on the edge, his lips parted to take ragged gasps of air.

"You don't have to," he began, breaking off when she took the tip of him in her mouth. "*Holy shit.*"

"Mmm," she hummed in response, loving his reaction. "I like how you taste."

He swore under his breath. "You taste better."

"Debatable." She giggled, sliding her lips down the side of his length, teasing him before taking him deep and sucking.

Groaning, he cupped the back of her head as her mouth slid down his length and back up, using her lips to apply pressure.

"You don't have to," he panted in a voice like gravel. But the tension of his body belied his words.

Emma withdrew, his cock leaving her mouth with a pop. She rubbed the head of it against her breasts, sliding it between them and pushing her breasts together.

Following her lead, he pistoned back and forth.

"That's good," she crooned in praise. "But I want you to fuck my mouth first and then me."

Emma loved the sounds he made when she sucked him off.

Her words were like a match to gasoline. Garrett's nostrils flared and he nodded sharply. Reaching out, he took her hair, wrapping it around his wrist. Using the hold, he guided her, urging her over his cock faster than she'd been going—although not as deep.

She tried to slow him down, so she could urge him a little farther, but he stopped her, telling her without words that he wanted it fast and hard. She compensated by pressing her lips more firmly around him, shaping her mouth to make him moan.

He let her suck him for a few minutes before he pushed her back onto the mattress. "I ca-can't," he panted, crawling over her.

His body covered hers. Emma welcomed the weight of him pressing her down, even as strong hands ripped her panties.

"Don't stop," she pleaded when he paused to push down his pants. "Like this."

She took hold of him, wrapping her fingers around his length and wiggling until he was poised just at her entrance. Then he was forging into her, still dressed but open and bare where he needed to be.

Emma arched up, welcoming his thickness and heat. She clutched at his shirt, urging him to thrust.

Not that he needed the encouragement.

Garrett's control was threadbare. Undulating under him, she tugged him down with his shirt, pressing his bare chest against her breasts and drawing her up until the whole length of him was gripped tight inside her.

The friction of his shirt and pants against her naked skin added another layer of sensation to what was already too much pleasure.

The push and pull of him was addicting. Every drive built that delicious friction higher and higher, until she was crying out, her cunt throbbing around him. The orgasm broke her open even as he pinned her down, rocking and grinding her into heaven.

She felt more than heard his muffled cry. His hot breath fanned her temple and his shaft jerked, sending a spreading warmth that overflowed her, spilling out onto the sheets.

Emma fell back on the mattress, her legs splayed open, muscles lax, incapable of movement.

Garrett groaned and rolled off her. Summoning the energy to turn her head, she checked out the glistening skin of his chest and abs with satisfaction. "I brought some of your ties in my overnight bag."

Twisting, he lay on his side, a little pucker between his brows. "Thanks. But you know I keep part of my wardrobe here, including spare ties."

"Oh, I know." She stretched, enjoying the way his eyes moved over her body. Hungry and reverent at the same time. "I just wanted to make sure you had enough."

His head lifted off the mattress, bemused. "Enough for what?"

The grin she gave him was downright wanton. She turned on her side and ran her toes up his pant leg. "That depends. How strong is your headboard?"

Chapter Forty-Seven

EMMA

Emma dozed on and off throughout the morning, rousing when she felt her hands being bound to the headboard.

"It was your idea," Garrett reminded her, his breath against her ear.

There was plenty of slack in the ties and she was comfortable. But despite the amount of sex they'd had last night, her body warmed at the thought of fulfilling his fantasy to this extent. "It was. But where did the blindfold come from?"

A dense but airy fabric had been slipped over her eyes.

He pushed the blindfold up onto her forehead, his grin that of a man temporarily satiated after last night. But they both knew the hunger was there in the background, like a firecracker ready to be lit.

"It's a sleep mask," he said. "I keep enough clothing and supplies on hand in this room to pack for a weeklong business trip in case I need to go somewhere on short notice."

"You haven't done that since I met you," she said, testing her bonds.

"No, I've cut back."

A pang went through her. "Because of me."

He was afraid of leaving her alone because of her health issues.

"*Hey.* No need to make that face," he said, smoothing the line between her brows with his fingers. "The kind of traveling I'm talking about is not the soothing vacation kind. They're more like a marathon—two or three days of back-to-back meetings. The only nice thing about it was getting to try new restaurants. Or at least that's what I would tell myself afterward, so I wouldn't dwell on the fact I saw nothing of the cities I was in. Just the inside of various boardrooms. And trust me, after a while, all of those look distressingly the same."

Emma tugged her hands out of the soft ropes Garrett had so diligently tied.

She grinned at the look on his face. "I don't know where you learned to tie knots, but babe, you suck."

He groaned and buried his face in her neck, his muffled laughter sending puffs of hot air into her hair.

She put her hands on either side of his face, nudging until he raised his head. They shifted until they were lying side by side.

"I don't want to hold you back."

His eyes flared and he inched closer. "That's what you think?"

"If you need to leave town for work, you should go. I don't want to be the reason you miss out on some big deal or negotiation."

"I won't because all the big negotiations are done for the time being."

"Really?" she asked, her lower lip jutting out. The urge to bite it was irresistible so he promptly did.

"I do mean it," he said when he'd released the luscious treat. "There's still work to do, of course, that requires travel but nothing so sensitive that I need to handle it in person. I always planned on delegating the busy work to my employees. I've started doing just that."

He shifted closer, stroking the down on the side of her cheek. "However, this does bring up a good point. How would you feel about taking trips here and there—once you're feeling up to it? If your doctor clears it."

"That would be nice…" She trailed off, an idea occurring to her.

He stroked her hair. "What is it?"

"I was thinking, maybe we could invite my family to join us somewhere the way you do with your aunt?" she suggested. "Not at the same time, of course."

"No, never at the same time," he agreed with a widening of his eyes. "But of course, we can invite them somewhere nice. Hell, they can come here. I can charter a jet for them. They could be here tomorrow."

She hugged him. "You are the sweetest man in the world, you know that, right? But Stella's starting kindergarten soon and probably shouldn't skip if we can help it."

"I had no idea she was that big."

Garrett had caught quick glimpses of her sister a few times when he'd come into the room as she video-chatted with her baby sister, but Emma hadn't had them speak to each other yet.

She should introduce them soon. Especially as it appeared they were going to be staying married.

"Yes, she's growing up so fast." Downcast, she folded her hands.

"Don't kids usually turn five before the start of kindergarten?" he asked.

"Colorado has a later cutoff date than California—it's October there. She's growing up too fast for me. I'm sorry I'm missing so much of it. But coming here was a chance to start over without all the accident baggage. I felt bad leaving Stella, of course, but I could only help so much with her. If I tried to babysit and got a headache… well, I didn't want her to take care of me, you know."

Because that had happened more than once, and it had been *awful*.

"You had to focus on your health first. I'm sure your mother understands that."

That much was true. "Mariana is the one who encouraged me to move. She wanted me to have my own life. But she does appreciate the money I've been sending." She'd sent all of her wages from the part-time work and half of her weekly allowance.

"Does she know about the college fund yet?"

"What college fund?"

"I started one for your sister. Your mother doesn't have to worry about her schooling anymore."

Emma's mouth dropped open as he began to relate the particulars.

Her sister had the Rolls Royce of college funds. Stella could go to any school in the world with the account he'd set up for her.

The room was still spinning. "Mom is going to go ballistic."

He settled against the pillow more deeply. "Won't she be relieved knowing it's taken care of? I *am* family now."

Emma wrinkled her nose. "Uh… she still thinks ours is a marriage of convenience, that we did it for the insurance."

A line appeared between his brows. "You haven't told her that it's real now?"

She sighed. "That seemed like one of those things you should do in person."

"*Okay*," he said slowly. "When is the next school break?"

"Thanksgiving."

He frowned. "That's more than two months away."

Garrett paused and she knew what he was going to say. Because she couldn't deal with going back to Verdant Falls. Except her mother didn't live in Verdant Falls anymore. Mariana had moved one town over. It had been closer to the hospital where Emma had convalesced.

"Perhaps they can come sooner. Colorado isn't far. A long weekend would be a good start."

"If my mother's work schedule allows."

"Of course." He stroked down her arms. "So… is this all right?"

"Leaving me tied up in your secret bedroom so you can come and take your pleasure between meetings? Is that what you mean?"

Garrett nodded, a very innocent expression on his face. "Yes, please."

Emma laughed and held up her wrists. "Then you better practice those knots."

"Googling it now," he said, taking out his phone. "Do you need to go to the restroom first? Need some food?"

"No." She'd used the facilities in the predawn hours while he was still sleeping. It had been easy. Because his knots did suck. "But I am starving," she added.

"Of course you are. I'll order us some breakfast."

Emma turned very hot for another reason. "From *De Olla*?"

"Err… yes. Unless you want something else?"

"Well, I could go for a Danish for breakfast. And the *café de olla* of course. It's just funny. I feel like I'm playing hooky *at* work. Except I'm doing it naked, playing harem girl for the boss' pleasure."

Garrett leaned over her, pressing kisses down her neck. "This is usually where I vehemently deny being your boss in any way, shape, or form, but I'm half tempted to go get that *De Olla* apron. I'd love to fuck you in it. The apron and nothing else."

"No," she squealed as he reached a particularly sensitive spot. "I could never wear it at work again after. I'd have to ask Hector for another, and then he'd ask me what happened to the first one."

She twisted her head to press her face against her arm, squirming.

"I'll get you another one. I'll get you ten."

Emma giggled. "Not a *De Olla* one. Any other kind." Any apron she wore would be ruined, just like the suit he had been wearing last night.

"Okay," he agreed a little too readily. "I will have one delivered before lunch, so be ready," he said, punctuating his words with a light spank before leaving the room to order breakfast.

She waited for the click, signaling the door had closed before scooting up on the bed, trying to strike a pose that was both comfortable and enticing.

After all, she wanted her husband to enjoy the view.

Chapter Forty-Eight

EMMA

She fell back against the sheets, out of breath with the anonymous apron tangled around her neck. Emma felt a tug and lifted her pleasure-drugged head so Garrett could pull it off.

He withdrew from her body as he backed away. "I'm going to leave you like this now, my cum still flowing from your body while I shower. I have twenty minutes before my next meeting. Is that okay with you?"

"Mm-hmm," she murmured. "Fix my mask."

He adjusted the eye-covering as she made herself comfortable, raising one leg and leaning it against one of the pillows so that it lay open, leaving her pussy wet and exposed.

Harsh breathing filled the room. "You're going to be late," she reminded him.

"Yeah," he rasped. "Until later."

Feeling very smug and not a little sore, she lay back, luxuriating in the softness of the bed as the shower started. She was still shifting around, making herself comfortable while he dressed. He groaned more than once as she stretched on the bed.

Why was it you could feel when someone's eyes were on you? Garrett's gaze was almost physical. She could almost feel it, a glancing touch skating over her breasts and thighs.

"Remind me why I thought this was a good idea," he said, frustrated as hell. He ran out of the room, the door closing firmly behind him.

Emma spent the whole day naked, an experience both bizarre and decadent.

She lazed about on the bed, undoing the very loose knot of her bindings once or twice to use the facilities and to eat lunch with him when he brought it.

Other times he would come in and he would touch and stroke, fucking her if he had enough time between meetings and other important tasks.

It must have been late afternoon when he came in again, rousing her from a light sleep. But this time he didn't move toward the bed.

She was naked, her nipples stiff despite the fact Garrett had turned up the temperature so she'd be comfortable. Her legs were open, exposed to him, the proof of their earlier lovemaking sticking to her skin, just like he wanted.

"Garrett?" she asked, her voice groggy with sleep.

The air moved. It was followed by the sound of the door closing.

Confused, she turned her head and pressed against her arm to nudge the mask up. The room was empty.

Emma lay back and sighed, figuring Garrett must not have heard her, his mind on his work. It was a busy day for him. He'd been popping in and out, watching without waking her to savor the picture she made. But she didn't mind. That was why she was here, to give him what he needed on his terms.

It was her gift to him.

He didn't return until late afternoon with elaborately prepared sushi rolls for an early dinner.

Emma was starving but she let Garrett feed her one piece at a time while her hands remained bound. When they were done, she stretched out in silent invitation, and he stripped down and fucked her one more time before cleaning up and changing for one final meeting.

Feeling pleasantly sore and lethargic, she showered, letting the hot water soothe her overused muscles. Some of their sex had been rough and she'd been bound for a lot of it, but for the most part, Garrett had been very careful with her.

Revived by the shower, she quickly dried off and dressed. She gathered her things and put them back in her overnight bag before settling down to wait for Garrett.

After a while, she decided waiting in the bedroom was counterproductive to leaving the building, so she made her way to the front part of the office.

Garrett's shiny sleek desktop was password protected, so she settled on the couch with her phone, streaming a movie on the tiny screen.

Look at you, you fancy bitch.

As little as three months ago, the phone screen would have been huge to her. More than adequate to watch a movie. Now, thanks to Garrett's many flatscreens, it was too small.

Soon you'll be putting on airs. Emma had read that phrase in a book and it had stuck in her head. It was too late, she thought, nestling deeper on the couch.

She was already a fancy bitch.

"Hey."

Emma looked up. Fletcher was standing at the threshold, holding a manila folder in front of him like a shield.

"Oh, hi," she said, putting her legs down and sitting up straight.

"I was looking for Garrett."

"I thought he was with you," she said.

"He was until ten minutes ago."

She lifted a shoulder. "I'm sure he'll be here soon."

Emma went back to her movie, expecting him to leave, but he didn't. After a minute she looked up and he was watching her with this weird considering expression on his face.

"I'm sorry, is there something I could help you with?"

"No." Fletcher shook his head. "I was just thinking. Life is…"

"Yeah?" she prompted when he trailed off.

"I was just thinking. Life is so weird." He scratched his thinning hair. "You know, the way things turn out."

Fletcher gestured to her as if she hadn't figured out who he was talking about.

"Seeing you like this," he continued. "Here waiting for Garrett like a… a…"

"A wife?" she asked.

"Yeah!" Fletcher's answering laugh sounded forced.

Emma pressed her lips together, the unpleasant realization that she'd been living in a bubble hitting her just as it burst.

Most of Garrett's friends were nice and supportive. They liked seeing him with someone. Except for Fletcher. He was from their hometown.

She didn't know what he saw when he looked at her, but she didn't like it.

Emma was about to ask what his problem was, but Fletcher was feeling chatty and was ready to tell her.

"It's just that you and Garrett were always at each other's throats." Fletcher leaned against the doorjamb with exaggerated casualness. "Seeing you this way, so domestic. I mean you're his *wife* now. It takes some getting used to. And to think it would never have happened without the accident."

Emma must not have looked as offended as she felt because he didn't run away like he should have.

"Because somehow I started working here?" she asked.

"No. Well, yes, but also no." Fletcher pushed away from the door. "I just meant you and Garrett, getting together."

"Because we were enemies," she said. Or because she had been a poor barista and Garrett was a billionaire?

"I guess that part isn't so surprising," he mused. "In retrospect, it's kind of obvious—all that bickering masking some sexual tension. At least on Garrett's part. Am I right? Without the accident, none of this would have happened."

Her blood iced over. "Actually, without the accident, we would have been together much longer."

Fletcher raised a skeptical brow. "You think so?"

Speaking in a normal tone took serious effort. "I take it you don't?"

"Well… no." He lifted his hands when she scowled. "I mean, it's a nice thought, but Emma, you don't know the way you were. So ambitious and stuff."

She was definitely starting to dislike this man. "And ambition is wrong?"

His head drew back. "Hey, no need to get offended. It's not a criticism at all. It's just ironic. Without the accident, you would be on Wall Street right now, kicking ass and taking names."

He rolled his shoulders before his expression softened. "Instead, you're here, happily married."

"*Because* of the accident?" she repeated. The back of her neck was so tight she was starting to get nauseous.

Fletcher had the grace to wince. "I just mean that if it wasn't for the accident, the two of you would never work. It would have been like Garrett marrying himself. This way he gets to spoil you and never has to worry you'll take off for the greener pastures of some high-powered job. It's like his wet dream come true."

She didn't need his significant glance at the door leading to the bedroom to get what he was ever so subtly implying.

Emma was Garrett's fuck toy, the former enemy who had, through some twist of fate, become his trophy wife. And not a very shiny one at that.

She was going to be sick. Hell, she had even served herself up to him at his office, his place of business.

"It's a good thing," Fletcher insisted. "The accident was a blessing in disguise. Garrett gets the wife he's always wanted. And you—it's like you won the lottery. You don't ever have to work. You just have to make him happy. And that's easy for you because you're the one he has been pining for. He loves you. Like *really* loves you."

Emma blinked, taken aback by his sudden intensity.

She stared at him, half in disbelief that he'd said all this shit to her, but also not surprised. Because it made sense. Not about the accident being a blessing. That was bullshit.

But what if she and Garrett did have a better shot with her this way? Emma, the broken doll, a cipher of her former self?

She was still reeling when Garrett came back. He and Fletcher spoke for a few minutes while she sat in protective numbness, waiting for him to be done with his important business.

Like a good little wife.

Chapter Forty-Nine

EMMA

She handed a pair of coffee frappes to the waiting teens with a brittle smile fixed on her face.

Emma had been fine covering the first part of Bethany's shift at the waterfront kiosk when the other barista had called her late this morning.

Garrett had gone off to work quite early and she hadn't been able to go back to sleep anyway, so she'd spent the early hours going over the papers she needed to apply to college.

Emma was *not* going to be a trophy wife. Yeah, she was a hot piece of ass, but she also had a brain. A broken one, but it still worked for the new stuff. Most of the time.

She was going to make the most of it. Finding the will to try was half the battle, wasn't it?

But Emma didn't kid herself. It was going to be a long war.

After a long deliberation, she had opted not to use her existing college credits or pre-accident coursework. Whatever degree she earned now had to be independent of that.

The decision had been a difficult one. She'd been so close to graduating. But Emma didn't remember anything from her old classes. Using the existing credits would have been dishonest. Moreover, she could very well be crippling herself, building a new career on knowledge and experiences she no longer had.

She didn't relish the idea of putting in another four years to get back to the same spot she'd been in before the accident. Besides, weren't some of the most successful businesspeople college dropouts?

But she wasn't comfortable enough to go without some sort of knowledge base. Which was why she was now looking at two-year associate degrees at all the local colleges. Perhaps marketing or business administration. She would rebuild her foundation in a useful and productive way while trying to decide what to do with the rest of her life.

However, trying to choose exactly what programs to apply to filled her with anxiety. There were so many choices. Time was precious. She knew that better than anyone. Emma couldn't afford to waste any of it.

The whole mess was giving her a headache. The cold wind coming through the kiosk service window didn't help either. It had given her an earache that made the pain in her head worse.

By the time Bethany arrived to cover the rest of her shift, Emma's head was splitting. Unable to do much else, she sat on the bucket, waiting for the worst to pass so she could head home.

"You look like death warmed over," Bethany said with her usual charm. "Can't you take something?"

"I already did." Emma had finally run out of her old pain medication a few days ago and started the new pills, taking one a few days ago and another this morning.

Bleary-eyed and slightly nauseated, she checked the clock above the service window. It was half an hour too early, but she couldn't afford to wait any longer if she was going to walk home.

"This stuff just doesn't work as well as the old prescription," she muttered.

Bethany shrugged. "Take two."

Emma must have looked like crap because the other woman voluntarily fetched her a cup of water.

"Thanks," she said, fishing out the prescription bottle from her pocket. "I just might."

GARRETT HANDED his edits of the latest contract of the Montevalle Resorts deal to the PA he'd just hired.

"Get this to legal and have them look over the changes. If they approve it, have them send it out."

The young man nodded, taking the folder and hustling out of the room.

When his former assistant had told him they weren't coming back, Garrett hadn't attempted to fill the position despite being slammed with work.

Instead, his brain had spun a little fantasy of Emma coming to work for him. She could help him in the office and learn the ins and outs of business at his side. He thought it might be a good way for her to dip her toes in the pool, before taking off and forging her own path.

Thank God Rainer had talked him out of that. It would have been a disaster, of course. He wouldn't have been able to keep his hands off her during work hours.

It was one thing to take her to the back bedroom when no one else knew she was here. But it would be quite another to do it if she was a regular employee.

It didn't matter that everyone knew she was his wife now. That just meant they'd be scrutinized more closely. The staff would be on the lookout for shenanigans. They'd take note when Emma was flushed or when a lock of hair was out of place, and they would correctly assume the two of them had been messing around during work hours.

No, his idea had been a bad one. He couldn't expose Emma to that kind of gossip and possible ridicule. She was his wife. He wanted his staff to treat her with respect. He would not have them snickering at her behind their backs because he couldn't keep it in his pants.

It was enough that she had indulged his secret love slave fantasy last week.

Garrett turned his head, looking at the door of the office bedroom as the memories flashed through his mind. But he ruthlessly shut them down.

Any longer and he would have texted her to come over again after everyone went home.

He had gone full sex fiend in that bedroom and would do it again if given the chance. When it came to Emma, Garrett was a glutton. He had to pace himself or she'd start to feel suffocated.

He'd also asked too much of her. Emma had been sore the day after spending the night at the office, enough that he'd noticed a tiny hitch in her step when she walked.

She'd also been suspiciously quiet. Had she been too embarrassed to tell him he was an animal?

No, Emma wasn't shy about calling him on his bullshit. If he'd gone too far, he would have gotten an earful. Still, a little moderation and a heck of a lot more discretion were in order.

Of course, Emma likely had her own opinions on the matter. She didn't hide her desire for him and was an enthusiastic participant every time they had sex. He just needed to make sure that she was comfortable yanking on the reins when his lecherous ass went off the rails.

He was going a little crazy, making up for lost time.

Shaking his head, he made a mental note to talk to Em as soon as he got home. It took him a good ten minutes, but he managed to put it out of his mind and got another couple hours of work done.

He was looking forward to a quiet night at home when Bethany called, frantic and swearing like a sailor. "Emma is fucked up!"

Chapter Fifty

GARRETT

Adrenaline flooded Garrett as he jumped the curb, illegally parking the Range Rover next to the construction site entrance where Bethany was waiting.

The barista was standing next to a heavily muscled construction worker with more tattoos and piercings than her.

"Hey!" she yelled, waving him over.

Garrett was already freaked out, but the look of panic on Bethany's face was a punch to the gut. "Where is she?"

"In there." The man jerked his thumb behind him.

The burly construction worker didn't look any calmer than Bethany, but Garrett wasn't given time to process that because the guy turned on his heel and started running.

He rushed past the chain-link fence securing the site, weaving around tractors and stacks of construction material faster than any man his size had any right to be.

Garrett and Bethany sped after him.

"What the hell happened?" he yelled as they went, thankful the Auric guys insisted on adding cardio to their workout regimen.

Bethany hadn't been clear on the phone. She just said that Emma had gotten dizzy and confused and had wandered onto a construction site.

"She had a headache and took some medicine. It seemed like a bad one so I told her she should take one more because she looked like hell. After she took it, she started babbling but nothing made sense. It was English but all jumbled and weird."

Shit. "How did she end up here?" he asked as they slowed to dodge around a lumber pile.

"I went to look for my phone to call an ambulance, but she jumped up and left. I swear she only had a twenty-second head start, but by the time I got out of the booth, she wasn't in sight. Then I saw her across the street, in front of these gates."

He spun his head, checking the crowded site. At least ten guys were milling around near the edge of a big pit. "Where the hell is she?"

The big construction worker they had followed grabbed him and pointed. "There!"

Garrett followed the line of his arm, confused. The only thing in that direction was a gaping hole.

And that's where she was, standing on a rickety-looking grill stretched over an unfinished basement. She was awake and looking around, but it was clear she either didn't see or understand her surroundings. Her expression was terrifyingly blank.

"*Fuck*!" he swore. "Em—"

Bethany elbowed him. "Not so loud. She's confused and high from the pain meds. The construction guys already tried to grab her. She backs away whenever anyone gets close—"

He raised a hand and nodded, ice sheathing his veins. "Okay, I get it," he breathed.

Emma wasn't standing in the middle of the small grill. She was on the edge. If she took more than one step back, she'd fall into the pit to the concrete basement floor. It must have been the start of the subbasement because it was a two-story drop, not one.

"We had stopped construction for a few weeks because of a lawsuit," the construction worker whispered, also worried about startling Emma.

"We just resumed yesterday and started pulling the covers off the basement before installing the rebar for the next floor. She must have come in after one of the trucks. No one noticed her until she was already over the pit. Her friend here chased her, but she was too far ahead and now she's there," he added, panic on his rough features.

"Did you call the fire department?" They needed ladders and ropes, and God knows what else.

"My super is on the phone with emergency services to see if they can bring one of the inflatable things they have people jump into. You got here first."

The Harbor Police must be on their way now. This was their jurisdiction. But Emma's position was so precarious. Even if they made no noise, they still had to climb ladders to get down into the subbasement.

All the activity might be enough to scare her. Emma could fall at any second.

"I am going to talk to her," he said, taking several steps to the right where the thickest metal beam began.

The grill was partially suspended over it. Emma was about twenty yards away.

"Emma," he said in a normal voice. "Baby, it's Garrett, your husband. Can you look at me? I need to ask you something. It's real important."

Ever so slowly Emma lifted her head. Even from this distance, he could see the glazed look in her eyes.

"Does your head still hurt? Don't nod," he added in case the motion jarred her. "Just say yes or no."

She didn't reply. Garrett swallowed and stepped onto the beam. "Never mind, baby. Stay there. I don't want you to move. I'm going to come to you."

"*Wait,*" Bethany hissed. She turned to the construction worker. "Do you have some rope?"

The construction worker didn't answer. Just turned and ran to a nearby truck. He returned holding a length of yellow plastic rope. Garrett took a few precious seconds to tie it around his waist, tossing the other end to the man so they could secure it.

He began to walk along the beam, one heart-stopping step at a time.

"You were right about the headache medicine by the way," he said in that same even tone, his movements slow but steady. "The new stuff is crap. You were better off with the old meds. But don't worry, I'm getting used to being wrong all the time. That's what marriage is, right? The wife is usually right. You more than most."

He was a little over halfway when Emma's head jerked.

The construction site got so quiet he could hear the construction crew sucking in a collective breath, the sounds of the traffic in the surrounding streets dimming.

"Married?" Emma asked in a slurred voice. She was looking at him now, the puzzled expression ripping him to shreds.

Garrett froze, his heart flying out of his chest, doing a nosedive to the pit. The medication had messed with her so badly that she'd lost her memory again.

Everything they'd built in the last two months was gone. He'd been erased. Again.

Garrett broke out into a cold sweat. "Yeah, baby. I'm your husband. You're my wife. We live just a few blocks from here. We should go there now."

He racked his brain, wondering what the hell he could tell her, what would be enticing enough to make her stay put. "We need to feed Meowmus Maximus. He's our cat."

Her eyes narrowed, suspicion darkening her features. "You don't like cats because your aunt's Persian used to hide under the couch and wait for you to pass him on the way to the bathroom. He would jump out and scratch you up."

Garrett damn near fell off the beam.

Emma might not remember that they were married, but she remembered that bitch, Duchess. He hadn't mentioned that demon beast once since they'd been married. No, this was a story he'd shared with her years ago.

Emma remembered something from *before* the accident.

He willed his heart to stop racing. "Yeah, that cat was a little shit.

But Meowmus isn't quite that bad. He's little more than a kitten. Just a baby. We're still training him."

"To do what?"

Emma's voice was clearer now. He risked a quick look at her face, continuing to inch along the beam. She hadn't snapped out of it but her eyes were less clouded.

"The usual. Not to scratch the furniture. Or the legs of my suit pants. He likes to go into my closet and pull them down off the hangers so he can make himself a nest."

Emma huffed, shifting her weight.

"Don't move," he begged. "I'm almost there."

She took an audible breath, frowning. The fogginess was retreating. It was good news, but Garrett was worried she'd come to and be surprised enough to lose her balance. He had to get to her before she realized where she was.

Four more yards. "Since we're out now, what do you want for dinner?"

Her head drew back. "Dinner?"

Ignoring the drop below them, Garrett reached out, tugging his wife into his arms. He pressed her against him and shuddered. "Please don't move," he breathed into her hair.

In the background, he could hear a mixture of cheering and applause. And sirens.

"Garrett, I can't breathe."

The words were muffled because her face was pressed to his chest.

He gave her a bit of space so she wouldn't smother. "Baby, I'm going to pick you up now. I want you to wrap your legs around me, okay? Then I'm going to carry us back the way I came."

Garrett tested the grill under her feet, relieved it seemed solid enough to bear his weight many times over. He kept holding her as he picked her up, urging her legs up and around his waist.

"I did marry you," she mumbled into his shoulder as he hefted her aloft, adjusting her weight more securely.

At least she didn't phrase it as a question. That was some comfort.

"Yes, you did."

Keeping a tight grip, he turned with small mincing steps. Ahead of him, the crowd was standing quietly, except for Bethany who was gesticulating wildly.

"C'mon," Bethany mouthed, hopping up and down.

Ignoring her, Garrett picked a spot above her head—a sign on a concrete wall—to focus on. Keeping his breath shallow so he wouldn't jostle Emma, he began the careful trek back.

His wife's warm breath puffed through his shirt. "You tricked me into marrying you."

"Uh, yeah. I suppose I did," he admitted. "But you're pretty happy about it now."

There was a very long pause. Too long.

"I guess that's true," she finally said.

Damn it. She had to stop yanking his heart out of his chest and then putting it back while he was walking over a two-story deep pit.

"I love you more than anything," he said, cradling her head to his chest. "Do you believe me?"

She hesitated, raising her head a touch. "Yeah."

"Good. Please keep that in mind for the foreseeable future."

They reached the edge of the pit. "Why?"

Garrett took two more steps, reaching terra firma, and kept going straight to the ambulance that had arrived in the interim. "Because I'm tying you to our bed for the next month."

There was the softest of huffs. Laughter. "Been there, done that."

It was a good thing he was on solid ground because the relief he felt was enough to weaken his knees. She remembered him.

Dear God, thank you.

When a uniformed firefighter stretched out to take her from him, Garrett didn't let them.

Emma blinked as Dr. Saha's replacement shone his penlight into her eyes.

"And you don't remember anything after taking your pills? Nothing about the construction site or why you went there?" Dr. Desjardin asked, putting the light away and smiling placidly at her.

She shook her head. It didn't hurt anymore, although she did still feel a bit fuzzy as if someone had replaced her gray matter with cotton wool.

"Just my head hurting and then having a weird conversation with Garrett."

One that had taken place on a rickety metal rail suspended over a twenty-foot-deep hole. She was glad her brain couldn't supply a clear picture of that.

"I heard your boyfriend was very heroic." Dr. Desjardin twisted a little, casting that benevolent smile at the man hovering over his shoulder.

Garrett glowered back. "I'm her husband, not her boyfriend."

The doctor's smile dimmed a touch. He turned back to her with a noticeably less effusive bedside manner. "Of course. And you're not feeling any numbness anywhere? Not your toes, fingers?"

"No. Only my head is fuzzy. Like I'm hungover."

"That's to be expected under the circumstances. But don't worry. It will pass quickly."

The doctor continued to check her reflexes and other responses.

"Why the hell is that expected?"

Garrett didn't look or sound angry, but she recognized that flat expression on his face. This is the hard-ass CEO, she thought.

"I thought these new pain meds were supposed to have fewer side effects than the previous ones," he added, his tone accusatory.

"They are," the doctor replied, pretending to be unbothered by the billionaire about to bite his head off. "But complications can arise when they aren't taken as directed. Didn't Dr. Saha or the pharmacist who filled the prescription explain the need to transition to them slowly?"

Emma frowned, trying to remember if either of those people had said that about the pills. "I don't think so. But it could have been in the papers that came with them."

All her medication came with FAQs and disclaimers, but she rarely took the time to go through them beyond a cursory glance.

She'd been on the same meds so long there hadn't been a need.

Dr. Desjardin frowned. "They should have explained that in person when they prescribed them. The abrupt transition between medication types can lead to episodes like this."

"But I had taken them at least once before." She looked over at Garrett, apologizing with her eyes. "I didn't think it was that big a deal."

"I didn't either," he said, his face grim. "Dr. Saha didn't mention it as far as I know. But I had one of the PAs that works for my company pick up the medication. If the pharmacist had any instructions, they didn't pass them on."

Uh-oh. Emma had a feeling that PA was about to find themselves in the crosshairs.

"It's more likely the pharmacist didn't say anything," she said, willing it to be true. For the poor assistant's sake.

He didn't reply. "Do we need to change her meds back to the old ones?" he asked the doctor, still glowering.

Dr. Desjardin shook his head. "No, I don't think that's wise. Going back and forth is what led to this. Emma should be fine on the new meds provided you step back on the dosage."

He explained they should buy a pill cutter to slice the tablet into fourths, taking one piece to start and then steadily increasing the dosage until her body was habituated to the new medication.

He continued to offer other advice, being particularly thorough in an obvious effort to thwart any future accusations of malpractice.

She couldn't blame him. Garrett's suit screamed, 'I have expensive lawyers.'

After they were done, he called the car service so he could sit with her in the back seat.

Emma was glad he did, tucking her under his arm to cuddle.

"You might have to carry me upstairs," she warned. "Every limb feels like it gained a hundred pounds."

Garrett pressed his lips to her hairline. "Done," he mumbled, wrapping his arm tighter around her. "What do you think of Desjardin?"

"He seems okay." She tipped her head back to look at him. "Why do you ask?"

"I don't like him."

"The medication thing isn't his fault. Dr. Saha might have told me about building up to the dose and I forgot. Or maybe it would have happened anyway, even if I had done it the right way."

"Today took ten years off my life," he growled. "But that's not what I'm talking about."

Emma didn't hear anything after the first part. It made her stomach hurt. "I'm sorry," she whispered.

His hand reached up to cup the back of her neck. He squeezed lightly, his touch reassuring. "*Hey.* It wasn't your fault. Never think I blame you. I'm simply reacting to what might have happened. I almost lost you today and I'm deflecting by focusing on the doctor and his inappropriate behavior."

His what now? "What are you talking about?"

"The good doctor was clearly upset to learn that you're married."

He rubbed his fingers on her neck again, the touch distinctly possessive this time.

She would have laughed if she had the energy. "That's crazy. He didn't say anything like that."

"I saw his reaction. That was disappointment."

"You were standing behind him!"

He sniffed. "I know what I know."

His jealousy was adorable. "Trust me, a woman *knows* when a man is interested in her—even one with brain damage. To him, I'm an interesting case. Traumatic memory loss like mine isn't that common. He doesn't want me. Not like that."

Garrett sniffed. "What he wants from you is a HIPPA violation."

Emma snickered. "I think you're projecting. I also don't think you know what a HIPPA violation is."

"Of course, I'm projecting. Doesn't mean I'm wrong."

Emma let her weight rest against his broad chest. "I'm sorry."

He squeezed her to him. "Don't be. The only person at fault is me. I shouldn't have been so eager to mess with your medication. From now on I'll take much better care of you."

His voice rang with self-recrimination.

Okay, she had to stop this before he spiraled. "I did some research after the fact. The new medication *is* supposed to be better. I wouldn't have taken it if it wasn't."

He was already shaking his head. She put her hand on his chest, over his heart. "You want what's best for me. And I know I don't always act like it, but I want that too. I got complacent with all my pills. I also stopped doing the exercises the physical therapist prescribed before I met you too. But I'm going to get back on track. I'll start working out and taking these new and improved meds."

"I shouldn't have insisted."

"They *do* have fewer side effects. Not just for me, but for a baby."
Garrett jerked.

"Or should I say developing fetus?" Emma bit her lip. "Dr. Saha mentioned that you had concerns about that when she first prescribed them. Which just goes to show how far ahead you were planning."

"No, I wasn't." He stopped and scowled—at himself. "All right, maybe I was. But it was too soon to consider making a baby. That hasn't changed. We need to focus on your recovery. There isn't room for anything else."

"So, you weren't planning on knocking me up?" she joked, but it was weak.

"Not yet. Someday. But not yet."

She looked down at her lap. "It *is* too soon. But it won't be always. If we want to try for a baby in the future, I can stop taking the meds."

"*No.*" He reached over, taking her hand at the wrist and positioning it over his heart.

"My headaches are less frequent now," she pointed out. "In a couple of years, I might be able to manage without medication."

"I would never ask that of you. I can't stand seeing you in pain."

He took a deep breath as if bracing himself. "As for whether your pills are okay during pregnancy, examining every contingency is what I do. It's a personality flaw I've managed to turn to my advantage in my work, but when it comes to our relationship… I don't want it to cause friction."

She put her fingers on his. "Garrett, it's okay. I've come to terms with having a billionaire stalker."

He stared at her a second before bursting into loud, hoarse laughter.

"I love you," he said, wiping the corner of his eye.

She reached up to caress his cheek. "Good. Carry on."

That earned her another deep belly laugh. Then he hauled her into his lap and kissed her.

She put her arms around his neck. "You know we have been sitting in the parking garage for the last five minutes."

"I do." He reached out and opened the door. "And now I'm going to carry you upstairs."

"I was kidding." Climbing off him, she got out of the car. "The last thing we need is for you to throw your back out."

Garrett kicked the door closed with a neat little maneuver and swept her up in his arms. "As if that's a possibility."

"Compromise!" she squealed as he swung them toward the elevator. "Put me down inside the cab."

His very put-upon sigh was his only answer. But he did as she asked.

Chapter Fifty-Two

GARRETT

He leaned forward to hand Emma her dinner plate. "How do you feel?"

His lovely wife picked up a fork and mimed stabbing him with it. "You have to stop asking me that. I'm *fine*."

That was mostly true. Several days had passed since the incident at the construction site. Emma had done as Dr. Desjardin directed, taking small doses of her pain pills to condition her body to the new medication. There hadn't been a repeat of the fugue state that had nearly ended her life.

According to the doctor, that meant she was in the clear now, but he advised keeping her close for the next few weeks.

It was a prescription Garrett could easily follow. He took some time off work and spent the next few days driving his wife insane by following her around the apartment, making sure she didn't trip, and pressing food on her every other minute.

Fortunately for him, Emma was in the mood to humor him. For a while. But now they'd officially entered the stabby utensil phase.

"I know." He sighed, looking her up and down. "And I apologize. I know I've been…"

"An overbearing butthead?"

"I was going to say prison warden."

"Yeah, that too."

She pointed the fork at him and wagged her eyebrows. "Don't get me wrong, I enjoyed playing naughty prisoner last night. But I can't have you busting in on me in the bathroom anymore."

He smacked his lips. "Hey, you were taking too long in that bath. And I thought you liked it when I climbed into the tub with you."

"You're right. That was fun," she acknowledged. "But you've got to ease up a little. On a totally unrelated note, when are you going back to work?"

He grinned at her. "I was thinking of something else when I asked about your health. Do you feel up to a trip?"

"Where to?"

"Verdant Falls."

Her lips parted. That was not the answer she had been expecting.

"Or rather just outside it—your mom lives in the next town over, right?"

Bemused, she nodded.

"And your little sister's birthday is coming up?"

Her face softened. "Yes. Stella's going to be five. I, uh, was going to wait till they came here to have a big blowout celebration."

"I know." Emma had been making plans for sightseeing over Thanksgiving break, including trips to the zoo and Sea World.

"We can still do that. But we can also go this weekend for her actual birthday."

Emma leaned back in her chair, chewing on her lower lip.

Garrett leaned forward, covering her hand with his. He understood her reticence only too well. "I know home is not your favorite place. You're far more vulnerable there. It's close enough to our hometown that anyone we see could be someone from your past and not knowing who they were to you must be deeply unnerving. But I'm going to be with you the whole time. Friend or foe, *I'll* know them and will be more than happy to run interference."

He watched the play of emotions on her face. Emma was so expressive. He could never take her to Vegas. She would be a terrible poker player.

"Not that we have to go into Verdant Falls at all," he continued. "I've been looking at Air BnB's. I found a few nice cabins a short drive from your mom's house. If we buy groceries and don't eat out, no one from Verdant Falls will know we're visiting."

She raised her brows. "Not even your aunt?"

That was a very good point. If Phil ever got wind that he'd been in town and didn't come by, she would skin him alive. "I might go see her for a quick visit. But she won't say anything to anyone if I ask her not to."

Judging from her expression, Emma wasn't convinced.

Garrett leaned over, reaching out to cover her hand with his. "But we don't have to sneak around either. If you do feel like going out, you'll do it with me at your side. Even if someone had an axe to grind with you—and that's a big if—they would never dare approach my wife."

Emma released her lower lip with a pop. "I guess that's true."

"But?" He knew there was one.

"If we want to spend time with Stella, we should stay at my mom's. She moved right after I got out of the hospital, but I do have a room at the house. It'll be a little cramped and your feet might hang off the edge of the bed, but we would manage."

Emma leaned forward, a sparkle in her eye. "If we were still fake married and maintaining separate bedrooms, it would be different. But the whole point of the visit is to introduce you to my family as my husband…"

"And spoil your baby sister with presents," he interjected.

Guilt flittered across her face. "*And* break the news to my mom that this marriage is real…"

Garrett's heart dropped to his feet. "She still doesn't know?"

Emma hesitated. "Well, my mom has been stressed out about something lately. I'm pretty sure she's been fighting with her current boyfriend—whoever he is. She hasn't mentioned anyone by name, but she talks a lot about men being pieces of crap. It didn't seem like the best time to tell her that our marriage is about more than health insurance now."

He suppressed a groan. "If that's the case, do you think it's wise to be in her house, shacking up under her roof?"

"Shacking up is what people who *aren't* married do," she corrected. "And it might be a little awkward at first. But now that I'm thinking about it, it's better to face this head-on. The sooner my mom sees us together, the sooner she'll know that we're the real deal. Plus, it will give me more time with Stella. I miss smushing her little face with kisses."

Garrett masked his disappointment, refusing to let her see it. There went his plans for lovemaking in front of a fire…

"If you think that will help Mariana get over any reservations she might have, then we'll stay with them. As for face-smushing kisses—I guess I can share with Stella for a few days. But I'd like to claim a small percentage of lip action if you can squeeze it in."

Whatever discomfort he might experience this weekend was worth the look on his wife's face right now.

And who knows, maybe once she was within a stone's throw of their hometown, she might want to take a closer look at her past.

Emma had remembered the story he'd told her about Phil's cat. Maybe if she went back home, relaxed and without fear in the company of her husband-slash-bodyguard, she might remember more.

She popped out of her seat to plant a rushed kiss on his cheek. "I'll call them right now to let them know we're coming!"

He kept the smile on his face until she was out of sight. Then he pulled out his phone to cancel the booking he'd made for the luxury two-story cabin by the river, the one that reminded him of the one his family used to own.

His father had sold that cabin years ago.

At the time he hadn't been sorry to see it go. Remembering his time with Emma in that place had been painful. So he'd celebrated the sale with a drink, telling himself it was for the best. Moving on was the healthy thing to do.

Garrett regretted letting it go now. According to his aunt that cabin had been his mother's favorite place in the entire state. Her father had built it.

Had his father bothered to get Phil's permission to sell it? Had she profited from the sale?

He had no idea. Garrett really should have asked these questions earlier. Berating himself, he shot another text to his PI.

It seemed Emma wasn't the one who needed to reevaluate things in their hometown.

Chapter Fifty-Three

GARRETT

Emma's mother's house was the tiniest two-story structure he had ever seen. It stood in the middle of a crowded block with homemade concrete sidewalks.

It was an odd layout for a residential area. So many homes set so closely together next to the roads while the woods stretched out behind them as if they were huddling together for protection against the elements.

Or more like the people who built these houses wanted to save some cash when they tapped into the city water lines. That was the only explanation for putting two streets worth of houses into one.

He spun in a circle, taking in the whole neighborhood. It probably hadn't looked so bad when they were new, but now, fifty years on, the clear signs of economic depression made for a grim little enclave.

The white wood paneling of each home was overdue for a paint job. Compared to the neighbor's houses, the Mendez home was in great shape, with a green patch of grass and no clutter in sight.

No HOA around here, he thought, noting the broken-down Honda on the dead lawn a few houses down. But he smiled at Emma when she turned to check his reaction, all the while making a mental note to check the crime stats for this neighborhood.

His wife would be devastated if something happened to her mother and little sister. Fortunately, she was too excited to notice his less-than-enthusiastic reaction to their surroundings.

"Why are we going through the side door?" he asked as she skirted the neat square of grass in front of the house to walk up the cracked concrete driveway.

"It's the kitchen," she said, waving him on impatiently. Emma fairly skipped up the steps, she was so excited.

He followed more sedately, determined to keep an open mind. He had to make a good first impression.

Sunlight streamed through a two-panel slider window on the left, illuminating a dated but scrupulously clean kitchen in white and yellow tile. But the crowded kitchen counters and cracked linoleum didn't detract from its overall cheerfulness.

The kitchen table was pine, with two chairs on one end and a cushioned bench on the other. A dark-haired woman sat on one of the chairs, a pile of papers in front of her.

Emma threw her arms out. "Mom."

Mariana Mendez turned around. She was a touch gray now at the temples and she might have gained a couple of pounds, but other than that she hadn't aged a day from their school days.

When she saw Emma, the tight expression on her face eased, the line between her brows disappearing. She jumped up to hug her oldest daughter, giving Garrett an unobstructed view of the documents on the table.

It was a pile of bills.

He hung back during the mother-daughter reunion. Squeals and warm hugs were exchanged. For a few moments, he let his mind drift. Would his mother have hugged him like that after a long absence?

She would have, right?

Phil's greetings were warm enough, he supposed. As for his father —*not* a hugger.

"I'm so glad you made it," Mariana said, finally breaking away. "I wasn't sure your boss would give you the days off so I didn't tell Stella you were coming. She's going to be so surprised."

"Oh, well, I have more days than I thought." Emma twisted to give him a meaningful look, a silent warning not to contradict her. "Garrett, this is my mom. Mom, this is Garrett."

Stepping forward, he set their overnight bags down on the floor. He stuck out his hand. "Thank you so much for having us."

Mariana nodded, smiling vaguely as if she didn't know what to make of him. "You're welcome. Thanks for bringing my baby home."

Emma snickered. "I am your grown daughter. Your baby is the birthday girl. Is she still at school?"

"Nope." Mariana pointed straight up.

Emma beamed and pulled away, twisting and squeezing his arm. "I'm going to say hi to Stella. I'll be right back."

She practically ran out of the room. The sound of pounding foot-steps rose as if she was running up a flight of stairs. Then he heard her walking directly overhead. A much younger-sounding feminine squeal followed.

Garrett smiled at Emma's eagerness. When he turned to Mariana, she was watching him, a crease between her brows.

Damn. She looked a lot like her daughter when she did that.

Be harmless. "Thanks so much for letting me tag along with Emma for the weekend."

"Oh, it's fine," she said, scrutinizing him as if he was a puzzle piece that didn't fit. "Always happy to welcome one of Em's friends. I hope you're okay on the cot. I, uh, didn't expect you to be so tall."

Well, there went the hope that Emma had prepared her mother since their talk.

Garrett was suddenly seeing a weekend of separate beds in his immediate future. That was not happening. He had to nip this in the bud.

"Thanks. Although, I should add that technically, we're more than friends. She did mention getting married, didn't she?"

The smile dropped off Mariana's face. "Yes. For the health insurance."

You handle tense negotiations all the time. Be polite but direct.

"It's, um, it's not about the insurance anymore. Although we might wait for Emma to come back down before we continue."

Well, that was smooth. He didn't want to have this conversation without Emma.

"Oh." Mariana's expression softened as she put two and two together. "You're a real couple. That's great. Emma hasn't dated anyone since…"

"Since the accident."

Mariana looked relieved. "Oh, good. I wasn't sure you knew."

He shrugged haplessly, fervently wishing his wife had prepped her mom a little better. "The fact she didn't remember me was kind of a dead giveaway."

Mariana crossed her arms, muttering something under her breath. The frown was back. "I thought you looked familiar. Are you from here?"

"I am… you actually worked for my aunt Philomena for a little while."

Recognition filtered, settling into the grooves of Mariana's mouth. This was not happiness to see him.

"You're a Martin," she said.

This was delivered in the same tone as someone announcing, 'Oh, you're a Nazi.'

Well, shit. This conversation was happening now. For some reason, he'd always assumed Emma would be here to act as a shield.

He cleared his throat. "Yeah. My mom was Iris Martin. Technically, I'm a Chapman."

Judging from her expression, this might have been worse, although he couldn't see why.

"I see," she mumbled.

He rubbed his temple, uncertain how to proceed. His mother-in-law was the woman his aunt blamed for the end of her marriage.

Garrett had been old enough when they broke up to know it wasn't that simple, but this was still excruciatingly uncomfortable.

Regardless of what Phil would say, he had to build a cordial relationship with this woman.

"We didn't formally meet before," he began. "But I saw you around town a lot. You and Emma. You were at our high school production of *Much Ado about Nothing*—because of the two grades she skipped, we were in a lot of the same classes."

Her head drew back, pivoting to look in the direction Emma had gone when a particularly loud squeal filtered downstairs.

"You were in the play?" she asked.

Garrett put his hands in his pockets, trying to switch gears and steer the conversation away from the contentious topic of his family.

"Yeah, I was Don John and Emma was a great Beatrice." He broke off. "I know Emma hasn't been all that receptive to reconnecting with anyone she knew before the accident, so the fact she married someone from Verdant Falls must be kind of a shock. There's a funny story about that. Well, sort of funny, depending on your point of view…"

He trailed off when the sound of thunder signaled Emma coming back down the stairs. For a small woman, she could make a racket.

Of course, that could have had something to do with the ricketiness of the structure. Even the child following her sounded like a pint-sized elephant trailing in her wake.

Add a building inspection to the to-do list. He'd pay for the contractor himself.

Emma burst into the kitchen a moment later, holding the hand of an adorable dark-haired girl dressed in a green sweater dress with a tulle skirt.

"Garrett, I want you to meet my baby sister, Stella."

Prepared to be charmed by a pint-sized Emma, Garrett looked down. He took one look at the child staring up at him with her big brown eyes and felt all his blood drain to his feet.

Holy shit. Stella was the spitting image of his mother.

Chapter Fifty-Four

GARRETT

"Garrett?" Emma's voice sounded as if it was coming from very far away. His ears were ringing. Literally. That had never happened before.

Blinking, he tore his eyes off Stella, checking Emma's reaction. But she was smiling down at her 'sister,' no hint of tension in her expression.

Garrett swallowed the lump in his throat and stuck out his hand. "It's a pleasure to meet you."

A giggling Stella shook it, her tiny hand enveloping his index and middle fingers.

Her small touch sent a painful jolt of electricity running through his entire system.

"It's nice to meet you too," she said shyly in the voice of a cartoon princess before letting go to tug on Emma's arm. "C'mon, Em! I want to show you my new bike."

"Just a second, baby," she said, her gaze going from him to her mother in an obvious way. "I have to show Garrett to *our* room."

"It can wait," he rasped past the constriction in his throat. The sleeping arrangements were the last thing on his mind. "Go see the bike."

"Yeah! Let's go." Stella pulled Emma to the door.

"*Are you sure*?" she mouthed.

He nodded, waving them on despite the fact his heart was going a million miles an hour.

"I'm good," he lied. "I'm about to head out myself. I thought I would make a quick grocery store run. I think this baby's fifth birthday calls for champagne. You like champagne, don't you, Stella?"

His words were met with the tinkle of silver bells. "Yeah!" Stella cheered. "I do."

"That's what I thought," he said with a nod. Mouthing 'sparkling apple cider,' he fished out his car keys with numb fingers.

Dear God, he might need a consult from Dr. Douchebag Desjardin. Numb extremities. That was bad, wasn't it?

"Go play," he rasped. "I'll be back before you know it."

Emma gave him a weird look. She knew something was up.

"Go," he insisted.

"Okay." Emma let Stella tug her out the door with only one backward glance—a puzzled one, but grateful too.

He waited till they were gone to round on his hostess. "Please excuse me," he said tightly. "I have to check something out."

Mariana stared at him, alarmed. *Yeah.* That was the appropriate response.

He left before he did something he would regret. Garrett walked out of the house, waving to the girls without looking at them, hustling to the car.

Leave, as quickly as you can.

That was the smart thing to do. Not that other thing—going up to Stella and picking her up to peer into her eyes until the truth came to him.

This was crazy. He had to be wrong. That was Mariana's daughter back there. Stella was Emma's sister. Not her daughter. Not *his.*

But the look on Mariana's face just now. It had been as if she'd seen a ghost.

Well, so had he.

Evidence. I need evidence. Fortunately for him, some existed.

Garrett drove straight to Sally's Liquor. It wasn't called that anymore, but the new place still sold booze.

He glanced at the freshly painted sign, his lip curling. What did it say that the most prosperous business in this town was the liquor store? Not that he wasn't tempted to march in there and buy out their lot of whiskey. But he wasn't going to do that. He had work to do.

Lifting his cell phone, he pulled up the group chat he maintained with Rainer, Ian, and Elias.

> I need a favor ASAP. It's an emergency. Who is in town?

The universe was with him because the answers instantly poured in. Rainer was in a meeting in Los Angeles and Ian was on a plane. But Elias was free, and he was ten minutes from Garrett's apartment.

Elias called him the minute he was inside. "Okay, are you going to tell me why I'm here?"

Garrett sucked in a deep breath and closed his eyes, aware that what he was about to reveal made him sound like a lunatic. "I need you to go to my bedroom."

"Wait. Is this something kinky?" Elias hesitated. He'd been anxious, spurred on by Garrett's urgency. But now he was just his usual sardonic self. "Because if I'm about to walk into your room to find your blushing bride tied to your bed and I need to untie her, I warn you, I *will* enjoy it. Of course, I'll act like I don't. But I totally will."

Garrett grunted, but the pulsing fight-or-flight adrenaline coursing through him eased back. "This is the part where I would normally threaten your life, but there is no need. Emma and I are together in Colorado."

Elias' amusement ended there. "Are you sure that's a good idea? Didn't her doctors warn you about forcing memories to surface?"

Emma's doctors hadn't said anything of the kind. But that was almost enough to derail him. "No, and you watch too much TV. This isn't about that."

He sucked a deep breath. "I just met Stella, Emma's kid sister."

Elias grunted. "That clarifies nothing."

It was a good thing he was sitting down. Garrett was getting dizzy just contemplating saying this aloud. "I need you to go into my bedroom closet. I have some photo albums on the top shelf."

His aunt Phil had the family photos meticulously recreated for him almost a decade ago. He had never uploaded the JPEG scans they'd made to the cloud, but the fine leather photo albums the photography studio sent him were right there in his closet.

Garrett hadn't looked at them in years.

"I need you to find the oldest. Find the picture labeled 'Iris, first day of school.'"

His mother would have been five in that photo. That would have been the same age Stella was now.

"It should be somewhere in the middle of the album," he added.

There was no noise on the other end of the line.

"Elias, I really need a copy of that picture right now."

It was a good thing his friend was quick on the uptake. "Uh, yeah. Of course. *Wow*. Shit."

Garrett waited, trying to calm down. If he was right—no, he couldn't think about it now.

There was noise finally, rustling and stuff being moved around. "Have I ever told you you're a neat freak?" Elias asked.

"I'm not," he mumbled. "I just have a very good cleaning service."

"Shit, there's like a dozen albums here. Which one is the oldest?"

He pinched the bridge of his nose, picturing the albums in his head. "The spines have the years they cover printed on them."

"Oh, I see them." More rustling. "I think I got it."

An eternity later there was a click and then a picture popped onto his screen.

Everything stopped. He could feel every molecule of air in his lungs, the blood rushing through his veins.

"Well? Don't keep me in suspense. Is this what the kid looks like?"

His mother's hair and skin were lighter but the eyes and mouth and the shape of the nose were identical. They could have been twins.

"Yeah." He swallowed. "She looks just like this."

More silence.

"It could be a coincidence," Elias said. "A lot of little kids look like each other. Do you have a photo of Emma's kid sister? You need to do a side-by-side comparison to know for sure."

"Uh…" He'd met Stella for all of two minutes when Emma introduced her. Damn it, he should have offered to snap a picture of the two of them, to commemorate the occasion.

"Can you check Emma's old room? It's the one across the hall."

He waited.

"No, there's no picture frames out."

Garrett groaned. That was what he thought but had hoped he remembered wrong.

"I'll have to go back and take one." It wouldn't be hard. This was Stella's birthday weekend and Emma would want lots of pictures.

Garrett tried to start the car, but his fingers slipped off the starter button. He had to calm the fuck down.

He was doing a piss-poor job of that when the text chime he'd assigned to his wife dinged.

She had sent him a message, accompanied by a photo. It was a close-up shot of her and Stella, their heads pressed together.

> I just explained that champagne is alcohol, so Miss Stella has changed her order to cookies and cream ice cream.

Tears stung at his eyes, his throat thickening. Emma's timing was impeccable, as always.

With shaky fingers, he wrote back.

> Her wish is my command.

"I got a picture," he muttered for Elias' benefit before downloading and cropping the photo. Then he sent the side-by-side back.

There was a long low whistle. "That… that is a damn close match," Elias said. "You need to get a DNA swab to be sure."

He sat frozen, unable to comprehend anything but the most obvious and painful fact. "Emma lied to me."

Elias' answer was immediate. "Oh, hell no! You don't fucking know that."

Garrett flattened his free hand on his thigh to get it to stop shaking. "But she has to know."

"No, she doesn't," Elias spat. "Her head's all messed up. Or did you forget you married a woman with amnesia?"

Garrett closed his eyes. Could it be that Emma believed Stella was her college boyfriend's baby? Is that why she hadn't told him?

That didn't make sense. Emma had to know he was a better contender for the father, right? He'd laid out their past sexual history in excruciating detail.

And Mariana—what the hell was going on with her? Why had she gone along with this? Or had it been her idea?

"I know this is all kinds of fucked up, but whatever you're thinking, *stop*," Elias ordered in that tone that he reserved for ordering his private security soldiers around.

"For all you know, her mom slept with your uncle or something and we're looking at a cousin right now. Stranger things have happened."

"My mom didn't have a brother," he said tonelessly. Nor did she have any male cousins.

But Elias had a point. Conjecture would only drive him mad. He needed the truth, and he needed it now.

"I gotta go."

"All right, but don't go all half-cocked with Emma. There must be a reasonable explanation for the resemblance."

He shook his head at Elias' mental one-eighty. "I thought you said marrying her was crazy. That was you, right?"

"That was before. She makes you happy so don't do anything stupid to jack it up. Go back and have a nice calm conversation with her. And get that DNA swab."

If he was right, the DNA swab was pointless, but he would get it anyway. His lawyers would hound him if he didn't.

"You're right," he decided. "I am going back there for a good long talk."

Just not with Emma.

Chapter Fifty-Five

GARRETT

Garrett parked the car across the street from the Mendez home, startled to realize that he had no memory of driving there.

He checked the side of the house. Emma and Stella were nowhere in sight.

Shit, the ice cream. Taking out his phone, he ordered it, tacking on some champagne, several appetizers, and a full gourmet meal for good measure.

He had a feeling Mariana wouldn't be up to cooking after he got through with her.

Garrett found her in the kitchen, washing dishes. She turned to him with a pensive expression but tried to smile.

She wiped her hands on a dish towel. "Emma and Stella are upstairs playing Legos."

He sat at the table, grateful for small mercies. This conversation would be easier without them. "That's good. Because I need to speak to you."

He took out his phone and pulled up the quick side-by-side photograph. "So… did you lie to her or is my wife lying to me?"

Mariana startled. "*What?*"

He slid the phone to her.

Brow puckering just like Emma, she picked it up. The moment of recognition hit her like a freight train.

"Oh my God," she breathed, the phone shaking in her hand.

"I know that child is not yours."

His voice was flat and much colder than he intended. But that couldn't be helped. It felt as if his skin was peeling off.

It seemed Mariana was feeling the same. The trembling in her hands had spread to her entire body.

"Sit," he said, more gently this time.

Too shaken to disobey, Mariana slid onto the bench across from him.

He set his hands on the table, folding them together. "Tell me the truth before they come back."

Mariana opened her mouth, her eyes going from him to his phone. "*How?*"

His head drew back. "How do you think?"

She sucked in a harsh breath, almost wheezing. "I can't believe this."

Mariana wasn't the only one. Good God, he had a child—a five-year-old child. And Emma hadn't told him.

"You're not Stella's mother," he said with more composure than he felt. "You're her grandmother. *Emma* is Stella's mother. And I am her father."

But Emma hadn't told him. That was the hardest part of this whole mess.

Hell, he knew she had struggled in the aftermath of the accident, but how could she go along with this pretense that the girl was her sister? Or was he wrong about that?

Please let me be wrong.

Mariana leaned forward, casting a nervous eye in the direction of the stairs. "Are you sure Stella is yours? Really sure?"

Garrett tapped the picture. "She's the spitting image of my mother at that age."

"I can see that," Mariana mumbled, looking all around the room with a lost expression. She gripped her hands tightly together. "I had no idea you two even knew each other back then."

"We were high school rivals," he explained in a low voice. "But high school *ended*."

He wanted to push for explanations, but instinct told him to wait. Mariana was already on the edge. Too much pressure and she would crack.

Mariana picked up the phone again, zooming in on the picture.

"The resemblance is uncanny." She looked up, her face and tone softening. "She's gone, isn't she? That's what your aunt said…"

She leaned back, clearly regretting mentioning the woman she'd wronged.

"My mother died when I was seven," he confirmed. "But thanks to Aunt Phil, I have all her pictures."

Mariana couldn't quite meet his gaze. She reached for a bottle of water and swallowed some.

"Please tell me how this happened."

How had everyone in this town come to believe that Stella was Mariana's daughter? "Emma has no idea, does she?"

Mariana closed her eyes, tears glistening at the corners. She shook her head.

Garrett released a shaky breath, every muscle in his body unclenching. For some reason that made them ache but that was fine. Good even. This was going to be okay.

Except for the self-flagellation he so richly deserved. He should have never doubted Emma. She had always been honest with him. They had never lied to each other. Not once.

He'd forgotten that in his shock today.

Besides, he had a much bigger problem to deal with. Emma had no idea she was a mother. "It was the accident, wasn't it? She doesn't remember having Stella."

The timing was right. They spent most of Christmas break together at his cabin. Spring break had fallen the third week of March. But she hadn't come home right away because she'd been freaking out about something.

I guess I know what that was now.

Emma must have discovered she was pregnant while she was away at school. That last month of phone calls. He hadn't imagined her distraction. Jesus, she must have been so scared, worried about what he'd say.

Had she doubted him? Did she think he would turn his back on her and the baby?

Garrett had been planning on asking her to marry him, but his plans had been amorphous. He hadn't talked to her about what was then the distant future. Their relationship had felt too new for such serious discussions.

He should have spoken to her about marriage anyway. If he had, she would have felt more comfortable in confiding in him.

She was going to tell you about the baby in person. That had to be why she was in the woods. You didn't tell someone they were going to be a father over the phone. At least Emma wouldn't.

But why didn't she say anything about him to her mother or one of her friends? If she'd told someone they were seeing each other, Mariana would have put two and two together.

He would have known about Stella.

"We got into a huge fight," he admitted in a distant voice.

God, he'd been such an asshole. "Her ex-boyfriend was in her dorm room when I called one night. She said they were working on a project together for one of their classes, but I didn't believe her. I assumed the worst and we argued. I thought we'd fix things when she came home but I never heard from her again. When she didn't return my calls, I thought she chose Edward."

Damn the man's timing.

Mariana buried her face in her hands, scrubbing it hard before lowering them with a shaky exhale. "Emma was acting weird on the phone. But she was in college—she was overdue for some sort of meltdown. I had no idea she was pregnant until the doctors told me in the hospital. They gave her a test when they admitted her."

The sound of a little girl laughing made him jerk in his seat. He gazed at the ceiling. A moment later, Emma joined in.

They sounded like they were having the time of their lives.

The sound wrapped around his heart, squeezing it in a vise. It hurt so bad, under any other circumstances, he would have suspected a heart attack.

Garrett closed his eyes and took a deep breath. Yes, this was a royal fucking mess. But those were his girls upstairs. *His.*

He would fix his family.

Hands fisted, rage filled his chest when he realized how close he'd come to losing them both.

"She could have miscarried when the car hit her."

Mariana swallowed audibly, rocking back a touch. "When the doctor first told me she was pregnant, I thought that might be better."

His feeling about that must have been all over his face because Mariana pushed her chair back a few inches, her features hardening. "You don't get it. I thought my baby was going to die, her baby with her."

Garrett tried to unclench. *She's right.*

He couldn't judge her. If anything, she should be coming down on him. He hadn't been there. Mariana had. She lived through a terrible thing, believing she was about to lose her daughter and granddaughter.

In a very real way, she *had* lost Emma.

He took a deep breath and leaned forward. "I understand that, I guess. What I don't get is why Emma thinks Stella is her sister."

Mariana threw a panicked look over her shoulder at the stairs, but there was no thunder. The girls were occupied upstairs.

She collapsed back into her chair. "It was touch and go the first few days. I didn't leave the hospital that entire first week. I was afraid to shut my eyes because I was convinced Emma would die while I was asleep."

Garrett had experienced more than one nightmare about Emma's accident. This was worse. The retroactive terror at everything he'd almost lost was going to stress-age his organs by a decade.

"But she didn't die."

It was as much a reminder to himself as it was to Mariana.

"No, but she didn't wake up either."

"I know. She was in a coma."

"For almost six months."

"*What?*" he hissed, flattening his hand on the table. "Six what?"

Mariana nodded. "Months."

Fuck, the hits just kept coming. "I thought the coma lasted a few days—a week at the most."

"No. It was… endless," Mariana said, her youthful face gray.

"The doctors had given up on her. They told me to get ready for her to die. Not in those words, of course, but it was all over their faces. They would hedge, couching every conversation in doctor doublespeak."

She put her hands on the table, as if bracing herself on it. "But one didn't do that. His name was Stanley. He gave me hope when he told me this story he'd heard of a pregnant woman waking up from a coma when she went into labor."

Garrett's mouth dropped open. "Is that what happened?"

Mariana nodded, the memory lightening the tension in her features.

"Well, sort of. Her vitals began to change when she began false labor pains. She gave birth in this weird sort of half-conscious state. It wasn't until a few days later that she opened her eyes. But it wasn't an instant thing like in the movies. She was in and out for weeks."

Holy shit. That was unbelievable. And so fucked up.

Garrett really should have grabbed a bottle at the liquor store. "She has no memory of giving birth?"

The look on Mariana's face was a mix of too many emotions to dissect. "I did tell her."

He held up a hand. "Hold up. *What?*"

"When she woke up," Mariana began. "Like really woke for longer than a few minutes—I told her. But her memory of those first few months after waking up is fragmented. It's all a blur to her. Emma doesn't remember our conversation, or any others from that time."

Mariana's youthful face was turning haggard. "That was before I realized how badly she was hurt. All I knew was that she was awake and seemed alert. But Emma could barely speak or move. She couldn't even eat without help. Hell, she had to relearn how to walk."

He'd guessed some of this after reading her medical records but hadn't understood the full extent. "And you decided not to tell her again when she remembered?"

It wasn't meant as recrimination, but his words pissed off Mariana nonetheless.

"You weren't there!" she cried. "You don't know how hard it was. For both of us. Emma had to work so hard to get just a sliver of her life back. It took *years* for her to get to the point where she could take care of herself again. Emma had enough to worry about. So did I, taking care of Stella."

She shot to her feet, beginning to pace the short length of the kitchen.

"I apologize," he said after a long minute. "I didn't mean to imply that you did anything wrong. Far from it. You did everything right."

He gestured for her to sit back down. She did, but not before taking a detour to get a few beers out of the fridge.

Mariana slid one in front of him, but he didn't open it. His stomach would have rebelled.

"You could have given Stella up," he said after a long silence. "No one would have blamed you."

"I thought about it," she admitted, wiping her eyes. "But I couldn't do it. For a long while Stella was all I had. Emma had woken up, but it took so long for her to come back to herself."

Her voice broke. "You have no idea how hard she had to fight."

No, he didn't.

"Thank you," he whispered. "For keeping them safe."

"Oh." Mariana sniffed, straightening. "Well, they're my family. You don't have to thank me."

"Someone should."

Her laugh was sudden and a bit manic. Mariana clapped a hand over her mouth to stop the disturbing sound.

"Why Stella?" he asked.

"Huh?"

"The name Stella. Why did you choose it?"

"Oh. Because of Stanley."

Garrett looked at her blankly.

"Stanley, the doctor," she reminded him. "He and I spoke often when Em was in her coma. He told me once that he was named after the Brando character in *A Streetcar Named Desire*."

Garrett snorted. "His mother named him after *that* Stanley?"

"I hadn't seen the movie at the time, but he told me a little about it —he even imitated that one scene, pretending to rip his shirt off." She shrugged. "I liked the name Stella."

Under the circumstances, it could have been worse. The doctor's mother could have been a *Gone with the Wind* fan. He couldn't imagine saddling his child with the name Scarlett.

He'd known more than one stripper who went by that name, back in his partying days.

"Stella is a good name. I can live with Stella."

Mariana stilled. "What do you mean by live with?"

"What do you think I mean?" He pointed up at the ceiling. "That's my kid up there. Not to mention the fact that through some trick of fate, I am now married to her mother."

It was his turn to get up, but the kitchen was too small for him to pace. "I lost Emma for far too long. But she's finally mine and I'm not letting go. I'm not letting *either* of them go."

Mariana's sky was falling. Her eyes filled with tears. "I can't tell Emma the truth now! She wouldn't understand."

"Then we'll make her understand," he bit out. "But things can't go on the way they have. Emma has to know the truth. And Stella needs to know me. She needs her father."

Mariana was already getting up, ready to bolt. He reached out, putting a restraining hand on her shoulder. "I know this will be difficult, but you know I'm right."

Her breaths were coming too fast. If he didn't stop her, she was going to hyperventilate and pass out on him.

"Mariana, I'm not going anywhere. Emma is my *wife*," he stressed. "They will understand. We'll do it together."

"You will be there?"

He nodded. "Yeah. And I'm going to help with everything else."

Bewildered, she snatched her beer off the table. "What else is there?"

Garrett gestured to their surroundings. "Let's start with this house. It's a rental, right?"

Mariana's expression grew tight. "Yeah. I rent from my friend. He owns it."

It was the way she said it that clued him in. *Well, shit.*

"You're talking about Teddy Bronson, aren't you?"

She didn't look at him. Just nodded.

Well, isn't that just perfect? His aunt's ex-husband owned this house.

Chapter Fifty-Six

GARRETT

He held his breath as his daughter blew out the candles on her birthday cake, almost bursting into simultaneous laughter and tears when she couldn't quite manage to do all five at once.

Five years.

He'd missed five fucking years of her life. And not just him. Emma had missed a lot of those years too, through no fault of her own.

According to Mariana, the home they lived in did belong to Theodore 'Teddy' Bronson.

Teddy was Phil's second husband. A decade her junior, he was the son of a good country club family who latched on to his aunt Phil on a cruise. They were married a few months later. He'd moved to Verdant Falls to be with her. But his real goal had been to become a real estate mogul. Using some of his aunt's capital, he'd opened a small office in Verdant Falls.

That was how Mariana had met him. She'd been the supervisor of a small crew of house cleaners. They got the contract to clean Teddy's rental properties.

Of course, Mariana hadn't told Garrett *how* they'd gotten involved. But he knew Teddy Bronson by reputation. He'd also seen him in action before and after the divorce.

While he didn't believe Mariana to be entirely blameless in the matter, Teddy was a piece of shit.

Bronson wouldn't have hesitated to use his position of authority to pressure a woman into an affair.

As bad as he felt for his aunt, the affair was the last thing he cared about. What mattered was Teddy's involvement in his daughter's life.

"He knows Stella isn't mine," Mariana had explained before the girls came back downstairs. "I took Emma to a hospital at the other end of the state—they had the facilities she needed for long-term care. Teddy was the only person who came to see us. For a while. But when I decided to claim Emma's baby as my own, he got mad and stopped coming around so much. It caused some problems for him, you see."

It was official. Fate was a bitch with a well-developed sense of irony. "Because everyone thought he was the father."

Mariana shrugged helplessly. "He told me I was being paranoid, but I couldn't help it. I thought Emma had gotten involved with someone bad and they had hurt her. Letting everyone believe Stella was mine was safer."

God, how did he even begin to unpack all of that? "I'm sorry it caused problems in your relationship."

"I'm not." Mariana straightened to her full height. "But I don't want to talk about that."

And yet Teddy was still in her life today.

"When did he come back?" He needed to know.

She looked down at her hands. "A couple years later. Emma was in and out of the hospital and I couldn't work as much. I had to cut back my hours with the cleaners."

She didn't come right out and say it, but the affair must have made her less desirable as a cleaning woman too.

It was one thing to have an attractive woman come and clean your home. It was another to hire one known for getting involved with other people's husbands.

Garrett didn't think his aunt would have badmouthed her. That would have been an acknowledgment of the affair. But Verdant Falls was a small town. People would have known, and Mariana's life would have been that much more difficult. Especially financially.

Or at least it would have been until Teddy came back, riding to the rescue.

"Can I ask what the state of your relationship is now?"

Mariana worried on her lip, chewing on it too hard. "He still owns some properties. I sometimes see him there, while I clean, if they're still vacant. I don't like him coming here. Neither of us wants Stella to think he's her dad."

He couldn't express how relieved he was to hear that.

"Good. That's good," he said before giving her a long, hard look. "Are you happy?"

Mariana frowned, at a loss for how to answer. "Is anybody?"

He leaned forward. "How do you feel about moving?"

The girls came down before she could answer. They were ready to celebrate, and Garrett hadn't been about to let them down.

He'd had vague plans of sitting them down after cake and telling them the truth, but Emma started to feel bad during dinner. She'd gone to bed that night with a full-blown headache and woke with one as well.

The delay was killing him.

Garrett was close to bursting. He was both excited and terrified to tell Emma the truth. But when she didn't improve by lunch, he couldn't bring himself to do it. He had to break this news as gently as possible to soften the blow.

When she didn't improve after lunch, he did the next best thing. He fetched Emma's medication and put some food on her bedside table. Then he took everyone else out so she could rest.

A group of kids from Stella's kindergarten class met at the park regularly on Saturdays. She played with them for all of ten minutes before demanding he push her on the swings. He happily did that for a solid half hour before asking Mariana to give them a little space at snack time. She was reluctant but did as he asked.

Garrett had a new plan. Tell Stella first, then they could tell Emma together once she was feeling better.

His aunt Phil would have to be last. She wouldn't like that, but it couldn't be helped.

"Where is Mommy going?" she asked as Mariana retreated to the edge of the park, pacing near the parking lot.

Garrett took a deep breath, examining the five-year-old. She was wearing a pink corduroy jumpsuit with a long-sleeved white shirt. Over these was a thick fleece jacket that had seen better days. A gray beanie with a white pompom on top completed the ensemble.

She was adorable and perfect. And he was about to upend her entire world.

"I asked Mariana to give us a little time alone. I wanted to talk with you."

Stella was a brilliant little girl. "About Emma?"

He put his hands on the table. "Yeah. Kind of."

Her little face grew unspeakably sad. "Is Auntie Em sick again?"

Goddamn, she was killing him with that little pout. "She isn't sick exactly, but she gets bad headaches because of her accident. You know about that, right?"

Stella gave him a solemn nod. "Em hurt her head."

"Yes," he breathed. "Yes, she did. She has problems because of it. One of the big ones is with her memory. Emma doesn't remember anything from before her accident."

"She has 'nesia."

"Yes!" Garrett wanted to pick her up and squeeze her, but Stella wasn't ready for that yet.

That's okay, he told himself sternly. They had time now.

"Yes," he repeated more calmly, surprised to find that he was sweating. "Emma has amnesia. Which means she doesn't remember things that were important, including one big secret. It was the most special secret in the entire world and the accident made her forget it."

Stella's eyes grew huge. "Really?"

Her little lip turned down. "But no one will ever know it 'cause she hurt her head."

Garrett forced himself to breathe in and out. He leaned in. "Well, the good news is I was able to figure out the special secret."

Stella leaned forward too, mimicking him. "What is it?"

"Well, it's about you, baby girl."

Stella's sudden disdain was worthy of a teenager. "I'm not a *baby*."

"Oh, of course not. Silly me," he apologized, lightheadedness making him giddy.

"It's just that I don't know any other kids, so you seem small to me. But I stand corrected. You're a big girl. Five whole years…" He trailed off, his throat aching. "I'm sorry I missed them."

Stella watched him with huge brown eyes. Such a familiar shape. And the curve of her mouth. *Damn.* He looked just like that when he was confused.

He cleared his throat. "I have to tell you the special secret now. And it's going to be hard to understand. Stella… the woman you call mama isn't your mama. Mariana is your grandmother."

Yeah, that scowl was real familiar too. He saw it in the mirror all the time.

"Emma is your real mama," he continued, trying not to rush through the words. "You are Emma's daughter. That's the super special secret—the one the accident made her forget."

Stella twisted behind her to look at Mariana.

"Your grandma Mariana will tell you all of this is true in just a minute. Because the secret is so big, I'm not done with it yet."

The sweat was trickling down his back now. But there was no help for it. "You see, I am not just Emma's new husband. We were boyfriend and girlfriend before her accident."

He paused, searching for the right words and not finding them. In the end, he just blurted it out.

"Stella, I'm your dad."

"*What?*" The earsplitting screech made him flinch.

He chuckled, the noise scratchy to his ear. "I am your father. And Emma is your real mom. But because of her accident, no one knew. Emma didn't get a chance to tell me she was going to have a baby before she got hurt. Which is why I didn't know about you. If I had, we would have met a lot sooner."

The little girl stared at him. She didn't even blink.

"Stella, do you understand everything I just told you?" he asked, giving her what he hoped was a reassuring smile. "I know it's a big and very weird surprise."

Stella's mouth opened so wide Garrett was sure he could see her tonsils. He braced himself for another shriek.

"Emma is my mom and you're my *dad*?" This last was delivered in that same eardrum-destroying frequency as her last scream.

"Wow, that's a serious talent kid," he said, massaging his throbbing ear with a smile on his face. "Remind me to see if you can make crystal shatter."

Actually, that would be cool. They might have to try that.

He was about to launch into the speech he'd begun working on in the car, about how he wanted to be a part of her life and how he'd like to see a lot more of her.

He wasn't sure he should broach the subject of moving yet, not until he'd broken the news to Emma. But Stella was already on her feet, and she had a plan of her own.

Before he realized what she intended, Stella was running toward the group of school kids she'd played with when they first arrived.

"Hey, Tyler!"

She busted into the circle of tiny people clustered near the slide, pointing her little finger at a stout blond boy, channeling his aunt Phil to a T when she yelled, "I told you I had a dad! He's right here and he's way better than your dad!"

Garrett blinked, his mouth dropping open. He looked over at Mariana, who winced but didn't move. Seeing no help there, Garrett got to his feet, hurrying when Tyler began to push her away.

"Everyone knows you don't have a dad! My dad says your mom doesn't even know who he is!"

Tyler reached down to grab a handful of sand, throwing it at Stella and the other kids, who began to yell and shout.

That little shit!

Garrett ran as other adults began to converge on the group. But his anger lost some of its self-righteous steam when Stella brushed her face off and charged the blond-haired turd, shoving him to the ground and leaping on top of him.

"Ah, hell."

Garrett sprinted, reaching Stella just after she started pounding on the kid. He snatched her up just as Tyler's parents hit the edge of the sandbox.

"Uh, sorry about that," he apologized, panting, a squealing and squirmy Stella slung over his shoulders.

Tyler's dad, a short pudgy guy with a receding hairline, puffed up, opening his mouth to tell him off. But he shut his mouth when Garrett stepped closer, unintentionally looming over the smaller man.

Despite the man's incipient paunch, Garrett had more than thirty pounds on him. But his was muscle, not fat.

The thin blond woman with him, presumably his wife, took one look at his face and began to smack her husband on the arm repeatedly with the back of her hand as if to say, "*Look! Look!*"

"I told you my dad was better 'cause he's bigger and he has more hair!" Stella yelled, struggling to get down to continue pounding Tyler.

Garrett pressed his lips together to keep from laughing. Taking a better hold of his errant daughter, he cradled her against his chest with one arm and cleared his throat.

"Again, I'm so sorry. She's just… excited."

"It's not a problem," the mom said breathlessly.

He tilted his head, snapping the fingers of his free hand as he finally recognized the woman. The voice had jogged his memory. "Oh! Hey. It's Sharon, right?"

Sharon Moore had been a year behind him at Verdant Falls High. The man with her was a little familiar too, but the receding hairline was throwing him.

"Yes," Sharon said.

She looked from him to Stella and then back to him, her eyes widening so big she looked like an owl with a pituitary problem.

"Uh, wow. I never expected to see you here. Like this." She broke off to smack her husband one more time. "Look, honey, it's Garrett Chapman!"

They waited, but *honey* just stood there slack-jawed, so Garrett refocused on Sharon. "How've you been?"

"Good, good. We moved here after high school. It's a better school district. Isn't that right, Dennis, darling?"

She nudged her husband with a high-pitched chuckle.

Dennis finally closed his mouth. But it was a brief reprieve because he promptly opened it again to put his foot inside.

"Stella is *your* daughter?" he asked incredulously.

His plan to play this close to the vest while he broke the news to Emma and his aunt crumbled around him. But he went with it.

"She is," he said, standing taller. Because this remarkable little girl —who was already so much like him and like Emma—was something to be proud of.

Stella shifted in his arms, leaning her head on his shoulder as she gripped his collar with her little fingers.

"I told him," she whispered in his ear.

Garrett put his hand on her back, rubbing it soothingly. "Yes, you did, baby girl."

She didn't complain about the nickname this time.

Dennis darling wasn't done showing off his IQ. "You and *Mariana Mendez?*"

"No, idiot," Sharon muttered, a mortified blush flooding her face. "Him and *Emma.*"

Dennis stared at her blankly, then sucked in a deep breath. "Oh. *Oooh.*"

He shook himself like a dog. "Oh, wow. That's, uh, that's news. Really big news. You and Emma Mendez."

Tyler the turd, who had finally realized no one was paying attention to him, picked himself up and ran off.

"Yeah," Garrett said, wishing she was here.

"So, you and Emma are *together* together?" Sharon asked, a bright *I can't wait to tell everyone I know* smile pasted on her face.

Garrett nodded, with not a little regret. He could picture the gossip emanating out from these two like a tsunami, but the big secret was already exposed.

Sharon might be a terrible gossip, but she had been friendly to Emma as far as he knew. Her curiosity was understandable.

He decided to go with it, to try and control the narrative. "Yeah, we just got married."

This was too much for the inquisitive Sharon. She stared at him for a full ten or twenty seconds, processing, before rushing to congratulate him.

"Oh my God! How exciting," she said, wishing him luck with genuine enthusiasm.

Dennis echoed her, gesturing to his head. "And how is Emma now?"

"Mama-Emma has 'nesia," Stella said before he could reply. "And her head hurts."

Garrett gave them a weak smile. "What she said. Emma is home with a headache. But she's come a long way since the accident and continues to improve all the time. She has excellent doctors now."

He leaned forward conspiratorially. "I'd appreciate it if you kept all of this to yourself for a day or two. I'm moving some big chess pieces here and I'd strongly prefer that certain parties don't learn about this yet."

"*Oh.*" Sharon, always quick on the uptake, nodded. "Of course."

"Thank you," he said, this smile stronger and far more genuine.

Hoisting Stella a little higher, he began to walk away, waving goodbye as they went.

Sharon took a step to follow him. "I'm so glad Emma is doing better! Please tell her the Browns said hello."

"Will do."

He walked down the hill to his car, gesturing for Mariana to join them. Sighing, he dropped the smile after he fastened Stella in her booster seat.

Park time was over. His careful timetable had just been blown to pieces. Some damage control was in order, but he couldn't help feeling a tad smug.

Stella thought he was a better dad than darling Dennis.

Given Tyler's sand-throwing proclivities, that was a low bar, but

Garrett had been a father for less than a day now. He'd take whatever victories he could get.

Chapter Fifty-Seven

EMMA

Her headache receded as the afternoon began to wane, but it was beginning to get dark before Emma finally felt human enough to open her eyes.

Guilt immediately set in. She had been home for less than a day before her stupid head wrecked things.

Stop that. You didn't ruin anything.

They were her thoughts, but Emma heard them in Garrett's voice. Yes, her quality time with Stella and her mom was dwindling fast. But Garrett could fly them over for Christmas in addition to their Thanksgiving visit.

Not that she'd wait that long to make it up to them. She would begin now, starting with getting out of bed.

Pushing herself up, Emma managed to sit up only to have to lie back down when a wave of dizziness overcame her.

Okay, a little slower. Stella had waited this long to play family with her stuffed animals, hadn't she? Besides, they would have way more fun at Thanksgiving when she and Mariana came to San Diego.

She just hoped Garrett was getting along okay. The last thing she'd wanted to do was abandon him to her mother's tender mercies.

Not that Mariana would be outright rude or unwelcoming.

However, her perception of men tended to be influenced by how well her relationships were going. Emma wasn't sure how she'd cope with having a man with Garrett's presence around without her to act as a buffer.

It might have been better if he'd taken the opportunity to go and visit his aunt after taking Stella to the park. She'd fully expected him to, but she could hear him moving around downstairs. That heavy tread on the wood was unmistakable. That and he appeared to be having a very animated conversation with Stella.

She couldn't hear the words, but the tone was everything. It sounded like bright sunshine, even through the floorboards. Emma took a moment to marvel at the miracle of falling in love with a genuinely good man.

Her savoring was cut short when a flurry of small footsteps signaled Stella's imminent arrival. She was groggy, but happy as Stella pushed her door open, sticking her little face in the crack.

"*Psst.* Are you awake?" Stella said in a loud whisper-shout.

Emma rolled over. "Hey, peanut."

Stella gasped and turned to look behind her. "She's awake!"

The bed bounced and a warm sparkle-clad body pressed against her.

Garrett appeared at the threshold. He stopped and stared at them with an arrested look on his face. He lifted his phone, snapping a picture with an oddly wistful smile.

He walked around the bed and climbed on her other side, wrapping a hand around her waist before pressing a kiss to her hair. "Do you feel better?"

"A bit foggy but much better. Give me a minute and I will wash up and come down." She turned back to Stella. "I'm sorry I missed the park."

"It was fun!" her sister chirped. Then she made big eyes at Garrett. "Now?" she whispered.

"Almost," he replied.

Bemused, Emma turned to look over her shoulder at her crafty husband. "What do you two rascals have planned?"

"It's not a plan. It's your secret! We know your secret!"

Turning back to Stella, Emma furrowed her brow.

"You do?" she asked, playing along. "What is it?"

Garrett cleared his throat loudly.

"We have news," he said with mock solemnity. "It's going to be hard to hear, and even harder to believe. But it's real and we're here for you."

He looked past her. "Okay now, Stella."

Stella could barely contain herself. She took a big gulp of air and squealed, "You're my mommy!"

Emma blinked. She opened her mouth, but nothing came out.

"And Daddy Garrett is my papa!"

A nervous laugh escaped but Emma killed it. She was going to correct her when Garrett squeezed her arm. She turned to face him, and everything stilled at the dead serious expression on his face.

His fake gravity wasn't an act.

He began to speak but her frozen brain didn't process what he was saying. She only registered small snatches like *spitting image*, *dimple*, and *worried about*.

A slow blink and then a small hand was on her cheek.

"Are you okay?" Stella's worried little face appeared over her. "Papa, I don't think she's happy."

Papa! Stella had gotten confused playing her family's game and somehow, she'd taken Garrett with her into fantasyland.

Emma shook her head, ready to explain how this was all a mistake when she caught movement out of the corner of her eye. Her mother was standing in the doorway.

Mariana's eyes were red, shining with unspent tears.

She raised a shaky hand to her mouth, but not before Emma caught what she mouthed. *"I'm sorry."*

Oh my God.

Emma bolted upright, her head swimming. She was vaguely aware her breathing was far too fast to be normal. The room was spinning.

Strong hands pushed her gently but firmly back down on the mattress.

The ceiling continued to whirl above her and began to darken. But small hands were touching her face and Garrett's voice in her ear, saying over and over, *It's okay, you're okay.*

She couldn't let go. Emma beat back the dark, taking shallow breaths.

She blinked and Stella's concerned face was replaced with Garrett's.

Emma raised her arm—which for some reason weighed like a hundred and fifty pounds—and touched his face.

His features softened, almost glowing with warmth and love. Or they were soft. Until she flattened her fingers on his face and pushed him away—*hard*.

"Sorry," she mumbled, groping until she curled her arms around Stella.

Emma clutched her daughter's little body to her chest, hugging far too tightly.

But Stella didn't complain. Her little face was inches away and she was beaming at her.

Stella nuzzled her, ecstatic with the best birthday present she could have possibly received.

Her dad.

Chapter Fifty-Eight

GARRETT

Keeping an eye on both Stella and Emma proved impossible but he tried long enough to make him cross-eyed.

Relax, he scolded. Stella was just riding her bike. But his heart started pounding out of control when she and Mariana disappeared down the street.

Garrett forced himself to sit back. His mother-in-law had the situation in hand. She'd been raising the kid alone for the past five years, for fuck's sake. He could survive ten minutes.

Emma turned to him, her eyes wide. "Should we follow them?"

Yeah, there was a reason he loved this woman. He laughed nervously, pulling at the collar of his sweater before thinking better of it and taking it off altogether. "That's harder than it should be, right?"

He plucked at the cotton of his shirt, lifting it up and down to get some air circulation. "I didn't know my daughter existed yesterday morning, and today I am sweating when I can't see her."

Emma had said very little since getting out of bed. But she had eventually let Stella go, which he took as a good sign.

Now she put her hands on her head and staggered to the porch, where a worn wooden bench covered by a cushion looked over the front lawn.

"How did this happen?" she asked, dazed. "Why didn't my mom tell me the truth?"

"I think she tried," he said. "But you were in really bad shape when she did, and the memory didn't stick."

"How could I forget that?" she cried, her throat thick with tears.

Garrett scooted closer, wrapping his arms around her. "You had a traumatic brain injury. It's a miracle you recovered."

"But I did. I got better." Emma sniffed, wiping her cheek. "She could have told me later."

He wished she had, but he also understood why she hadn't.

"Mariana was scared. Part of her has always believed that the father of your baby was a bad guy—bad enough to run you down in the woods."

Emma closed her eyes, an inarticulate sound escaping as she let her head tip backward. "I keep thinking I'm dreaming and I'm going to wake up."

Garrett squeezed her arm. "Right there with you. But it's real and we're going to handle it."

He hoped that sounded confident enough. They were going to be a family.

Emma twisted to face him, a pleading anxious light in her eyes. "And you're sure she's ours?"

He swallowed, but not because he wasn't sure. It was what he had to show her.

"One hundred percent," he said, taking out his phone. "These are going to be hard to see—I sure as hell had a difficult time with them. But you should see them."

Thumbing the screen, he flipped to the pictures Mariana had sent him.

"Your mom took pictures of you at the hospital, to chronicle your progress."

"My what?"

It was better to show her. Grimacing, he turned the phone so she could see it.

Emma gasped and snatched up the phone.

It was her in the hospital, in a bed, hooked up to an IV and a bunch of wires to monitor her vitals. The sheets had been pulled taut over her in the shot, enough to discern the start of her pregnancy.

Garrett rubbed the back of his head. "The belly gets bigger in the later shots."

Emma groaned and bent over the phone, scrolling to the more recent photographs. Her pregnancy belly swelled more and more until the final one, where an anonymous nurse hovered nearby with a tiny, wrinkled baby nestled in the crook of her arm.

"*Shit*." Emma shoved the phone back at him. Then she snatched it back and swore again. "This is crazy."

"Not as crazy as this," he said, gently prying the phone from her hands. He went back to the side-by-side of his mom and Stella and showed it to her. "That's my mom."

She stared at it open-mouthed. "I guess we know why you're so sure."

"Yes, my mom is five here." He put his arm around her. "I don't think we need a DNA test to prove she's mine."

She shook her head and then frowned. "But you are very rich. Do you want one anyway?"

He shrugged. "It won't change anything for anyone except my lawyers."

She looked at him sharply. "Right, then do it. I don't want anyone to doubt her."

"They won't," he promised. "Even if she weren't the spitting image of my mother, if I say she's my daughter, then she's my daughter."

Emma swallowed. "What if I want the test?"

"We don't need it."

"I might," she said in a small voice.

Her mind wasn't going to rest until he agreed.

"All right. Then we'll do it. But you need to take my word on something—you were madly in love with me. You weren't with anyone else."

She smacked him in the arm. "You weren't that sure a few weeks ago."

He took her hand, guiding it to his mouth and pressing a kiss to each of her fingertips. "I was an immature jerk back then. I've grown up since then."

Emma rolled her eyes, but her lips turned up at the corners. "Right."

"I have." He laughed, even though he felt more like crying. "I have aged like a decade since then."

Seriously, his heart couldn't take much more of this.

She shuddered, the aftermath of too much emotion. "You became a father."

"And you a mother."

Emma put a hand over her heart. "I've been a bad one. I wasn't even here this past year."

He pulled her into his side, squeezing her tight. "You did the best thing you could have possibly done. You went to San Diego to find me, so I could fall in love with you all over again."

Pressing his forehead to hers, he took her scent deep into his lungs. "Although to be honest, I never stopped."

Emma softened momentarily but she wasn't done freaking out. "What if that hadn't happened? I still wouldn't know Stella was mine. And no one would have ever realized she was yours. All because I didn't tell you I was pregnant."

No, they weren't going to play that game.

"You were going to," he said. "You didn't get a chance."

That was why she was in the woods. She'd been on her way, and some asshole had run her down and snatched five years from them.

More actually. Was pregnancy really nine months? Because he thought he'd read somewhere it was more like ten.

He could feel himself getting pissed off. But he shoved those feelings back. He couldn't let that anger poison the here and now. They had a future to focus on.

"Our daughter is brilliant, by the way."

And ballsy. She wasn't afraid to take on a boy taller and heavier than her. But she'd need a better fighting technique because soon the boys would be too big.

Hell, puberty was going to come way too soon for his comfort as well. Garrett didn't have the full twelve or thirteen years other dads got to prepare.

"Some jiu-jitsu classes might be in order," he said. "Or better yet, kickboxing."

You could do more damage at a distance with kickboxing.

Garrett turned to find Emma staring at him. She fluttered her lashes. "Is this the first father of a daughter meltdown I'm seeing? Or did you also lose it at the park and forget to tell me?"

"First." And sadly not the last.

Emma ran her fingers through her hair. "God, we're going to be parental disasters."

"No, we're not," he protested. "Well, maybe we will be at first. But we'll muddle through."

She closed her eyes and nodded. "I do think Stella is better off now that everything is out in the open."

"Yeah," he agreed. "Plus, I think she likes having a dad."

"Look at you puffing up like Superman." Emma grinned. "And you don't have to tell me she loves it already. I'm pretty sure you're the reason she's accepted all this so quickly."

They looked at each other. He opened his arms and she scooted against him, resting her head against his shoulder.

"I never realized how hard it must have been for her, not knowing who her dad was. Although, I guess it's good my mom never made up a story for her."

Yes, he agreed silently. They had gotten lucky. But she was also right that it must have been hard on Stella. She was only in kindergarten, and it had already been an issue.

Also, fuck small towns.

"Was it hard for you, not knowing?"

Emma's brows puckered. Then she rammed her shoulder into his. Not hard. But hard enough. "I know who my dad is!"

"Oh." *Fuck.* He cleared his throat apologetically. "I didn't realize you knew that. Where is he?"

She shrugged. "Seattle or Oregon. Someplace rainy. With his new family."

"Oh." *Find a new syllable, dude.* That one was getting stale.

He cleared his throat, trying to decide what to say.

"And before you ask, no, he's not in my life at all. Not since I was two or three," she said, a hard look on her face. "He did deign to visit after I got out of the coma. I was in physical therapy, and he came by for the first and last time since he left us."

"How did that go?" he asked, ignoring the buzz coming from his back pocket.

Her face displayed a distinct lack of enthusiasm. "He stayed a couple of hours and left. He didn't mention Stella. She wasn't there. But he was extra-judgy about Mom and her boyfriends so there's a good chance he thought she was hers. He's a born-again Christian now —so holier than thou. He was ten years older than my mom when they got together. Just another hypocrite if you ask me."

She sniffed. "Anyway, that was enough father-daughter time for me. He's welcome to stay the hell away."

"Noted. No holiday invites for your dad."

"Those two things do not and will not ever go together."

She paused before giving him a wry smile. "I'm afraid all things father are on your head."

He offered her his pinky. "I got this. I promise."

She wound her own smaller pinky around his. "I know. Thank you. Why does your phone keep vibrating?"

Garrett gave her his most winsome grin. "Because I put it on silent."

Emma's lips compressed.

"All right. Well, speaking of disasters," he began brightly, checking his phone. "I've gotten three texts from my aunt Phil in the last hour."

Her pupils flared. "Did you tell her?"

"Not yet," he said with resigned smile. "I knew it was too much to hope that Sharon and darling Dennis could keep their mouths shut."

Emma was starting to look nauseated. "Should we go see her?"

"Not today."

Her head drew back. "Your aunt is blowing up your phone and you're not going to see her today?"

"No." Garrett was certain. "Today is for us. Well, for you. I had last night. But you got some big news today, so I'm going to turn off the phone entirely and we are going to go inside your mother's house and order a fantastic dinner for us and our daughter."

He paused. "Your mother is going out tonight."

"Of course she is," Emma mumbled.

"I think it's good. Generous even. We get to spend time with Stella alone, so she can get used to us as parents. How does that sound?"

"Like your aunt is going to hunt us down and kill us."

"Let me handle Phil," he said, rising and holding out his hand.

They were walking inside when he snapped his fingers. "*Body-guards*! In addition to putting Stella in jiu-jitsu, we're going to hire some bodyguards to keep an eye on her."

"Oh my God." Emma covered her face with her hand.

"Okay, how about a tutor with a law enforcement background?"

Emma gave him a very wifely look of derision.

But Garrett was not about to be deterred. His one true love had been run down like a dog in the woods. Because of it, they had missed one thousand eight hundred and twenty-four days of their child's life.

If Garrett was ever going to sleep again, he needed to make plans and get some security protocols in place.

"I know some mercenaries. Maybe they can take turns babysitting. No? How about a nanny with martial arts training?"

Emma continued to ignore him, heading to the kitchen. But that was okay. He'd keep working on her.

If any law enforcement officials passed them now, they would assume he had kidnapped Emma. One look at her face and they would think she was getting ready to jump out of the moving car.

They might be right.

The car was climbing up the hill on the way to his aunt Phil's house with Stella riding in the back seat in her booster seat with the tablet he'd had shipped overnight.

A pair of pink sparkly children's headphones sat on her head. They had cat ears that flashed with multicolored LED light, a function he'd turned off almost immediately.

"You can wait outside while I speak to Phil," he assured his wife in a low voice after checking the rearview to see if Stella was listening. "I can signal you once the coast is clear."

Emma turned to him, a slowly moving backdrop of evergreen trees behind her. "Do you think that will happen today? Or even this year?"

Garrett wasn't about to lie or massage the truth for Emma. "It will be awkward. She'll be unhappy at first. But once I explain things to her, Phil will get on board."

Despite her formal country club manners, Phil loved him. She'd accept his family. He just needed to lay out the facts before she started in on him.

"I don't remember her, of course, but I know how my mom feels about her," Emma added in a low voice. "She isn't going to welcome us."

"I won't deny those two have an ugly history," he conceded. "But that bad blood is between them. We are not a part of it."

"I doubt your aunt will see it that way. Just look at me." Emma waved a hand over her face. "I'm my mom fifteen years ago."

"You may resemble her, but you are *Emma*," he stressed. "My wife. The mother of my child. Never forget that."

She made a rough sound in the back of her throat. "Just signal me if we should start running."

They pulled up to his aunt's house a few minutes later. Phil lived in a massive three-story American Colonial in the wealthy enclave of Verdant Falls. Situated right next to the river, it was known locally as the 'White House.'

The original structure had been built by another family at the turn of the century. It had been purchased by his mother's people in the thirties.

Since then, it had been expanded multiple times until it had become this three-story monolith, one that appeared coherent and whole thanks to the work of some of the best architects in the state.

His father had sold the house Garrett had grown up in right after he'd gone to college. But it hadn't mattered to him. He may have slept in that other house, but this place and the cabin down the river had been more of a home to him.

Garrett stepped out of the car, hurrying to the other side to open the door for his girls. Stella reluctantly let go of her new tablet in favor of the stuffed owl that was her favorite toy.

As they'd discussed, Emma took Stella's hand, taking the path on the side of the house that led to the back garden and the koi pond designed to withstand Colorado winters.

He knocked at the front door and was admitted by Consuela, who introduced herself as the housekeeper.

Phil had always employed a cook, but the live-in housekeeper must be a recent addition. However, given the alternative, using the same cleaning service that used to employ Mariana, it was not unexpected.

When his aunt didn't come to meet him, he walked through the house, searching for her.

Phil was in the back living room, watching Emma and Stella walk around the garden.

Emma was keeping her distance from the house, so she couldn't see his favorite relative watching them with her arms crossed in silent judgment.

Phil didn't even turn around before beginning to lecture him. "Do you have any idea how many people have called me to say that you've been seen in town? In the company of that *woman*, no less!"

"That isn't Mariana Mendez out there."

His aunt spun on her heel.

Despite losing her summer tan, Phil was looking well. She had what people called good bones, like his mother. The sisters had resembled each other a good deal, although Phil had narrower, more aristocratic features.

And a soupçon more judgment.

"I know that," Phil scolded. "Don't you think I know the difference?"

She raised her fingers, pinching the bridge of her nose in a telltale gesture of stress.

Garrett pulled her into his arms. "Hi," he mumbled into her expertly colored hair.

Softening, she leaned against him, hugging him tight before pushing him away. "I'm waiting for an explanation."

"I apologize for not saying more in my text, but I have quite a story to tell you now."

She recrossed her arms. "I don't think there is anything you can say to explain why, of all the people in the world, you chose to get involved with that woman's daughter."

Trust Phil to make *that woman* sound like the worst curse. "What else did people call to tell you?"

Phil threw her arm out, pointing to the pair next to the gazebo. "Wasn't that enough?"

Nope. Not even close. "Maybe you should sit down."

Phil covered her face with her hands. "Please don't tell me you're going to marry Emmaline Mendez. Don't you dare."

Garrett straightened his shoulders. "I already married her. It's been a few months."

Phil staggered to a brocaded wingback chair, collapsing gracefully. "Are you trying to hurt me?"

The genuine pain in her voice dug into his gut like claws.

He sat on the matching ottoman in front of her.

"No, I'm not," he said with gentle firmness, putting his hand on hers. "This has nothing to do with you or her mother. It's about me and Emma and the fact that I love her. I have since high school."

"What?" Phil's face twisted skeptically. "You barely even knew her back then."

"I didn't talk about her, but I knew her," he corrected. "We didn't get together until much later. We had a brief relationship when we were in college."

His aunt opened her mouth to interrupt. He held up a hand, forestalling her. "*Please*. I promise I will tell you everything you need to know, but first I have to ask, did you know about Emma's accident?"

Phil blinked. "The hit-and-run in the woods?"

He'd expected that answer, but it was a blow nonetheless.

"Garrett? What's wrong?" Phil asked, alarmed by the expression on his face.

He took a deep breath, trying to get ahold of himself. "I am upset, but I get it. You didn't know she was important to me."

He looked up to find his aunt wide-eyed, watching him like a woman taking out her garbage only to be confronted by a bear next to the bins.

"That woman—Mariana—left town after the accident," Phil said carefully. "I heard the daughter was in the hospital for a long time. I... I would have mentioned it had I known that you were interested."

"It's my fault you didn't." He'd been too fucking proud and secretive.

He was man enough to admit he should have been more open about his relationship with Emma. Not just with his aunt, but also his friends from high school. Instead, he'd gone scorched earth on anything to do with Verdant Falls after Emma had stopped calling him.

The only exception was his partnership with Fletcher, but he hadn't needed to come home to reconnect with him after college. Fletcher had sought him out.

He had no one to blame but himself for losing Emma for so long.

"I saw Emma again by chance in San Diego, working in my building," he told Phil. "She hasn't fully recovered from the hit-and-run. I wanted to take care of her. She needed health insurance. So I talked her into marrying me eight weeks ago."

Phil glowered at him. "That sounds like something your father would do."

He didn't dignify that with a response.

His father would *never* have married Emma. He'd have set her up as his mistress for a year or two before replacing her with a newer model.

"I won her over eventually. But the hit-and-run caused memory problems. Emma lost everything from before the accident."

Phil straightened in her chair. "I hadn't realized it was that serious."

He was relieved to hear that. If she'd known the extent, he'd keep blaming himself for not questioning her on old town gossip.

"It was bad," he said, his voice growing thick with incipient tears. "When she woke up from her coma, she had no memory of being pregnant or giving birth. She was in no shape to care for a child. Her mother decided to tell everyone the baby was hers."

His aunt's questioning stare scoured his face, before transforming into a grimace of horror.

"That's not funny!" she snapped.

"I'm not joking." He wished he was.

Phil jerked forward in her seat. "Everyone knows who that child belongs to."

Yeah, the supposed sins of the previous generation were far more believable than the truth.

"I know why you think that. The rumors that she was Teddy Bronson's child must have been everywhere. But Stella is *my* daughter."

Phil jumped to her feet, her face set. "I don't know what lies that woman has been spinning but she can't be yours."

He frowned, struck by a sudden thought. "Did you ever confront Teddy about Stella?"

"No," Phil scoffed. "There was no need. By the time I learned she existed, we were already separated. The divorce proceedings were well underway!"

Then Stella hadn't been the straw that broke the camel's back. That had to be a blessing, right?

"It's obvious you've never taken a good look at Stella. That's understandable—"

His aunt waved her hand in his face like she was flagging down an inattentive waiter. "The girl is Teddy's! That rat even bought them a house—one he paid for with the divorce settlement I was forced to give him."

"He makes Mariana pay rent."

None of his explanations about Stella seemed to be getting through to her, but this did.

"*What?*" she cried.

It was time for the photo. Garrett showed it to her, but Phil shook her head adamantly.

"This is Photoshop. Or that new thing they are talking about. The thing from *The Terminator*." She snapped her fingers. "AI. This is AI."

Garrett rose to his feet, tugging her to the glass doors.

Stella was on all fours next on the flagstones surrounding the koi pond. He couldn't hear what she was saying but it appeared as if she was having an animated conversation with her mother.

"Stella is here, in the flesh. I want you to look at her, not her picture, and tell me what you see."

Frowning, Phil went to the desk, taking out a pair of glasses he'd never seen. She perched them at the tip of her nose and peered out the window.

He knew the moment she saw the resemblance.

Clutching the glasses more firmly on her face, she turned to him with a gasp. "Good Lord. That's *me*."

It was true in a way. The sisters had looked a great deal like each other, but he thought Stella resembled his mother more strongly.

"There's a lot of the Martins in Stella," he acknowledged. "She's very smart and sweet. And she's going to be a real ballbuster when she grows up. But neither Emma nor I can take credit for any of that. We've known she was ours for all of forty hours."

That caused visible consternation.

"Why did that wom—" Phil stopped, catching herself. "Why did Mariana let everyone believe Stella was her child?"

Because her life experience has taught her to expect the worst from people.

"She thought Emma's accident wasn't an accident," he explained, launching into a brief sketch of what happened all those years ago, all the doubts, her fears. How hard Emma's recovery had been.

"She did the best she could," he finished. "It was a very stressful time."

"Yes, I can imagine."

Phil folded her hands together. She was quiet for a moment before she cleared her throat. "Well, it's getting cold outside. I think it's time you called your wife and daughter inside."

"Thank you," he murmured.

His aunt smoothed her sweater, nodding in acknowledgment. "I'll go tell the cook that we'll be having hot chocolate in the sunroom."

Garrett raised his brows. "Make mine Irish. I think everyone old enough to vote could benefit from one."

Phil huffed, not quite laughing but close enough for him. "You're not wrong."

Chapter Sixty

GARRETT

The pines crowded the car as he drove, making the stretch of woods darker than it should have been at this hour of the afternoon.

It was easy to imagine it at night, the moonlight fighting a losing battle to illuminate the dirt tract.

Garrett gripped the wheel of his rented Range Rover, wondering where exactly on this godforsaken road Emma had been run down.

"Asked and answered," he growled to himself as he spotted Sheriff Warner's 4x4 parked a few dozen yards ahead.

He slid his vehicle behind him, a short stretch with room for a shoulder on what was a wide single-lane track this deep in the woods.

The sheriff waved as he approached.

Jesse Warner had always dressed the part of local law enforcement, favoring jeans and plaids even in his off time when Garrett used to live here. But he'd leaned hard into the sheriff persona since, adding boots and a Stetson to his repertoire.

Garrett stuck out his hand to shake but the sheriff bypassed it, giving him one of those backslapping hugs peculiar to overcompensating men everywhere.

"Thank you for taking time out of your day to see me," Garrett said, pulling away as soon as it was polite.

Jesse tipped the hat back a notch. "It's not a problem. I had some time this afternoon."

But his expression didn't match the easy words. Or that hug.

"I haven't been back here since college," he said. "I appreciate you showing me the scene."

"Of course." Jesse shifted his weight, sticking his thumbs in the belt loops. "But before we start, I need to ask—is it true? What I'm hearing about you and Emma?"

If Phil heard, it made sense that Warner had too. The small-town grapevine worked at the speed of light.

Garrett nodded, unable to help the satisfaction from creeping into his expression.

"Yeah. Sorry I didn't lead with that. I was waiting to tell my aunt before spreading it around town. Emma and I are married now. If it hadn't been for her accident, we would have been married all this time. That's why I'm so invested in learning everything I can about it."

He explained to Jesse what Emma had been doing on this road that night, their fight, and how he'd made the mistake of his life leaving town the next day.

Jesse whistled, scratching his head. "That's quite a story. But it's good that you and Emma were able to work it out."

"Yeah," he agreed, although he felt that simple summation downplayed the hand of fate. Emma coming back into his life was nothing short of a miracle.

"Can you walk me through the accident?" he asked. "And what happened after?"

The other man jerked as if Garrett had interrupted some deep thought.

"Yeah, sure."

Jesse moved to the middle of the road, his posture altering subtly as he shifted into sheriff mode. He gestured south, in the direction of the former Mendez home.

"The night of the accident, Mariana had gotten out of work around eleven to find Emma gone. She left a note, but midnight rolled around and Mariana still hadn't heard from her. That was late for Emma, so

Mariana started texting, offering to pick her up. They only had one car —that gray Corolla, remember?"

"Yeah, I do."

Did Mariana still drive that old beater? There hadn't been a vehicle in the driveway. He'd assumed the family car was in the standalone garage in the back, but he hadn't checked what was in it.

Mental note, get grandma a reliable new car ASAP.

"When Emma didn't text back, she started calling but Em didn't pick up," Jesse continued. "According to Mariana, that was pretty unusual. Mari always said Emma was the responsible one, and she was the flaky one…"

Jesse paused as if waiting to see if he would comment on the pet name.

Garrett wasn't stupid. He wasn't touching that situation with a ten-foot pole.

"Next, she called around to Emma's friends, but none had heard from her. That was when Mariana called me. She asked me to start checking the roads between their place and town. We both assumed Emma was on foot and her phone battery had died. Without the flash-light on it, she would have had a hell of a time maneuvering through the woods."

"Yeah, no kidding."

He remembered that about this place. Unless the moon was right overhead, it would have been pitch-dark, the only light sporadic patches where the moonlight was able to break through the trees.

"We thought everyone who could have given her a ride was accounted for." Jesse stepped back, pivoting to face north and the direction of Garrett's old cabin. "Truth be told, if I'd known about the two of you, you would have been a prime suspect—a poor but beau-tiful young girl with the richest guy in town…"

Garrett should have been offended, but he couldn't blame the guy. "Fair enough. But for the record, it wasn't me."

Although in retrospect, the accusation would have been welcome. If one single fucking person had told him about the accident…

He sighed. Yeah, he really had to stop playing that game.

"I know. Mainly because dozens of witnesses put you at your cabin during the accident window."

Jesse squatted for a second, picking up a rock. He turned it in his hands. "You hadn't been home in a while, so the party was big news. I was going to check later. But at the time, I thought it more likely that Emma was walking home from somewhere else."

Garrett nodded. "You said Mariana found her."

"Yeah." Jesse threw the rock past the tree line opposite the ridge. "I was searching the southern trail. It winds a bit more but lets out close to the library and café. But Mariana took this road and spotted some damage over here."

Pivoting, Jesse walked a couple of yards, gesturing to a spot on a thick pine at the edge of the road some dozen yards from the shoulder.

"It's healed over now, but there was some obvious splintering just here, white and fresh. It stood out in her headlights, so she got out to investigate, using the flashlight on her phone."

Jesse crossed the road, stopping at the edge. Below them was a steep drop-off.

The trees were thinner along the slope but that hardly mattered. Emma only had to tumble into one of those. It would have been like hitting a concrete pillar.

"Mari found her near the bottom, bleeding from the head but breathing."

Garrett's imagination was far too good. In his mind, he saw Emma's beautiful face, covered in blood, her body crumpled and broken.

His jaw was so tight it felt like it might shatter. With effort, he pushed the nightmare images away.

Yes, they had lost years, but Emma was safe now. Garrett was going to make damn sure she stayed that way.

Both his girls would be protected.

He cleared his throat. "Thank God for Mariana."

Jesse grunted an assent, his eyes distant. "The EMTs went down with a stretcher and neck brace. Emma had a broken arm and some cracked ribs. But the head injury was the worst of it. Emma needed a specialist, so she got transferred to Denver. Mariana went with her."

He kicked a small stone down the slope. They watched it fall, coming to a rest halfway down before he spoke again.

"She didn't come back here. Mariana gave up her lease, using her savings and some donations to stay on in Denver until Emma was well enough to be left alone. I thought she was going to come back, maybe find a new place since their old place was occupied, but she moved one town over instead."

His mouth tightened.

"With baby Stella," he added, his voice noticeably rougher. "Once Emma got out of the hospital, she joined them. Which leads me to a rather uncomfortable question. But I gotta ask. About Stella…"

Garrett couldn't help being surprised at the unasked question. He knew Jesse and Mariana had dated, but it must have fizzled out much earlier than he thought, or else the sheriff would have known the answer to the question he was asking.

"Stella is mine," he said. "Mine and Emma's. She was a few months pregnant at the time of the accident."

Jesse's face contorted.

He may as well have punched the other man. Jesse staggered back, his face turning gray.

"Emma delivered Stella in Denver," he continued in a softer voice, conscious that he was delivering one hell of a blow. "The labor pains may have helped rouse her from the coma. But when she woke up, she had no memory of being pregnant. She couldn't even speak yet, let alone care for a baby. So Mariana took the infant."

Jesse grunted, wiping his face. Garrett felt bad, but Jesse had to know the truth. It was better to rip off the Band-Aid. Trying to ease into it wasn't going to make it any easier for the man.

"You never did track down the driver of the car," he continued. "Once Mariana realized Emma was pregnant, she connected the baby with the accident. She thought the father might have run Emmy down. Little did she know I was having a literal pity party just a few miles away, drowning my sorrows in cheap beer and overpriced whiskey because of a stupid misunderstanding."

"Huh." Jesse processed that. "I guess that's a good enough reason to keep the baby's parentage a secret. But I still can't believe Mari didn't tell me."

Garrett didn't know what to say to that, so he decided nothing was better. Clearing his throat, he gestured down the incline, beginning a careful climb down to the area Jesse had indicated earlier.

"Was it around here?"

"Yeah. Just to your right." The sheriff pointed a few feet from him. "We're not sure where she hit her head but as best we could figure, her leg struck that tree, stopping her descent to the bottom. I know it sounds weird, but that might have been lucky. The bottom has some big stones that could have done a lot more damage."

Garrett turned, scanning the bottom of the incline. *Christ.* Jesse was right. Those boulders were fucking huge.

Swearing under his breath, Garrett crab-walked across the uneven ground, one leg higher up on the slope to maintain his balance.

Seeing how much trouble he was having, Jesse wisely decided to stay where he was. His traction would have been shit in those cowboy boots.

"We scoured the ground around her thoroughly in the days following. Aside from her phone, there was nothing down there."

"No auto glass on the road? Like from a headlight?"

Jesse shook his head. "Just the paint transfer on the tree."

Garrett began to climb back up, glad he'd busted out his hiking boots for this. "How high was it?"

Jesse put his hand out, helping haul him up the last few feet. "What was that? I missed it."

"The paint transfer on the tree." Garrett brushed off the dirt on his knees. "Was it at sedan or truck height?"

"Sedan is my guess, although it looks to be about truck height now. But that's only because the tree has grown. Come see."

They examined a faint scar on the trunk, which was just above his waist.

"The paint was an extremely common shade of black," Jesse said with a frown. "It was used by multiple car makers. It was the only clue. We didn't find any clear fresh tire tracks. The ground was too hard-packed. The few impressions we had were confused. The clearest looked older and were likely made during the rain we had weeks earlier."

Damn. No wonder the trail had gone cold.

Garrett scanned the road. It did bend sharply here. It *was* possible the driver hadn't seen her. Especially if she'd been wearing something dark.

"I suppose it could have been an accident," he muttered. "She might have jumped off the road to avoid getting run down, her injuries a result of hitting one of these trees."

"The first doctor to examine her believed the arm break was a crushing injury, but if she hit one of those trees just right, then yeah," Jesse agreed. "They could have been caused by the tree and not the car. But the fact that the driver never took their vehicle in for repair means they were aware of the accident or learned of it after the fact."

"Yeah." He didn't dispute that.

But he wanted to go back and tell Emma once and for all that her accident was just that. For her peace of mind. And his.

"I just wanted to tie up loose ends before we close this chapter and move on," he said, voicing his desire out loud. "I should have known we wouldn't get this tied in a neat bow."

Jesse squinted in one of the rare patches of sunlight. "Frustrating as shit, isn't it?"

"Yeah." He took a final look around and shook his head.

It probably was an accident. Part of him didn't want to accept that because that meant he had no villain to fight. And he dearly wanted someone to blame—aside from himself.

Can you kick your own ass?

Shaking off that mental image, he turned back to the sheriff. "Did you remember to bring Emma's phone?"

"I did."

Jesse jerked his thumb at his SUV. "It's a Motorola model commonly given away when you sign up for a phone plan. I had it dusted for prints and swabbed for DNA but got nothing that shouldn't have been there. As for the data, I had it sent upstate to see if they could pull anything off it. But they weren't able to get it to start, so fair warning your experts may not fare any better."

"I know it's a long shot, but I have seen Toya Almari, the specialist at Auric Security, work miracles."

Jesse looked skeptical. "I doubt it will shed any light on the accident, but like I said on the phone, you're welcome to it. It belongs to Emma, broken or not."

There was also the fact the statute of limitations for a hit-and-run had come and gone well before he and Emma reconnected.

"I know. At best, I'll see a string of my texts to Emma. But I need to cross every T."

Jesse nodded, sticking his thumbs in his jeans pockets. "Well, if you discover any deep dark secrets on it, you'll let me know."

"I will," Garrett promised. "Although, I suspect I know Emma's biggest secret now."

The sheriff stared at him for a second before nodding in understanding. "Ah. Yeah, of course. Stella. Wow, I hadn't even stopped to think about the implications of her being yours—you're probably going to take her with you."

"Oh, hell yeah."

That wasn't even a question in his mind. His wife and daughter belonged with him in San Diego. He was already researching the best kindergarten schools near his place.

"What about Mariana?" Jesse asked. He cleared his throat with a slightly strangled sound. "She'll be alone."

"Oh, Mariana's coming." Garrett wasn't about to split her and Stella up. "I've arranged for her to have one of the condos on the floor below our penthouse."

Jesse's lips parted. "You did?"

"Yeah, we all agreed that it's best for Stella if we all stay together. Besides, I'm pretty sure Mariana is ready to put Colorado in her rearview."

Jesse rocked back on his heels. "But what about her house and... and her relationship with that Bronson fellow."

Well, shit. Garrett wasn't going to get out of discussing his mother-in-law's love life after all.

"Mariana hasn't exactly said where she and Teddy stand, but she did say she'd like to be out of here before he gets back from the Bahamas," he confided. "So my guess is it's not good."

Jesse scowled. "What about her house?"

The sheriff's effort at casual needed a lot of work.

"I don't know where people got the idea that the house belongs to Mariana. She *rents* it from Teddy. Yeah, it's a bit cheaper than market rate but she does pay him."

Garrett even knew the dollar amount. He'd found the check stubs in one of the kitchen drawers when he'd been looking for a spatula to make Stella pancakes.

He hadn't intended to snoop, but the bill drawer had given him a pretty good idea of Mariana's financial picture.

Garrett ran a hand through his hair. "Anyway, after raising my daughter for the last five years, I decided Mariana deserved an early retirement. The condo will be in her name, all expenses paid. She still wants to babysit, of course, and now she can be there for Emma too, for any doctor's appointments I can't make."

Jesse raised his brows, taking it all in with slow blinks of the long dark lashes that had made him very popular with the ladies. "Wow. That's a lot. Lots of changes, I mean."

In for a penny, in for a pound. "Can I ask you something?"

Jesse put his hands on his hips. "Shoot."

"Keep in mind that this is coming from the jackass who didn't know he had a kid because of one stupid fight," Garrett began. "But I'm a little surprised you didn't know about Stella. You were investigating the hit-and-run. Did you not go see Emma in the hospital?"

The pregnancy would have been obvious at some point.

Jesse's face tightened. "It's a fair question. I did see Em when she was at the local hospital, but I didn't ever go up to Denver."

The sheriff kicked the ground with the tip of his cowboy boot. "To tell you the truth, me and Mari weren't talking a whole lot during that period."

He adjusted his Stetson, scrubbing his reddening hairline. "I had started seeing Kelley Ames around then, long enough to fuel rumors that I might pop the question and marry her. Mari avoided me when she saw me in the street. I heard she started seeing Bronson again just after the accident. He kind of swooped in, riding to the rescue. I didn't like it, but…"

He trailed off, his face dark. "Everyone thought Stella was his."

"And you were still playing the field."

Jesse scowled. "It's not like Mari and I didn't stay friends."

Garrett nodded. But he couldn't help but think that *Mari* no longer thought of Jesse in those warm terms. She would have told the sheriff the truth if she'd trusted him.

"And I *did* check in after Emma came back from the hospital!" Jesse's voice was getting louder. "Mariana could have said something then—at the very least to tell me her theory that Emma's baby daddy ran her down. It would have given me a new lead."

"As the baby daddy in question, I kind of wish she had too. But it was a crazy time, with Emma in the hospital. Even after she went home, she had to go for endless rounds of physical therapy." Garrett sighed. "I'm just glad Mariana kept Stella. For that, I'll be eternally grateful."

His philosophical response didn't rub off on Jesse. The man wasn't done venting. "To my knowledge, Bronson denied being Stella's dad once or twice to some of his cohorts, but it was pretty half-hearted."

Garrett made a noncommittal noise, leaning against the car door.

He wasn't about to tell Jesse that Teddy *had* gone to Denver, visiting Mariana several times during Emma's pregnancy. It would have sounded too much like censure.

He tried again to bring the man back down, so he could grab that phone and get back to Emma, but Jesse wanted to keep complaining. He went on for a while about Teddy and his growing reputation as a slumlord.

Garrett, however, was already aware of what Teddy had been up to. He'd had his people keep track of the man's business dealings, in case Teddy ever decided to pester his aunt again.

However, Jesse was really warming to the topic, as if Garrett's questions had broken open some sort of dam.

He put up his hands to interrupt the rant. "Jesse, I know this thing about Mariana not being Stella's mother is throwing you. You were close once and she didn't share this very pertinent detail. I'm sure it also burns that Teddy knew and you didn't."

"But she let Bronson—"

Okay, enough. Garrett slashed his hand through the air. "Do I have to say it aloud?"

Jesse crossed his arms. "Say what?"

There was no good way to do this, so he kept it as short as possible. "That I think my mother-in-law may have prostituted herself so she could keep a roof over my daughter's head."

Jesse dropped his arms, closing his mouth.

Garrett grimaced, shoving his hands in his pockets. "It's just a theory, of course. Mariana hasn't said anything remotely like this. But from the way she talks about Teddy and the speed at which she's packing, it's obvious she wants to blow town while he's out of the country."

Jesse stared at him for a minute. Then he stalked to his vehicle, climbing in and slamming the door. He drove away in an aggressive cloud of dust.

"Okay then," Garrett told the trees with a sigh. Then he swore.

Jesse hadn't given him the phone.

He finished dusting off his clothes and headed to his rental, wondering if there was any way he could beat the sheriff to Mariana's house.

Chapter Sixty-Two

EMMA

"Mommy, are you still mad at Mama-Grandma?" Stella asked.

Emma jerked, studying her daughter in the dim light of the cramped pantry. "What? No. I'm not mad."

"Then we aren't hiding from her?" Stella asked, blinking those impossibly long lashes at her.

The conjoined Mama-Grandma wasn't a mistake. Stella had started calling Mariana that last night and Garrett had encouraged Emma to embrace it.

"The situation is complex and she's only five," he said. "As long as you're not hurt, I don't think there's any harm in it. Stella will get it all sorted out in her head once she gets used to us as parents."

Emma had agreed, assuring him it didn't bother her. But secretly her stomach had nose-dived to her knees. Because she was Mama-Emma now.

Motherhood had hit her like that moment of free fall when the coaster dropped.

Emma had done her best to be a supportive and loving sister in the past few years. But once she moved to San Diego, she'd been so wrapped up in her own life, trying to establish some semblance of independence.

The fact that she'd diligently video-chatted with Stella every week didn't seem like enough. Not now that she knew the truth.

A little hand crept into hers. "Are you sure we're not hiding?"

Emma sat on the upturned bucket Mariana used as a stool, pulling Stella into her arms.

"Well, maybe we are a little," she admitted. "It's just that Mariana, Mama-Grandma, keeps apologizing for not telling me about you."

Emma kissed her forehead, taking a deep sniff to draw her baby's scent deep into her lungs. "I want you to know that I would never have left you if I'd known you were my baby."

Stella put her little hands on her cheeks. "It's okay, Mama-Emma. Papa said it would have been superhard to be a normal mama with your broken head."

Blinking back tears, she smiled at Stella. "That's true. But I would have tried. Because I will always choose you. *Always*."

Stella widened her eyes. "But you had to go so you could find Papa! So he could come and be my papa. And I'm glad he's my papa! He's the bestest!"

Emma bit her lip, mentally counting all the papas. She rubbed her cheeks against her daughter's baby-soft hands before pressing kisses all over them. "You're right. He *is* the bestest. And you're going to love his apartment. It's bigger than this house."

Like four or five times bigger.

Stella tilted her head, pursing her rosebud lips. "Will I like my room?"

"Yes!"

Emma pictured the bedroom she'd slept in when she first moved in with Garrett. Stella probably wouldn't like sleeping right across the hall when she was a teenager, but for now, they wanted her close.

"We're going to get all new furniture for it," she promised. "And lots of new clothes. It's warmer in San Diego but still gets chilly by the water."

Stella's eyes lit up. "Can we go to the store to pick a new bed?"

Somehow, Emma doubted there was a store Garrett would consider good enough for his baby girl.

"We'll find one with the best things. And if you don't see something perfect, we'll find someone to make it."

Knowing him, Garrett would have a list of bespoke carpenters on file.

Stella squealed, excited. They left the pantry, chattering about pink beds and princess sheets.

Emma pulled out her phone and showed her different styles and decoration ideas until Stella got sleepy and went down for a nap.

Hovering over her sleeping daughter, she pressed one last kiss to her little hand before forcing herself to stop.

There would be time for kisses later. For now, there was something else she had to do.

Stella had picked up on her reluctance to speak to Mariana. That wasn't good. Emma was going to have to start untangling the knot of emotions choking her every time she thought about how long Mariana had kept her in the dark. For all their sakes.

Bracing herself, she found Mariana upstairs in her bedroom, packing up her things. Clearing her throat, she waited until her mother turned around, her hands full of shoes.

"You know Garrett offered to hire movers. You don't have to lift a finger."

Mariana gave her a tight smile. "I want to sort things myself. Most things I'd like to get rid of or donate."

They stared at each other, both seemingly at a loss as to how to go on from here.

"Want some help?"

Mariana nodded, some of the tightness of her muscles easing.

They hadn't been alone since the big revelation. Garrett had given them privacy to speak, of course, but he'd still been in the house, just a few rooms away. And it wasn't that her mother *hadn't* explained. Mariana had told her everything last night after Stella went to bed, going over the entire situation in halting words, along with her rationale for not telling her the truth.

Her mother had genuinely feared that her pregnancy had been the reason she'd been run down. She had been picturing an affair with a married man, someone determined to get rid of the evidence of his indiscretion at any cost.

Emma didn't need to speculate on why her mother's brain went there. If she was being honest, she wasn't mad about it.

If someone had asked her which was more likely—an affair with a married man or one with a handsome eligible billionaire, she would have ticked the box next to married man as well.

There was also the fact Emma hadn't been capable of caring for herself, let alone a baby. She knew that in her head. It was just harder to tell that to her heart.

Emma had never felt so mixed up. Her emotions were like a hurricane with her at the epicenter. If she stepped out of the calm center, she could be swept away, smashed against the nearest hard surface.

Emma pictured her skull cracking against a concrete wall, the image so clear and real.

Yeah, she might not remember the accident, but somewhere in the recesses of her brain, there was an echo of it. Maybe it was encoded in her cells now, imprinted by the car that hit her like an unexpected dose of radioactivity mutating her DNA.

Shaking off that morbid thought, she refocused on her task, lifting various items of clothing and knickknacks so her mom could vote and veto, sorting them into three piles: going to San Diego, going to Goodwill, and going to the trash.

"There's nothing you want to set aside for friends?" she asked when the Goodwill pile threatened to topple over.

"Not too many of those," Mariana said matter-of-factly. "None of the women around here would want this stuff anyway."

She wanted to ask why but Emma kept her mouth shut, merely nodding and continuing to sort as if her life depended on it.

They made excellent headway. It helped that they didn't have to worry about the furniture. Except for a few pieces, most of it would stay with the house as it had come furnished. It would stay on for the next tenant.

She and her mother had finished clearing the closet when the sound of a car engine roaring up the drive drew her to the window. Emma had been expecting Garrett, not the sheriff he'd gone out to meet.

Sheriff Warner had come out to see her a few times before she moved to San Diego. He would check in periodically, in case she remembered anything about the accident.

She had thought it odd in the beginning. The visits never lasted more than a few minutes—a bit of small talk followed by a few questions that could have easily been asked over the phone.

There had been that weird tension she couldn't decipher every time Mariana and Jesse had been in the same room together.

Emma quickly realized those visits hadn't been about her.

But while Mariana later admitted to a past relationship with the younger man, she never went out with him again. She never even called him by his real name, always referring to him by his title.

Emma had been afraid to ask what happened between them.

"It's the sheriff," she warned.

Mariana's face went blank. Emma made a motion to go to the door, but her mother stood and brushed off her hands. "I'll go see what he wants."

Chapter Sixty-Three

EMMA

Emma waited until the footsteps receded. Wide-eyed, she took up vigil by the window.

Garrett arrived just as Mariana went out the front door, parking their rental on the street to avoid blocking the sheriff's vehicle.

Jesse Warner climbed out of his SUV, standing in front of the hood with his arms crossed.

She could picture Garrett's expression without seeing his face. It was clear in his posture. He had not wanted this to happen.

The sheriff didn't move to the house or make any other moves, friendly or otherwise. He was waiting for Garrett to go inside.

Her husband paused by her mother, inclining his head and saying something she couldn't hear.

It better be an apology.

Her mother gave Garrett a curt nod. He was not forgiven. Mariana dismissed Emma's billionaire husband like a queen banishing an unruly subject.

Emma caught his grimace before he came inside.

She waited on tenterhooks, torn between running down the stairs to meet him and staying at the window to watch the drama play out.

"Why does the sheriff look angry?" she asked the moment he entered the room.

Garrett made a rough noise in the back of his throat.

"My fault," he grunted.

But he didn't explain. He simply swept her into his arms, kissing her and squeezing her half to death.

Something about the tightness of his hold, the urgency of it, warned her that Garrett was going through something.

"What happened?"

"I met Jesse at the site of your accident," he mumbled into her hair.

"*Oh.*" Emma hugged him back. When he had said he was going out to meet the sheriff, she had assumed he'd be going to the man's office.

A shudder passed through him. "The steepness of the slope, the closeness of the trees, and that fucking scar on the tree trunk where the car hit it brought it all home. I could have lost you that night. I *did* lose you that night."

"Not forever," she said into his chest, deciding not to tell him about her trip out to see the accident site.

She'd gone with her mother about a year after she'd gotten out of the hospital. But that wooded road had been as foreign to her as any other place.

He didn't answer her, tightening his hold until it was almost painful. But Emma didn't complain. She let him take what he needed.

The sound of raised voices made them turn their attention back to the window.

"What exactly did you say to the sheriff?"

Garrett wrapped himself around her as they gazed down at the strained tableau playing out on the driveway.

"I knew your mother dated him, but I didn't realize he was still so invested. I think the announcement that she was moving caught him off guard."

Emma frowned. "They're not seeing each other. They haven't in years as far as I know. And I think that was his decision."

Her mother's behavior during the sheriff's earlier visits had been too guarded and brittle, so unlike her usual warm and flirty self around a handsome man.

Emma hadn't needed a blow-by-blow to know that her mother had been badly hurt.

Garrett pulled the curtain wide, perhaps to make it obvious to the pair that they had an audience.

Not that either of them bothered to look up. They were too engrossed in their argument.

"He mentioned something about not being ready to settle down, but I think we can assume there was more to it. Jesse seemed surprised to hear that Mariana was renting this place from Teddy Bronson."

Emma wrinkled her nose. "Why?"

Garrett paused, squeezing her shoulders. "Have you met Teddy?"

"In person?" Emma thought back. "Once or twice maybe. He came to collect the rent. But my mom usually mails it to him or drops it at his office."

She knew her mother dated him sometimes too, but Mariana dated a lot of men, never getting serious about any. She flittered between them like a glittery bird, having fun, not letting any of them touch her too deeply.

The sheriff was the sole exception to that rule.

"If Teddy Bronson ever comes around, send him to me," Garrett said. "Neither you nor Mariana needs to speak to him. In fact, I'd rather you didn't."

Emma tilted her head to study him. "Do you think he's dangerous?"

"Not physically." Garrett rubbed her shoulders reassuringly. "But he's a smarmy asshole. There's no need to expose yourself to that. Either of you."

"Okay," she agreed, wondering if their life would always feel this tangled.

"Hey." Garrett cupped her cheeks in his hands. "I have an idea. I think we should hire a therapist."

"Like couples therapy?"

"No. All of us. You, me, Stella, and Mariana. Group sessions and separate ones too. In every combination possible."

She laughed. "Because we're so messed up?"

Garrett squeezed her to him. "Don't get me wrong. I wouldn't trade us for anything. But there's a hell of a lot to unpack between each of us. I know in my gut that it's been too easy with Stella. Her little life has been upended. And even though she seems to be taking it well, we're going to have issues down the line. It's inevitable. I just want to get us off on the best footing possible."

Emma nodded but felt like she had to warn him about Mariana. "I'm not sure how my mother will react to the idea of therapy. She always said that's what bartenders are for."

Garrett lifted a shoulder. "Sometimes just talking about your issues is enough. But other times you need more than that. I've never been to therapy, but I know enough people who have benefited from going. It doesn't have to be a big thing. Sometimes it's just a safe space to decompress. I think we could all use that."

Emma let her head fall on his chest, picturing the hurricane inside her mind all too clearly. "I think you might be right."

He pressed a kiss to her forehead. "I'm glad you agree. Now if you don't mind, I'm going to go hide from your mother."

She laughed. "Because you lured the sheriff here?"

"It's more like he was sideswiped by something I said and ran over here uninvited to confront her." He sighed heavily. "She might be mad for a while."

"She'll forgive you when she sees her new place."

Garrett had already shown her some pictures. The condo he was going to give her mother was spacious, with a great view of the city at night and a balcony facing the Pacific. In short, it was a miniature version of his penthouse.

"Well, until then, please excuse me for making myself scarce."

"There aren't many places to hide here," she pointed out.

"Which is why I'm going to Stella's room. Not only do I get to watch our baby sleep, but there's also the bonus of Mariana not yelling at me in front of her."

Emma put her hand over her heart as he left. The way he said he'd watch their baby sleep—like it was a privilege—just melted her heart. Also, they were going to give Stella a complex, hovering the way they did.

Yup, therapy was a really good idea.

It had gone quiet outside. Emma glanced out the window, surprised to see that the sheriff was still there. He and her mother were still arguing, but it was now being conducted in voices so low she couldn't make out a word.

Mariana seemed very calm. It was Sheriff Warner who seemed emotional. And angry.

Then her mother said something that made the sheriff step back.

Mariana turned on her heel and went inside. When she didn't return to her bedroom, Emma went to find her.

Mariana was in the upstairs bathroom, lying in the tub fully clothed.

Emma sat on the closed toilet. "That bad?" she asked.

Her mother stared straight ahead. "That man shouldn't have stirred the pot."

"Garrett is sorry."

"I meant Jesse."

Emma had a hard time thinking of that tall bearded man as Jesse.

The sheriff was built like a lumberjack, with pale-brown hair mixed with gold. He had a matching beard that wouldn't have looked out of place on a Viking.

"How did he do that?"

Mariana shook her head. "It doesn't matter."

But Emma had already guessed what had set the sheriff off. "He's mad because we didn't tell him about Stella."

"In part."

Garrett had told her many people assumed her mother's long-running affair with Teddy Bronson had led to Stella.

"I'm sorry if the rumors about her parentage stood in the way of your relationship."

Emma hadn't realized how sorry she was until this moment.

In her hurt, she'd thought mainly about herself and Stella, what they had missed out on not being able to be mother and daughter. She should have thought about the sacrifices Mariana had made to keep Stella with her.

The financial burden was the most obvious one. But Emma hadn't considered the ramifications to her mother's personal life. Why would she? Her mother had kept dating different men. Mariana treated them like interchangeable cogs.

She hated to think that this mess had cost Mariana someone she had genuinely cared for.

But when she said as much to her mother, Mariana laughed, the sound edged with glass.

"Never worry about that, Em," she said, the look on her face heartbreakingly bleak. "He may be acting like a jackass now, but the fact is Jesse Warner was never a serious prospect. I'm eight years older than him. And even if he'd been ready for the things I wanted with him, he wasn't about to go there. Not with me."

She grabbed a small washcloth from the side of the tub. It was stiff, having dried in the shape it had been dropped in, but Mariana didn't care. It absorbed tears just as well as a freshly laundered one.

"Jesse was always gunning for the spot of sheriff. That's an elected position around these parts." Marianna sniffed, wiping under her eyes. "And they would never elect someone who got serious about the town whore."

"*Mom*," Emma said sharply. "You aren't a whore. Garrett is right. If you lived anywhere else but this small Podunk town, no one would even comment on your love life."

"I had an affair with a married man," her mother pointed out.

"That was a mistake," Emma acknowledged with a wince. "But according to my husband, it's one Teddy made with several women. Not just you. He was a serial cheater."

"Maybe," Mariana admitted. "But I should have tried harder to avoid him."

How? Emma wanted to ask. Teddy owned this house. He'd been her boss. Mariana's livelihood was still tied to him. The cleaning company she worked for depended on his business.

"As for Jesse," Mariana continued. "He's been dating Samantha Corning for almost half a year now. She teaches elementary over in Verdant Falls and is exactly the kind of woman the town wants their sheriff with. He must think so too, or he wouldn't have gone to Denver to shop for rings last month."

Emma's sympathy for the sheriff dried up in a snap.

How dare that jerk fall for someone else? The temerity of him coming around, acting all butthurt as if he was the wronged party! No way. Screw that noise.

"You know what?" Emma said, standing and putting her hands on her hips. "We're ditching this town tomorrow."

Mariana frowned from the tub. "I thought we were going to stay through the weekend to pack."

Emma slashed her hand through the air. "Not anymore. We already sorted everything important. Let the movers come and box up the rest. We'll leave Post-it notes on everything that goes to charity or the dumpster."

Reaching inside the tub, she tugged on her mother's arms until Mariana climbed out.

"You have a whole new life waiting for you in San Diego, including a gorgeous new apartment to furnish. We'll let the pros handle the rest of this mess. And if one of them tosses a match on what's left after we blow this popsicle stand, all the better."

Mariana stared at her for a moment before smiling weakly. "I wouldn't go that far. But leaving tomorrow is sounding damn good to me."

Emma wrapped her arm around her mother's shoulders. It was easy. They were the same height.

"Then that's what we'll do."

Chapter Sixty-Four

EMMA

They had flown to Colorado on an airline that was part of Garrett's investment portfolio. But when their numbers doubled, he made arrangements for a charter flight to take them back to San Diego.

As impressive as first class had been, flying commercial didn't hold a candle to traveling on a private plane.

"It seats eight, but this way we can take all of Stella and Mariana's essentials," Garrett explained when they arrived at the tarmac and saw the gleaming Gulfstream jet. "The movers can deal with the rest."

Keeping an excited Stella in her seat proved to be a challenge, but Garrett managed to corral her long enough for take-off and landing.

Once they were safely on the ground in San Diego, he unclipped her seat belt, taking her little hand so the cabin crew could safely open the door without a five-year-old barreling into them.

"Goodbye, sweetie!" the flight attendant said, pushing open the door to reveal a ladder leading down to the tarmac of a private airstrip.

"Bye!" Stella chirped, swinging her and Garrett's clasped hands, her smile so big and bright it lit up the cabin.

Garrett murmured his thanks to the pilot and crew before stepping into the bright San Diego sunshine just ahead of her and Mariana.

The sound of cheering caught them all completely off guard.

Pausing on the top step, Garrett turned back to her with a grin. "You gotta come see this."

He swung Stella into his arms, carrying her down the stairs to hoots and hollers.

Bemused, Emma followed more slowly. Her lips parted at the sight of the crowd holding balloons, toys, and a huge banner that read, "Welcome home, Stella!"

Rainer and George were there, a huge stuffed bear tucked under Rainer's arm. They were surrounded by the Auric co-owners and their soldiers, many of whom she'd met at the wedding.

Elias Gardner whooped, pushing his cousin Ian forward. In his arms, he held a huge pink unicorn. The pair swooped in with coordinated movements, almost as if they were attacking someone—which in a way they were.

Stella's happy squeal could be heard over the crowd as Elias presented her with the unicorn like a knight bestowing a prized steed to his regent. He even kneeled.

"Who are all these people?" Mariana asked in a bewildered voice. "And why are they reenacting Beatlemania?"

Emma sniffed, waving a hand over her watery eyes. "These are some of Garrett's friends and business partners."

Mariana scanned the crowd with wide eyes. "Jesus, where did they grow them?"

"I think a lot of them are ex-soldiers," Emma said, acknowledging the hit to the hormones the men made as a group.

Every single man in the crowd was six foot or taller, all fit and muscular.

"They work at a private security company Garrett invested in. He also trained with them at one point."

She explained the history a little until she noticed Mariana's anxiety.

Emma leaned over. "None of them are going to judge you for keeping Stella's identity a secret. There was no way for Garrett to know she was his before now. They're all aware of this."

Mariana's brow smoothed a touch. "I guess that's true."

Emma gave her mother a reassuring squeeze before herding her toward the group.

A small figure broke away from the crowd. George ran over, intercepting them to give Emma a fierce hug. "She's so beautiful I want to cry."

Emma nodded, instantly tearing up again. "She is. She looks like his mom."

"I know! I saw the side-by-side pics." George wiped her eyes, turning to Mariana. "Hi! I'm George. I live next door to Emma and Garrett with my husband Rainer. But you're going to be just below us—right next door to my dad."

Mariana thanked her, before jerking to face the crowd when Stella squealed.

Emma turned to see her daughter being passed around from man to man, occasionally tossed high in the air by the burly ex-soldiers.

Being Garrett's daughter, Stella lapped up the attention as her due, giggling and screaming her delight to the world.

"I don't care how big they are," Mariana said. "If they drop her, I will be kicking some ex-soldier butt."

"They would never," George swore. But she turned around and scolded them to stop.

Garrett took Stella back from a blond man named Mason, another familiar face from the wedding.

He hoisted Stella on his hip, displaying his baby girl so proudly it brought tears to her eyes. The men clustered close around them, their genuine joy at the friend's good fortune written all over their faces.

George put a hand over her heart. "Oh my God, I think my ovaries just exploded."

"Agreed," Emma said. "Mine physically hurt."

They went to join the crowd, the festive atmosphere turning into a parade, then a party at their penthouse.

George and Rainer had warned the chef they shared to prepare a feast, but the crowd consisted of a literal army, so they quickly plowed through the trays of mini beef Wellingtons, charcuterie, dumplings, and other finger foods.

More food and drinks were ordered from a wide selection of restaurants. Their choices were dropped off by a steady stream of delivery people until the crowd was finally satisfied and then some.

They would be eating leftovers for a week. Even the arrival of the *De Olla* crew didn't make a dent.

"I can't believe you had a kid and didn't even know it," Bethany marveled before jabbing her elbow. "But good job on getting knocked up by a future billionaire."

She gave her coworker a speaking glance before Bethany decided it would be more fun to pick up a few mercenaries.

Even Pedro showed up with Hannah Cho on his arm. Emma couldn't think of an odder couple, but she knew they were probably thinking the same thing about her and Garrett. In the end, she just hugged him and thanked them both for coming.

Sometime during the festivities, Emma and Garrett broke away from the crowd to show Stella her room.

Ian and Elias had put all the stuffed animals they'd brought to the airport in the bedroom across the hall. The king-sized sleigh bed she had slept in was gone. In its place was a smaller white four-poster bed complete with a pink bedspread. The filmy canopy curtains were artfully tied to the posts, completing the picture.

Stella squealed in delight. "It's the princess bed from the picture!"

Emma didn't know where Garrett had found it, but it was the same dream bed they'd found on Google, which she had saved by texting him the image.

Stella pushed out of his arms. Mariana managed to intercept her long enough to wrangle her shoes off. Their daughter broke away to leap onto the bed, giving it the trampoline treatment with the biggest smile on her face.

"I was going to wait to replace the bed," Garrett explained. "But the other one was just too high. I wanted to make sure she wouldn't hurt herself if she fell out of bed."

"You also added carpet." It was plush and thick with extra padding underneath. If Emma jumped where she stood, she'd bounce too.

"A wise move in retrospect, don't you think?" he asked, his head movements tracking the amount of clearance Stella's feet were gaining with each jump.

He had a point.

She was about to tell Stella to stop jumping. Plush carpet or not, she shouldn't be encouraged to go buck wild like this. But when she turned back, Stella was curled up on her side, fast asleep.

"*What?*" she asked in disbelief.

"Yeah, she can go out between blinks," Mariana informed them matter-of-factly. "And she sleeps like the dead so be prepared to shake her awake when she's enrolled in school again."

She and Garrett stared at her mother, his expression of shock mirroring her own.

Mariana smirked. "The reverse happens too. She'll wake up and go from zero to sixty in nothing flat. Make sure to have your coffee first."

Emma snickered. "We'll remember that."

Garrett slipped a key into her hand. "I thought we would walk Mariana to her place as a family, but this might be a good time, while Stella is napping."

She turned to her mother. "What do you think? Do you want to see your new home?"

Mariana smoothed her hands over her shirt. "Sure," she said. But her voice was hoarse.

Garrett grinned. "Follow me."

But her husband's guests made a smooth exit impossible. After the second time they were stopped, Emma tapped him on the shoulder. "It's okay. I think my mom might prefer to see it without an audience."

It was the right choice.

When Mariana entered the apartment downstairs, she covered her mouth with shaky hands, her eyes shining with unspent tears.

"Holy shit, look at this place."

The three-bedroom apartment was much smaller than the penthouse, but the clean lines, wood floors, and large picture windows deliberately echoed the space above.

Her mother drifted through each room, which had been sparsely furnished with elegant and comfortable-looking furniture in neutral shades. Emma had been assured everything was stain-resistant.

Garrett had shown her pictures of everything on the plane, but she hadn't been prepared for the open brightness of the space. It was a literal clean slate, furnished just enough to be livable right away.

"Garrett said you're welcome to change anything you want," she assured her mother. "He has this decorating firm he's going to use to finish Stella's room. They'll do whatever you want in here. But the kitchen and the bathrooms are already stocked with food, linens, and toiletries. I think you'll like the bed in the master bedroom. Also…"

She tugged her mother's hand and led her down the hall. "I know I should show you your room first, but this one is important too."

Emma opened the door, revealing a spacious bedroom with high hermetically sealed windows and no balcony. A second child's bed dominated the room. This one had an elaborate headboard shaped like a circus tent complete with pastel-striped curtains that stretched over the top half of the bed.

"Holy shit!" her mother exclaimed. "Your honey bunny doesn't do anything halfway."

"No, he doesn't. Also, for the love of God, please never call him that again."

Her mother laughed. "Yeah, it sounded bad to me too."

"We didn't think you'd mind if we carved a space for her here straight off the bat," Emma began when Mariana walked around the bed, touching the bedspread almost reverently.

"We want Stella to know she has the option to come and be with you whenever she wants."

"Of course I don't mind." Mariana turned with tears in her eyes. "I know, I shouldn't have tried to be her mother, but thank you for not taking her away from me completely."

Emma walked over to bed and sat down on it, gesturing for Mariana to do the same.

"Stella *needed* you to be her mother. I wasn't capable of it when she was born. Hell, I'm not entirely sure I am capable of it now. I'm still going to need your help. And not just with Stella. With life. But now you'll hopefully have a chance to find the one you want for yourself too. Whatever that looks like, Garrett and I want you to have it."

Mariana rose, reaching to run her hand over the satiny surface of the dresser. "It's like winning the lottery. I don't know that I deserve all of this."

Emma snorted. "I know the feeling. But Garrett deserves to have the wife he loves. And Stella deserves her dad. So, the two of us are going to have to find a way to accept our good fortune without beating ourselves up about it."

Mariana bent to pick up the stuffed unicorn Elias must have brought down, hugging it to her chest like a shield. "I guess we do."

"I think Garrett was right."

"About what?"

"We all need therapy."

Mariana wrinkled her nose. "Therapy? Really?"

Emma wound her arm around her mother's. "It can't hurt."

"I don't want to," her mother admitted. "But if you think it will help Stella…"

"I do." Emma tugged her to her feet. "Why don't we go see your room now?"

Mariana grinned, the anxiety in her expression melting away. "I'm excited."

She didn't have to tell Emma it had been a long while since she had felt that way.

She stood and put her arm around her mother's waist, leading them across the hall.

"That's probably the right reaction," she said before pushing the master bedroom door open.

Chapter Sixty-Five

GARRETT

Meowmus Maximus had found a new human. The moment the little shit met Stella, he ditched both Garrett and Emma in favor of their cuter hybrid counterpart.

Not that Garrett minded. Less time in close contact with the beast meant fewer allergy pills. Truth be told, he was rather smug about the whole thing because it proved his point about cats.

Dogs were clearly superior in the loyalty stakes, while cats could and would switch allegiances on a dime.

He said as much to Rainer one gray weekend afternoon when Emma was out furniture shopping with her mother. He and Stella had spent a lazy day watching Saturday morning cartoons. Then they went next door to Rainer and George's for brunch.

Their small beast, who was equally at home in that penthouse, accompanied them.

"I never did go through with my plan," he told his friend as they sat on the couch, drinking one of Emma's special coffee blends.

George and Stella were sitting on the floor, busy entertaining Meowmus with the absurd assortment of cat toys he'd accumulated.

"What plan was that?" Rainer asked, his eyes on his wife.

"The cat," he confessed in a low voice. "Meowmus just reminded me that I intended to talk Emma into going around Verdant Falls with me to see if it would jog her memory.”

“Didn’t you decide that was a bad idea? Because it upsets her?”

“It does,” he acknowledged. “But that was before they changed her medicine, before the construction site.”

Rainer shifted to face him with an expression that could have curdled milk. “What about that near tragedy made you think she would want a trip down memory lane? Except for your sorry ass, she’s been firm about keeping the past she can’t remember in the past.” He leaned forward, lips firming. “Or do you intend to force the issue now because of Stella? Because I’m not sure that’s a good idea.”

“I don’t intend to force anything.” Garrett wasn’t a complete idiot. “But when Emma recovered a pre-accident memory at the construction site, I thought it all might be coming back. But so far, it’s the only one. I wasn’t going to push in Verdant Falls, just support her if she wanted to take a look around.”

This earned him another scowl.

“I’m sure that’s what you’d like to believe,” Rainer warned. “But that unspoken expectation would be there. And Emma’s astute enough to recognize that for what it is.”

His friend came closer, pitching his voice lower so the girls wouldn’t hear him. “You now have a beautiful daughter in addition to your beautiful wife. I don’t want to watch while you screw it all up by reaching for some idea of perfection.”

That one hit home. “The way I always do, you mean?”

“Perfect only exists on paper and in your memories,” Rainer murmured. “It’s not a thing of the present. And trying to plan your future around it isn’t just borrowing trouble. It’s inviting it home and letting it crash on your couch.”

Grunting, Garrett took a sip of his coffee, savoring it despite the heavy conversation. Damn, Emma could pick a bean.

“What memory was it?” Rainer asked.

“Hmm?”

“The memory Emma recovered?” Rainer prodded. “You never actually said what it was.”

"Oh, the thing about the cat." He set the mug on the side table. "Not this one. My aunt's old Persian."

Rainer sat up. "You mean how the cat would lie in wait for you, hiding under the couch?"

"Yeah." He laughed. "Emma remembered the story I told her when she was in college. The little shit would wait for me to pass by on my way to the bathroom. Then it would leap out to claw the shit out of me. Fucker always did it in the middle of the night when I was half-asleep with a full bladder."

He'd accidentally pissed himself a little one time. But he didn't tell Emma that.

Rainer didn't join in the laughter. "*Shit*. Emma didn't remember that. I told her that story."

Garrett stilled. "What?"

Rainer sat up straighter. "I shared it with her when she came over to pick up Meowmus after we cat-sat early on. She was commenting on how you didn't seem to like the animal and was wondering why you would adopt one. I said at least this one didn't lie in wait to ambush you and ended up telling her the whole story."

The once excellent coffee swirled in his stomach unpleasantly. "You told her this before the construction site?"

Rainer nodded.

Fuck.

"*Hey*," Rainer hissed. He pointed an accusing finger, wagging it in his face. "That right there. You shut that shit down and you do it now."

He scowled. "What did I do?"

"Your disappointment is clear as day. If Emma sees it—"

"She won't," Garrett interrupted.

"Make sure she doesn't."

Rainer's expression softened. "Look, I know how hard it must be. In your shoes, I'd be invested in my partner remembering her past too. But you've already salvaged the most important parts of it," he added with a significant look at Stella.

Rainer was right, of course. "Yeah," he acknowledged. "I did. I won't forget that."

They sat in silence, watching George and Stella play for a while longer.

Rainer was right. Having Stella and Emma with him was more than enough. They were his future, one he didn't fully deserve. But he would sure as hell try.

"Hey, what is up with your partner?" Rainer asked after he'd finished his coffee.

Garrett raised a brow. "Emma is out shopping. I told you that."

Rainer rose, heading to the bar to pour himself a glass of water. "I meant the far less cute one—Fletcher. He hasn't been around much."

Garrett followed him, taking his mug to the sink. "He's fine. Probably tired as hell and resenting me a bit. He offered to hold down the fort for me at work so I could have this time with Stella and Emma. I'm grateful to him."

Rainer grabbed the mug, washing it so his cleaning woman didn't have to. "He's handling your current deals on his own?"

Leaning against the bar, he nodded. "He wants to help. He knows it's a crucial time for Stella."

"Forgive me for saying it, but Fletcher is not usually that selfless." Rainer sniffed. "Although, I suppose it makes sense—in this case. Otherwise, he'd be here, trying to be in the thick of things in that thirsty way of his."

"In this case?" he echoed.

"No doubt he's feeling a little shitty about what he said to Emma." Rainer set the clean mug on the rack hidden on the top of the bar.

Garrett's pulse picked up. "What the hell did he say to her?"

Rainer raised his brows. "She didn't tell you?"

"No. She didn't tell me anything."

"Ah." Rainer scratched his head. "Well, try and not go all agro on Fletcher. For what it's worth, I don't think he realized he was being an asshole. I'm sure Emma would like to forget it too. It hurt her feelings, but she got over it."

He was going to have to strangle his best friend. *Tell me what he said.*

Rainer grumbled something unintelligible under his breath.

"Keep in mind I heard this secondhand."

Rainer raised his head, checking that George and Stella were still occupied. "Fletcher came by to talk to you about something and found Emma in your seat, waiting for you. He stuck his foot in his mouth the way he does, implying that her accident was a blessing in disguise."

"How the fuck was it a blessing?" He'd lost the love of his life *and* his child for five fucking years.

Rainer wiped his hands on the towel. "He thinks that you two wouldn't have made it as a couple without the accident, because of Emma's ambition. She was gunning for Wall Street before the head injury, right?"

"And? I would have been right there with her."

"I know that. But Fletcher suggested that both of you in high-powered positions would have been too stressful."

"So, we would have broken up? That's total bullshit."

"It probably is," Rainer agreed. But he heard the hint of doubt.

"All right—things *might* have been a little harder," Garrett acknowledged. "But we would have made it work."

Especially if they'd both known Stella was on the way.

"Hey, you're preaching to the choir here. I wouldn't bet against you and Emma." Rainer huffed as if amused. "You don't know how you look at her sometimes."

"Untrue. I'm well aware I stare at her like a lovesick jackass—kind of how you look when George walks into the room in a new dress."

Rainer pitched the towel at his head. "Hey, I'll have you know she gets that in her ratty grease-stained coveralls, too."

He turned his loving gaze to his wife. George glanced up as if sensing his regard. They exchanged one of those married looks, a moment of shared intimacy. At least until the furball pounced on her, forcing her to turn back to the game she'd abandoned.

"I'm glad you have this too," Rainer said with genuine emotion. "No offense but you were starting to worry me."

As little as three or four months ago, he would have been annoyed. But he knew better. Him before finding Emma again versus him now—there was no comparison.

"I'm happy." That was all there was to it.

"That's good. That's really good." Rainer gave him an assessing once-over. "Although, never in my wildest dreams could I have seen you as a father. But you're handling being a dad rather well."

"I wouldn't go that far," he muttered. "I've been cramming child-rearing books like nobody's business but have yet to remember a damn thing when it matters. Like when she wakes up in the night and wants one of us to get in bed with her until she falls asleep. According to the books, we're to reassure her but be firm that she's to go to bed alone."

"Didn't work?"

"Hell no. Emma ended up sleeping with her till morning."

He loved his baby girl so much already but that was not a pattern he wanted her to fall into. Nor did Garrett want to encourage Stella to crawl into their bed if she woke up scared.

In all the craziness of Stella's homecoming, he and Emma had been forced to turn the dial down on their sex life—not a pattern he wanted to maintain.

Not that he hadn't taken a few steps to remedy the situation. Pulling Emma into the coat closet yesterday had been lots of fun. Still, he had a very large and comfortable bed and he wanted to use it.

"Do I have to do something about Fletcher?" he asked.

The messy beginning had been his fault, of course. If he hadn't accused Emma of industrial espionage, Fletcher wouldn't have become prejudiced against her.

But the man should have corrected course by now. He and Emma were married, for Pete's sake. Garrett couldn't have his business partner upsetting his wife.

"Your call," Rainer said. "But you know how awkward he can be. God knows he tries, but he's never really fit in with the rest of our crew."

Garrett wouldn't have put it in quite those terms. But even he had to admit that Fletcher wasn't his first port of call when he needed help. The man next to him was.

"Elias said he's been riding my coattails since high school."

"There is some truth to that," Rainer admitted with some reluctance. "And it's something he seems to be aware of, which can't be a comfortable headspace to be in constantly. That doesn't mean he hasn't been a decent partner to you. He'll relax about the Emma situation soon enough. In the meantime, he's trying to make it up to you the only way he knows how."

"That he is."

It made sense. His business partner had been trying to make amends when he stepped up to handle their workload. But Garrett would have to keep a closer eye on that situation. And he needed to speak to Emma about it as soon as she got home.

That was his intention anyway. Until Stella decided to derail his plans.

Chapter Sixty-Six

GARRETT

The night began on a good note. Great, in fact. Emma and her mother were spending the day with his decorator, going from showroom to showroom to finish up Mariana's place while he stayed home to watch Stella.

It was the first time he'd watched her on his own for more than a few hours without George next door to back him up if he needed it. The mechanic was busy with a new project that had a strict deadline.

Aware that he was still a little nervous about going it alone, Rainer and Elias had offered to come over, but he'd declined their generous offer.

Garrett was a father. He needed to learn how to be one without a safety net, so he asked Fletcher to shuffle things so he could work from home again.

Stella obliged him by playing quietly on her new tablet or with Meowmus on the carpeted area in front of his desk. He'd had the decorator put some beanbags there for Stella to have her own space in his office.

He wanted her to feel welcome there.

The decorator had wanted to make the beanbags leather in a dark-maroon shade to match the furniture. But having a kid meant making sacrifices. Even if those sacrifices came in bright-pink faux fur.

Stella's good behavior allowed Garrett to tackle another project while he was home.

Ever since finding out he had a five-year-old kid, he'd been scrambling to catch up. Now that Stella was settled in their home, the next crucial item on his list was to line up the best grade school possible. Their goal was to enroll her in January when the next semester started.

Getting Stella into a premier private school midyear proved tricky, even to someone with his resources. He'd put his assistant on it, but the matter still required his personal attention.

Strings had to be pulled. In the end, it had been Elias who'd held the most important one—his stepmother, Rosemary Gardner.

Rosemary was a true old-money socialite, the second wife of former Governor Graham Gardner, Elias' adoptive father. She was a woman with hundreds of friends. One of these sat on the board of the private school his assistant had earmarked as the best in town.

A quiet word from Rosemary and a spot suddenly opened up.

His relief at having that settled was substantial. But because Stella wasn't starting until the new year, Garrett had decided to hire a babysitter who could double as a tutor.

He knew it was just kindergarten, but he didn't want her to fall behind. The tutor-slash-sitter would ensure her transition in January would be seamless.

Or at least that was his plan.

Garrett had no intention of dumping all his parenting responsibilities on an employee. He could barely handle having Emma and Stella out of his sight as it was. But he'd taken Emma's words on her mother's porch to heart.

He couldn't hold on too tight, so he was trying to begin as he meant to go on.

Garrett would have to go back to the office soon. Fletcher couldn't shoulder the workload alone. But finding someone whom he trusted around his family was going to be a tall order, so he didn't waste any time in setting up interviews.

He should have done a better job explaining the situation to Stella.

She had caught on to the fact he was interviewing babysitters immediately, of course, after the first woman came in.

But Garrett hadn't liked that applicant's vibe, so he had the next set of applicants run through the gauntlet of Auric's background check. It was part of the service they provided to new and existing clients, one he hadn't taken advantage of before.

Once the pool had been vetted, Garrett resumed interviews, trying to time it so he got at least twenty minutes alone with them first. Then he had Stella come in so he could gauge their rapport.

As long as they had the Auric seal of approval, he could afford to take Stella's opinion into account.

They had just met the day's final candidate when Emma and Mariana arrived home, exhausted but pleased with the progress they'd made. Mariana's place would be completely furnished in a matter of days, a cause for celebration all around.

They were halfway through dinner when Stella pricked their collective balloon of happiness with her sterling silver Tiffany & Co. baby fork.

"Why don't you come down for a Disney princess movie marathon after dinner?" Mariana suggested. "We got the best pink pillows to cuddle up on the floor."

Stella surprised them all by turning it down and shaking her little head solemnly. "Papa will be sad if he can't kiss me good night," she declared, rather decisively for a five-year-old.

Aware that Mariana had been missing Stella something fierce, Garrett pointed out that a sleepover did not preclude a goodnight kiss from either of her parents.

"That's the great thing about having your Mama-Grandma just one floor down," he explained, injecting as much enthusiasm as he could muster into his voice. "We can come up and down whenever you want."

"Yes," Emma added, setting down her fork. "You should think of it as one big house. So you can go with Mama-Grandma now and we can come down to carry you to bed."

"No. Because Mama-Grandma's not my mama," Stella announced. "She's a liar!"

There was a collective intake of breath.

"Baby girl," Garrett began, glancing at Mariana's stricken face. "That's your grandma you're talking about."

Stella's cheeks turned beet red. "She told everyone she was my mama. But she's not!"

Well, shit.

Emma looked as crushed as her mother. "She did that to protect you, baby. Remember when we talked about that?"

Stella inhaled, the jut of her chin disturbingly familiar.

Dear God, she's me at that age.

"She's a liar!" his daughter shouted. "I want to stay with you and my real mama!"

Garrett rose, plucking his daughter out of her chair. He carried her to the living room as Stella screamed at her grandmother.

"I didn't know my papa because of you!"

Emma and a shell-shocked Mariana followed him. His mother-in-law was already in tears, her hand over her mouth.

He sat on the couch, holding Stella in his lap. Emma took the seat opposite them, trying to soothe her with murmured reassurances.

But Stella didn't want soothing. She wanted to stay mad. Garrett knew that feeling better than anyone, but her anger was misdirected.

He searched for the right words but settled for the bald truth. "Stella, what happened wasn't your grandmother's fault," he said firmly, repeating it until she quieted down enough to listen. "It was *mine*. I was the one who made a mistake. And it was huge—the biggest one I ever made."

He jiggled her on his knee, wondering if anything was getting through.

Judging from the stubborn little lines of her face, it wasn't. "Do you want to know what it was? No? Well, I'm going to tell you anyway —I didn't come back."

Garrett met Emma's eyes, his words for her as much as their daughter. "I should have known that something was terribly wrong when your mother wouldn't return my calls after our fight. That was the biggest clue in the entire universe and like a giant stupid-head, I missed it. Because there is literally nothing that your mother loves more than arguing with me."

Emma laughed, her eyes bright with unspent tears. "Still do. Sometimes."

"You see, baby girl, if anyone is to blame, it's *me*," he stressed. "And with your mama in the hospital for so long, your grandma Mariana did the best thing she could think to do—she took care of you. Long enough for all of us to find each other again. But now we're all together and we can be a family. One with a mama, a papa, and a grandma."

"And an Aunt Phil," Emma added.

Garrett snapped his fingers. "Yes, her too."

He should have included his father on that list too, but he didn't have the energy to explain what 'estranged' meant.

Stella turned to her mother. "Mommy, don't be sad," she said when she saw the traces of tears on Emma's cheeks.

She gave Stella a watery smile. "I am a little sad but mostly happy. We're allowed to be both."

"Oh." Stella pushed her head back into his chest. "Does that mean I can be mad *and* happy?"

"Of course, baby girl. I'm mad and happy all the time," he said.

Stella wasn't comforted by this.

"Are you mad at me?" she whispered, her lower lip trembling. "Because I won't stay with Grandma?"

"No, never," Emma added, squeezing in next to him so she could wrap her arm around Stella. "We want you with us all the time. But we're not the only ones who love you. Grandma took care of you for a long time, and she loves you sooo much. We know we have to share."

Stella thought about it. "I can watch a movie with Grandma. But then I'll come back here to my room, and you can tuck me in."

"That sounds like an excellent plan." Garrett smiled, rubbing her back. "You're quite the negotiator."

He and Emma turned and said the same words at the same time.

"She gets that from me."

Chapter Sixty-Seven

EMMA

Collecting the dishes on the table, Emma said a prayer of thanks that Garrett didn't keep a permanent maid on staff. Tonight would have been ten times more awkward with an audience.

Garrett hugged her from behind. "Hey," he muttered into her hair.

Emma closed her eyes and leaned against him. "Hey. Are they settled?"

"Yeah. They're curled up in front of the TV with a bowl of kettle corn and Stella's favorite princess movie."

"*Moana* again?" Stella had been watching that movie on a loop for the last week.

"No, the one with the long magic hair."

Stella's favorite movie had changed again, and she'd missed it?

Emma hung her head. "I should know that."

"Nah." Garrett took the last dish from her, setting it on top of the stack. "It shifts every few days. So do the names of her favorite stuffed animals because Stella herself forgets what they are. Once that stops, then we can feel bad about forgetting them—because we will. We're human. It's inevitable."

She groaned. "That doesn't make me feel better."

It also didn't sound like the man who had been cramming parenting books like he was studying for finals.

"I know. But that's normal too." Garrett raised his hands and began to rub her shoulders. "I know tonight was upsetting, but I think it's a good thing that Stella is comfortable enough to fight with us."

Twisting at the waist, she made big eyes at him.

"I'm serious," he insisted. "She's brave and she stands her ground. The parenting books say that's the sort of thing we should encourage."

The corner of her mouth lifted, but it wasn't a smile. "Somehow, I doubt they meant letting your kid scream out their feelings."

"No. That part we'll have to work on," he acknowledged. "Not that I blame her. There's been a few times I wanted to scream about all of this too."

Emma turned, standing on her tiptoes to wrap her arms around his neck. She pressed her face into his chest, mumbling against his pecs. "It's a lot. But she was overdue for a meltdown."

"Yeah," he agreed. "After the sitter, the next thing on the list will be finding that therapist."

Emma was about to tell him that he'd done just fine without one, but what the hell, it couldn't hurt. She could use the guidance. And, as they saw tonight, Mariana might have been parenting longer, but she wasn't going to have all the answers. Especially when the problem stemmed from the fact she used to claim Stella was hers.

Garrett returned her embrace and then some. She pulled back when his hands began to roam in a distinctly non-comforting way.

She lifted his head to tease him when he cupped the back of her neck. His mouth covered hers aggressively, his hold growing possessive.

Emma broke away, concerned at the increasing desperation of his touch. "Garrett, what's wrong?"

"I…" He was panting, his face flushed. "I…"

She cupped his face. "What is it? You can tell me."

"I am not jealous."

Bewildered, she flattened her hands on his chest. "Of who?"

"Our kids."

Emma raised her brows and laughed a little hysterically. "I know you mean Stella, but under the circumstances, can you please confirm that we do not have more children?"

His cheeks tightened with chagrin. "We don't. It just hits me sometimes—Stella is always going to be our priority. She and whatever other children we have. And there's nothing wrong with that."

"But?"

He stared at her for a long moment. "But we just found each other again. And we didn't get a whole lot of time alone together before we became parents."

Garrett dropped his hands before changing his mind. He reached for her, gripping her waist tight. "I'm a selfish bastard."

Oh, Garrett.

She pressed a kiss chin. "You are always going to be the most important man in my life. I love you."

He slid his hands down her body before lifting and setting her on the thick glass surface of the dining room table.

"I love you, too. Never doubt that… especially after what I'm going to do next."

"And what's that?"

He pressed his forehead to hers. "Some very dirty things."

Emma snickered, but it turned into a moan when he reached under her skirt to remove her panties, stroking her expertly as he went. He stuffed them in his pocket before moving between her legs.

She opened her arms, trying to embrace all of him.

"How long is that Disney movie?" she murmured, the languorous heat spreading as he gathered the midnight fall of her hair and wrapped it around his fist.

"Not long enough. Let's make the most of it," Garrett used the handhold to tilt her neck to the side, exposing the length of it for his mouth.

Emma's eyes were threatening to roll into the back of her head. She leaned into his embrace, revealing more of her neck and pressing her breasts into his chest.

It was like she flipped a switch. Garrett started tearing at her clothes, pulling the sides of her black wrap dress like he was opening a present.

"You're so beautiful," he whispered, tugging her bra straps down. He didn't even bother to undo the lacy confection. He simply pushed it down to her waist, out of his way.

Garrett's large hands covered her bare breasts. Lips parting, she arched like a cat, her empty sheath tightening in response.

Her hands went to his zipper. He pulled away just far enough to watch her undo his pants. The sound he made when her hands released his hard length sent a pulse through her that dampened her panties.

She started to wiggle out of them, but Garrett pulled them to one side, fitting his length to her entrance.

"Too fast?" he asked, stroking the head of his cock against her clit.

"*No.*" Emma's fingers dug into his back as he pulled her to the edge of the table and began to penetrate her.

Crying out, her legs squeezed around his hips. His thick cock surged, stretching the snug walls of her sheath to their limit.

"You're so wet, baby. It's so good." Garrett pressed closer, beginning to fuck her in earnest, rocking in and out.

His mouth skittered across her hairline, the kisses interrupted because he wouldn't stop, his thrusts just this side of frantic.

Emma didn't care, even though he'd gone from zero to sixty in nothing flat. No, it didn't matter because she'd caught his urgency. He was the only one who could do that to her, turn her on so fast and so hard it was like she was burning.

Her breath was ragged as she clutched at him, trying to envelop as much of him as she could. "More," she panted. "Please, more."

His muscular body pushed against her, the cloth of his still buttoned shirt abrading her nipples and breasts.

"You never need to ask." Garrett pressed an open-mouthed kiss to the corner of her lips, tracing a line with the tip of his tongue to her ear. Emma squirmed, laughing and clenching around him at the same time.

He groaned as Emma squirmed, adding an undulation to try and caress him as best she could.

"It tickles," she whispered, giggling when his whiskers rubbed against the sensitive skin next to her ear.

Growling, he lunged, taking her earlobe between his teeth.

"This won't but it may throb." His hand slipped between them, his thumb pressing firmly on her clit and rubbing.

Emma gasped, her nails digging into his shirt, her heart picking up in time with Garrett's ministrations.

"That's right, baby," he said between ragged breaths as her head fell back. "Just lie back and take the pleasure your man gives you. Because this one's for you. The next one though—that's when I'm going to ask for too much from you. But you'll give it to me anyway."

He punctuated his words with an extra-deep thrust. Shivering, she cried out as her orgasm splintered her into pieces.

Garrett held her close while she sobbed and shook in his arms. When the last spasm died, he grinned at her, slowly pumping in and out one more time.

"You didn't come."

He usually didn't hold back, letting her orgasm carry him over the edge too. But she knew that look in his eye. She was in trouble.

His hand cupped her cheek. "Remember when I said I'd ask for too much?" he asked, pressing a soft kiss to her lips.

Emma was already stripped bare. She stared at him, all her heart, everything she felt for him shining there. No shields or defenses.

"There is nothing you can ask for that I wouldn't give you."

His head drew back, his teeth worrying his lower lip for a moment. "Keep that in mind."

Withdrawing, he reversed course, taking her hands to help her hop off the table.

She expected him to lead her to their bedroom before he put his hands on her shoulders and bent her over the table.

Emma turned her head. "I know you're excited, but we have done *this* before."

Garrett didn't smile like she expected. "Not like this," he rasped.

He put a hand on the back of her neck, turning her face down. She was looking at the polished floorboards when he moved, crawling underneath the table.

"What are you doing?" she asked, her view blocked by the width of his shoulders. Garrett crawled back a few steps, revealing his phone.

The camera app was open, her face and bare breasts reflected in the little screen. Garrett met her eyes before turning back to the phone and adjusting the zoom until only her face and the top of her décolletage were visible.

"No one but me will ever see this—I swear it," he vowed through the glass before getting to his feet.

Emma should have said no. But Garrett had never asked her for something like this. And she believed him when he said no one else would ever see it. His word was solid.

Speaking of...

Another giggle escaped which earned her a low rumble from Garrett. He put his hand on her bare back, pressing the rock-hard length against the silkiness of her cheeks.

"So, this is funny," he said, his fingers leaving a trail of tingling skin in his wake. "But it might not be as hilarious in a minute."

With that, he entered her in a long smooth stroke. Emma's lips parted, all her nervous hilarity dying.

She caught sight of herself on the small screen below. The woman on the screen didn't look like her. Yes, she wore her face. But this sex goddess with the sharp sexual awareness in her eyes could have been a stranger.

And then Garrett withdrew, pumping back. He began to fuck her at a steady pace, each stroke punctuated with an audible slap.

The tiny Emma stared up from her phone screen. Even at that size, she could see herself, skin pink with a telltale rosy blush, kiss-swollen lips open as she panted, an animal reduced to nothing but sensation.

Stroke after stroke, she watched herself being pleasured. But Garrett had her pinned down, so she could barely move.

Emma wanted to give as much as she got but had to do it with tiny motions of her hips, as much as he allowed. That and her interior muscles, which she was using to great effect judging from his groans.

The first spank surprised her. "Bad girl," he rasped.

He was close, she could tell, so she squeezed him again and was rewarded with another spank.

Garrett pulled her back off the table another inch, just enough to work a hand between her pussy and the edge of the table. He began to work her clit in time with his thrusts, making her cry aloud.

Emma forgot she was being recorded. She forgot everything except Garrett's heat at her back and the hard length of him pounding into her.

Hands flat on the glass, she turned her head to face the camera. She could no longer see it, but this wasn't for her. Her lips formed the words so he would see them later. The same three, over and over again, claiming him even as he did the same to her.

Her body was burning, pulsing with his every push and pull when he pressed close, grinding and shouting. His cock throbbed, hot seed spurting inside her as he came. A few more strained hard thrusts and she was coming too, that hot tight knot at her core exploding in wave after wave of pure bliss.

When she recovered, she was face down on the table, the glass too fogged for her to see. There was cold at her back and a shadow of movement under the table. The phone dinged as Garrett stopped the recording. Then he put the phone in his pocket before picking her up and carrying her to their room.

An hour later, after a long session in bed, he showered and went downstairs so he could carry their daughter to bed too.

Chapter Sixty-Eight

EMMA

She finished sorting the mini cups of green coffee beans in order of quality before checking her cheat sheet from the ICI, International Coffee Institute.

"Yes!" She pumped one hand in the air and did a celebratory jig around the kitchen island.

Ever since she'd decided to pursue coffee roasting as a career, she had been researching all aspects of the business, including pursuing a Q-grading certification.

These were the people who were able to sort beans by type and quality *before* they were roasted. It was a crucially important skill set to have, and every roaster and green coffee importer employed at least one.

She'd gotten the idea from her husband. Every time he drank a cup of something she'd selected and prepared, he would compliment her, saying she knew how to pick a bean. Once she realized just how important that skill was to her career plans, she had begun to research whether that was true. And according to the kit she'd had specially couriered by the ICI, it was.

This was significant. If she could refine this skill, she could build a business around it. A little importing and bean roasting enterprise.

Garrett kept encouraging her to try, offering himself and his friends up as a sounding board whenever she needed.

At first, Emma had fielded these offers from him with skepticism. That was before. Now she accepted them because that was how *they* had succeeded.

Garrett's friends didn't spring forth from the womb as titans of industry. Even Rainer and Elias, who had been raised with family money, took what they'd been given and pushed it to new heights. And they'd done it by helping each other.

Like them, she had that desire to create, to work toward something bigger than herself. Her little enterprise didn't have to be huge, just hers.

Yes, her husband was going to provide a little seed money. But Emma was going to be smart. It was going to be a one-woman operation while she laid the foundation. Once she had things in place, she'd hire one or two others.

Both Kyle and Bethany had expressed an interest in getting on board. They both wanted to be 'on the ground floor' of something.

"Woman, I don't want to be shlepping coffee to people in five years," Bethany had told her.

The tattooed barista had been serving at *De Olla* café at the time. She ignored the uncomfortable looks of the customers she'd just handed coffee to. "By then they better be bringing it to *me*."

Emma warned Kyle and Bethany to keep their expectations low. She didn't intend on building the newest coffee empire. It wasn't going to be the next Starbucks. But they could carve out a niche that could sustain and fulfill them and still leave time to have a life. To enjoy their families. Because no matter what happened, Emma would be there for Stella.

She also wanted to be there for herself. It wouldn't be much of a life if she worked herself into the ground. Which meant she needed a solid plan. She wouldn't rely on hopes and wishful thinking.

Emma was continuing her associate degree in business, taking classes remotely for the time being. She'd also had lunch with a few of Garrett's friends, including the owners of Auric, who were involved in many entrepreneurial efforts, not just their security company.

Until last week, she hadn't known Elias was a founding investor of one of those DNA ancestry sites. He'd talked to her about it and a few of his other businesses, letting her pick his brain with a patience she wouldn't have expected from such a tough, taciturn guy.

Elias had been open and full of helpful suggestions she could apply to any fledgling business.

It had been, in some ways, easier than talking shop with Garrett. Not that she wouldn't take her husband's advice. But that must be the nature of marriage—it was easier to accept that kind of guidance from an impartial third party.

Garrett seemed to instinctively understand this. Or at least he pretended to, she thought with a wry grin. She knew he was dying to overload her with advice but was making a superhuman effort to restrain himself.

Instead, he offered the rare suggestion, pointing to a resource she would find helpful, then standing back to let her figure things out for herself.

Happy wife, happy life. A motto to live by.

Satisfied with her progress on the bean test, she checked a few more things off her list: research into eco-friendly pour-over filters and Scandinavian coffee cheese, Kaffeost. That sounded like the weirdest combination. But it combined two of her favorite things so she wasn't about to write it off.

Just where did one find Scandinavian cheese in the most southern part of Southern California?

After bookmarking likely cheese shops, she began to clean up the kitchen in preparation for dinner. Stella and her mother were at the zoo with George's father, Ephraim, who was Mariana's neighbor on the floor below them.

Despite their age difference, Mariana and Ephraim had hit it off, becoming fast friends. Maybe because they both had daughters who had married absurdly wealthy men, who also happened to be best friends.

Ephraim was at least two decades too old to be a love interest for Mariana, which was a pity. Emma wanted her mother to find what she had. But falling for her new bestie's father was asking for too much.

Nevertheless, the two bonded over their changed circumstances, normal people now one percent adjacent.

Ephraim was a big fan of the zoo, and San Diego had the best one as far as he was concerned. He had an annual pass and had suggested taking Stella on a special backstage tour that allowed them to feed the giraffes, which were her favorite animal.

Stella had been thrilled. So had Mariana because Ephraim had purposefully made it a grandparent thing, leaving Emma and George out of the invite so they could get some work done.

Emma planned on having Stella's favorite dinner on the table when they got home—chicken fingers and buttered pasta. It was a dish simple enough for her poor cooking skills, leaving Chef Mohammed free to take orders from the other building residents.

Garrett was going to be bringing their favorite sushi home for dinner, a feast large enough for all the adults, save for Ephraim, who didn't eat anything raw.

She had just taken the chicken fingers out of the freezer when the front door opened and closed. It was still too early for her mother and Stella to return. But Garrett was in the habit of rushing home unexpectedly if he got a spare hour or two at work, especially when he knew Stella would be busy with her grandmother.

Emma poked her head out of the kitchen, expecting to see him. But the living room and bar area were empty.

Rustling noises came from down the hall. But they weren't coming from the bedroom.

"Did you forget some—" Emma stopped short in the office. The man rifling through the desk drawers wasn't Garrett.

"Fletcher," she said weakly when Garrett's partner looked up, dismay in the deep lines of his face.

"Oh, hi, Emma," he said, shifting to hide a box behind him.

Only a corner of it was visible, but the bit she could see was distinctive. It was that FedEx box that had arrived from Colorado this morning, the one from Sheriff Warner.

She rested a hand on the doorjamb. "What are you doing with that?"

Fletcher's sudden smile was all wrong.

"This?" He moved his arm, holding the box out in front of him. "It's nothing. Just some contracts Garrett asked me to pick up."

"No, sorry. That's the wrong box," she told him. "That's not work-related."

The smile dropped off his face. "Oh, I know *that*," he said, scoffing. "The contracts are already in my briefcase."

He knelt behind the desk and lifted a matte black attaché case. It looked like the kind used to store portable nuclear weapons.

"Legal needs these contracts today," he continued, stuffing the FedEx package inside. "I'm taking the box to work as well because Ian is going to swing by to pick it up."

She frowned. "I thought Elias said he was going to handle it."

That's what her husband had told her earlier.

Fletcher's eye twitched. "No, that's wrong. Ian handles logistics."

"But–"

"It's *Ian*," he snapped, his face hardening. "Ian does all the tech stuff."

Emma's lips parted, all the blood leaving her extremities, street racing to her heart which began to pound out of control.

When Auric was brand new, Ian *was* in charge of their technical division. But he had long since turned things over to Toya Almari, a security specialist who could make computer code sing and dance like a badass black pied piper.

But Fletcher wasn't friends with the Auric men. They were polite to him, but not enough to make him privy to the inner workings of their company.

Toya didn't like parties, preferring smaller, more intimate gatherings. The only reason Emma had met her was because she'd been to dinner at Elias' house.

Contradicting Fletcher at this point would have been incredibly stupid. She pasted a smile on her face.

"Okay. My mistake," she said, grateful that her voice was even. "I'll just leave you to it."

Emma had taken two steps back when Fletcher swore and hung his head. When he looked up, the wrongness in his eyes had grown, the black eating at his icy-blue irises like an oil spill in the arctic.

She needed to get the hell out of here. *Now.*

Chapter Sixty-Nine

EMMA

She turned to run, but it was too late. Fletcher hurled the case at her head.

Yelping, Emma lifted her hands, her palm slapping it out of the air by sheer chance. It struck her thigh as she twisted to run, sending it flying in front of her.

The case bounced off the doorway, ricocheting out of the room. The case spun on the hardwood floor, sliding down the hallway like a hockey puck.

She stopped, gaping at it. Emma looked back long enough to register that Fletcher was wearing a similar one, disbelief twisting his normally placid features into a grotesque caricature.

Slowly, they both turned to look at the case, then back at each other.

Emma broke her stupor, snatching it up by the handle and running flat out to the living room.

She managed to clear the hallway when the pounding behind her turned into a blow. Her body went flying, tumbling down the two steps into the sunken living room.

Her face smashed against the floor before the rest of her body.

Stunned, Emma lost her grip on the case. It went flying under the coffee table. Every muscle in her body froze, tensing up to protect her after the fact.

It was only a second, but that was long enough for Fletcher to catch up. But the man spent his days behind a desk. He wasn't as physically gifted as Garrett or the rest of his circle. Unable to check his momentum, he ended up tripping over her, his foot connecting with her ankle.

He might as well have kicked her. Emma groaned, scrambling to her feet, the pain in her ankle radiating up her foot.

Forget the damn case. She had to get out of there.

Emma took a few steps, wincing when her injured ankle threatened to give out on her.

Fletcher grabbed her leg, his hand a vise. Emma cried out, twisting to kick him away with her good foot. But her kick went wild. She lost her balance, landing on the floor on her butt.

Then he was on her, grabbing at her hands and using his body weight to press her into the floor.

"Get off me!" she screamed. Emma couldn't use her arms, so she pushed her legs into the carpet, trying to buck him off.

"Just stop," he growled, slapping her face so hard it made her ears ring.

Emma sobbed, still fighting, but it was weaker now.

Fletcher might not have been a strong man, but he was stronger than her. When he hit her a second time, the ringing stopped and her head lolled, her cries muffled, as if they were coming from a great distance.

For one terrifying moment, the world flickered, darkening. But the pain didn't lessen. Emma clung to it, clawing her way back to consciousness, continuing to cry out until her voice strengthened, turning into a scream.

"No, no, quiet," he begged.

Spittle fell on her face as Fletcher wrapped his hands around her neck.

Emma screamed louder, the noise a roar in her ears. The world began to blur at the edges and she couldn't breathe. Scrabbling, she dug her nails into his cheek, going for his eyeballs.

Suddenly, the weight was gone. Fletcher flew to the side as a booted foot rammed into his side.

Coughing, she looked up, expecting and praying to see Garrett. But the dark-haired blur was too vicious and sharp.

Elias.

He turned to her, a quick split-second check before rounding on Fletcher, growling. The sound could have come from a demon straight out of hell.

Garrett had told her a secret once when he'd had one too many whiskeys. Elias was former black ops.

She shuddered. This look on his face—like Fletcher was prey. This expression had been the last thing some men had seen before they died.

Elias snarled, stalking the smaller man. "What the *fuck do you think you're doing?*"

Taking a deep pained breath, Emma rolled onto her hands and knees, scuttling backward.

Fletcher rose but went down with one punch. He landed with a meaty *thunk.*

Emma kept crawling away, her brain remaining unconvinced that she was safe until she hit one of the little tables next to the fireplace, knocking it over.

"Emma."

Strong hands reached for her, helping her up. Elias' face sharped into clearer focus.

"Are you okay?" he asked, his eyes latching on to her neck. "*Fuck.* No, you're not. It's okay. Don't try to talk."

Before she could answer, there was a distant crash.

They both turned in time to see Garrett come in the front door. His coat hung off one shoulder and he kept glancing behind him toward the elevator.

"Fletcher nearly mowed me down. What's wrong with him?"

Elias spun and swore when he saw her assailant was no longer on the floor. He sprinted for the door. "Stay with her!" he yelled.

Emma could see the moment Garrett realized she was hurt. His face went blank, icily remote.

It was far more terrifying than Elias' more explosive anger.

He snapped his head to the open door and for a split second, she thought he was going to run after Elias. But he didn't. He ran to her instead.

The moment Garrett's arms wrapped around her, the dam broke. She burst into tears, noisy sobs that were barely muffled against the muscles of his chest.

"It's okay, baby. I've got you. It's going to be okay."

He picked her up and carried her to the bedroom, setting her on the edge of the bed and holding her close.

Emma didn't know how long she cried, but it felt like a long time. Her body ached everywhere too, even in places that hadn't hit the floor.

"I—I d-don't know w-what's wrong w-with me," she whispered, forcing the words past her swollen throat.

Garrett tightened his hold. "Adrenaline. But you don't have to worry. Whatever the hell Fletcher was up to is never going to happen again—because I'm going to kill him."

This would have normally been the part where a normal upstanding citizen protested but Emma didn't. Shuddering, she fisted her hands in his shirt.

"He came for the phone," she said, grateful that her voice sounded normal. But holy shit it hurt to talk.

Garrett frowned. "What?"

"The phone Sheriff Warner sent. The FedEx box was in his briefcase."

Garrett's hands tightened on her as she told him the rest.

"I found him going through your desk. He hid it but I saw. He tried to play it off, saying you sent him for it, but I guess I didn't look convinced because he threw his briefcase at me and… and…"

Emma stopped because the expression on Garrett's face now was going to haunt her in her dreams.

Yeah, she didn't care that Elias was an experienced killer. That's what black ops meant and although her husband always tacked on 'former' in front of it, Emma didn't think there was anything former about it.

But when came to her, none of that mattered. Garrett would always be the more dangerous one.

The atmosphere darkened, the universe warning her that Elias was back. He stomped into the room a minute later. "I lost the fucker!"

"*What?*" Garrett seemed more shocked by that than the fact that his business partner of almost a decade had attacked her without warning. "How the fuck did that happen?"

Elias glowered, flinging a hand up. He pressed his phone to his ear and began barking orders, starting with bringing him Fletcher Sweeney's head on a pike.

Every Auric employee on the West Coast was being mobilized for the search.

Drained and hurting all over, Emma stumbled to the bathroom. She hadn't looked at herself in the mirror since it happened.

The bright bathroom lights revealed the rapidly darkening ring around her neck. It was going to be black and blue for weeks.

Garrett appeared in the reflection behind her. Wordlessly, he wrapped his arms around her, pulling her into the steel of his embrace.

Elias entered with two glasses of whiskey in one hand as he continued to bark orders into his cell phone. He stopped to press the glass into her hand.

"Drink," Garrett ordered when she stared at it.

"It's not for you?" she asked, her brain sluggish.

"No, it's not. Drink."

His hands took the glass from her unresisting fingers. Garrett crouched, putting the lip of the crystal to her lips. He urged her to drink it all, and she did, despite the burn in her throat.

When she was done, her fingers had stopped shaking, though the occasional shudder still racked her body.

Elias put his phone down, shaking his head. "He won't leave the city. I promise you that."

Emma raised her brows. Considering the international border with

Mexico was less than twenty miles away, that was going to be impossible. It had to be a white lie to placate her furious husband.

Or at least she thought it was until she took in their expressions and read murder there.

"The team doctor is on his way." Elias downed the whiskey in the other glass. "What the fuck happened? Why the hell did that asshole attack her?"

"Fletcher took the phone Warner sent," Garrett informed him in a flat voice.

Elias didn't get it at first. When he did, a few emotions crossed his face, settling on an anger that was only eclipsed by her husband's.

"Don't worry. He won't get away."

Garrett rose, resting a hand on her shoulder. "No, he won't. It doesn't matter what hole he tries to hide in. We will find him."

Chapter Seventy

GARRETT

The question of whether Emma would be forced to sleep in the apartment where she was attacked became moot when George came home. She coaxed his wife into taking a sedative and marched her out the front door and into her and Rainer's apartment.

"I put her over there," Rainer gestured to the largest spare bedroom when Garrett came in. He was carrying a sleeping Stella over his shoulder.

"Thanks," he said, laying his baby girl next to Emma on the California King.

Stella cuddled instinctively against her mother's body.

Their daughter had been so worn out by her day out at the zoo that she hadn't noticed the tense atmosphere of all the adults around her. She thought they were having a fun sleepover at George's house.

As for why her mother was too tired to greet her, she just thought Emma had another one of her headaches. He promised they'd all sleep in one big bed, with Mom in the middle, which more than made up for any disappointment.

Garrett watched them for a long time before leaving them curled up next to each other. He would join them shortly. But first, he had business to attend to.

He walked back to their place. In the space of a few short hours, the penthouse had been converted into a makeshift Auric headquarters.

At least half a dozen of their soldiers were scattered across the living room, a few on the phone, working their local contacts while others were on military-grade laptops doing God knows what.

Ian had arrived while he was over at Rainer's. His best friend was here too, while George and a few men watched over his sleeping family.

The pair were getting a debrief from Elias.

Elias was still furious with himself for letting Fletcher get away. Garrett was frustrated about that too, but he was angrier at himself.

Fletcher had been a huge part of his life since high school. He'd followed Garrett to college, seeking him out again after they went to different business schools. Garrett had built a billion-dollar business with him.

And all this time he'd been a fucking snake in the grass. He'd stabbed Garrett in the back, a wound so old he hadn't even felt it for years.

If Emma hadn't come back into his life, he would have *never* known.

And thanks to him, Fletcher had plenty of fuck you money. Enough to disappear and make a life anywhere in the world.

Hell, the asshole might even get plastic surgery. That's what Garrett would do in his shoes.

He paused halfway through the living room, stopping at the recliner where Toya Almari was typing away on a laptop so hard it was like she was trying to punch through the keyboard.

"Thank you for coming," he told the former intelligence operative in a voice like sandpaper.

Toya looked up at him, her expression fierce. "You and your girl don't have to worry. *I've got this.*"

Nodding, he went to the bar, shaking his head when Rainer offered him a drink.

Neither Elias nor Ian had drinks either. The three of them wanted to be ready when they finally ran Fletcher to ground.

"His place is empty, nothing in his safe," Ian reported. "Some of his clothes are gone but both his cars are there. The ex-girlfriend hasn't heard from him in weeks."

"He wouldn't get into a vehicle we could trace that easily," Elias muttered, his hand kneading something—one of Stella's toys, the squishy kind that were multiplying like gremlins in her room.

Elias was using it as a stress ball.

"How long has he been planning it?" Rainer said, narrowing his eyes. "Running away, that is?"

He paused when all eyes trained on him. "On some level, he's been waiting for this shoe to drop ever since you told him about the phone."

Elias ran a hand over his dark hair. "I wonder what the hell is on it."

Garrett had a few guesses, but he refused to speculate. It would just make him rage out, and right now, this icy plane of thought was better. Letting yourself run too hot was how mistakes were made.

Murder should always be committed in cold blood.

"He did have a plan," Garrett acknowledged, thinking back to Fletcher's behavior over the past few months. "The moment Emma came back into my life, he must have realized he was on borrowed time."

Ian made a rough sound in his throat. "He must have been shitting a brick."

"Yeah. Till I gave the piece of shit the perfect excuse to have *me* drive Emma away—all that idiocy about her being a corporate spy."

He stilled, the ice in his veins growing even colder. "He had to have known about her amnesia. He knew the whole fucking time."

"Shit," Rainer muttered, his tone of surprise indicating this hadn't occurred to him.

"He thought he was safe," Elias said after a short sharp silence. "Years passed without any cops beating down his door. He must have kept tabs on the sheriff's investigation, enough to know it hadn't gone anywhere."

"He had no way of knowing Emma wouldn't recover her memory

once she saw him again," Rainer pointed out. "Why didn't he bolt then? Why stay and risk discovery?"

"And leave his comfy life and all the money that came from working with Garrett?" Elias scoffed. He threw him a knowing look. "You carried that bastard for years. Without your wheeling and dealing, he would have been a mid-level accountant at some no-name law firm or worse."

Garrett pressed his fingers to his temples. The pressure had stopped building, but he still felt the edges of his brain pushing against the inside of his skull.

And then something else occurred to him, making it snap.

"Did he know about Stella?" he rasped, his heart beating wildly out of control. "Did that fucker know Emma had my baby and *not tell me?*"

The atmosphere in the room chilled even further as the men exchanged grim looks.

How had Fletcher looked him in the face every damn day at work all the while with that knowledge boiling in the back of his brain? How had the guilt not eaten him alive?

Garrett didn't wait for an answer. He marched into his office and unlocked the bottom desk drawer.

He sat down in his leather chair and pulled out his gun safe. With swift, precise motions, he took out his Glock and began to break it down, methodically cleaning the individual components.

His friends followed him into the office. Ian took one look at him readying his weapon and closed the door behind him.

"Whoa, slow down." Rainer was turning green. "You don't know if any of that is true. You said it yourself—the only people who knew Emma had your baby were Mariana and that scuzzy ex of hers."

Garrett took a deep breath, setting down the shammy he was using.

Rainer bent to flatten his hand on the desk. "I don't think Fletcher even knew about you and Emma. You didn't tell *anyone.*"

Garrett didn't need that dagger to the heart at this particular moment. It wasn't as if it didn't already have its own designated space there, like a custom-made sheath.

Still hurt pulling it in and out though.

Ian cleared his throat. "I hate to give that fucker the benefit of the doubt, but I agree with Rainer. Fletcher is too much of a coward to hide something that huge from you. He wouldn't have the balls."

The others agreed, but Garrett resumed polishing, reassembling the gun with the speed and precision Mason, the Auric team leader, had taught him.

Rainer stared at him like he was a bomb about to go off. "No matter what he knew and when he knew it, Emma wouldn't want you going to jail for killing Fletcher."

"Like we would let him get caught," Elias muttered with a snort.

Garrett met his eyes, a silent thank you passing between them. Ian looked grim, but he didn't protest.

Rainer, meanwhile, was predictably worried. He yanked at the collar of his shirt like he wasn't getting enough air.

Elias rolled his shoulders, his neck red as a brick. "I'm gonna get a refill," he announced, waving his crystal glass before leaving them alone.

"Don't mind him," Ian said when his cousin disappeared. "This whole thing, seeing Fletcher attack Emma, brought back some shit he'd rather forget."

Rainer nodded, but his expression grew speculative.

Garrett knew what Ian was getting at, but he kept his mouth shut. As far as he was concerned, Elias was more than entitled to his secrets.

Their fourth returned with a double in hand. "Given all these revelations, I think you need to call your bank like yesterday. I wouldn't put it past Fletcher to raid the corporate accounts."

Garrett raised a brow. "He doesn't need to. He has enough of his own money."

"A lot is never enough for some people," Elias pointed out. "This is the end of the line for him. He'll go for the nuclear option."

A few phone calls proved Elias right.

Fletcher *had* embezzled money from Next Chapter. Ten million dollars directly from the payroll and expenditure accounts.

The first chunk of money had been taken the day after he married Emma—within hours of Garrett calling to give him the news.

He calculated the full amount stolen. All the air left his lungs.

Yes, Garrett was a billionaire. But that was on paper, the wealth tied to his business. Moving all the pieces he needed to keep these accounts solvent was going to keep him busy for hours. Possibly days when he should be out looking for the bastard.

He was the closer that brought in the big business, but Fletcher was the one who dotted the i's and crossed the t's. And his partner had been smarter than he'd given him credit for.

Garrett looked forward to shoving some of those t's down the bastard's throat. He just had to find some sharp enough.

This could have been worse. Had Fletcher started earlier, or had he been a little bolder, he could have entirely wrecked Next Chapter. As it was, Garrett was scrambling to meet his commitments.

"The embezzlement is not bad news," Ian told him the next day.

Bleary-eyed from spending most of the night at his computer, he eyeballed his friend. "How do you figure that?"

"This amount of money is like a spotlight to someone like Toya who can follow no matter where he goes. We'll trace his personal accounts too. They're already tagged. Trust me, there's no hole deep enough for him to hide in."

That might have been true, but Fletcher had been his partner for the better part of the decade. Garrett was the one who knew him best—what cars he liked to drive, his addiction to hair growth elixirs, his favorite meals…

His lips parted, the memory of a whitewashed building and red-tiled awning suddenly clear in his head. "There's a place across the border we have to check."

Chapter Seventy-One

EMMA

Stella was playing with her dolls in front of the fireplace. Emma knew she should be playing with her, but she couldn't. All she could seem to do was sit on the couch, staring at the carpet.

Was that indentation from when Fletcher knocked her down or when Fletcher hit the floor?

What if there was blood they couldn't see? She should have checked with her phone flashlight. Because Elias had punched Fletcher *so* hard.

Emma turned to George, her trepidation bleeding into her tone. "Should I be letting her play on the carpet? What if there's evidence on it?"

George's face curdled as she leaned forward to give the carpet a thorough inspection. "I don't see anything. Do you want me to arrange for it to be cleaned?"

"I think we should. Just in case." Emma pressed her thumbs to her temples. "Maybe they should do the whole living room."

She wanted every spec of Fletcher's DNA removed from the apartment. "Would calling in a crime scene cleaner be too extreme?"

"*Oh, Emma.*" George's thin but surprisingly muscular arms

wrapped around her. "It's going to be okay. The memory of it will fade —trust me."

Emma knew George spoke from experience, but it was different for her. This attack had occurred in their *home*.

"It's not me. Not really." Emma fought back tears. "I am having a hard time having my baby play here in this space."

She watched Stella, willing herself to calm down. It didn't seem possible. "Maybe we should stay downstairs in my mom's place for a while."

George's brow creased. "If you think that's best. But let's get those cleaners in here too. We can replace the entire carpet."

Emma was still mulling that over when the men came out of the office.

They moved like a pack of wolves—smooth, coordinated, and utterly silent. And not just the two who ran their own private security company. Garrett and Rainer were moving the same way, the elite training they'd undergone with the others suddenly obvious.

It freaked her out.

Emma was on her feet and across the room before she knew it. "Where are you going?"

Garrett's hand brushed her hair aside, but his face didn't soften.

"Toya checked out a place Fletcher owns in a little town down the Baja Peninsula called Puerto Nuevo. He bought it on a whim because he liked the restaurant downstairs. The electric meter started up the day he disappeared."

"It did?"

That didn't sound right. The one time Fletcher had spoken Spanish within earshot of her, haranguing a waiter at the wedding, he'd mangled every word.

"Are you sure? He doesn't seem the type to subject himself to any sort of inconvenience."

Fletcher was the type of American who'd get annoyed if anyone spoke anything other than English, even if he was the one in a foreign country.

"He isn't, but it's still in his name."

"Aren't a lot of other places too?" Garrett had multiple homes. It made sense that Fletcher would too.

He stroked her upper arms. "Yes, but given the timing, we have to check it out."

Emma stepped closer and fisted a hand in his shirt. Part of her wanted to cling harder, to tie him to the furniture. "Are you sure you should go? Can't Elias and Ian go check? It's what they do."

Garrett took her hand, his hold light as he pressed his thumb to the center of her palm. "I'm the one he fucked over. I have to go. But I don't want you to worry. We'll be taking every precaution."

That just made her heart race faster.

"What does that mean?" She checked that Stella was still occupied before leaning closer to whisper, "That you're going to wear body armor?"

His hands came to rest on her shoulders. "Yes. And we're taking an entire team with us—guys Rainer and I both trained with. They're pros. You have nothing to worry about."

She cast her nervous gaze across the room. George and Rainer appeared to be having a very similar conversation by the couch.

Emma gripped his shirt a little tighter. "I know better than to try and stop you, so I'm not going to. I don't care if it looks stupid—wear a helmet. And it better be bulletproof."

He put his hands over hers. "It will be. Not that I'll need it. He's probably not there. But if he is, it's not going to be just me gunning for him."

Garrett gestured to the militia mobilizing around them. Computers were being packed into secure cases, vests, and tactical belts stored in heavy packs.

She took a deep breath, trying to find comfort in the preparation. Her husband did have a point. Fletcher had no idea of the shitstorm he'd brought down on his head.

"But what if he's hired someone?" she asked. "Like a bodyguard?"

"He could hire a whole team, but they won't match ours."

Garrett pulled her flush against him, speaking directly into her ear. "Trust me on this. We'll be fine. Because my world is finally right with you in it. You and Stella. Nothing on God's green earth will keep me from getting back to the two of you."

Tears made his handsome face blur.

"Okay," she agreed with a sniff. "But if the worst happens, I expect you to use Elias as a human shield."

"I heard that," Elias called out.

"You were meant to," she shot back, humor replacing the worry in her eyes.

Elias stalked over, growled, and picked her up in a bear hug.

Emma squealed and slapped his arms. He put her down and they smiled at each other with the kind of affection usually reserved for siblings.

"Brat," Elias scolded before kissing her on the forehead. "Don't worry, we've got this. Your man won't get a scratch on him."

"He better not," she called after them.

But she couldn't help reaching for George when the woman joined her at the doorway. Together, they watched the men file out.

It didn't occur to her to wonder why none of them were armed until much later.

Chapter Seventy-Two

GARRETT

They didn't cross the border in the traditional way, by vehicle. There was no way they wouldn't have been arrested with all the guns and gear they were going to need. But that didn't matter. Ian and Elias had connections all over the world.

Their man in Tijuana arranged to borrow a boat registered to a fishing outfit working out of the coastal town of Ensenada. Elias, the former SEAL, took the helm. When they landed, his man, Juan Carlos, met them at the dock, directing them to two large vans full of gear.

They climbed into the first van with three other guys, all dressed in Mexican police uniforms.

Garrett didn't ask if they were genuine. Knowing Elias and Ian, these guys would be the real deal, trusted men well-compensated for their time.

"The top floor of the building is all his suite," Juan Carlos said when they got into the van, their destination a short ten minutes away. "The meter is still pulling electricity, and no one has come in or out since we've been watching."

Ian took his bag, exchanging a look with Elias before turning to him. "He should have run farther."

"Damn right, he should have," he muttered, pulling the nearest bag to him to check his gear, which they had been warned not to put on until they were in the building.

Rainer followed suit, as did the rest of the team. They were going in eight strong, with their Mexican counterparts taking surveillance positions, some outside but most in the building, which they couldn't clear without making a lot of noise and attracting more attention than they wanted.

The locals in uniform would ensure the other residents didn't interfere or come to harm, while they went in quiet, climbing nine stories. They stopped in an empty apartment just below the penthouse to gear up.

"Still no movement," Juan Carlos murmured as they lined up in the living room. "The front door is the only viable entrance. Scaling the balcony will attract too much attention."

Garrett nudged Rainer, who slipped a military-grade thermal camera out of his bag. He pointed at the ceiling. "There's a heat source but it's not much above ambient."

Ian examined the image. "We go in regardless—he could be in the tub or behind a glass wall. Either way, he's probably alone. This other image is not warm enough to be a person."

Nodding, Garrett slipped on his bulletproof vest, and because he promised, a helmet. The others donned their gear as well, checking their borrowed FX-05 *Xiuhcoatl* guns before forming a single line, with Elias taking point.

However, their preparations weren't needed.

Fletcher *was* in the apartment.

His rapidly cooling corpse was spread-eagled in the center of the living room floor, a gun in his hand, the source of the gunshot wound at his temple.

A tape recorder lay on his other side.

Chapter Seventy-Three

GARRETT

"Consider this my confession."

Fletcher's voice sounded thin and tinny on the cheap device.

Everyone but Elias was back downstairs, dressed in civilian gear once more, their weapons and everything related to their raid removed by Juan Carlos and his men before they called the police to come for the body.

"By the time you get this, I'll be long gone to a place you'll never find me," the recording continued. "But I wanted you to know that I never meant for this to happen. None of it—I still don't know how it all went wrong."

There was a pause in the recording, long enough for Ian to growl. "By being a cowardly *asshole*."

Rainer grunted his assent, but Garrett kept staring at the recording as Fletcher's voice kept on making excuses and apologizing before getting back to what he wanted to hear.

"As you might have guessed, Emma's phone had a text I didn't want you to see."

Fletcher sighed. "It wasn't what you think. All I did was offer her a ride. She usually said no, but I guess she was in a hurry that night. I didn't know it was because she planned on meeting up with you. That wasn't on my radar at all. When I picked her up, I assumed what any guy my age would. I thought we were on a date. But it all went wrong…"

There was a long silence and Garrett thought that was all the explanation he was going to get, but Fletcher continued.

"I didn't do *anything*. I just went for a kiss and she acted like I was attacking her. But I wasn't. I would have kept driving her to the party. *She's* the one who stormed out of the car."

Another pause. "I didn't mean for her to get hurt. I don't even know how she did. One minute she was in front of the car and the next she wasn't."

Because the fucker ran her down!

He'd known this was what had happened when Fletcher took the damn phone. But hearing it out loud was like a punch to the gut.

Fletcher's lucky he is already dead…

"I swear I only grazed her," Fletcher said, contradicting his earlier claim of ignorance. "She must have assumed I was trying to hit her— she's the one who jumped down that damn ravine. But I wasn't aiming for her. I was just trying to get out of there, maybe kick up a little dust to get her dirty. That was all."

The static of the recording was the only thing they heard for another long beat. "I swear I had no idea Emma had been hurt that bad. I expected her to show up at the party later that night—you even asked me who I was looking for, remember?"

Garrett didn't but that mattered fuck all. Mentally his hands were wrapped around Fletcher's throat.

"You gotta believe I never knew you were together. If I had, I swear I would have said something. But when she turned up working in our building of all places and didn't remember either of us… well, there was no need to confess."

There was a scraping noise as if Fletcher had wiped the recorder on his shirtfront. "Yeah, I know how fucked up that was, but it was like I had a get out of jail free card. You would have done the same thing."

The hell he would have.

"I'm not going to lie. Having Emma around freaked the shit out of me. And you kept getting closer and closer to her. So I did my best to make sure she didn't stick around. But that blew up in my face."

He and Rainer frowned at each other. What had Fletcher done, besides be an asshole to Emma?

"Then you told me the sheriff was going to send you the phone. I knew I had to get rid of it. Emma was supposed to be at the zoo. You said everyone was going."

"Him attacking Em was your fucking fault?" Rainer scoffed. "Jesus, he's lucky he's dead."

From the looks on Elias and Ian's faces, that was a common sentiment.

Fletcher's high strained voice continued. "I keep going back to that night. I would change everything if I could, but I do stand by what I said to Emma at the office. If she'd gone to business school like she wanted after college, you would *not* be married. The Emma from high school would have left if you got in the way of her goals. But because of the accident, she's different now. More content."

Unfucking-believable. "I lost her and my daughter for five fucking years, you asshole!" he yelled at the recorder.

It was as if Fletcher could hear him. "I didn't know about the kid. That was a big fucking shock. I swear I didn't know."

Garrett grabbed the recorder, hurling it at the wall. The flimsy device broke into pieces.

No one said a word.

He thrust his hands into his hair. "Excuse me. I need some air."

Chapter Seventy-Four

GARRETT

He burst into the street like he'd been shot out of a cannon. He was vaguely aware of Rainer and Elias at his back, but they gave him room as he strode to the widest free space nearest them, a small plaza on the other side road.

He walked the length of it over and over, trying to get ahold of himself before they made the trek back home.

I should call Emma. She needed to know that the nightmare was over. But his brilliant wife was going to ask him the same question he was asking himself.

Why the hell had Fletcher bothered to steal all that money if he was contemplating suicide?

It didn't make sense. Garrett paced for several minutes, turning that over in his mind when he felt someone watching him. And it wasn't his crew keeping an eye on him.

This scrutiny wasn't friendly.

A tall older man with a full head of white hair was discreetly monitoring him. He was dressed in khaki shorts, a sleeveless white shirt, and aviator sunglasses.

He looked like any other tourist that frequented this small seaside resort. Except for the way he was tracking Garrett's every movement.

On impulse, Garrett stalked to the opposite end of the plaza, taking out his phone.

The man was smooth, concealing his interest behind those aviators. But Garrett had been taught surveillance detection techniques by the best. He knew when he was being surveilled by a professional.

If Rainer was surprised to get a call from him when he was less than a hundred yards away, he didn't show it.

"Don't look at me or make it obvious in any way, but do you recall Emma's description of the man who scared her? That insurance investigator?"

Across the plaza, Rainer turned his back, facing Ian and Elias to include them in the conversation. "She told George he was tall with white hair."

"Hmm," he murmured.

"Are you thinking what I'm thinking—flowered shirt in the café?"

Garrett shrugged for the white-haired man's benefit, but he continued in a low voice. "Fletcher had a fixer of some kind. He mentioned him in the recording. He said he'd done something to break me and Emma up. But that it blew up in his face."

"The fake insurance investigator was meant to apply pressure," Rainer said, catching on. "He told her that as long as she was living with you, they would suspect her of insurance fraud because she couldn't afford to live in that building."

"And instead of letting her find a new place to live, I married her, ensuring she didn't go anywhere. Fletcher's plan to separate us failed."

Ian's voice was low, but he was standing right next to Rainer, so Garrett heard him through the receiver. "We can't be sure that's the same guy."

"Test," he muttered. "Walk in his direction, the three of you. Gamma formation."

The maneuver was one they'd practiced with the Auric team. It was just three men walking… but with extreme prejudice. Garrett knew from experience that seeing that wall of muscle bearing down at you was one of the more intimidating experiences in life.

His friends did menace very well.

But the man in the flowered shirt was a very cool customer. He saw the guys coming and rose nonchalantly, grabbing a leather satchel at his feet as he did.

The white-haired man could have been sauntering in a garden for all the emotion he showed. He didn't make a mistake. Not until he looked up and saw Garrett standing in his path.

Their suspect had kept his eyes on what he perceived to be the bigger threat, his three well-trained friends. Little did he know the biggest threat was him.

He'd taken advantage of the man's distraction to cut off his escape route.

"Hello, Inspector Folsom," Garrett said, grabbing his arm. "I believe you've met my wife."

For one long moment, Folsom didn't react. He simply stared at Garrett, nothing in his expression to give himself away.

Garrett had been expecting a denial—not the telescoping baton the older man whipped out, attacking without wasting time on protests.

He blocked the overhand blow, but Folsom was already running. Pivoting, he gave chase, pounding after his quarry.

He was at least fifty yards ahead of the other guys. Garrett ran for all he was worth, chasing Folsom through a warren of tiny streets. But the slippery older man knew the area better, cutting through the less touristic parts of town before bursting onto a flagstone-lined walkway crammed between two buildings.

Folsom was spry for his age, but Garrett was younger and faster. He grabbed the white-haired man by the shoulder, spinning him around.

The fake insurance investigator managed to twist away. But he knew he wasn't going to get away now. He did the only thing that could give him any sort of leverage—he took a hostage.

"Come here," Folsom yelled in English, snatching up the closest person to them—a small boy who'd been sitting on the ground with his back against the wall separating the walkway from a steep drop into the ocean.

Small colorful packages of Chiclets went flying—the boy must have been selling them. The child screamed, a high piercing sound that penetrated his eardrums like a stiletto.

Garrett flinched as Folsom pivoted and held the child in front of his chest like a human shield.

Fuck. He was still alone, the lack of footsteps telling him the others had taken a wrong turn.

He put up his hands. "I don't have a weapon," he lied, acutely aware of the knife strapped to his utility belt. "Let the kid go."

Folsom looked him dead in the eye. "I didn't do anything wrong. It was just a job—scare your girlfriend so she'd move out. That was it. I didn't hear from Fletcher again until he called me last night, asking me to get him papers so he could get out of the country under a new name. I came to deliver them, but he didn't answer."

He lowered the boy a fraction to check his reaction.

Garrett narrowed his eyes, recognizing the lie for what it was.

Fletcher had called this man to fix his problems. But Folsom must have smelled the desperation on his former partner. Garrett was willing to bet that the bag Folsom was holding had been packed by Fletcher—and held a hell of a lot of cash.

"Let me guess," Garrett began, keeping his hands up. "He was dead when you got there."

Folsom, or whatever his name was, knew no one was buying his story.

Garrett could see the moment of decision in his eyes. *No!*

He was already moving when Folsom hurled the boy over the edge of the rampart.

The sound that came out of his mouth was so loud his ears didn't process it. Garrett lunged after the kid, who was screaming bloody murder.

His hand grazed the child's fingers… *and he missed.*

The bottom of his chest felt like it had fallen out. Until he realized that while the child disappeared over the edge, the high-pitched screaming continued.

Garrett slammed against the waist-high wall of the rampart, looking over the edge even as Folsom's running footsteps signaled his escape. He didn't consider going after him. His only thought was for the child, who was still crying out.

The cliffside here sloped down at an angle. The kid had slid down but managed to find a foothold in the patchy earth. His little brown hand was clutching a clump of weeds half a story down.

"Garrett!" Rainer was sprinting to him.

"Over here," he yelled back, swinging a leg over the lip of the waist-high wall.

"What the hell are you doing?" Rainer slammed his hands on the rough concrete edge of the barrier.

"Do you have rope?" he asked.

"No, I don't," his friend panted. "Maybe the others do, but we split up when we lost sight of you."

Then he couldn't wait. No longer wasting time on words, he used careful handholds and every trick he'd learned in Auric's climbing gym to make his way down to the kid.

He ignored the yawning void at his back, calculating their odds if they plunged down to the picture-perfect blue ocean below.

"*Va estar bien*," he said, trying to reassure the boy, who was startled enough at his use of Spanish to stop crying. "*Aggarate de mí.*"

Reaching out, he snagged the child's arm just as a black rope dropped onto his head. He looked up, silently thanking Rainer and Ian who had just appeared above him.

Leaning forward to hug the wall, he tied the rope into a swing, working it around himself and the little boy. Then he nodded to the pair above him, letting them pull him up, using his free hand and booted feet to help as best he could.

When they reached the top, the little kid broke away, running as far from them as he could.

"Wait," Rainer called after him, picking up the discarded box of gum and chasing after him.

Knowing his friend, the kid would be caught and paid handsomely for every Chiclet pack. He turned his attention to the remaining man.

"Did you catch Folsom?"

Ian shook his head. "We caught up just in time to see him toss the kid over. I doubled back for one of the bags of gear, expecting to have to trek back to Fletcher's for it. But Juan Carlos was on our heels. He handed over one of our packs."

"And Elias?" He hadn't seen the other member of their quartet in a few minutes.

"The three of us separated a few streets back because we didn't know which turn you'd made—he's still looking," he said, holding up his cell phone. "Rainer spotted you and Folsom first. I was one street over but came when I heard the kid yelling."

A few minutes later Elias tracked them down, sweaty but not out of breath—a testament to his fine conditioning. "I think Folsom had a boat out here. Juan Carlos' men saw one departing from one of the little piers fishermen use about half a mile down the waterline."

"Are they sure it was him? Do they still have it in sight?"

He shook his head. "It was going fast and no, they didn't see who was on it. We're sending out boats in pursuit. And Juan Carlos is still looking on land, tapping his local network of informants."

But hours later, they had nothing to show for their search. The small armada of boats they assembled found nothing as well.

Folsom was in the wind.

Dusk was falling when Garrett threw in the towel. "Let's get the hell out of here," he told the others. "We'll let your contacts continue the search and take Fletcher's body for an autopsy. We'll see what the exam says about the cause of death."

In the meantime, his wife was waiting for him.

Chapter Seventy-Five

GARRETT

Elias was quiet on the boat ride back. He was at the wheel, staring off into the horizon with a pensive expression on his face.

"Did you have a chance to examine the body before the cops came?" Garrett asked.

"Yeah." Elias fished out a scrap of paper with a bunch of numbers on it. "This will likely belong to the account Fletcher used to stash the money he stole. I took the liberty of texting these to Toya. She's already tracking it down."

"He converted some of it to cash," Garrett said after thanking him. Folsom had been clutching on to that bag for dear life, but he must not have searched the body. He hadn't found the account number.

"Not all of it. It would be too heavy," Ian pointed out. "It won't take Toya long. We told her to start with the usual suspects—the Caymans and Switzerland."

It turned out to be both.

Toya quickly demonstrated why Auric paid her so generously, tracking the stolen funds to two newly established accounts. Fletcher had transferred half to the Grand Cayman bank and half to Credit Suisse in Zurich.

She also found more than a dozen calls to the same number in Fletcher's phone history. The number was traced to a burner phone.

The details fell into place quickly after that. Richard Folsom was a pseudonym. No one by that name worked for the state of California as an investigator.

"The most reasonable explanation we came up with is that Folsom was some kind of fixer," he told Emma after the Auric investigators had the chance to dig deeper. "Fletcher must have called him for help to get out of the country and set up somewhere else."

"And he got double-crossed?" Emma asked, a line between her brows.

Garrett nodded. "We've recovered most of the money he stole thanks to Toya's skills and Auric's contacts. But at least a million is missing. We think he took that out in cash and drove down to Mexico, waiting for his fixer to take him to his new life. Folsom, or whatever his real name is, must have seen the cash and taken advantage of the opportunity."

He had explained how the man had escaped by endangering a child. She understood, of course, and had told him in no uncertain terms that he'd made the right choice. But she couldn't hide her worry about the man who got away.

"Are we still in danger?" she asked, pressing close to him. "Folsom knows where we live."

Garrett pressed a kiss to her hairline. "Aside from the money, nothing ties him to Fletcher's death except our gut feelings. He staged the suicide like an expert. The Mexican authorities have it down as one, too."

She exhaled. "So, no one is looking for him for murder?"

He shook his head. "If he has half a brain, he'll stay away. If he dares show his face in these parts, everyone at Auric will be after him. He knows that."

Emma didn't look convinced.

Garrett slid closer to her on the couch, pressing his forehead to hers. "We'll be careful, but if you want to start looking for a house right away, we can do that. Someplace we can easily secure."

Emma frowned at him. "But this place *is* secure. You've removed Fletcher's fingerprint from the smart lock. And we trust everyone else on it."

His lips parted to argue. Emma put her hand over his heart. "I don't want to make you move. You love this apartment. *I* love this apartment."

But he wasn't convinced. "Stella should have a yard to play in."

"Stella has a huge bedroom filled with toys and a lifetime pass to the zoo. Not to mention the fact we're minutes away from Balboa Park —which may be the most gorgeous park in the world. Stella is fine here. So am I. Better than fine."

Garrett knew she meant it, but he'd also seen the way she had begun to stare at the carpet whenever she was in the living room.

Thankfully, George came up with the perfect solution to their dilemma.

Chapter Seventy-Six

GARRETT

He pressed his nose into Emma's hair, hugging her lush body to him.

"Good morning," he murmured when he felt her stir.

"Morning." She turned around in his arms, hiding from the sun by pressing her forehead into his chest.

"Still not used to the sun on this side of the bed?"

Much to his satisfaction, she burrowed deeper. "Nope. You called the guy, right?"

"I did," he assured her, taking advantage of the close contact to run his hands all over her. "He's coming on Saturday to install the contact paper."

Emma had been right when she said they both loved his apartment. But every time she'd sat in the living room, she'd grown quiet and withdrawn—even after he replaced the carpet. It was as if she couldn't help but relive her attack.

Garrett wanted to move. He'd even called a real estate agent to start scoping out properties. But Emma took that personally, telling him he was letting Fletcher win. She dug in her heels and refused to move to a new place. Thankfully, her new bestie George came up with a simple plan that solved all their problems.

They switched penthouses.

"They're almost identical apartments, with the same number of rooms and square footage," George pointed out. "And we've been meaning to do some redecorating in any case, including adding a room to display a few more of my engines. Why don't we just max out the number of movers and swap apartments?"

Fortunately for them, Rainer had gone for the idea.

It took a crew of two dozen moving men three days to shift their belongings the few dozen feet that separated their apartments.

If the movers thought they were crazy, swapping between two almost identical apartments, they kept their thoughts to themselves.

Georgia now had an entire room filled with pedestals to display her growing collection of car-related artifacts. This included two engines, over a dozen hood ornaments, and something she called the greatest innovation in carburetors the world had ever seen.

Meanwhile, Garrett and Emma had decided to knock down the wall between Stella's room and the extra bedroom next door, using a broad arch to delineate the two spaces. The side room would serve as a play-room now and a study area when she grew older.

The other two bedrooms down the hall were kept in reserve for a possible future nursery at Emma's insistence.

She was determined to have at least one more child. Garrett wanted one too, but he was determined to go the surrogacy route, to avoid additional stress on Emma's body. However, she was equally deter-mined to carry the child herself—which was why he was content to put the thing off.

But they kept the rooms available, just in case.

Despite keeping the penthouse as their primary residence, Garrett found he couldn't let go of the idea of giving Stella a yard. That was why they had just closed escrow on a spacious three-story house in Del Mar with a big walled-off garden and a private staircase down to the beach.

So far, they had only spent one weekend there, but he'd taken a thousand pictures of his girl's first beach day—the first one Emma remembered.

Garrett and Stella had built a sandcastle in front of the surf before climbing up the stairs to wash up and eat burgers. They grilled them on the sunny deck overlooking the water.

But the penthouse was still home. The only problem was that the sun came through at a different angle in the master bedroom first thing in the morning, one that woke them too early.

Rainer had used blackout curtains, but neither he nor Emma liked their view of the Pacific obstructed. That was why he was having a specialist come and install special UV contact paper compatible with their smart-glass windows and doors.

Until then, he pulled the navy Egyptian cotton sheets over his and Emma's heads, making a private cave for the two of them.

He ran his hands over her backside, glorying in the silkiness of her skin before rolling over her like a wave.

"Someone wants a very good morning." She giggled, wrapping her legs around his waist.

Garrett gave her his most charming grin. He nuzzled her neck. "Yes, please."

Emma ran her foot over the back of his calf. "Stella's going to wake up any minute. Do you think we can finish in time?"

He stripped out of the pajama bottoms he wore in deference to having a five-year-old. He pulled down the sheets before settling between her rounded thighs. "I do love a challenge."

His gorgeous wife smiled up at him, lingering drowsiness making the gesture slow and wanton. "Well, then step right up, challenger," she said with another giggle. "I'll have to think of a suitable prize if you win."

He stretched out over his wife, his touch flagrantly possessive. "Oh, I already won."

He ended up being grateful to the intrusive sun, which had woken them a full half hour ahead of schedule.

Garrett made the most of every minute, driving his luscious wife to a panting orgasm just before the alarm went off.

They dived into the shower together, returning to the bedroom just in time for Stella to poke her head inside, asking for breakfast.

Whistling a happy tune, he set the table while Emma got Stella dressed for her big day. The pair entered the room wearing matching sweater dresses and new UGG boots in deference to the dreary January weather.

Stella's hair was in pigtails. She was the most adorable thing he'd ever seen. But seeing her take Emma's hand, the two of them walking toward him with such similar smiles—the sheer perfection of the moment knocked him flat.

"Did you start the coffee?" Emma asked.

When he could finally take a breath, he held up the freshly branded bag of Baby Bella Beans. "You mean the first batch of your special blend? Hell no, I wouldn't dare."

Rolling her eyes, Emma took the coffee from him, busying herself at the shiny professional-grade espresso machine while he fetched Stella her breakfast.

He watched his wife handle the shiny chrome espresso machine like a pro.

To say Emma was particular about her coffee was an understatement. He never quite got it right. But he flipped a mean pancake. And those were Stella's favorite.

Emma and her little crew had busted their butts to get the specialty batch of beans out for the Christmas season. *De Olla* had stocked it at their café and their kiosks, and it flew off the shelves. Garrett had been lucky to reserve a few boxes before they sold out.

"Eat a whole one in case you don't like your lunch today," he told his daughter, pouring syrup on her pancake when she sat down to eat. If he let her do it, she'd empty half the jug onto her plate.

"Don't tell her that."

Emma kissed Stella on the forehead before handing him a steaming mug and going back to the machine to make her own. "You're going to eat lunch in the cafeteria with all your new friends—I hear the food is really good."

"I hope so," Stella said primly, picking up her fork before attacking her pancake as if all the food in the world was disappearing. Garrett followed suit, with enough gusto that his wife muttered something about living with a pack of wolverines.

"At least she's not nervous about today," he said around a mouthful of pancake. It was a shame the same couldn't be said for him. Garrett was a ball of nerves.

Emma, predictably, was a rock.

After breakfast, they piled into the Range Rover and drove to Francis Perkins Elementary, the best private primary school in the county.

Stella was starting kindergarten, on the first day of the spring semester.

"You need to stop making that face," Emma whispered to him as he climbed out of the SUV. "She's not worried now, but if she sees how anxious you are, she'll start panicking. You know she's like a sponge."

"I'm not anxious," he protested.

"You're sweating," she said, surreptitiously wiping his brow with the lens-cleaning cloth she used for her sunglasses before making room for their daughter to walk between them.

Emma took Stella's right hand and he took the other after helping her with her furry panda backpack, a gift Mariana had bought her at the zoo.

"I still think we should have waited," he muttered over his daughter's head. "She could have kept on with the tutor for another semester. There would be more new kids starting school. Right now, she's the only one."

"It's going to be fine, Papa," Stella said, having caught all of that with her sharp five-year-old ears. "I want to go to school."

Melting completely, Garrett gave her a wan smile. "I know, baby. And you're going to do great."

"I am." Stella beamed. "I love school!"

He chuckled. "She gets that from you," he told Emma as they entered the main office to find out where Stella's class was.

Letting her walk inside it took nearly everything he had.

"See," Emma said, pointing through the window once their daughter had skipped inside. "She is already making friends."

Scowling, Garrett approached the window, the tight knot in his gut loosening when he saw the teacher had taken his baby to her seat at a table with three other kids.

It had been less than a minute, but Stella was already chatting a mile a minute with the little girl seated to her right, a black-haired girl with an impressive braid.

He studied the elaborate coiffure with a critical eye. "We need to watch hairdo tutorials on YouTube."

Emma laughed, taking his arm. "*That's* your takeaway? Not that our beautiful baby is more than ready for school and already making friends?"

He grunted noncommittally, giving the other parents—some of them openly eyeballing them—a polite nod, but not engaging in conversation. Making other parent friends could wait, once he wasn't a jumble of nerves and regret.

The bell rang. Emma waved at Stella one last time before dragging him to the front gate.

"You really have to loosen the apron strings," she teased as they crossed the parking lot.

He gave the crowded hallway the side-eye. "There are more kids than I thought. What if she gets bullied?"

Emma paused. "Then we'll deal with it. Or better yet, we'll teach her how to deal with it."

She looked up at him, wrapping her arm around his waist and squeezing. "Don't worry. It will get easier once the next one comes along."

Garrett nearly tripped, his heart hammering. "Don't joke about that. My heart can barely take being in two places at once—half with you and half with Stella. But that's it. No more."

She smiled, a glint in her eye.

His shoulders straightened. "You are joking, right?"

With a sphinxlike smile firmly in place, Emma climbed into the Range Rover. She beckoned him to join her with one perfectly manicured finger.

As if he would ever do anything else. "Baby, tell me you're joking…"

Emma set her purse inside the console divider, closing it before reaching for her seat belt. "What should we name our next child? I like Serena for a girl, but what do you think about Gabriel for a boy?"

Garrett stalked to the passenger side door, throwing it wide. "Woman, are you pregnant or not?"

Still no answer. Just that little smile.

She blew out a breath, the air displacing her thick bangs. "Fine. I'm not… yet. But someday soon I will be. And your heart will get used to being in three places at once. That's the great thing about them—their infinite capacity to grow."

His shoulders dropped. "You're killing me," he sputtered. "You know that, right?"

Emma fluttered her lashes, that familiar twinkle in her eye. "You love it."

"God help me." He sighed, his muscles relaxing as he reached around to fasten her seat belt. "I do. I really do."

And it was true. Emma drove him crazy in all the best ways.

It no longer mattered that she didn't remember their beginning. Garrett was going to fill the rest of her days with fantastic new memories. Her and Stella both.

His girls.

EPILOGUE

Elias

Elias pored over the stills he'd printed out from the surveillance footage taken from the lobby of Garrett's building.

He hadn't told his cousin or his friends he was still pursuing this, but after seeing the man who called himself Richard Folsom, he hadn't been able to stop himself.

Elias was like a dog with a bone. When he sank his teeth in something, he couldn't let it go. Not until the matter was resolved… or completely crushed if necessary.

When it came to Auric, he was the one who decided if it was necessary. That was part of his job. He had a feeling this was going to be one of those times.

I know I've seen this fucker somewhere, he thought, examining the picture for the thousandth time. He just couldn't remember where.

He was still staring at the photograph when the call from Albuquerque PD came in.

Elias couldn't believe what he was hearing at first, so he made the detective repeat himself a few times.

"My DNA has come up in connection to *what*?"

"A murder," Detective Garcia repeated. "Your DNA has come up in connection with a homicide."

The End

FOLLOW ME FOR UPDATES ON ELIAS' story, True Crime Billionaire!
www.authorlucyleroux.com/newsletter

ABOUT THE AUTHOR

A 7-time Readers' Favorite Medal Winner. USA Today Bestselling Author. Mom to a half-feral princess. WOC. Former scientist. Recovering geek.

Lucy Leroux is the steamy pen name for author L.B. Gilbert. Ten years ago Lucy moved to France for a one-year research contract. Six months later she was living with a handsome Frenchman and is now married with an adorable half-french 9yo who won't go to bed on time.

When her last contract ended Lucy turned to writing. Frustrated by a particularly bad romance novel she decided to write her own. Her family lives in Southern California.

Lucy loves all genres of romance and intends to write as many of them as possible. To date, she has published thirty novels and novellas. These include paranormal, urban fantasy, gothic regency, and contemporary romances with more on the way.

www.authorlucyleroux.com

amazon.com/author/lucyleroux

facebook.com/lucythenovelist

x.com/lucythenovelist

instagram.com/lucythenovelist

bookbub.com/authors/lucy-leroux

www.ingramcontent.com/pod-product-compliance
Lightning Source LLC
Chambersburg PA
CBHW071430190726
48292CB00001B/181